TARA TAYLOR QUINN

THE 2ND LIE

MIRA®

Recycling programs for this product may not exist in your area.

ISBN-13: 978-0-7783-2838-4

THE SECOND LIE

For questions and comments about the quality of this book please contact us at Customer_eCare@Harlequin.ca.

www.MIRABooks.com

Printed in U.S.A.

For Rachel Marie Reames—the daughter I gave birth to, raised and will love through eternity.

Dear Reader,

Kelly Chapman is about to open one of her most private and intriguing files. She's sharing them one by one in the hope that they will be of interest to discriminating readers everywhere. Kelly first presented herself—and these gripping case files—to me a couple of years ago.

Kelly is a psychologist and expert witness. She's helped to prosecute criminals guilty of all kinds of heinous acts. And she's testified for defense attorneys representing innocent people accused of crimes they didn't commit. Kelly is in demand all over the country, but she's lived in the same town (Chandler, Ohio) all her life—not counting the years she was away at college—and has friends she's known forever. At home Kelly is happily ruled by her four-pound toy poodle, Princess Camille, who, on most days, allows Kelly to address her as Camy.

The Second Lie took me by surprise. I was halfway through writing the book and still didn't know what was going to happen, how things were going to end. It's fair to say this book was an exercise in trust as I sat down every day and wrote, believing that the plot would take care of itself. And it did!

You're about to meet Maggie Winston, a fourteen-year-old girl whose story is only too real. And you'll meet Samantha Jones, the thirty-three-year-old single cop who will stop at nothing to protect the people she's dedicated her life to serving. Maggie is Kelly's client. Sam is her friend. The rest…well, I'll let you find out for yourself.

I hope you enjoy *The Second Lie.* I love hearing from my readers. You can reach me at Box 13584, Mesa, Arizona 85216. Or though my Web site, www.tarataylorquinn.com.

Tara Taylor

1

I couldn't find a pencil that hadn't been chewed on. So what if the existing ones all bore my own teeth marks? Sometimes a girl just needed fresh wood.

I'd already seen four patients that day, had worked at the soup kitchen during lunch—my turn to wash dishes—and book club was that night and I hadn't finished the book, in spite of being up half the night trying.

And right then, critical on my list was that none of my desk drawers had unused, which for me meant unchewed, pencils. Okay, so the habit was somewhat disgusting. I acknowledged it. At least I faced my issues.

"Deb?" I punched the phone intercom system—a system that had come with the office and had been around, I suspected, since before color television.

"Yeah?" Deb Brown, my assistant wasn't the most professional employee around. But she was loyal and compassionate, which made up for any lack in her office etiquette.

"Have we got any pencils out there?"

"No, but you've got a call on line one. I was just going to buzz you when you buzzed me."

"Go get some new pencils, would you?"

"Now? I'm in the middle of billing."

"Now. Please. If you don't mind."

"Heck, I don't mind. It's eighty degrees and sunny outside."

"But make sure you only walk as far as your car," I told her. The one store in town that carried office supplies was three miles away and Deb had been known to make that hike.

"Okay," Deb said, and clicked off.

Why the store was closer to the highway seven miles outside town instead of downtown where people worked was beyond me. The only businesses out by the interstate, besides farmland, were an economy hotel, a truck stop and a family diner. If you considered a greasy spoon filled with truckers a "family" diner.

Picking up a pen, pulling one of four or five notepads toward me, I took my call on line one.

"Dr. Chapman?" The caller was female. Sounded older than a teen. At a guess, in her early thirties.

"Yes?"

"My name is Lori Winston. The counselor at Chandler High School referred me to you."

Jim Lockhart had sent several troubled teens to me over the past five years.

"You have a son or daughter in high school?" I asked, mentally reviewing my assessment of her age.

"A daughter. Just starting high school this month. But I can't pay you," the woman continued. "I barely got enough money to pay lot rent and utilities."

Jim knew that when it came to kids, I'd work pro bono anytime.

Insecure, I jotted down about Lori Winston, because I always made notes about whatever popped immediately to mind when dealing with my clients. Or pretty much anyone I talked to.

Low-income.

First impressions were sometimes vital.

"You and your daughter live alone?"

"Yep."

Independent, I added, thinking of the thirteen- or four-teen-year-old I had yet to meet.

"For how long?"

"Since she was born. Took me three years to save up for this trailer and it's not much. Two bedrooms. And a hole in the bathroom floor. But we do okay most of the time. It's just comin' up with extra that's hard.

"And before you ask, I had her when I was sixteen. Had to quit school 'cause I couldn't afford a babysitter without working full-time. Seems everyone wants to turn up their noses at us, and if you're one of 'em, then fine, we don't need your help."

"No, wait." I frowned, quickly put pen to paper. *Defensive home environment.* "I'm happy to help—at no charge." I said what I figured would mean the most so I could keep the needy mother on the line. "And I'm not judging your situation," I added. "My mother also quit high school to have me."

Right here in Chandler.

"And you turned into a doctor?"

Well, a doctor of psychology, anyhow. "Yes," I said.

"You'll understand Maggie, then. Lots of folks don't. They look at me and figure she's white trash, too, without bothering to learn what she's about. Not that I'm trash or nothin'—I'm not. But I know what people say about me. I hear them."

"Maggie's your daughter?"

"Yeah. She's fourteen."

Maggie. Cute name. Weary mother.

"How's she doing in school?"

"Straight A's so far."

Responsible.

"What about sports?" Seemed like every kid in the county played something. There wasn't a whole lot else for them—or their parents—to do. Some of the people in Fort County seemed to put more emphasis on games and practice and working out than they did on homework and attending class.

"She was a cheerleader in junior high and made the junior varsity team at Chandler, but she quit when practices started. Said she was bored with it. They have to pay to play now that the tax levy failed, so we couldn't afford the extra, anyway."

I looked at my notes. Nothing stood out. So I asked the obvious question. "Why do you think your daughter needs a counselor?"

"I think something's going on with a guy. An older guy."

"Can you explain that?"

"Used to be she said she was going to graduate from college before she got serious with a guy. Said she wasn't going to let anyone slow her down, or stop her from bein' whatever she wants to be, which is fine by me. She thinks guys in high school're dumb, anyway. But now she's talking like 'having a partner could make life so much better' kind of stuff." The mother mocked the daughter's tone.

"What did she mean by that?"

"Hell if I know."

"Did you ask her?"

"Yeah. She said, 'It's obvious.'" More of the mocking

tone. "And there's no guy in high school who's gonna be talking that way. Not puttin' thoughts like that into her head."

I wasn't as sure of that.

"Then last week I found a condom in her purse," Lori Winston continued. "She said they gave 'em away free at school last year and she keeps it for safety purposes. 'Like what?' I asked. Like if she gets raped, she's going to pull it out?"

"Do you think she's sexually active?"

"God, I hope not. She's only fourteen and I know that's not the way to go. I've told her. Over and over. And used to be she listened. But I don't know about her anymore. That's why I'm calling you. Other than this, Mags is the greatest kid ever."

"Has she ever had a boyfriend, that you know of?"

"No. She's always said boys are dumb. Now she's saying boys aren't worth talkin' to till they're grown-up and past some hormone something-or-other—and that's what scares me the most. She's dressing different. Paying more attention to her looks. When I ask her if she's seein' someone, she says, 'Course not.' But I don't believe her. There's a man in my daughter's life. A man. Not a boy. A mother knows these things."

I wished I could believe the woman was wrong. But at this point, I couldn't disagree with her that a liaison with an older man was possible.

"Has she ever been in trouble with the police?" I thought of my high school friend, Samantha Jones, who was now a Fort County deputy. She might know if Maggie Winston was hanging out with a bad crowd.

"Of course not. Like I said, she's a good girl, Dr. Chapman. She's never given me a bit of worry until now, except for maybe that she's too sweet. People use her, always asking for help and she never says no. She'd be real easy for some guy to take advantage of, if you know what I mean."

"I'll be happy to see her if you think she'll talk to me."

"She will if I tell her to. When?"

"Any day this week. I can stay late if I need to."

We set a time for the next afternoon. And I hung up. A psychologist's life is often difficult, but never more so than when you're dealing with a child.

The man inside the elegant whitewashed home was armed and dangerous. He'd already killed his wife. Samantha had been the one to find her body on the back porch. The dead woman still had a cell phone clutched in her hand, her call to 9-1-1 showing on the screen.

Now, crouched against the cement foundation, Sam held her department-issue cell phone to her ear while three other deputies surrounded the house. They'd secured the area. And called for the county's hostage team, such as it was. But out here, what they had was pretty much what they had. Ben Chase and Todd Williams had a little more training than the rest of them; that was it.

And Williams, the dickhead, was on his honeymoon. Who'd have thought her old partner would've gone and got married right when she needed him most?

"Answer, dammit," she whispered through gritted teeth, listening to the monotony of ringing that she'd been hearing on and off for the past five minutes.

"Hello."

She almost dropped her phone. "Mr. Holmes?"

"Get them guys outta my yard or I'll blow my head off."

"We're here to help you, Mr. Holmes. We've seen your

wife. She's hurt. We have to get her to a hospital." Was lying to a hostage against the rules? Samantha couldn't remember. "We need you to put down your gun and come out, and we'll do everything we can to help you."

It was so dark out here, she couldn't be sure if there was some animal moving in the brush—a cat, maybe— or if she was just seeing shadows.

"You got money to pay my mortgage?" Holmes shouted in her ear, following the question with obscenities. "You gonna get my truck back for me?"

"There are programs to help you with all that, Mr. Holmes. But we can't do anything if you stay inside with that gun."

"You can't do anything, anyway." The man's voice had dropped so low she could hardly hear him. "I killed my wife. You think I don't know that? I killed her."

When she heard the distinctive and unmistakable sound of a .410, followed by breaking glass falling on pavement, she prayed that her fellow officers hadn't been anywhere within range.

"Mr. Holmes? Are you okay? Mr. Holmes!"

"I told you to get those guys outta here."

"Mr. Holmes." Samantha put every bit of nurturing she could find into those two words. "Please put the gun down *now,* so we can help you."

Another shot sounded, and Samantha didn't need a phone to her ear to know the man had just blown off his own head.

Kyle Evans liked the country.

Sitting outside at night, unwinding from a long day of farming, communing with the stars and the air that told him what the next day would bring, was heaven compared to living in a city where he'd be surrounded by people even if he lived alone.

Not that he lived alone. Or had ever lived in a city. Or even a small town.

No, Kyle was a farm boy from his head to his toes. Chandler, with all its busybodies and people milling around, the traffic, the fast-food places—that were now staying open twenty-four hours, for godsake—tore at his nerves.

Late on the first Monday night in August he was sitting out back, a few cold beers for company. He sat in a pine rocker he'd built himself across from the other pine rocker he'd built himself, under the hundred-year-old maple tree. His grandpa had set him in the lower branches of that tree before he could walk.

He'd been climbing it by the time he was four. Shimmying up it, hugging the bark so tight with his arms and knees that he'd damned near skinned them. But a few scrapes and bark burns were worth the view from the top. He could see the entire farm from there. Could see his daddy fifty acres away, if there were no leaves on the trees and his old man was on the big tractor.

He could see the cows in the farthest pasture.

He'd once saved a foal from up in that tree. He'd seen a fox coming over the hill toward the horse pasture and had hollered for his grandpa, who took Kyle and the .22 out in the truck, shooting the fox from thirty yards away, right before it lit into the new foal.

The carcass had hung in his father's office until after Kyle graduated from high school. It was in the barn someplace now.

He'd downed his second beer, was considering whether to go into the house for a third or just call it a night, when he saw lights in his drive. Since it was a long drive, he had plenty of notice when someone came to visit. At night, anyway.

His decision made because he recognized his visitor, Kyle went in for the beer. He took a moment to make sure his grandfather was still tucked into bed, asleep, which was how the confused ninety-two-year-old spent most of his time. Then he brought out the rest of the six-pack. There was only one person who'd have the audacity to interrupt his peace this late at night.

And only one person who drove up the gravel drive like a bat out of hell. An officer of the law ought to know better.

It's private property—I'm allowed to drive fast, Sam always said when he bothered to call her on it.

One look at her face tonight as she stepped out of her reconditioned '77 Mustang, and Kyle knew he wasn't going to call her on anything.

Normally he hated the sight of her in the manly beige slacks, shirt and tie that made up her Fort County deputy uniform.

Not because of the manliness, but because of what they represented. The job. The danger. Her obsession.

Tonight, he hardly noticed her apparel.

Beer first and then talk, he'd learned when she had that wild look in those familiar blue eyes. The look that asked him if she was insane. Or the world was.

The look that told him she'd been seeing something really ugly while he was staring at the stars.

She grabbed the beer he handed her and sat down without a hello. Lying back in the handmade pine chair she used so much he thought of it as hers, she downed half the beer.

"How's Grandpa?" she finally asked.

"Better today. The swelling in his legs went down and

he made it to the table for all three meals. Bitched at me for burning the toast, too." He grinned.

"Did he know who you were?"

"I'm not sure. I was either me or my dad. He knew he was with family. I'm good with that." It was when the grandfather he'd grown up with as a second parent thought Kyle was a stranger that he struggled.

"Where's Zodiac?"

"In the barn. Lillie's ready to foal." And the German shepherd would alert him if there was a problem that required his attention before morning.

"You need to hire yourself a hand."

He held up the two he had, beer bottle included. "I've got all I need."

"Your father had two men, plus you and your grandpa, helping him."

"He had twice the land to work and the money to pay wages. I've got help coming for harvest. I can do the rest myself."

"You think you're gonna break even this year?"

"Maybe."

By next year, his time would be up. Either the experimental crop paid off or he had to find Grandpa and himself a new place to live.

Which would kill the ailing old man who'd never lived anywhere but this farm.

Kyle wasn't kidding himself. It would probably kill him, too.

He had one more year before the bank called his loan. One year to get his ass out of the hole he'd dug himself.

"You gonna tell me what happened tonight?"

"I was talking to a guy on the phone when he blew his brains out."

"Jesus, Sam, what happened?" In Fort County? Where

cops were called when mothers and daughters had spats. Kyle studied her expression, or as much as he could see in the darkness. "Why'd he do that?"

"Guess it was something I said."

2

Samantha debriefed with Kyle as best she could. She'd already written her report at the sheriff's office. There'd be a more formal conference with her superior in the morning, but that was mere procedure.

And if she had serious trouble coping, she could always call Kelly Chapman. It wouldn't be the first time.

Tonight, though, she needed the friend who knew her better than anyone. She needed Kyle.

"We found about an ounce of meth, spilling out of the bag, on his coffee table. There was a pipe on the nightstand in the bedroom. And a needle in the trash…"

Samantha took a long sip of beer, savoring the familiarity of the experience, the "country backyard barbecue everything's going to be okay" taste. She didn't see anything in the darkness around her, though she knew the shapes of Kyle's barn, a tractor, his truck.

"The place was torn up, shattered glass on a wedding photo. Looked like he'd been throwing furniture. Nice stuff."

Kyle hooked his foot beneath hers.

"His wife had a single bullet through her chest. She was about our age. Wearing a white blouse and jeans. Cute. I heard her call come through on the radio. I was only ten minutes away. She was already dead when I got there."

"Were you first on the scene?"

A dangerous position to be in. And she knew what would follow her admission—a lecture from Kyle.

"I'm telling the story here." She needed him on her side. "One of the rooms had bunk beds," she continued. "There were two young sons. They were spending the night with their grandfather."

The bottle felt good against her lips. She wanted to keep it there, keep sucking down the comforting taste of beer.

"Better slow down, girl. At the rate you're going, the evening will be over in less than ten minutes. Hardly worth the drive out."

According to her most recent alcohol-blood-level test—a self-requirement, not a departmental one—two was her legal limit.

Giving him a belligerent look, Samantha sipped again. "I'm telling you, Kyle, we've become infested with this crap. Meth is everywhere. Destroying us. It's all I'm seeing anymore."

"It's all you're seeing because of the line of work you're in." Kyle had never hidden his aversion to her career.

Nor had he stopped trying to convince her that his strongly held opinion on the matter was the right one.

"Don't start on me," she warned him.

"Now might be an appropriate time to take a good hard look at yourself." Opening another beer, he tossed the cap toward the cardboard six-pack container—scoring a clean shot. "I might be dense or backward or something, but last I checked, happiness didn't look anything like you."

"I love my job."

"That's why you're up late on a Monday night, drowning

your brain so you don't have to think about your day on the job?"

If he wasn't her best friend, she would have left.

"Like *your* work doesn't ever cause you stress?" He was the one who worried every day that he might lose his precious farm. "And it's not just because of the line of work I'm in," she added, skipping back to his earlier comment. "Meth use has become an epidemic. And not only with losers, either. This guy tonight—his neighbors say that up until six months ago he was an engineer at Samson pulling in a six-figure income." Samson was an aerospace plant forty miles from Chandler. "His father-in-law thinks he started using last summer. That's when his behavior changed, at any rate."

Kyle's silence usually meant she had his attention.

"I was talking to Danielle from Child Services yesterday, and she said that almost three-quarters of their cases have to do with meth in some way. Three-quarters of their cases, Kyle. Do you know many children that involves? It's scary."

"We live in a scary world, honey. Or most of you do. Look around you." He indicated the yard where they sat. "There's fresh air to breathe. Peace and quiet and stars in the sky. Maybe, after tonight's violence, you can appreciate life out here a little more."

"What I'm seeing in Fort County…" she began, ignoring his all-too-predictable comment. "I think it's worse than a lot of the rest of the country. Maybe not out West where the Mexican drug influence is so prevalent, but for this part of the country, we're way above statistics. Even our own. Meth use is up over one hundred percent from last year at this time."

"The economy's been in the shitter. What do you expect?"

"Drugs take money. Especially if they're being imported."

"So what's your explanation?"

"I think it's like you say—it's been a hard couple of years and many people are getting desperate. But I also think this stuff is being made locally. In large quantities, like in Mexico—more of a mass production approach, not the little mom-and-pop labs we've seen in the past."

"What makes you say that?"

"There's so much of it, for one thing. And the recipe that's being used, for another. There are several different ways to make meth, different ingredients that can be used. What we're finding here isn't as pure as the stuff that comes from Mexico. And also, it would have to come from here to make it cheap enough for the number of users we're seeing." She'd done her homework. And she was scared. "Ohio's been hit hard, especially the Dayton area, with NCR pulling out and GM leaving, and so many other factories closing. More people are out of work, a record number of them, searching for jobs that aren't there. They need money. A superlab, which is what the mass production meth labs are called, could support an entire factory's worth of workers. And good times or bad, there's always going to be a market for drugs."

He was staring out over the yard, his eyebrows drawn.

"Just because we've never had a superlab in this part of the country before doesn't mean there isn't one. As a matter of fact, it makes sense that someone from the West would take advantage of the situation here and get a lab set up, say, at the crossroads of Interstate 70 and 75. That's the ideal location for transport to all parts of the country."

He didn't respond.

"Desperate people do desperate things, Kyle. And…I don't know, aside from all that, I just have a feeling—"

"Women's intuition and police work do not go hand in hand," Kyle interrupted with another oft-repeated remark. "You'll get yourself killed thinking that way."

She'd scared him. His remark, focusing only on her last sentence, ignoring the facts, told her so.

"My intuition saved my life the night I knew not to approach a speeder I stopped until I called for backup." She'd handled them on her own many times before. And that night, she'd saved herself a bullet to the chest. Another officer, one who arrived wearing a bulletproof vest, took the hit, escaping with only a bruise.

"What would save your life is getting out of that uniform and staying out," he said, looking up into a tree with branches they could hardly see in the darkness.

Sam had once been jealous of those trees. And the fields. Back when she'd wanted Kyle to love her more than he loved his farm. She still wondered what he saw, what he felt, when he gazed out over his land.

Whatever it was, she couldn't see it. Even in daylight.

"You could've been killed tonight."

"No, actually, that was Chuck." Her closest friend on the force. "He was out front when the guy blasted the bay window. The bullet missed Chuck by a foot."

Because the other deputy had been crouched down. Thank God for good training.

"Will you be tracing this meth? To learn where the ingredients are coming from?"

"We'll send it out. We'll know in a couple of days if it's ice or not, but I can already tell you it isn't. From the way it was packaged."

"Ice?"

"The stuff that comes from Mexico. Like I said, it's a much purer form. And it's a lot more dangerous. Not that it matters our stuff is a lesser quality drug. The crap is spreading like a virus and at the rate we're going in our fight to stop it, it might as well be coming from Mexico."

"Here, this will help. At least for now." Kyle handed her a second beer, cap removed. "In the long run, if anyone can get them, Sam, it's you. You're the best damn cop I've ever heard of. Anywhere."

"Uh-huh." She took his praise with a grain of salt. "And how many cops have you been in contact with?" Their small group in Fort County and Chandler and a couple of the surrounding burgs. And only when he'd been with her or her family.

"I have a television."

"When's the last time you turned it on?"

"A couple of weeks ago when it looked like a tornado might be moving in."

The only way she'd been able to talk him into getting a satellite dish was by showing him the weather channel one night while he was at her place in town.

Sam had a double-wide modular she'd inherited from her grandfather—her dad's dad, a retired deputy—when he'd passed away five years before at the age of ninety.

"And it doesn't seem to matter how good the cops are," she added. "We simply don't have the money to go to war."

"But if the problem's local—it just means finding the labs, right? Like last year, when you were part of the sting that busted the woman in town who was making the stuff in her bathroom and selling it to kids at the high school."

If only it was that easy. The investigating was usually

the most straightforward part. "And that little bust cost the county almost six thousand dollars," she said, having a hard time pulling herself up after this latest testament to a fight they might not win. In her grandfather's day—hell, even in her dad's day—being a cop was about upholding the law.

Now, like everything else, it was about money.

"First, you pay law enforcement, and as you know, our budget's been cut in half in the past two years, but that's a whole other issue. Then you make the arrest. You house the perpetrator in a county facility. You pay for a trial—you pay to clean up the lab, which creates about six pounds of toxic waste for every pound of meth. And you have to do all of that for every single case, so then you pay for treatment for the perpetrator, which is usually required at sentencing. The county goes bankrupt before half the operations are shut down."

"You're telling me you don't have the money to stop these people. That you guys aren't even trying because you can't afford to?"

She drank some beer. She thought about keeping quiet because mum was the word around headquarters these days, and then reminded herself that she was with Kyle.

He might not like what she had to say, but she always tried to be honest when she talked to Kyle.

"It's not quite that bad yet, but yes, you're partially correct. We're working with such a small crew, we don't have much time to put into the investigations. And we have to consider whether one bust is big enough to be worth the expenditure of monies, or if we should just turn a blind eye and wait for a bigger bust that'll give us more bang for our buck."

"Sweet Jesus, Sam. I had no idea it had come to this."

"Not many people do. Except, of course, the operators. They seem to be multiplying like flies."

"In Fort County? We're out in the middle of nowhere!"

"A perfect cover for a superlab."

"I wish you'd quit saying that."

"If it's happening, my silence isn't going to make it go away. The only way to get rid of it is to talk about it. Find it. Go after it."

"And you really think that's what we have here? Some kind of mass production?"

"It's possible. I hope not."

"God, I hate your job."

Being a cop was the one part of her Kyle didn't understand. Or like. And that wasn't going to change. She'd given up hoping a long time ago.

"I'm kind of tired of it myself at the moment," she said, unfastening the top button of her shirt. "Mind if I take this off?"

His grin was slow and warm as he glanced over at her. "Do I ever mind?"

No. His fondness for her body had never been in question.

"I need you tonight, Kyle." He was *her* drug. Her escape. The place she came when she needed to find herself within the cop she'd become.

"Then you've got me, baby."

"Now?" Sam pulled her belt strap out of its loop.

"Any time you need me, Sam. You know that." It was the closest he'd come to telling her he loved her since they'd broken off their engagement for the final time thirteen years before. He'd been married and divorced since then.

She'd been promoted—twice.

Kyle didn't get embarrassed about much of anything. She loved how he just dropped his pants to use as a blanket for her bottom and made love to her right out there in his backyard. And then, wrapping her in clothes just in case Grandpa stirred, he carried her to the large oak bed he'd carved with his own hands and held her until she fell asleep.

In spite of the fact that she was a big strong cop.

"You ready?"

The girl nodded.

"Today's delivery is different. This guy isn't a parent, but he really needs what we can give him. Instead of going up to a house, you'll have to wait at the corner by the trash can and then, when he pulls up in his car and asks for directions, you write them on the bag and hand it to him."

"I know. I got it."

"You're sure you aren't afraid?"

"I'm sure."

"If this goes according to plan, I'll pay you double."

She nodded again.

"Remember what I told you? If he makes a move on you, drop the bag in the trash can, scream and run. If he makes comments but stays inside the car, just play along."

Another nod.

"No eye contact."

"Okay."

"You're a good girl. The work you do, it's vital to so many people. You understand that, don't you?"

"Yes, Mac."

"You know how those kids—and their parents— would suffer if they didn't have you? It's drops like the one today that let us finance the rest of them. That let me pay you."

"I know. It's okay, Mac."

"You're getting prettier by the day, and that worries me. You're going to have to be savvy, watch your back at all times, or you're of no use to us. Remember the self-defense classes. Promise me you'll practice what you learned or I won't be able to employ you anymore."

"I'll be careful. I promise."

She needed the money. She wanted to go to college and her mother didn't make enough to pay their bills. He understood that. But she had to understand something, too—that the world was a tough place.

"Good. I'm glad. I'd hate to lose you. You're by far the most promising teenager I've ever worked with."

Her eyes remained downcast.

She was the kind of girl you spent your whole life hoping to find.

And he'd met her now, like this.…

"Maybe someday, when you're a little older, we could, you know, hook up." He'd broken his number-one rule.

"Maybe."

In spite of everything he couldn't do—wouldn't do—he ran his fingers through her hair, allowed the palm of his hand brief contact with her cheek. And then he pulled back. There would be no involvement here.

But still…

"Would you like that? If we hooked up?"

She nodded again.

And he was satisfied.

3

Chandler, Ohio
Tuesday, August 3, 2010

In my office, I had this old chintz flowered couch in primary colors that should probably have been replaced. Most of my clients avoided it, preferring to sit in the chair across from me. But I didn't think that was a good place for Maggie Winston.

I didn't want her to feel isolated.

So when she arrived, all neat and clean and proper looking, I sat on the couch. And invited her to sit beside me.

I'd purposely left my pad and pen over on the desk, though I suspected I'd be desperate for them before this session was through. Still, kids tended to associate note taking with people who had authority over them and I needed Maggie to open up and talk to me.

She was a cute kid. Young woman, I amended as soon as she opened her mouth and thanked me for seeing her.

"You're welcome." I smiled at her.

"My mother told me to say that because we aren't paying you."

Cute and forthright. I liked that.

With chestnut-brown hair that hung halfway down her back, and dressed in a pink T-shirt and jeans, she looked like an ordinary kid, but Maggie's eyes were… calmer. Clearer. I guessed she had an awareness beyond her years.

Not surprising, given what I knew about her upbringing.

"I like your highlights," I told her. They were dark in the back, mostly in the under layer, and lighter on the top and sides. They were not maroon or blue or black like the highlights I'd been seeing on kids around town lately.

"Thanks. I did them myself."

"You did? They look great."

The girl nodded. "Mom hates them. She doesn't think I should have put them in."

"Did she buy the color?"

"No. I did."

"With your own money?"

"I didn't steal it if that's what you're thinking."

"I'm not thinking that at all. Listen, Maggie, you aren't here because you're in trouble. You understand that, don't you?"

The girl didn't answer, and she looked far too stoic for someone so young. I hated to see kids grow up too fast. Maybe because I'd had to.

Childhood should be fun, the only time in life for carefree self-centeredness.

"You don't have to stay," I said now. Maybe we needed to do this slow, in short sessions. If Maggie would even come back.

"I don't mind being here."

I was surprised by the girl's reply. Pleased, too.

"It's just that I honestly don't have any problems like my mom thinks I do, so we're wasting your time—especially since we aren't paying and all."

"It's my time. Why don't you let me worry about it?"

"Okay."

"So why does your mom hate the highlights?"

"She says they make guys notice me more."

"Is that why you wanted them?"

"Of course not. I wanted them because everybody else my age has highlights, and if I don't, I'll look like a poor kid. And when people know you're poor, they treat you differently."

In a town the size of Chandler, highlights weren't going to change what people knew about you. Maggie's trailer-park address was her giveaway. There were two mobile-home parks in the city. The one on the east side had privately owned manicured lots and a communal playground, clubhouse, swimming pool, basketball court and barbecue pit. The other, on the west side, was where Maggie lived. The units were old and rusty, their yards dirt patches with cars parked on them. The only communal area held overflowing trash bins.

"How do they treat you when you're poor?"

Maggie shrugged shoulders that appeared way too thin and fragile for the weighty world she seemed to be carrying on them. "You know, like you're not worth much. Some parents don't want their kids hanging out with kids like me. Like I'd be a bad influence. And they don't want their kids coming over to my house."

"Highlights aren't going to change where you live."

"It's not just that. Like if you're sick or whatever, your life is worth less than someone who has a lot of money to pay for medicine and stuff."

My hand reached for the pen that wasn't there.

"Have you or your mother ever been sick?"

"No."

"Has a child in your neighborhood been sick?"

"I don't know. We aren't close with any of them."

"Do you know someone who's been sick?"

The girl nodded.

"A friend of yours?"

She nodded again.

"You want to talk about it?"

Maggie shrugged, looked at her hands. "There's nothing to say, really. We were best friends. All through elementary and junior high. Jeanine was like me, living alone with her mom. Only her mom didn't have a job and drank all the time. Jeanine used to stay with us a lot. Until she got sick."

"What was wrong with her?"

"She got leukemia." Maggie had tears in her eyes when she glanced up. "She could have gone into remission, or at least not had so much pain, but they didn't have insurance and social services only did so much and then stopped."

"Did she die?"

"Yeah. Last year. At the beginning of eighth grade."

The girl didn't sob. She didn't even let her tears fall. She just sat there, wide-eyed.

"Have you done any grief counseling?" I asked. Her mother hadn't said a word about the death of Maggie's best friend the year before they were to enter high school together.

The information was critical. Starting high school was intimidating enough and without your best friend...

Maggie was emotionally ripe for someone to take advantage of.

"Not really, not anymore. They did some of that at

school for us right after Jeanine died. But I belong to this chat group on the Internet." Maggie grew animated for the first time. "It's for kids who are sick and can't get out to interact with other kids. One of my teachers told me about it last year. I talk to the kids that can't go to school. We're kind of like friends even though we don't ever meet or anything." The girl's eyes were bright with enthusiasm. "It's really helped a lot to talk to kids like Jeanine."

I had so many questions, but wasn't sure how long Maggie would be willing to speak with me. I decided to go back to the mother-daughter conflict.

"Why didn't you tell your mother the reason you wanted the highlights?"

"I'd rather she thinks I want to be hot."

Working with kids was difficult, sometimes excruciating, but their candor was refreshing. "Why would you want her to think something that upsets her when it's not true?"

"Mom's just, you know—she didn't finish high school. I mean, she could've if she didn't have me. She's smart and knows a lot about life and stuff, but sometimes she can't, I don't know, figure things out. And then she gets cranky."

"Cranky?"

"She yells and slams things and blames other people for stuff in her life."

"Who does she blame?"

"Depends."

"Does she blame you?"

"Sometimes."

"Give me an example of when that happens."

"Okay. When I'm doing homework and she tries to help and can't, she says it's because I didn't explain things right."

Unfortunately, it wasn't the first time I'd heard that one.

"What else?" I asked.

"Like the highlights. She doesn't get that people look down on us 'cause we're poor. She thinks I'm looking down on her if I say anything about fixing up our place. Or doing her hair. I bought her some makeup for Christmas and she thought I was cutting on her. Trying to change her. Like I thought I was too good for her." She shrugged. "I just figure it's better to let her think I'm interested in boys. It's what she expects, anyway."

"Why would she expect that?"

"By the time she was my age she'd already had sex."

I couldn't ignore the invitation she'd just handed me. "Have you had sex?" The offhand way kids talked of such intimacies was something I was used to. And worried about. But that was another issue.

"No."

I believed her. If her mother was right, and there was someone, which I was beginning to doubt, we'd caught the situation in time.

"Do you want to?"

"I'm a little curious, you know, about it. Some of my friends have done it and they say I'm missing out on a great part of life."

"So why haven't you done it?" I almost choked, asking that question of a fourteen-year-old. But I had several teenagers as clients. If I was going to help them, I had to meet them where they lived. Even if I hated the lodging.

I could guide. But not if I judged.

"I've never even had a boyfriend," Maggie was saying without much inflection.

"Do you want one?"

"One of the boys at school?" she asked. Her question made me curious. And a little edgy.

"Any boy." We needed to head out of the baby pool and into deeper waters.

"Boys my age are stupid, Dr. Chapman. Don't you know that?"

"Who doesn't know it?" I had to get her to trust me.

"My mom. People can be smart in some ways, but not in others. Mom, she's really smart when it comes to figuring out how to, I don't know, get away with stuff. But other things she just doesn't have a clue about. Like the way hormones affect boys and girls differently or that boys' brains don't catch up with girls' until they're out of high school."

She could have been spouting from a child development 101 textbook.

"Did they teach you that in school?"

"Uh-uh." She shook her head. "I read it on the Internet."

I pictured my pen writing furiously. *A lot of time on the Internet.*

"You said your mom was good at getting away with stuff. What kind of stuff?"

"You know, like the new law that says they can't shut off the electricity in the winter. Mom doesn't pay the bill in December so there's extra money for Christmas. And she's great at making up excuses when she's hungover and can't go to work. She comes up with really creative stuff and they believe her every time. She knows how to avoid the manager of the trailer park when our lot rent is late, and then when she has the money she takes it to him personally and acts like she just forgot. He always just smiles and tells her not to worry about the late fee. Sometimes he even asks her out for expensive dinners and she brings back a doggie bag for me. And she hooked us up to cable and the Internet without paying for it. That kind of stuff."

"She knows how to survive."

"Yeah. Like whenever anything breaks, she knows some trick to fix it, or else she calls someone over to do it for us so we don't need a service that charges a hundred bucks just to walk in the door."

"Where does your mom work?"

Maggie named the local department store. "She's a cashier, but that's just because she doesn't suck up enough to the managers to get a promotion. I keep telling her she should just do what they say and quit arguing and pretty soon she'll be calling the shots, but she doesn't listen."

We were getting off track, and that sense I have that tells me when something's surfaced was kicking hard.

"So you're curious about sex, but you don't like boys."

"I guess."

"Did I misunderstand?"

"It's not that I don't like boys—as though I like girls or something. I don't. I like guys all right. Just not…you know…immature ones."

And she was curious about sex.

Uh-oh.

Maybe Lori Winston was right about Maggie having a new interest. Moms often knew their daughters well.

I refrained from biting on a fingernail in the absence of my pen. Or a new pencil. It's just that I seem to relax more, hear more, when I'm chewing something. Or writing.

"Is there someone you like now?"

"No." Maggie seemed to be inordinately interested in a flower on my couch.

"You sure about that?"

For the first time, when the teenager glanced up, she avoided looking me straight in the eye. "Positive."

Okay. Well, I'd file that reaction. As soon as I could get to my pad and write it down.

I had nothing solid. No real clues.

Which put me right back to square one. Damn.

It wasn't my job to like or dislike my clients. Or to open my heart to them. But this was my town. I cared about the people who lived here.

And I liked this girl. I wanted to help her.

"Is there anything you want to talk about?"

"I paid for the hair color. It was on sale." Interesting choice of topic.

"How do you get your money?"

"I have a paper route." She named the local weekly that regularly employed Chandler teenagers. Like the larger papers used to do when I was growing up. "And I babysit whenever I can."

Maggie and eighty percent of the other female teenagers in this town.

We'd been talking for forty-five minutes. Lori Winston was due to arrive in another fifteen. Which didn't leave me much time.

"What else is going on in your life? Any concerns about starting high school?"

"Not really. I mean, it'll be all the same kids I went to junior high with. Just the teachers and building are different."

"Why'd you quit cheerleading?"

"Guys think cheerleaders are hot."

"And that's a bad thing…" At Maggie's frown—her first full-out facial expression since she'd been there—I added, "Because the guys who think they're hot are immature."

"Right," she said, and I was left feeling as if I'd just scored well on an exam. Sometimes my job was like being a soldier—you had to walk through some minefields to get the work done. You avoided them when you could, and prayed in case you couldn't.

"You said you read about teenage development on the Internet. And that you talk to sick kids online. Do you spend a lot of time on the Net?" Living alone with a working mother would probably give the girl plenty of opportunity to log on to what I considered the world's worst invention.

"Some."

"Do you talk to other people besides the kids?"

"Not much."

"But some."

"Yeah. I guess."

"Anyone in particular?"

"What is this, twenty questions?"

I'd just stepped on a mine.

"Do you know why your mother wanted you to come see me, Maggie?"

"Yeah. She thinks I'm doing it with an older guy."

"But you aren't."

"No. I told her that. But she doesn't believe me."

"Have you talked to any older men on the Internet?"

"I'm not stupid, Dr. Chapman. I know all about the sick stuff that goes on there. I stay away from it."

"If an older guy asked you out, would you go?"

"No. I'm too young."

"Would you want to?"

"Do I have to answer that?"

"No."

I waited, but Maggie didn't respond any further. I'd pushed as far as I could. The girl's entire demeanor had changed from willing cooperation to resentful suspicion.

"What else have you read about on the Internet?"

Maggie crossed her arms over her chest. "Just stuff. I read articles about all kinds of things."

"Do you smoke, Maggie?"

"Of course not. And I've never tried drugs, either. They're gross. And they'll kill you, too. That's what I keep telling my mom about her cigarettes. But she doesn't quit. Sometimes I think she'd rather be dead."

Did her mother do drugs?

"How about you? Have you ever felt like you'd rather be dead?"

"I'm only fourteen."

"That doesn't answer my question."

"Why would I want to die? I've hardly started to really live."

She had an edge.

"What do you and your friends do when you're together?"

"Hang out."

I had a choice. Let her go and hope I could get her to come back. Or try to help her and risk losing her.

"Do any of your friends know you like an older man?"

"Of course not. You think I'd tell them…"

Maggie stopped dead. And with a venomous glance, she got up and walked out of my office.

4

In the middle of lifting a bite-size piece of the most delicious-smelling pork to her lips, Sam paused. "What?" she asked, twirling the toothpick spear.

Her older brother, Pierce, wiped his hands on the white full-body chef's apron that was folded over and tied at his waist. "What *what?*"

"You're frowning."

"Sorry." Busying himself with the cooked pork, Pierce didn't elaborate. Sam stared at the big erase-board calendar on the wall beside him. Thursday, August 19. He had two functions that day.

"No, I want to know," Sam said, lowering the sample he'd just handed her. "What's on your mind?"

"Nothing." His fingers touched the food softly, gently, almost reverently, as he layered longer skewers with different-colored vegetables. Sam knew the finished product would look more like a work of art than the main course of the dinner he was catering that evening.

"Yeah, right. Nothing. And I'm quitting my job." Sam leaned on the cooking island Pierce had had installed when he'd remodeled the downstairs of the Victorian house they'd grown up in and opened his catering business.

She always stopped by during her lunch hour, hoping her brother would have something tasty to sample.

"What'd you think of the pork?" Pierce turned around. "You didn't like it?"

"I didn't try it. Not until you tell me what the frown was about."

"You, of course. It's always about you. But you know that."

"Me." Grumpily, she closed her teeth around the toothpick and slid the meat off. It was good.

Almost good enough to distract her from her bad mood.

"What about me, specifically, and why today?" she asked, softening her tone a bit as she snagged another piece of pork.

"You're becoming more and more like Dad every day. And you're worrying Mom. Have you even been upstairs to see her today?"

Pierce had renovated the house into separate apartments—one for him, one for their mother—on the second and third floors.

And her brother knew she hadn't been up upstairs. She'd come in the back door, which opened into the kitchen.

"What's the matter with her legs?" Sam groused defensively. "They still work, don't they? There's no reason she can't come down here once in a while to see me. She knows I'm going to be here. Every day. Like clockwork." Pierce babied their mother—just as their father had. He thought he was taking care of her, but to Sam, he was simply pandering to their mother's fears. Especially the fear that Sam was incapable of protecting herself.

But that was a twenty-year argument she definitely didn't have time for today.

Pierce folded a long piece of foil over his skewers.

"And how am I like Dad?" she asked when it became fairly clear that he'd relegated her "mother" quip to a "not worthy of response" status.

"You're obsessing."

No, she wasn't. Pierce could accuse her of many things—and be at least half-right. But not this time. Obsessing led to mistakes. And in her line of work, a mistake could mean death.

Peter Jones, their father, had found that out the hard way. He'd let a personal tragedy cloud his professional judgment.

"Anyway, is this just a personal observation, or did Mom put you up to it?" Living alone upstairs with too much time on her hands, Grace had perfected the art of worrying.

"We've talked about it, but the observation is mine."

"Just for the sake of clarity, what am I supposedly obsessing over?"

"This idea that there's some big local meth operation. You're using your own resources and time to do unsanctioned investigative work."

"Who told you that?"

"What does it matter who told me? Are you?"

"No." She looked him straight in the eye.

He stared back. Hard. "You swear?"

"I swear."

Not to say she hadn't thought about it. It was something her grandfather would have done. And her dad, too. But times were different now. With the economic hardships Fort County had suffered over the past couple of years, there weren't enough cops to do the sanctioned work, let alone initiate their own investigations. "I'm pulling extra shifts just to cover my normal workload," she told Pierce.

"So what about the shooting?"

That had been seventeen days ago. Why bring it up now? "There was an internal investigation just like there always is when gunfire is involved. Everything cleared just as I knew it would. We followed procedure to a T when it went down that night."

"Have you talked to anyone?"

"Of course. Everyone who asks about it."

"I mean professionally."

She loved Pierce. Her mother, too. But sometimes they drove her crazy.

"I spoke to the county shrink the next day," she said. And then, relenting, added, "And I called Kelly, too."

His eyes narrowed and she knew she'd said too much. Rather than relieving his worries, she'd confirmed that she'd needed a shrink.

"So you are having problems with it."

Shrugging, Sam stuffed her mouth with pork, talking while she chewed. "A little trouble sleeping at first. Insomnia happens sometimes when a gun goes off in your ear while you're in the middle of a phone conversation."

She wasn't sure Pierce could understand a word of what she said with her mouth full.

Just as she'd intended.

She wasn't going to give her brother—or her mother or Kyle—the chance to mess with her head. They didn't understand that her being a cop was a good thing. The right thing.

Unfortunately, they were the three people she was closest to. Just her damned luck.

"Thanks for lunch," she said, grabbing another couple of pieces of meat. "Gotta get back. Tell Mom I said hi and not to worry. I'm directing traffic for a stoplight installation in Milburn today." The tiny village at the west end of Fort County only had one traffic light. Or would have by the end of the afternoon. It had a bar, too. And two churches. And that was it. Not a single gas station or grocery store that could be held up. Or a school for dealing drugs.

Pierce was frowning again. She tended to have that effect on the people in her life.

"The meat was great," she added, because it was true. And because she hated it when her big brother was upset with her, she asked, "Was that the new marinade?"

He didn't smile. "With Worcestershire and vinegar, yeah."

Maybe tomorrow she'd go to Hamacher's for lunch.

Kyle was in the barn with Lillie and the colt, sitting on an upturned feed bucket as he finished off the last of a peanut-butter-and-jelly sandwich his grandpa had made that morning for Kyle to take to school. A familiar figure filled the lighted doorway.

"Bob Branson, how the hell are you?" Standing, Kyle wiped his fingers on jeans that had already seen a full morning's work and held out his hand. Zodiac was there beside him, wagging her tail.

"Can't complain," the older man said, returning Kyle's vigorous handshake and at the same time reaching down to pet the German shepherd.

Halfway between Kyle and his father in age, Bob had been around for as long as Kyle could remember. He'd also been a lot heavier than he was right now.

"You've lost weight."

The man chuckled, patting his midsection. "I could afford it."

"How's business?"

Ohio was the second largest producer of eggs in the United States, and with more than five hundred thousand dozen shipped per week, Bob's local poultry operation was one of the state's largest. It was also where most of Kyle's feed corn crop ended up. Chickens ate a lot. Thank God.

And, even in a struggling economy, egg consumption hadn't declined.

"Business is good," Bob said, walking over to the stall where Lillie had just begun making a ruckus. She was still a little territorial when it came to her two-week-old son, Rad. The colt stood at the door of the stall, his head tilted curiously toward the new voice. "We've hired a couple of extra hands for city leaf pickup in the fall and have more orders for compost than we're going to be able to fill." Bob rubbed Rad's nose. "He's a good-looking lad," he said. "Right up to your old man's standards."

Kyle's goal was to fill his father's horse barn to capacity, then sell the good-quality quarter horses to families and farms across Ohio, just as his father had done.

"He's a start," Kyle said, though he wasn't sure he planned to sell the colt. Sam had taken a liking to the little guy. Which was why his name was Radiance. And while he could in no way refer to a colt of his by such a ridiculous name, even if Sam had chosen it, he could live with the shortened version.

"Has Grandpa been out to see him?"

"Of course," Kyle said. "I carried him out here the night she foaled. And a couple of times since. Each time he thinks it's the first he's seen the colt. But he knows Lillie."

"It's so hard…" Bob broke off. "Such a shame."

Grandpa was ninety-two. He'd lived a long, good

life. Kyle didn't want anyone feeling sorry for either of them.

"So what's up?" He studied his friend. Bob was a busy man. Too busy to stop by just to shoot the breeze.

Bob stared through the large open window at the back of the barn, and Kyle wondered if he was about to tell him he was sick. The man's jeans were hanging on him. And the forearms exposed by his rolled sleeves looked almost emaciated.

God, how long had it been since he'd seen the older man? Six months? A year? Kyle couldn't remember if Bob had been around when he'd stopped by the Branson farm last fall to finalize the details of a corn delivery.

And it wasn't as if the man came by to see Grandpa— which was how Kyle kept up most of his contacts these days.

His grandfather didn't like to leave the farm, and Kyle didn't like to leave Grandpa.

Bob was one of those people who felt uncomfortable seeing Kyle's grandfather in his current state.

Scared was more like it, Kyle figured. And he understood.

"Let's take a walk," Bob said, convincing Kyle that bad news was imminent. Let whatever disease he had be treatable, Kyle offered up by habit, though he was no longer sure anyone was listening.

Except maybe his old man.

"Show me the field."

"The field" was Kyle's experiment. His attempt to grow a hybrid feed corn that would produce double the starch per kernel—and cut in half the amount of corn necessary to produce a gallon of ethanol.

A dream that had become his last-ditch effort to save the farm, his birthright. Not that anyone else knew that.

Kyle had made two big mistakes in his life—both with women—and was in debt up to his throat. Seeing no other way out, he'd spent the last of his savings and hocked the farm on a chance to make a mint on a hybrid crop. If this year's crop didn't show some measure of success, he might have gambled himself right into bankruptcy court.

A five-minute walk later and they were standing in the field. Bob pulled back the shock on a ripe ear of corn, fingering one of the soon-to-be-plump kernels of corn he'd exposed. The man might be a chicken farmer, but he knew corn. And soybeans, too. He grew close to five hundred acres of each.

"One ear per stalk" was all Bob said. One ear was typical for feed corn—unlike it's cousin, sweet corn, which had multiple ears.

"Can't afford to share the nutrients."

"I thought soaking the seeds was going to increase the starch."

"That's the idea. And if this works, I'll be able to maintain one ear per stalk with double starch. That's still double output."

"Right." Bob checked another couple of ears. "And you aren't going to get a true comparison reading unless you're taking one-eared corn up against one-eared corn, since that's the standard for ethanol corn."

"So what do you think?" Kyle's father had thought Kyle was crazy when he'd first talked about his "schemes" back in high school. As Kyle remembered it, Bob hadn't been as skeptical.

"I think you might be on to something." The older man straightened. "I'll be waiting to hear how they test out. And in the meantime, make damned sure you keep this stuff away from my chickens!"

"Yes, sir." Kyle nodded, his expression serious, though

he knew Bob wasn't the least bit worried that Kyle would mix in the experimental crop with the regular feed corn he also grew.

Such a mistake, if it did happen, could be catastrophic.

"I plant and harvest them a week or two apart," Kyle added. "The crop that pays the bills comes first."

Turning, he and Bob headed back up the row to the dirt road that led to the barn, Zodiac at their heels. "I thought you should know that Viola and I are divorcing."

Kyle's scuffed work boots didn't miss a beat. His heart did. "What happened?"

His own mother had died before Kyle was old enough to remember her, and Viola Branson had partially taken her place.

"Me, that's what happened," Bob said. "I screwed up. Took a risk I shouldn't have. Got in too deep to stop myself in spite of Viola's many pleas. Thank God nothing I did hurt the business or my family's finances. Viola stood it as long as she could and then she left me. I got the papers earlier this week. My biggest regret is how much I hurt that girl, Kyle. I love her."

Kyle's thoughts scrambled with a hundred questions he knew he would never ask. "Where is she?"

"At Shauna's." The oldest of their three daughters. Not a place of her own.

"Maybe you still have a chance, then. As long as you've gotten out of whatever it was you were into." Horses? Tables? Women? "Maybe she'll come home."

"Nope. I'm not contesting it. She'll have her divorce by the end of next month."

"You're not fighting for her? After thirty years together?"

"Nope. I don't trust myself not to hurt her again."

What the hell was going on? But Bob's business was his own. He'd tell Kyle what he wanted him to know. Still, Kyle had one more question he needed to ask.

"Is there someone else?"

"Nope," Bob said again, his voice curiously flat. "Never has been. Since I first set eyes on Viola, she's been the only girl for me."

"Does she know that?"

"Yeah."

"And it doesn't make a difference?"

"Sometimes love just isn't enough."

Bob's words stopped the flow of Kyle's thoughts. He understood. Bob must have known he would.

Love hadn't been enough to get him and Sam to the church.

"Nope, and I'll never replace her, either," Bob was saying, almost to himself, as they approached the horse barn.

Kyle got that, too.

He wondered if Bob had any idea how much pain was coming.

Chandler, Ohio
Tuesday, August 24, 2010

I loved to skate. In-line skate, that is. When I was on skates, I felt strong. I could fly through the wind—be free. It was also my time for reflection and sometimes, as with so much in life, that which served me well was also the bane of my existence.

Tonight, that was the case. It was a glorious summer evening. The sun had been shining all day and was slowly disappearing in the west, leaving a trail of vivid reds and oranges and golds in its wake. Humidity was low. And the eighty-two-degree temperature hardly felt warm as the wind resistance my speed was creating lightly breezed against my skin.

I was on one of my favorite routes—an old railroad track that had been paved to make a bike/skate/running path that ran through four counties. The section I flew over wound through farm country, mostly cornfields, with stalks that were shoulder-high in places. Those same stalks would soon be taller than me. From spring planting until fall harvesting, I skated by, witnessing birth, growth and death. All in a few short months.

It kind of put my human existence in perspective. Add some time to the mix—several decades, I hoped—and that would be the pattern of my life, too. All of our lives. Just that simple. Birth, growth and death. And a new spring would come with fresh seedlings. New birth. New growth. And next fall, another death.

A never-ending cycle. As exemplified by the stalks of corn whizzing past in my peripheral vision.

I liked the never-ending part; it defied death.

I half chuckled—the half that could spare the air. Leave it up to me to turn a recreational skate and a few stalks of corn into a philosophical life lesson.

But it wasn't the lesson I was seeking that night, and I just kept "skating on my problems," as I referred to my habit of meditating on anything that was bothering me while I skated. Heck, who was I kidding? I skated on *everything*. From what my new office couch should look like to the fact that my household was ruled by a four-pound very spoiled toy poodle.

Whenever something puzzled me, stumped me, caused any kind of doubt within me, I "skated on it."

Sometimes I just "skated on it" for confirmation. Or for the courage to actually do whatever I was pondering.

That was tonight. I knew what I should do. I just needed the courage to do it. So much was at risk. A child's life.

Skating took away the fear. And any other distractions that clogged my thoughts. And…I could see that I had no time to lose.

My brake pushed against the black asphalt and, with knees bent, I took the stop like a pro, turned and traversed the two miles back to my car quickly enough to win a speed-skating race. I didn't even bother to wipe off the sweat sliding beneath the back of my sleeveless T-shirt before I was on my phone.

Sam picked up on the first ring. "Sam?" I asked, though I recognized her voice.

"Yeah?" My high school buddy sounded hesitant. Like I was a doctor bearing bad news.

Probably because she'd been a recent—mostly uncooperative—sort of patient. If you could call a friend seeking an M.D. referral for sleeping pills a patient.

"How are you?" I asked, because I cared. And to bug her, too. Maybe if I bugged her enough, she'd unload on me. It would be in anger, but I wasn't picky. Anger would open the door I needed to get inside and help her.

As a general rule, carefully directed anger could be a positive thing.

And if Sam got mad, she'd get over it.

"I'm fine."

"Sleeping?" Another thing I knew about Sam—she might lie to herself on occasion, but she wouldn't lie to me.

"Some."

"Better than you were?" I grabbed a pen out of the cup holder beside me and tapped the leather steering wheel of my spiffy new blue Dodge Nitro. I'd drive home, but it'd be kinda hard to push the gas with an in-line skate on my foot. I chewed the end of the pen instead.

"Not noticeably."

"I wish you'd come talk to me."

"I wish you'd give me a referral for sleeping pills."

"Uh-uh." Sam needed to deal with the demons keeping her up at night, not numb them.

"I'll probably be glad you said that at some point."

"Probably."

"Right now it kind of pisses me off. I mean, what are friends for?"

I was sitting in my SUV with the door open in a deserted parking lot on a country road—something Sam wouldn't approve of if she knew. "To have your back," I said, dragging my heavy feet, still in skates, inside and locking the door.

Sam's silence was compliance enough for me.

"I called to ask a favor," I said then, back to tapping my pen instead of chewing it. Sam and I had known each other since grade school. And we'd played basketball together for a year during high school before I quit to be a receptionist at the local assisted-living facility. (We'd called it an old folks' home back then.) Sam had spent more time hanging out at the police station and with her farmer friend, Kyle Evans, than with any of the other kids from school. But we'd stayed friends.

I'd always liked her. More importantly, I trusted her. Implicitly.

"What's up?"

"I've got a client who might be in trouble." At least, I hoped I still had a client. Maggie Winston had stood me up that day—for the second time, which was why I was calling Sam. I was worried I'd lost Maggie.

I filled Sam in on the original call I'd received from

Lori Winston and my first visit with Maggie. "I've seen her once since then," I added. "She stopped by my office without an appointment, and after I assured her that our conversations were completely confidential, she asked me some questions that left little doubt that she's interested in an older man. From what she said, I'm pretty sure she found him on the Internet."

"Do you think she's met him in person?"

"Yes."

"How sure are you of that?"

"Ninety-five percent. I know she met a man on the Internet. I know she's seen him in person, though it sounds like, as yet, there's been no physical interaction. I'm not even sure they spoke when she saw him. I know she's interested in an older man. She hasn't admitted that the man she met on the Internet and the one she has a crush on are the same person. Maybe the guy she's interested in is an unsuspecting teacher at school and the Internet thing is unrelated. At this point, I'm certain enough that something's going on to be worried. But I have no proof. That's why I'm calling you."

"Do you have the guy's name?"

"Nope."

"How about an age?"

"I think he must be past thirty." Maggie had mentioned a friend whose father was killed in Kuwait. Which meant the friend had to be a lot older than Maggie.

"You aren't giving me much to go on here."

"I know."

"Maggie Winston, you said her name was?"

"Yeah. Can you just keep an eye on her for me?"

"I'll see what I can find out."

Dropping the pen back into the cup holder, I unlocked the car door and climbed out. "Thanks, Sam."

"Yeah. You owe me."

"I know." I owed me, too. Another couple miles of skating. I was two short of my usual six.

"So how about that sleeping-pill referral?"

"Nope." If Sam really wanted a sleep aid, she could get it from her M.D. We both knew that.

"You suck at paying your debts...." Sam rang off before I could encourage her to stop by my office for a chat. Dropping my cell onto the seat, I locked the car and pushed off.

Sam was a great woman. Honest. Hardworking. Sincere. Maybe I'd stop by her place over the weekend. It would piss her off, but if I could break through that shell she'd been throwing up at me since I'd come back to town after college, all certified and capable of seeing through her, if I could help her fight the inner demons that drove her, she'd probably get over it.

Yeah—I bent my knees to take a bump in the path— if I could squeeze it in, I'd stop by Sam's on Saturday. If I was lucky, she'd have some of her brother's samples to share....

5

Sam had never studied finance. Had never been the least bit curious about what in the heck the Dow Jones industrial average really was. A cop's family was never going to be rich. Never going to need to know a whole lot about investments or savings or capital gains. So maybe the state's financial crisis, which filtered down to Fort County and the sheriff's department, had come as more of a surprise to her than some. Maybe others had been more mentally prepared for the cutbacks that made it tough for cops to do their jobs when crime was at an all-time high.

Hell, they were living in a state with one of the highest unemployment rates in the nation. Ohio was a manufacturing and farming state. Pretty much every major company in nearby Dayton had either closed or moved out of state over the past couple of years, leaving desperation and deprivation in their wake.

Pretty towns that had provided suburban neighborhoods for workers from the six GM-related plants in the city were now boarded up, paint peeling from the picturesque houses and foreclosure signs in the windows. Where flowers had once lined the streets, there were

now weeds. Tall weeds, with hairlike follicles and no
community money to mow them down.

Sam had patrolled these streets and seen the changes.
And along with the disappearing jobs, the growing desperation, they'd seen a huge hike in crime. In the current
economy, there was less money to pay for law enforcement, and fewer officers to contain the growing desperation. And desperate people did desperate things. Sam
didn't need to be good at math to know that the odds were
stacked against law-enforcement agencies.

Still, there was a good side. There always was if you
looked hard enough. Sam had learned that a long time
ago. About the time her father had been killed while at-
tempting to apprehend a man he thought was a pedophile
attacking a child. One positive thing was that he'd died
not knowing he'd attacked a father in the middle of some
good-natured roughhousing with his child.

And the positive spin on their current economic down-
swing was that Sam got a car to herself—when gas money
was available. There weren't enough deputies left on staff
for them to partner up anymore.

Which meant that she didn't have anyone watching
over her every minute of the day.

And that was one reason why no one, including Kelly
Chapman and Kyle, knew she'd been driving by the west-
side trailer park several times a day for the past week—on
duty and off. Listening to hunches was a lot easier if she
didn't have to answer any questions.

School was due to start just after Labor Day—only
six days away. If Maggie Winston was up to something,
chances were good that summer's end would escalate her
activities.

So far, Sam hadn't seen so much as a shoe print....

There she was.

The girl looked a lot older than the photo Sam had been carrying around with her for a week, clipped out of Chandler's 2009 junior high yearbook. But it was definitely Maggie.

Wearing denim shorts and a green short-sleeved shirt, her oddly highlighted hair down around her shoulders, and her feet in green flip-flops that matched her shirt, Maggie looked like any of a hundred teenagers out on Chandler's streets that day.

Sam slowed the white Mustang that was pretty much a member of her family. Pappy, her grandfather, had helped her rebuild the classic car ten years ago and it had never let her down.

The girl looked neither left nor right as she stepped down from the trailer she shared with her mother on the edge of the run-down park. Weeds and trash covered the common ground around the mobile homes.

The place was nothing like the flower-lined streets that surrounded Sam's double-wide model on the other side of town—a mere three miles away.

The only thing of beauty Sam could see here was the young woman striding with purpose toward the exit on the other side of the park. Rounding a corner, Sam was able to keep Maggie in sight mostly because of the lack of trees between them. She turned again, in time to see Maggie climb into the front passenger seat of a nondescript American-made two-door maroon sedan—2006, if Sam had her windshield moldings right.

Ohio license plate, DSL T77. Sam committed it to memory. One of these days she'd keep paper and pen handy to write things down.

Maybe.

When she got old and lost her ability to remember everything she saw.

She wondered if Maggie knew the bottom of her shirt was stuck in the waistband at the back of her shorts.

Keeping a reasonable distance, Sam followed the car. A female was driving. Blonde. And young, based on the glimpse Sam caught of her in her side-view mirror.

Out on the state highway that connected Chandler to several other small towns in Fort County before eventually leading to the big kahuna—Dayton—she was able to stay two cars behind the girls without any effort. Off duty until noon, she was in jeans and an oxford shirt and blended in with the rest of the world just fine as she tooled along under the speed limit.

If the girls were on their way to an adult rendezvous with some lecherous creep, they didn't appear to be in any hurry to get there.

"Probably just on their way to the mall," Sam muttered to the Mustang. And she could be at a desk at the station getting caught up on paperwork, which was what she'd planned to do with her Tuesday morning off.

And then she saw the sedan signal a turn. Mechanic Street. She knew the road. She knew all the roads in the county, but this particular street was more familiar than some.

She'd seen it written on a blood-spattered scrap of paper that was in the bag of things picked up off the floor of the Holmes family living room the night Mr. Holmes had shot his wife and then blown his own brains out.

One-oh-nine Mechanic Street. She'd investigated the place. The home was vacant, bank owned and for sale. She'd figured maybe Holmes, who'd had his accounts and mortgage at the same bank, had known the Morrises, the people who'd lived there. She'd tried to find them herself, but so far no luck.

The family had left no forwarding address and hadn't

bought another home, or registered for public utilities, like electricity and phone.

Mechanic Street was a dead end. Fifteen homes, a couple of dogs, mown lawns, landscape lighting, that kind of thing.

If Sam followed the girls down the street, her Mustang wouldn't go unnoticed.

"This is where we part," she told the car as she pulled into a convenience store on the corner. "Back in a minute." Climbing out, she locked the door, rubbing her waist with the back of her forearm as she did so. Feeling for the gun tucked into her waistband.

Check and double-check. Always. Pappy had been firm on that one. So firm that he'd once grounded her for a week because she'd forgotten her house key and had been sitting outside on their porch on Main Street, waiting for him and Mom and Pierce to get home from Dayton.

It had been broad daylight, and people they knew were out and about. Facts that she'd pointed out to him. Facts that had fallen on deaf ears.

When it came to personal safety, check and double-check. She'd never forgotten again.

Crossing behind the store, Sam cut through a field of weeds that had once been a strawberry patch—and a dog run when a breeder had owned the property—to the back side of Mechanic. The yards were well maintained with swimming pools and trampolines.

One, about halfway down, had a big new barn set at the far end of the lot. Sam scrambled through a wall of six-foot-tall shrubbery, catching her bun, and crouched behind the barn, peering out around the side.

And barely made it in time to see Maggie walk up the drive to a house across the street.

Sam had no idea where Maggie's friend was. She couldn't see the street.

Maggie stood on the front porch, speaking with someone behind a closed screen door. Either that or she was talking to herself.

Maybe the girls were picking up a third friend to go to the mall.

Before she could conjecture further, Maggie was back on the drive. Walking alone. Carrying nothing.

The girl looked straight ahead as she walked down the drive and was lost from Sam's view.

Feeling like a really bad rendition of a destitute private eye, Sam slunk back through the underbrush to her car.

As a general rule, Kyle tried to get errands away from the farm done in the early morning hours of Mondays, Wednesdays and Fridays, when the nurse he'd hired with the help of government assistance stopped by to check up on Grandpa. Twenty years older than Kyle, Clara could have held her own with his grandfather even in his prime. And she didn't mind staying an extra hour or so to allow Kyle time in town.

Today, the first Wednesday in September, he made it through the majority of their grocery shopping—buying mark-off brands of everything except the chocolate sandwich cookies that were Grandpa's favorites—in just under an hour. Now he was anxious to get back.

Clara had had to come early that morning to check Grandpa's blood pressure before he ate. Kyle would be monitoring it throughout the next twenty-four hours, something the doctor had recommended after Clara had called in the stats on Monday.

Kyle knew his grandfather's time was coming, and he liked to hang close.

Now that Chandler had a department store, where you could buy plumbing PVC, jeans, work boots and food all under one roof—and do banking, too—he could be a lot more efficient. Especially since the place was open twenty-four hours. Lucky for him, most Chandlerites weren't in a shopping mood at seven in the morning.

"Yo, Kyle, what's up?"

Just as he'd been enjoying having the place to himself... Kyle turned and felt a twinge of remorse as he recognized the owner of the voice.

"David. How are you, man?" The clean-cut, model-handsome man was already in the suit and tie that had been his trademark ever since he'd returned to Chandler with a brand-new law degree and bar certification ten years before.

He held up a bag of disposable diapers. "Rough night," he said with a half grimace. "Devon's been going at it from both ends for more than twenty-four hours now. I had to take the day off yesterday to help with him."

What did it say about Kyle that the attorney's plight made him envious? Not that he wanted any kid to be sick, but to be a father...

"And we just found out on Monday that Susan's pregnant again," David added, twisting an invisible knife. "Number five. I gotta tell you, man, it's mornings like these that show me what a smart guy you are. I gotta be in court at eight, and after missing yesterday, I still have briefs to review."

"Sounds like you need some beer and a good game of barn darts," Kyle offered.

"Now that's just what the doctor ordered." David grinned. "How about Friday night? Susan has the church ladies coming over for crafting."

Sam worked the late shift on Fridays. Not that it mattered. It wasn't like Kyle kept nights free for her.

"You got it," he told the man who'd helped him through his god-awful divorce. David had saved half the farm for him. If Kyle had confided in him about his first mistake, the one before his marriage, the lawyer would have told him he was a fool to fork out money to a woman without a conscience.

"What's this loser got?" Pierce Jones, Sam's older brother, elbowed David from behind.

"A drunken game of darts," Kyle told the man he'd once thought would be his brother-in-law. "You want to help me beat the crap out of him again?"

"Always. When?"

"Friday night."

The jeans and tightly fitting black T-shirt Pierce wore emphasized muscles that were mostly, in Kyle's opinion, wasted in that fancy kitchen of his. He looked more like a cop than chef. Maybe if Sam's older brother had followed in their father's and Pappy's footsteps, Sam wouldn't have felt compelled to do it herself. "I'll bring eats," Pierce added.

There were upsides to most things. If you looked hard enough.

"Why don't you bring that sister of yours?" David headed around Kyle's loaded basket toward the self-checkout stand that had just opened. "She distracts Kyle enough to give us half a chance."

"Right," Pierce said, his expression sobering. "More like she'd beat us all." He looked at Kyle. "Why the hell that woman can't see what's right in front of her…" Shaking his head, Pierce walked off toward the fresh vegetables—obviously buying ingredients for the day's fare, whatever that might be.

Kyle directed his buggy toward the bin of five-dollar movies to see if there was anything really old that might spark Grandpa's interest. Was it just a guy's lot in life, he wondered, to want what he didn't have?

6

He drove by her place. Just to make certain she was okay. Then drove by again, alternately wanting a glimpse of her and hoping to hell she stayed locked inside.

If nothing else, he had to get her out of that hellhole. She deserved far better than the trash-ridden rusted heap of garbage her mother called home.

School was going to be starting again in a matter of days. Later than most Ohio schools, which went back before Labor Day. Once she was in class, she wasn't going to be able to do as much work for him. She'd have to concentrate on her studies. He'd insist on it.

As he did with all of his crew.

But maybe he could get her a couple of more jobs this week. Slide her some extra pay. He'd tell her it was tips.

That way, he could keep his eye on her. Just to make certain she was okay. To put his mind at ease so he could get on with the business of living.

For now, she was all he thought about. In the middle of the night. In the middle of the day. Sometimes the feel of her cheek against his palm intruded when he was having sex.

He kept replaying those few seconds of contact over

and over. The softness of her skin. That touch had done things to him.

Remarkable, unbelievable things.

In all of his thirty-four years, he'd never felt like this.

But he wasn't going to be stupid about it. Emotional and physical attraction brought men down. Powerful men. Again and again.

He had his code. And wouldn't break it.

So he'd watch out for her. Pass her a little bounty when he could.

In the privacy of his own mind he'd entertain thoughts about the silky touch of her skin. Of her sweet innocent smile. Those eyes that saw so much. And sometimes peered up at him with a hunger, a longing, that was far beyond her years.

He'd keep his thoughts private. And he'd be very, very careful.

Sam didn't like being kept up nights by questions that wouldn't go away.

And so on Thursday she was at work before the lights were even turned on, looking for answers.

Answers about the upswing in drug use. Answers about Maggie. Hell, she'd be happy to find answers to questions she hadn't yet asked.

She had to know. Knowledge was control. Protection. For her family and her town. Maybe her father or Pappy was sending her messages. Maybe the Fates were. Maybe it was just her instincts. Whatever. But Pierce was right about one thing.

She couldn't let the drug thing go. She'd been talking with a man when he blew his brains out. A man who'd just killed his wife. A man who, by all accounts, had been an

upstanding successful citizen, a good husband and father
with a happy family.

Chuck Sewell was at the station already. Putting in
extra hours just like she was. Like her, he lived alone.
And, like her, he wasn't letting the Holmes case just go
away.

"You know, if it had been an isolated event, maybe
I could get beyond it," Sam told her colleague as they
went over a list of all the local and state drug dealers they
knew.

"A more than one hundred percent increase in drug-
related cases this year is a little hard to ignore," Chuck
said. "We're going to have to get dogs out to the schools
more often even if it means we have to come in off shift.
And give harsher first-time sentences when we catch
someone. We have to get the word out or we're never
going to be able to put up a fight."

"Have you talked to the sheriff about this?"

"I plan to this morning. I'm on my way to meet him
for breakfast. You want to come?"

Samantha declined, but only because she had more
work to do before her actual shift started.

"Tell him I totally agree with you and will work whatever extra hours he needs. On my dollar."

Who else, if not those sworn to protect, could find
answers and put a stop to the escalating rate of crime?

"Got it," Chuck said. "We'll get these guys, Sam, I
promise you."

Sam believed him.

And then there was the challenge of Maggie.

At least Sam had a place to look for answers. She knew
the address that the teenager had visited the day before.
All she had to do was look it up.

She typed in the number on Mechanic Street.

David Abrams. A good guy.

She'd heard he and his family had just moved to a bigger house.

Relieved, Sam grabbed her phone. Dialed. It was a sure bet that Maggie's visit to the home two days before had nothing to do with either an older man or drugs.

But maybe David could shed a little more light on the girl herself.

Maybe.

She had David on the line before she'd even brought up the next computer screen.

"Is it too early?" she asked the attorney she'd hand-picked for Kyle when he was about to lose his beloved farm to his witch ex-wife. David was straight up. Smart as a whip.

One of Chandler's shining stars.

And he loved his wife, Susan, who happened to be Chuck's sister.

"Of course not—what's up?" David said in spite of the fact that it wasn't yet seven. He liked to prepare before 8:30 a.m. court. Or maybe he left home early to avoid the morning chaos of four young children. He hadn't seemed as eager as Susan to pop out babies one after the other.

Of course, that could just be Sam's take on it. She couldn't imagine a woman wanting to do that to herself.

"How's Susan feeling?" Pierce had told Sam the news of the Abrams' impending fifth child the day before at lunch.

"Good. No morning sickness so far this time."

"And how about you? You ready to do it all again?"

"Susan does most of the work," he reminded her. "And if she's happy, I'm happy."

Not quite a glowing testimony to fatherhood.

"I'm just being nosy here, but I was wondering what you know about Maggie Winston."

"Maggie Winston? I don't know the name. Who is she?"

"A fourteen-year-old kid. She was apparently at your house the other morning." She told him when.

"Oh. That was probably Glenna's friend. She's the only person I know of who stopped by. Susan never mentioned the girl's name."

"Glenna?"

"Glenna Reynolds. She's been helping Susan out all summer and wanted to bring a friend of hers who's willing to pinch-hit whenever Glenna can't make it. It's her senior year and her mom's sick so she'll have a lot on her plate. But she doesn't want us to find another nanny. She needs the money so she's trying to find a backup instead."

Babysitting. A normal teenage activity.

Sam had been wriggling around on her belly like a worm doing surveillance on a potential babysitter. Not the victim of a pedophile.

"Did the meeting go well?"

"It was brief. Susan had already done some checking and didn't like the girl's background. She started to tell me about her, but Devon's been sick all week and we just never got back to it. Why, is the girl in trouble? I can ask Susan for more details if you need them."

"No. No. Don't do that. There's no problem. She's a good kid. A friend of mine just mentioned something...."

"Well, now that I know she's just fourteen, she wouldn't have worked for us, anyway. Susan and I need a sitter with a driver's license. That way we can leave our van behind when we go out and know that all the kids would have a safe means of transportation in case of emergency."

Leave it to David to think of everything.

Chandler, Ohio
Thursday, September 2, 2010

I was facing a full day. Starting in about ten minutes. Back-to-back clients all morning, the soup kitchen at lunch, followed by the forty-minute drive to the airport and a flight to Denver, where I'd be assessing a young woman believed by the defense attorney who'd hired me to have inflicted physical abuse on herself and then blamed his client—her husband. Not the best domestic-abuse defense, but possibly the truth. I suspected the young woman could be suffering from a form of Munchausen syndrome.

People with Munchausen—named in 1951 after a German cavalry officer in 1700 who was a teller of tall tales—had a severe need for attention and invented illnesses or injuries to get it. To them, doctors and hospitals were like a bar to an alcoholic.

It was a tough one. You had a young woman with severe bruising over sixty percent of her body, a swollen face and a broken arm—which would certainly elicit jury sympathy. And a young man who stood to have his life irrevocably changed for the worse when he'd possibly done nothing more than fall in love with a sick woman.

Or…you had a moneyed and privileged young man who could afford an imaginative defense attorney—and could afford to fly in an expert witness from Ohio—who'd come up with a way to beat his wife and get away with it.

I could be morally responsible if my testimony set a wife beater free and he eventually killed the woman.

But the thing that got me was that the woman didn't have a single injury on her back—a place she couldn't reach. If she were being attacked, wouldn't she have turned her back on her assailant? Just to deflect the blows?

I—

"Boss?" My ancient intercom system buzzed.

"Yeah?"

"That WT woman's on line one."

WT? What was with Deb lately? "Excuse me?" I knew what the acronym stood for—white trash. You couldn't grow up in a redneck county without hearing the terminology. But that didn't mean it was or had ever been acceptable. And certainly not in my office.

"Lori Winston."

Maggie's mom.

"Okay, I'll take it… And…Deb?"

"Yeah?"

"I don't ever want to hear *WT* again. Ever."

"Sorry."

I should have hung up. But, come on, this was me. And my receptionist had just acted out of character.

"Is everything okay with you?"

"I'm not sure."

"You want to talk about it?"

"Maybe. Not today."

"I'm here, you know that. Any time of the day or night…"

"I know. Now get the phone before that woman hangs up and comes down here and I have to tell her that you're with a client."

I picked up the phone.

Lori Winston was—how had Maggie put it—*cranky*. It was the way she got when she didn't understand things, her daughter had explained.

I was leaning more toward the idea that fear prompted Ms. Winston's raised voice.

"Calm down," I said softly. "I want to help."

"Don't tell me what to do. I'll calm down when I'm good and ready."

"Okay." I could live with that.

"I want to know why there's a different condom in my daughter's purse."

I didn't ask why she'd been in her daughter's purse. Or if Maggie knew. The answer to both questions was pretty obvious. Lori Winston was a mother worried about her only child.

And no, Maggie didn't know. Otherwise, she would have been on the receiving end of this tirade instead of me.

"Maggie went for her high school orientation this week, right?"

"Yes."

"It's a new school year. Maybe they give the girls an opportunity to pick up a condom to protect themselves. Just in case."

I knew they did. Though I didn't agree with the practice. But that was another issue. One I didn't have time for today.

The outer bell sounded. My nine o'clock was here.

"I just want to know what you know." I didn't appreciate Lori's tone, but recognized the panic underlying it. The woman was a single working mom who was afraid she was losing control of her teenager.

I could hear Deb speaking with Marc Snyder. A young man who'd done two tours in Iraq and was having trouble finding a place for himself back home in Chandler. Chances were, he wouldn't wait long. Marc couldn't stand to be anywhere for very long right now.

"What I know is that Maggie's a good kid," I assured Ms. Winston. She'd called me to speak about her child. She was Maggie's legal guardian. I could, ethically, tell her anything I knew. "Like you, I worry about her, not because of Maggie, but because of her age and society...." And her home life, which was the best Lori Winston could make it, but still not great. "Just to be safe, I had a friend of mine check up on her and—"

"A friend? Who?"

"A female deputy with the county who—"

"You had the cops watching Maggie?" I had to hold the phone away from my ear. Even at arm's length, I could make out every word. "I didn't say you could do that. You put watchdogs on my house? How could you?"

"That's not what I said." I had no idea if Sam had checked out Maggie's trailer park, but I suspected she had. Sam was thorough.

"Just call them off, you hear?" the woman screamed. "Great. This is just great. Next thing you know, somethin's gonna go wrong out here, or somewhere, and Maggie'll be blamed. I can't believe you did this."

"Ms. Winston, I assure you, I didn't do anything." I got firm, something I didn't often do, but could if I had to. "Maggie's not on any list. No one but my friend knows about this. It wasn't an official thing. I just wanted to make certain Maggie was safe. And so far, she is. I thought you'd be glad to hear that. The most Maggie has done besides her paper route is look for a babysitting job."

"Really?"

"Really."

"You're sure?"

"As sure as I can be. This is a small town. If Maggie were in trouble, I think we'd know. But she's at a vulnerable age. I can't promise that trouble won't come. I'd really like it if you could talk her into coming back to see me...."

I rang off just as the bell attached to the front door

sounded again. I hadn't been quick enough. My client had left. I had to chase Marc a block to get him to come back for his appointment.

And was glad I did. The soldier had a bottle of pills in his pocket that he'd been tempted to take. He left them with me.

7

Sam was at her desk early again Friday morning. Sharing doughnuts and coffee with Chuck.

"You make the best damned coffee of anyone I've ever known," Chuck said. "I swear, Sam, you should open a shop. They'd be lined up out the door."

She'd brought two thermoses into work with her and, as usual, shared them with Chuck.

He was looking at his computer screen and Sam at hers, trying to find some common connection between recent drug busts. Area. Method. Packaging. Bills used. Age of dealers. Time of day.

Any pattern at all.

Sam chuckled. "Right. If I opened a coffee shop, I'd be crazy with boredom in a day. And bouncing off the ceiling with a caffeine high from drinking too much product."

"Would be kinda like an alcoholic opening a bar, huh?"

"Kinda."

"Well, I'll be damned." Chuck sat back, staring. He started jotting notes on the pad in front of him.

"What?" Sam wheeled her chair close enough to see

his screen. He was looking at a profile from a recent arrest. "Sherry Mahon? You know her?"

Sam read the screen. Thirty-five. The dishwater blonde looked ten years older. She was divorced. Had a couple of priors for solicitation. And was currently a guest of the county for possession of enough methamphetamine to keep an average-size client base high for a week.

"Yeah, I know her."

"She from around here?" Sam had never seen her before.

"Trotwood."

"Who is she?"

"Kyle didn't tell you?"

Sam froze, coffee cup halfway to her lips. "Kyle? My Kyle?"

"Yes, Deputy, your Kyle," Chuck said. "Though I still don't know why you won't just admit that you guys are in a rut and get over him and give me a chance."

"You're getting your chance, buster," Sam said, handling the comment as she always did—like Chuck didn't mean it. The man's heart belonged to the wife who'd left him for a man who worked a desk job. Everyone at the station knew that. "Tell me what Kyle has to do with this woman."

Chuck closed the screen. Moved on to another.

"Chuck."

Sitting up straighter, he turned his back to her.

"It has nothing to do with this," he said.

"Tell me, Sewell, or you've had your last cup of my coffee. Ever."

He turned, the compassionate look in his eyes scaring her.

"Tell me," she repeated.

"I never would have said anything if I'd thought for one second that you didn't know."

"Know what, dammit?" He was trying her patience. And after another mostly sleepless night, she didn't have a lot to spare.

"It was a long time ago, Sam."

"How long ago?"

"Fifteen years."

"And?"

"You'd just given Kyle his walking papers."

"Which time?"

Chuck's grin was only half-convincing. "Yeah, well, at the time, Kyle really thought it was over."

Sam thought back. She'd been eighteen. "It was right after I'd told him I was joining the academy," she guessed. She'd given him her ring back. And come begging for it two days later, knowing she couldn't live without him. He'd said the same about her and the next few weeks had been perfect. But looking back, she was able to see that that first break had been the beginning of the end. They'd broken up a few times over the next two years while Sam had been training to be a cop—until the final time when they were twenty.

"That was the time," Chuck said. "A bunch of us took pity on him and hauled him out on the town. Our goal— get him so drunk he couldn't feel the pain."

"I'm guessing you didn't have to work real hard to get him to cooperate."

Kyle had always loved his beer. And in their younger days, he hadn't had the maturity to drink in moderation.

But then, neither had she.

But this wasn't about alcohol consumption. "Where does this Mahon woman come in?"

"She and a friend of hers were all over us. All night.

We blew them off to the point of being rude, but a couple of days later Kyle came to me, telling me he'd slept with her. He was a little worried he'd caught something. But mostly, he was petrified that you'd find out. Especially after the two of you patched things up."

"He never told me."

"It wasn't something he was proud of."

"I can't believe he didn't tell me."

"I thought he would have, Sam. I guess he didn't want to risk losing you all over again. You guys were already on thin ground. I heard she came after him later, claiming she was pregnant, or some such thing, but he never said anything to me about it. And even if she was, there was no way to pin that on Kyle. The woman was a professional. Who knew how many men she'd been with?"

Coffee had never made her feel sick to her stomach before.

Sam sat there, afraid if she moved she'd throw up. Kyle. Her Kyle. The fact that he'd slept with another woman and not told her hurt. A lot. But she could understand. Sort of. While she'd been home after their breakup, devastated, unable to go on, an emotional mess, he'd been out fucking another woman.

He might have a child out there somewhere....

And he'd never told her.

She told Kyle everything. He claimed that he did the same with her.

But he hadn't.

"Hey, Sam, like I said, it was a long time ago."

"I know, Chuck." Gingerly pushing her chair back to her computer she added, "It's no big deal. I'm just surprised."

Shocked. She felt as if she'd just lost her best friend.

All this time, she'd thought Kyle was her soul mate, when she didn't know him at all.

He'd screwed a woman who'd grown up to become a prostitute and a possible meth dealer. Sam had never figured she'd find a lover of Kyle's on the Fort County inmate list.

"If it makes things any better," Chuck said, "I've never seen or heard of the woman until right now. It's not like she hung around or anything."

That didn't make Sam feel any better.

Sam went home. Showered. And with a fresh cup of coffee in hand, she signed on to the Internet from the laptop on her kitchen counter.

Sherry Mahon was in the past. Fifteen years past. She couldn't hold Kyle responsible for something he'd done as a kid. Something he'd done after she'd broken up with him.

Of course, then she'd gone back and blubbered all over him and begged him to return her ring and he'd never said a word. Not even later, when the woman had told him they were going to be parents.

Kyle and Sherry Mahon.

Not Kyle and Samantha Jones. And then there was his wife. Amy—the young girl he'd married just months after that final breakup, just months after Sam got her uniform and badge. He'd been twenty, on the rebound, and determined to have the type of life he wanted. A farm life. With a farm wife.

In her entire life, Samantha had slept with only one man. Kyle Evans. He, on the other hand, had screwed multiple women. Maybe he still did. How would she know? Hell, she'd practically lived in his back pocket before his marriage and she hadn't known what was going on then.

How in the hell would she know what he did with his penis these days?

Anhydrous ammonia. Concentrate, Sam. Focus. You're looking for methamphetamine ingredients. Mostly household chemicals like phosphorous and anhydrous ammonia, substances common to particular trades. Like truck driving. And farming. Both were prevalent in Ohio.

Logging on to a secure site, she found what she was looking for. A listing of all purchases of anhydrous ammonia in Ohio over the past year. The list was long. Mostly farms. Or farmers. Some names she recognized. Quantities were all in line with farm acreages, which were listed.

Except…

Sam stopped. Blinked. She was certain she'd transposed numbers for one particular name that was making her see red at the moment.

Kyle Evans.

She refocused. The numbers didn't change.

She moved on to other chemicals—to methanol. She saw the name again. And dropped her head onto the breakfast bar.

But she couldn't stay there.

Uh-uh.

Not now.

Not when she was finding it hard to believe anything about the man.

She was too furious at the coincidence and the lies and deceit to think straight about the link between Kyle and a woman who'd just been arrested for possessing large quantities of methamphetamine.

Sam grabbed her car keys and slammed out the door.

Thank goodness she'd showered. Pulled on jeans and a clean blouse with her police-issue black walking boots.

At least Kyle wasn't getting the old sweats she'd worn to the station that morning.

"What in the hell has happened to this world?" she asked the Mustang—partially because it didn't talk back to her. Was this what happened when you left your twenties behind? Nothing made sense anymore?

She'd thought that as she grew older, she'd get smarter. So why had she had things all figured out in her twenties, but couldn't understand life anymore?

She was not going to cry.

Crying was for sissies.

And women who'd just found out a man had betrayed them. Sam had broken up with Kyle more than a decade ago.

Still…she'd trusted him. Would have bet her life that he had her back.

But did he really? He hated her career. Hated her uniform.

Yet those things pretty much summed up Samantha. Her career was her life.

How could you say you were there for someone when you didn't even like what the person did? She thought he was her best friend, but a friend would never lie that way.

"Sorry," she muttered to her car as she settled both hands on the wheel and pushed her foot to the ground. The old Mustang gave her its all and roared up the long drive to Kyle's house. In another week or two, he'd be out harvesting, but this morning he should still be in the house, seeing that Grandpa was back asleep in bed if it was a bad day, or comfortably settled with blankets and pillows propping him in front of a movie on the TV. Or maybe Kyle was out in the barn with Radiance and Lillie. The colt was more than a month old and already showing promise that a second generation of Evans family horse breeding had begun.

Kyle came walking out of the barn to meet her. Good. Meeting him in the kitchen where she'd spent so much time as a kid, eating his grandpa's homemade chocolate-chip cookies and feeling more at home than she had in her own house, would have made what she had to say too difficult.

How could Kyle have done this to them? How could he have gone off and forgotten everything he was about, forgotten his morals and his…whatever…and fucked a prostitute? And if he had to screw around on Sam, how could he have done it without protection?

"Sam?" His frown marred an otherwise gorgeous face. "It's eight in the morning. What's wrong?"

She'd always thought Kyle's willingness to look her straight in the eye spoke of the absolute honesty between them. She'd cherished that.

Had his father known about Sherry Mahon? Did Grandpa know? Not that the dear old man would likely remember now.

"In the past six months you purchased large quantities of anhydrous ammonia.…" She stood, hands down at her sides, keeping her open car door between them.

Right. The ammonia. In an alarming amount. And an ex-lover in jail for possession…

Part of Sam knew she might be overreacting. Part of her didn't care.

And some small portion of her heart was trying not to cry, needing to hear what Kyle had to say for himself.

"That's right." He named an amount. A little higher than her figures. But in a quick search, she might have missed something.

"And methanol…"

Again, the amount he named was higher than she'd thought.

Which struck the fear of God in her.

She looked around at the farm owned by a man she wasn't sure she knew.

He had the perfect setting. The perfect reputation. The perfect cover—a cop as his best friend. And he needed money, though he wouldn't tell her exactly how bad things were. She'd seen the signs. Even his beer was the cheapest on the market.

"You've never ordered those chemicals in such large quantities before." Having grown up as a part-time member of the Evans family, Sam knew a bit about farming. And over the past weeks, with Chuck's help, she'd done her homework about methamphetamine production.

Crossing his arms over his flannel shirt, Kyle stood— square shouldered, feet spread, a full seven inches taller than her—and scrutinized her as if she was a bug on Zodiac. Tired as she was, she had a flashback to another time, same place. They'd been about fourteen. She'd come out to ride his father's prized mare—she was the only one allowed, because she was light enough.

While helping her down, Kyle had stolen a kiss. She'd never been kissed. At first, he'd looked as shocked as she'd felt. But in the next instant, he'd changed. He'd stood, arms crossed, staring her down like he was doing right now, as if daring her to find anything wrong with his behavior.

"You've…used…anhydrous ammonia…as fertilizer."

"That's right."

"But this year, you planted less field and ordered twice as much."

"Yes."

Why the hell didn't he say something she could sink her teeth into? Something she could scream at him for?

She could hardly yell at him for having had sex once fifteen years ago with another woman.

He stood there, all long-haired, clean-shaven he-man. Why didn't he just take her to bed?

No. She hadn't thought that. Didn't want that. Not now. Not like this.

But she remembered another time—the day she'd come back to Kyle begging for her ring. They'd made love that night. Again and again. Kyle had been more tender, more…everything. He'd touched her as if she was an angel from heaven.

She'd never forgotten.

"In all of my research I haven't found one practical use for methanol on a farm—at least, not in the quantities you ordered."

"Okay."

"I'm guessing you haven't taken up a sudden interest in racing cars, right?" Methanol purchases were common in the world of racing. At least, that's what she'd read on the Internet.

"Nope, can't say I have."

"Why are you being this way?"

"I might ask you the same thing. You look like hell, by the way. Rough night?"

"I…didn't sleep much."

She could sense him closing in on himself. There probably weren't any physical signs, but she felt his withdrawal just the same. "Who's the lucky guy?"

They both knew that some day there'd be other people in their lives. Neither of them wanted to grow old alone.

"Kyle, if you're in trouble, you know you can come to

me...." She'd do what she could. Anything she could. She loved him.

She was begging again.

And she wouldn't break the law for him. He knew that.

"I'm not in trouble."

"Can you explain to me why you are suddenly purchasing large quantities of chemicals used to make methamphetamine?"

"Yes."

"Then why haven't you?"

"You haven't asked."

Okay, not technically, but...

Kyle pulled her forward and shoved the door shut. "You come blazing out here when the day's barely begun, with all this distance between us and accusation in your tone, and you have the nerve to think I owe you anything?"

What was this? She'd never, ever felt unwelcome on the Evans farm. Not even during the months Kyle was married. "Twenty years of friendship stands for nothing, I guess."

"Exactly what I'm thinking." The hurt in his eyes said far more to her than the words he'd shot back at her.

"You're right. I'm sorry." She looked him straight in the eye. "Really sorry." And scared as hell, too.

He stood, arms crossed over his chest again, saying nothing.

She had a ton to say. About a woman he may or may not have seen in recent years. About lies of omission and possible offspring. About faith and trust and betrayal and...

She was hurt. Not a good time to unload.

"Will you please tell me why you bought the chemicals?"

"You want the technical version or the more general one?"

"Let's start general."

"The methanol I bought was derived in part from glycerol. Glycerol is a base of sugar, which is high in starch. Methanol is also a gas that, when combined with other things, can be used as a denaturing agent. I experimented and used my final product to soak my prototype seeds. And then soaked them in anhydrous ammonia. All before planting. I also used the ammonia as fertilizer. If you buy in quantity there's a price break. As you already know, my theory is that I can grow corn that has twice the starch per kernel. If I can come up with a way to do this, the cost of producing ethanol could be cut in half. Or at least severely reduced."

He wasn't making meth. Thank God. He wasn't supplying his ex-lover. Oh, thank God. He was…

"Those chemicals are dangerous, Kyle. Long-term exposure could kill you—heck, even short-term exposure—or make you really sick. You ingest five teaspoons of methanol and you could go blind. Or die. Or—"

"I know. That's part of the reason I'm starting out small. And I'm working alone so I'm not exposing anyone else."

"You aren't a chemist. These things should be left to trained scientists. In laboratories. Where everything is protected."

If anything happened to Kyle…

"I know what I'm doing, Sam. I do have a degree in chemistry, remember?"

Yeah. She'd forgotten. He'd double-majored.

"I've been talking about this since high school. Where you been?"

"Here. I listened." Sort of. "I just didn't realize that your project involved methanol." Or anything really dangerous. She should have paid more attention.

Cared more.

Same old story with them. The farm was Kyle's life. To her it was the kiss of death. Death by boredom.

"I'm sorry I doubted you. Not that I did, really." Okay, she had. And it didn't help that Sherry Mahon's name had muddied the waters. When she calmed down enough to be rational, she would ask him about the woman. "I'm just tired. And going crazy with this meth thing."

"I thought you were leaving that alone."

"I can't, Kyle."

"Sam…"

"I'm telling you, with the quantities we're seeing, I know there's some kind of mass production going on around here. Chuck thinks so, too. At least, he thinks we're getting large shipments from someplace and is as determined as I am to put a stop to it."

"You've been at this all night, haven't you? Investigating?"

"I've been studying. Going through records. Yeah."

"Be careful, Sam. You're going to end up like your dad."

And that's why she hadn't told him in the first place what she was doing.

"This is different, Kyle. And I *am* careful. Meth has been killing people in Fort County over the past two years and the numbers are increasing. It won't be long before it starts hitting our friends.…"

"If it's that bad, why isn't it all over the news?"

"It is."

But then, Kyle didn't watch the news.

* * *

Kyle was particularly eager for Friday night's dart game after his encounter with Sam. Growing up on a farm had taught him that life was like a business. It created daily jobs that, when done well, reaped worthy rewards. And then you moved on to the next one.

Life on a farm taught you early that there would always be another chore. The work was never done.

An addendum to the lesson had been added at some unknown point: meeting responsibilities brings fulfillment. Reward.

Playing darts was neither a job, nor a responsibility.

So Kyle, being Kyle, filed it in the reward category and got on with it.

He supplied the beer—enough to last them through a heated competition without putting any of them over the legal driving limit.

Even in pleasure, responsibility ruled. Kyle was okay with that.

He was also okay with wiping the barn floor with his opponents. In a testosterone-laced contest, Kyle was clearly the master. The trouble with David and Pierce was that they tried too hard. The trick was just to relax, grip the barrel lightly, let the dart flow and trust it to do its job.

"Fish face." Pierce grinned as David scored eight measly points, taking his three-twenty down to three-twelve. Scoring less than nine on a single turn was sometimes called a fish. Not fish face. But two legs into the match and a few beers later, who cared? At two-eighty, Pierce didn't have a lot of room to talk, anyway. Kyle was sitting on twenty—a count down from the five-oh-one they'd all started at. He had to hit it exact—with a three-dart throw.

"At least I'm no whale," David shot back, swigging on his beer as he rubbed in the fact that on two different occasions Pierce had scored less than three points on his turn. A whale.

"One of the many problems with the two of you is you aim for the bull's-eye." Kyle stepped up to the line, the barrel of his first dart resting familiarly against his thumb and first two fingers. Keeping his eye on the five, he hit it once. Then twice. And went for the double.

Which he scored with a perfect glide.

"Leg and match, guys. You want another?" He collected his darts.

"No way, man." Pierce shook his head and pulled a twenty out of his pocket with a rueful grin. "You remind me of my sister," he said. "Don't know when to quit. Damn good thing the rest of us are here to keep you in line."

Kyle pocketed the twenty. And the one David handed him, too.

"What's she up to now?" he asked, not sure he wanted to hear anything about Sam. He was relaxed. Feeling good. Wasn't even sure why he'd asked.

"Obsessing."

Kyle wasn't surprised Pierce would say that. Nor did he want to get involved. "About the existence of a superlab here in Fort County?"

"So she's talked to you, too."

"Yeah." He wasn't going to say more than that.

All trace of fun was gone from Pierce. His face was lined with a worry that had been years in the making.

"A superlab?" David, who'd gone over to run a gentle hand along Rad's neck, turned back to them.

"My sister has it in her head that there's some mass methamphetamine production lab around these parts.

One large enough to supply the whole county and beyond...."

"Wow. I hadn't heard. I thought everything came from Mexico."

"You and everyone else," Pierce said.

David shook his head. "Sam's usually spot-on. Is there any validity to her concern?"

"Not that I know of," Pierce was quick to point out, as if by making the idea sound far-fetched, the whole problem would just go away.

"She was present when some executive, high on meth, blew his head off," Kyle said.

"The Holmes case?" David asked.

Kyle wasn't surprised he knew the story. It had been in all the papers. Minus the names of the officers present. "Yeah."

"And from that she figures there's a lab nearby? Because of one user?"

"Pretty much," Pierce said. Kyle let the statement stand, though he knew there was a lot more to it than that.

Pierce shook his head. "My sister's a great cop, but she's too much like my dad. She gets an idea in that thick brain of hers and she won't let it go."

"So what's it hurt to have her poking around?" David was frowning, and Kyle wondered how hard it was to be the father of four kids—soon five—in today's world.

He wondered about being the father of one kid.

"The worst that's going to happen is that she won't find anything," David said. "And if she does, she earns a few steps up the ladder for doing a great job and keeping us all safe."

David wasn't predisposed to worry about Sam like he and Pierce were.

And put the way David had said it, Sam's obsession didn't sound so...wrongheaded. Or threatening.

His shot to her about her dad had been cheap.

Which meant he owed her an apology.

Dammit.

8

Friday nights in Fort County during the fall were extra busy. Anyone would think the high school football players were professionals, given the number of fans who turned out for the games. There were more adults than kids.

The county, and Chandler city police, ran extra patrols from August through late October, mostly on the lookout for potential DUIs. There'd been two separate fatalities from one small-township K-to-twelve school the previous year. Three weeks apart. Both sixteen-year-olds. Both under the influence.

But alcohol hadn't been their drug of choice.

Toxicology reports had come back with dangerous levels of methamphetamine in both cases.

Tonight was the season opener and Chandler's team was playing at home. Sam wasn't disappointed to draw her alma mater for patrol duty. Besides her regular shift duties, she could keep an eye out for Maggie Winston.

In full uniform, her long brown hair up in its customary bun, Sam stayed well behind the bleachers as she avidly watched the scene for illegal activity.

At an event like this, she might expect fights, underage drinking or drug use and, God forbid, rape. Two rapes had been reported in the county last football season. One by a teacher. The other a date rape.

In both cases the accused had pled out. Sam hated that part of the law. She and her fellow officers risked their lives to get crud off the streets and then the judicial system, to save time and money, gave the offenders reduced or suspended sentences in lieu of a costly trial.

Kicking at a rock with the edge of her black steel-toed boot, Sam watched out of the corner of her eye as a couple of teenagers—one male, one female, approximately sixteen years of age—slipped under the home team bleachers. Necking sessions weren't illegal.

And she wasn't a voyeur.

But something about the way they were feeling each other up caught her attention. The male put his hand in the pocket of her navy hoodie, and the female put hers in the back pocket of his jeans. When their free hands remained at their sides, Sam started moving closer.

The students were lip-locked and didn't notice her approach.

Sam barely heard the roar of the crowd. The world consisted of three people. Her. And the two teens she was watching. There…

The male withdrew his hand from the female's pocket and Sam caught the sheen of plastic before it was masked by the navy fabric.

The couple parted and Sam moved in, hoping, even as she did so, that she was wrong. That the worst that would happen was that these two kids were going to be embarrassed at being caught feeling each other up.

"Hold it." She planted herself directly in the path of the young man, who was turning to leave.

"What?" He was freckle faced—not shaving yet—with short dark hair that looked as if it had been cut at home with a bowl for a guide. "I'm sorry, ma'am," he added when he saw her uniform, his gaze landing on the gun at her waist. "Did we do something wrong?"

"That's what I'm here to find out." Sam flipped her radio to Send so that Chuck, the only other officer covering the game, could hear everything that transpired. "What were you two doing under here?"

The girl, blonde, blue eyed, stood silently. Now that Sam had a closer look, she saw that the kid was much younger, maybe twelve.

"We were…you know… I just kissed her. Is that, you know, against the law or something?" The young man's voice resonated with fear.

"What's your name?" Sam asked.

"Shane Hamacher."

Sam looked at the girl. "And you?"

"Nicole. Nicole Hatch."

"Are you MaryLee Hatch's daughter?" Sam had gone to school with MaryLee's younger sister. And, like the rest of the county, had been saddened when MaryLee's husband had been killed in a motorcycle crash in the middle of a poker run—a planned event where motorcyclists have to stop at five to seven predetermined points along a ride, collecting cards at each one. The rider with the best poker hand at the end of the ride wins a prize. Sometimes cash.

In Hatch's case, they'd been riding for charity—the Fort County sheriff's office.

"Yes, ma'am," Nicole said. It was one of the shakiest answers Sam had ever heard.

"What's that in your pocket, Nicole?"

The girl reached for the left pocket of her hoodie, pulling it inside out. "Nothing."

"Not that pocket, the other one."

Sam was looking at the girl, but didn't miss a beat as Shane Hamacher made a break. With a quick side step, she stood solid as he bumped into her. Hard.

"Hold it right there," she told him, ready to grab his arm if he attempted to flee a second time.

Tears streamed down Nicole's face but she didn't move, didn't say a word, as Sam reached into her pocket and pulled out a plastic sandwich bag containing about a gram of little white crystals that resembled a cross between quartz and crushed ice.

Methamphetamine.

"How much money did she just put in your back pocket, Shane?"

"I don't have any money. I don't know what you're talking about. I've never seen that stuff before." The boy leaned in for a closer look at the bag in Sam's hand. "What is it?"

"He knows what it is." Nicole was a smart girl—refusing to cover for her dealer. "He charged me a hundred dollars for it."

"Show me what's in your back pocket, Shane."

The boy could have made things difficult. He could have resisted. Instead, he pulled out five twenties.

And Sam, using her radio to call Chuck over for backup as she pulled out her handcuffs, saw him already approaching, his face grim.

It was sometime after three by the time she finally finished her shift and made it home.

She hadn't seen Maggie Winston all night.

Chandler, Ohio
Saturday, September 4, 2010

I'd been so busy Thursday, I hadn't gotten around to calling Samantha to tell her to stop any further surveillance of Maggie Winston. I tried phoning her twice on Friday, leaving messages that hadn't been returned.

Which gave me the perfect excuse to stop by her place after Deb and I returned Saturday morning from skating part of the seventy-two-mile trail that crossed southern Ohio. After dropping Deb off, I didn't bother going home to shower and change.

Sam had seen a lot worse than a thirty-three-year old in bike pants, a T-shirt and a wrinkled black hoodie. She'd seen me dripping with sweat after basketball games. And once I got home, I was staying put. I had a book to read for book club and I was going to get it done this time without staying up half the night before the meeting. Besides, Camy had been alone far too much this week and I'd promised not to leave her except for the skate.

The promise and a eucalyptus treat I'd presented as I'd walked out the door seemed to appease my four-pound princess enough to have her grudgingly climb up on her bed to wait for me.

She wouldn't be so accommodating if I went home and then left again. Worse, she'd be sad and hurt and she didn't deserve that.

Camy didn't know it yet, but I wasn't going out that night. And even better, she was going to have company. A psychology doctoral candidate I was mentoring was coming over.

Sam didn't answer my first knock. I stood on the solid-wood white front porch, admiring the white wicker furniture and colorful flowers and whimsical wind chimes. How did the woman manage to save the world and make a beautiful home for herself at the same time? The contrast between the work Sam did and her house came as no surprise to me.

There were two Sams. The great, but hardened, cop. And the sensitive woman locked inside who was allowed to come out occasionally.

She answered my second knock.

"Kelly? What's wrong?" Sam's long hair was mussed around her face. She wore flannel pants, a white tank top and nothing else.

"Did I wake you?" I'd never have knocked twice if I'd known she was sleeping. I thought she'd seen my car and was avoiding me—thinking that I'd come by to nag her into a session. Not that I blamed her. I was going to nag her.

"Yeah," Sam yawned. "My night rotation is on Friday."

"You work days."

"With the cutbacks, we each take one night a week."

"Hey, I'm really sorry, Sam," I said, backing up. "Go back to sleep. Now." Damn. The woman comes to me suffering from job stress-induced insomnia and I go and wake her up.

"It's okay." She came outside barefoot, in spite of the chilliness in the air. "I'm due up in half an hour, anyway. I promised Ben Chase I'd watch his kid play soccer. What's up?"

Ben Chase. One of her fellow officers.

"You want to put some coffee on?" I asked, still feeling badly. "I can wait."

"You want some?"

"No. I don't drink the stuff. Diet cola's my caffeine addiction."

"Wish I had some to offer you, but…"

I shrugged. "I have one in the car. I'll get it."

"Then if you don't mind, I need my first cup of coffee before I can think."

Sam moved around her kitchen like a professional barista. Three different machines sat on the counters. She poured ground beans in one of them, then scooped, poured and frothed.

I sat on a stool at the island counter and watched in amazement.

She turned, steaming cup to her lips, and caught me staring at her. She grinned.

"You know I like my coffee."

"Looks like you have some of your brother's genes, after all."

"My mom insisted that we both spend time in the kitchen with her. I needed the coffee just to stay awake through the ordeal." Sam slid up onto the stool next to me. Despite her grumbling, I suspected my friend was an excellent cook.

"You sleeping any better?" I asked her.

"Some." And then, since I wouldn't let her escape my gaze, she said, "Not really."

"You ready for some help?"

"Are you finally going to refer my prescription?" She sounded less than hopeful.

"No, but even if you won't come talk to me, I'm going to advise you to cut back on the coffee. That stuff won't be fazed by a hapless sleeping pill."

Silence ensued.

"I've been ordered to call you off," I said.

"Off what? By who?" She hadn't lowered the cup from her lips. Just held it there, nursing it.

"Maggie Winston's mother, Lori. She doesn't want you watching her house, her daughter or probably even this town, based on her vehemence." I told Sam about the unexpected turn the call had taken Thursday morning.

"Since I'm not on any official order to keep Maggie under surveillance, I can hardly be called off, can I?"

She hadn't disappointed me. "No, but you have the areas you're assigned to and—"

"I'm obligated, by moral code, to patrol any part of this county that I think might need protecting."

I didn't ask if that was police moral code or Samantha Jones moral code. Didn't make much difference.

"I might be overreacting here, Sam," I admitted. "Unfortunately, there are probably dozens of fourteen-year-olds on the verge of having sex and you can't watch out for all of them."

"No, but if Maggie comes to you and tells you that she's had sex with an older man, instead of just thinking about it, then what?"

"Then I report it to the authorities. I have to. You know that."

"The authorities. That's me."

"Yes."

"So you can call me in after the child's been hurt, but it's somehow wrong for you to do so when there's still time to avert disaster?" The deputy rose, whipped up another cup of joe for herself.

"Well, obviously I don't think so." I raised my voice to be heard over the machine. "I called you, didn't I? I just want to be clear here, and—"

"You're clear. We're clear. It's all clear."

The irony of the situation was no more lost on her than it was on me. Because *after* Maggie was the victim of a pedophile, I'd be called in officially, too. Or some other psychologist would be.

"I just want to know what the mother is hiding," Sam said, coming back to join me. Her eyes were more alert. "She wants you to invade her kid's brain, her confidences, but the second you start looking outside your office, the dogs are called off."

"I know. It bothered me, too. You'd think she'd be overjoyed—or relieved, at least—to think that Maggie has a free bodyguard."

"Albeit a part-time one."

"Right."

"When do you see Maggie again?" Sam pulled a foot up to the rung of the stool, resting her cup on her bent knee.

"I don't. Unless she calls or stops by."

"Let me know if she does."

"Of course. And you're going to keep watching her?"

"I think I'll step things up a bit. See what the mother's so desperate to hide."

I was glad to hear that. Overjoyed. And relieved.

"I'd best get going," I said, standing, diet cola in hand. "Camy's waiting."

"You need to get a life, my friend," Sam said, not budging as she smiled at me. "It's a beautiful Saturday morning and you're rushing home to a dog. Furthermore, you think your dog is aware that you're on your way home. She has no concept of time."

Sam was wrong about that. "Camy's a princess, not a dog. Just ask her. And princesses have schedules."

"Seriously," Sam said, pinning me with that look she had. "It's been, what, two years since you've had a date?"

"Six months. I went to that dinner in Columbus, remember?" It had been a professional thing, but I hadn't gone solo as I usually did.

"With some guy old enough to be your dad and you haven't seen him since."

"We didn't have a lot in common." He was a professor at the university where I mentored.

"Let me set something up with you and Chuck," Sam said, repeating an offer I'd heard before.

"I don't want to date a cop." Too much danger. Too much risk. And Sam couldn't argue with that one. It was why she was still single.

"You're thirty-three years old and have never had a long-term serious relationship," Sam said, as if I didn't know. "People are going to start thinking you're gay."

"They are not." I laughed at the absurdity. And then said, "I'm not." Just in case.

"I know you're not. Sheila Grant would have had you by now if you were."

"Sheila is happily taken."

"Which brings us back to you." Sam sobered. "I worry about you, Kel. You're hardly ever alone, but you're always alone."

"I don't feel alone," I told her. "A woman doesn't need a man to be complete, Sam. I thought you, of all people, understood that."

"I do. It's just…at least I've got Kyle. I don't know what I'd do without him."

I was horrified when Sam's eyes filled with tears. Samantha Jones didn't cry. Ever. It was like a rule or something.

"What's going on? Has Kyle found someone else?" It was inevitable. They all knew that he wanted a wife. A family. Always had. Even in high school, when most of them were raring to leave town and see the real world, Kyle had been the odd one out, wanting nothing more than to get married and stay on his farm forever.

Samantha shook her head. "It's stupid. I'm just tired and overreacting."

"To what?"

She looked straight at me. "Did you know that Kyle slept with someone else the weekend we broke up after I signed up to go to the academy?"

I was stunned. "No way," I said, falling back against the couch. "Kyle? Who was it?"

"At least I'm not the only one who didn't know about it." Sam's voice was bitter. I didn't like the tone coming from her. Wasn't used to it.

"Who was it?" I asked again. "Kyle never wanted anyone but you. Everyone knows that."

"Yeah, well, he had someone. A prostitute. Though I don't think she was one then. Supposedly she got pregnant."

"Supposedly?"

"That part's just rumor."

"Then that's all it is," I said. "Come on, Sam. If he'd gotten a woman pregnant, he'd have a child in his life. You know Kyle."

"Do I?"

Sam looked like a lost vulnerable kid—nothing like the Sam Jones I'd known since grade school.

9

Sam stopped by Sunday night. Zodiac greeted her outside, but Kyle waited in the house for her.

"Where's Grandpa?" she asked, standing in the doorway of the kitchen.

"In bed."

"Is he asleep?"

"I'm not sure. I pulled up the bars about ten minutes ago." He'd had to resort to a hospital bed six months earlier because his grandfather kept trying to get out of bed in the night. The old man's knees gave out on him more times than not these days and he'd taken a couple of potentially serious falls.

"Mind if I check?"

Kyle motioned toward the bedroom directly off the kitchen—his grandfather's room for as long as he could remember—then followed Sam.

"Hey, Grandpa!"

"Suzy, my girl. Come, come." His grandfather patted the side of the bed and Sam settled beside him, taking his wrinkled hand in both of hers.

Zodiac lay on the floor at her feet.

Suzy. Kyle's mother. A woman who'd died so long ago he couldn't even remember her.

"You're a good girl," Grandpa said, his toothless grin, so rare these days, big and broad. "My boy, he needs you." The old man looked at Kyle.

"I know, Grandpa, that's why I'm here," Sam said, playing along. "Now tell me about your day. How was dinner?"

"Good. I burned the buns, but the roast made up for it."

Grandpa hadn't burned buns in thirty years. Or cooked in two, other than making peanut-butter-and-jelly sand-wiches for Kyle at random times. And they'd had ham for dinner.

"Tell me about Gretel, Grandpa. About the time the two of you ran away to the fair…"

Kyle stood there, listening as his grandfather talked about the love of his life, who'd died before Kyle was born. When it came to his late wife, the old man didn't forget a single detail.

His voice filled with strength—and his eyes with peace. Sam asked questions, actively engaging in stories she'd heard almost as many times as Kyle had, until the old man fell asleep.

And then she headed back to the kitchen, standing there awkwardly.

"I just came to…apologize…again for the way I came at you on Friday." Her gaze scanned the kitchen. "I'm just tired, you know, and worried, and—"

"Forget it, Sam."

She looked at him, then quickly glanced away. "I… You… I don't want to lose you, Kyle."

"I'm guessing since you haven't lost me by now, it's probably not going to happen," he said, wishing she'd just be Sam and mouth off to him about doing something stupid like buying dangerous chemicals, or berate herself for being paranoid, and then take him to bed.

That's what they both needed.

"I…"

"Let it go, Sam." He needed her tonight. He'd had a call from the doctor Saturday morning. The blood pressure tests they'd done on his grandfather that past week hadn't been good. Any exertion at all—even eating—raised his blood pressure to dangerous levels. And he was already on the highest dosage of medication.

Nodding, she turned toward the door. "Okay, well, I just… I'm sorry."

She left. And didn't glance back.

Kyle was still pondering the ex-woman of his dreams Tuesday morning as he tackled the storage barn. Sam was acting as if she didn't know him. Like he'd sprouted horns. All because he'd purchased some extra chemicals?

Chemicals that could be used to make meth.

Could Pierce be right? Was she really becoming irrational like her father? So afraid that if she didn't rid the world of scum, her loved ones would be at risk.

He'd known Sam's father. Had liked him. He hadn't seen any sign that the man was obsessive. But then he'd only been ten when Peter Jones had been killed. Still, from what Kyle had heard, most folks were shocked when Sam's dad had gone off the deep end and gotten himself killed.

Surely the same thing wasn't happening with Sam.

Kyle didn't want to think so. But when he'd finally put his foot down, told her she had to chose between being a cop or his wife, she'd chosen to be a cop.

And if she'd given him the same ultimatum—staying on the farm or being her husband?

No, Kyle wasn't going to spend another morning going around in circles with that one.

Cleaning the barn was much easier.

The house only got dusted or vacuumed when Sam grew sick of looking at the mess and cleaned it herself or if he called a woman from town to do it. But Kyle did his best to keep up with the barn.

The fact that he'd had to climb over the small tractor, snow blade and the tiller, then step over some shovels, a half-used bag of mulch and the dump trailer just to get to the small insecticide sprayer he was looking for, told him it was time to reorganize.

A good hour later he'd cleaned and refilled the horse feed and seeding bins. Spare bags of both feed and seed were neatly stacked, extra horse tack and medicines were all in their proper cabinets and he had a small path cleared through the rest of his mess.

Which was more than he could say about the situation with Sam. He didn't want to marry the woman. They'd been down that road. But he couldn't imagine life without her.

He decided to tackle the chemicals next. When he went to hoist the fifty-five-gallon carbon steel tank of methanol so that he could sweep the cement slab it rested on, Kyle almost fell backward with the force of his own strength.

He'd used enough force to lift fifty-five pounds, but the tank felt like ten.

With a frown, and an unusual sense of foreboding, Kyle lifted the tank again, rocking it slightly back and forth.

He'd noticed the tank was a little lighter the last time he'd checked, and he'd put it down to evaporation. But forty gallons of gas did not evaporate from a sealed tank that quickly.

What the hell was going on?

Was he mistaken? Had he used more gas than he'd thought? Purchased less?

Shaking his head, Kyle set down the tank and headed for his office—what used to be the formal dining room in the house his grandfather had built for his Gretel seventy years before. He knew he wasn't mistaken. Sam had just thrown the sales figures at him on Friday. Not something he was likely to forget.

Checking both his purchasing accounts and the record of use he meticulously kept for all of the hazardous, seed, feed and medicinal products on his property, he verified what he already knew. He'd stored that last fifty-five-gallon tank of methanol on the cement slab poured specifically for that purpose. And he hadn't touched the tank since.

Call Sam.

Kyle reached for the phone and set it back down as the full implications of that Friday morning visit slammed into him.

Sam believed meth was being made in large quantities in the area.

Kyle had purchased a larger quantity than usual of two of the key ingredients.

And now he was missing a substantial amount of one of them.

How would that look to a woman obsessed with finding this lab, even though her colleagues weren't so sure it existed? Chuck Sewell was the best cop around next to Sam and equally concerned about the county's drug problem. But according to Sam, Chuck believed there was a huge increase in the amount of the drug being imported.

One thing was for sure. Right now, especially after Sunday's visit, Kyle didn't trust Sam to believe him when he told her that he had no idea what had happened to the gas. Or to help him. He didn't trust his best friend to have his back.

Still, methanol was a dangerous chemical. Improper exposure to the gas could cause dizziness. Nausea. Nervous system disorders. Eventual death.

And he had forty gallons of the stuff unaccounted for.

Back out in the barn with his inventory list, surrounded by his "toys," as Sam had once called his equipment and tools, Kyle calmed down a bit. Methanol was dangerous, but only if mishandled. If the extra gas were anywhere around him he'd have begun to react to its presence within hours.

If nothing else, his nostrils would have bothered him.

And if someone had taken it? In the first place, it wouldn't have been all that easy to get it off his property. And in the second place, the whole idea was ludicrous.

He wouldn't even have considered theft if Sam hadn't planted the seed of suspicion in his head. Methanol wasn't exorbitantly expensive. But had someone needed it for a valid and good reason and couldn't afford it?

Or was the thief involved in an illegal superlab?

What if Sam was right? What if the missing methanol was tied in some way to a dangerous drug operation?

He had to alert the authorities.

He couldn't be convicted for something he hadn't done. Hell, he had no idea how to make meth. Had never even seen the stuff. Even if Sam was nuts enough to arrest him, he'd be able to prove his innocence.

And his corn was going to be ready to harvest by the

weekend. Which was the other reason he was in the barn that morning—making his way to the combine to make certain that the belts were tight and to adjust and oil the roller chains.

This harvest was critical if he had any hope of becoming financially solvent. He had no family to fall back on. No brothers or parents or in-laws.

He had a grandfather who was dying.

And if he didn't make a profit, they might not even have their home.

The corn had tested at twenty-two and a half percent moisture content the day before. At an average loss of three-quarters of a percent per day, and a minimum kernel damage at nineteen percent moisture, he'd have to be out in the field by Saturday.

He already had a couple of guys set up to help him.

Waiting any longer than Saturday and he'd be looking at an ear droppage of ten to twenty bushels per acre, a potential loss he couldn't afford.

And that was it. There was no way he could afford to be in jail—even for a day—while they proved that Sam had overreacted.

Besides, how could someone have accessed his land and his barn without him knowing it? Zodiac wouldn't allow it. And the storage barn was kept locked.

Kneeling down at the edge of the large cement slab, Kyle glanced over the rest of the chemicals stored there. Insecticide. Pesticide. All on pallets. All in solid containers, no rust or potential leak sites. Though it took time he didn't have, he checked each one against the sheet he'd brought out with him. Nothing else was missing.

He studied the fifty-five-gallon tank as if it could give him an accounting of the missing gas.

And then he noticed it. The cap was firmly closed, but

the rubberized seal around the hose insertion area didn't look even. On closer inspection, Kyle started to breathe a little easier. It appeared as though something had been gnawing on the cap. The back side was whittled away. Which meant that the methanol had been exposed to air. For months.

Air facilitated evaporation.

He should have noticed the damaged seal straight off. Should have checked for it. Would have checked if Sam hadn't made him so damned paranoid.

He'd been fretting over jail time just because he'd never before heard of a varmint breaking a seal on a methanol tank.

But he had a bigger problem. A much bigger problem. The past hour had made it abundantly clear to him that Sam had destroyed the trust between them, something that not even their broken engagement or his marriage had done. And trust, once broken, couldn't be fixed.

Watching Maggie Winston any chance she got outside of her regular duties over the next week took time away from Sam's hunt for evidence of a meth lab. But it didn't take her mind off the problem. Or Kyle. Sitting alone in her cruiser, or the Mustang, gave her too much time to think.

She was going to have to talk to him. Sherry Mahon had been part of their lives for fifteen years, and Sam hadn't even known it. Now she did.

What if Kyle had had a child with the woman? And abandoned it?

They needed to talk.

Chandler had built a new high school facility since Kyle, Kelly and she had graduated. The property, along with an initial building fund, had been donated, and the town had resoundingly passed a tax levy. The new facility—just outside city limits—boasted a state-of-the-art sports facility, football field and computer lab.

Sam volunteered herself for the high school dismissal speed-control detail that the county ran every single day. That way, she could watch for Maggie. And avoid talking to Kyle.

Catch a speeder, save a life, had become the county's most important focus of late as a result of multiple teenage deaths due to excessive speed the previous year. The program was valid. Worthwhile.

And, like everything else, had become about making money. The more speeders they caught, the more bills they could pay and the more services they could offer.

Of course, the more speeders they caught, the busier the courts were. Running courts cost money, too.

As did issuing warrants and tracking down those offenders who didn't bother to show up to the justice party in their honor.

It hadn't been difficult for Sam to land the duty that week. It was one of a cop's most boring assignments, largely consisting of sitting in a pull-off on a country road and monitoring the equipment on her dash.

On occasion, she would wave at someone she knew as they passed.

She got to admire the stalks of corn that prevented her from seeing much beyond the road. And imagine the fall colors that October would soon be bringing.

She'd listen to the drone of the police radio, the most dangerous news the broadcast of a possible theft at the local budget department store.

And she drove herself crazy trying to find a lead in her hunt for the superlab. She was missing something.

Her thoughts were interrupted as she noticed for the

third time that week the same car that had picked Maggie up when she'd gone to David's to see about a babysitting job.

All three times, Maggie had been in the passenger seat.

On Monday, Sam hadn't thought much about it. The girls were friends. Maggie didn't have her license yet. Glenna most likely gave her a ride home after school. Routine.

But they'd headed away from Maggie's trailer park.

Probably had an afternoon babysitting job.

Or a rendezvous with an adult male?

Jumping to conclusions was a sign of bad police work. And could get people killed.

On Tuesday, Sam had seen Maggie in the car again. On a different road. She'd decided to follow the girls.

The friend had dropped Maggie at the newspaper office, then drove off.

A few minutes later, Maggie had come out with a bike and a load of papers. Sam followed her for a few minutes, but she was just delivering papers.

On Thursday, when they drove off in yet another direction, Sam followed the girls again. And when they crossed the county line, so did she, careful to stay far enough back that if they noticed her, they wouldn't feel threatened.

They ended up at the Tri-County Sports and Tennis Complex. Not so unusual for an after-school activity. Keeping kids off the streets had been one of the big selling points of the complex when it had come up for a tax vote.

But Kelly had specifically said that Maggie had quit cheerleading and was not involved in sports.

Maybe she'd meant high school sports. But there was

no way Lori Winston could afford tennis lessons for Maggie.

Driving slowly, Sam stopped across from the complex when the girls pulled into a parking spot.

Maggie got out alone and went into a small wooden building. When she came back out, she was carrying two tennis rackets and a small duffel with an emblem of a tennis ball on the side.

Sam recognized the duffel. She and Chuck had played tennis at the complex a time or two. Rented balls were kept in those duffels.

Another dead end. And this time in a county vehicle. On county time. Across the county line. She had to stop her surveillance of Maggie Winston. At least, to this extent.

She'd found nothing on the girl's mother, either. Lori was something of a deadbeat—spent a little too much time at the local bar. No warrants. No record. Long time on the job. No obvious influx of cash.

Putting the cruiser in Reverse, Sam turned to back up and caught a glimpse of Maggie out of the corner of her eye. The girl was heading to the tennis courts while her friend drove away.

Another kid, male, approximately sixteen years of age, had just exited the equipment building with a similar duffel. He went out to the courts, as well.

Sam watched as a couple of other teenagers arrived, went in for balls and walked toward the courts.

None of them were wearing tennis clothes—just denim shorts and T-shirts and tennis shoes.

And as she watched, she noticed that none of them could play tennis worth a damn, either.

They paired off. Volleyed balls back and forth. There

was no coach. No organization. Just a bunch of balls flying around.

And a bunch of kids staying off the streets.

10

With Zodiac in the passenger seat beside him, Kyle drove the old black truck that he'd had since before his divorce to a meeting of the local corn growers association. Generally he sat at the back of the room, nodded politely to his nearest neighbors, chatted with Bob Branson's sons-in-law if any of them were present and voted.

The small community association played a significant part in Ohio's political system, lobbying for the rights of farm growers. From getting locally grown produce included as part of a federally funded food-assistance project to applying for drought aid, the association had become a powerful force.

Kyle had already done a stint as president of the local organization—winning the election by a landslide, mostly because he'd been the only one running. He expected to be called on to run again. There was no statute of limitations on terms served in their group. And if they called, he'd accept, though the position was time-consuming.

Today, however, his goals weren't far-reaching. They didn't extend as far as the community, or even the men in the room.

He wanted to be certain that he didn't have a chemical problem on his farm.

He paid attention to the business at hand, which concerned a vote that was coming up on the November ballot that the farmers of Ohio did not support.

He'd sent out flyers and had done his stint at the county fair that summer to add his support to the farmers.

Now it was a matter of waiting for the lobbyists to do their last-minute campaign blast.

Updates were delivered at the meeting. New business discussed. Old business discussed. The treasurer, Kyle's nearest neighbor, James Turner, gave his report. They'd earned enough during their ice cream fundraiser at the fair to see them through another year. An impressive feat considering the cost of lobbyists in a failing economy.

And then the floor was opened.

And Kyle stood.

"All of you know me. Most of you well enough to be certain that I am an honest man."

People turned around to face him. Heads nodded. And with that encouragement, Kyle continued.

"I discovered some chemical missing from my barn a couple of days ago," he said.

The room fell silent, the mood suddenly grim. Farmers were aware of their vulnerability to theft and took reports of it seriously. For most, farming was not a get-rich life, and theft, if it was severe enough, could ruin a man quicker than bad weather or insect infestation.

"I also discovered a faulty valve. I'm considering the loss the result of evaporation due to the leaky valve, but it was significant enough that I want you all to know what's happened. And if any of you have seen someone on my farm without me, or know of anyone using methane, I hope you'll inform me."

Several men came up to Kyle as the meeting adjourned, James Turner among them.

No one had seen anything out of the ordinary. They asked questions and gave advice, but no one acted the least bit suspicious.

And he now had a loyal posse on the outlook for unusual chemical possession. They'd check with their kids. Their wives. Ask around. And, Kyle knew, they'd be watching his place like a hawk.

Just as he would do for them.

This was life. Not the frenetic world that Samantha Jones inhabited.

Here you knew who your friends were.

Chuck and Sam were on football duty again Friday night—in a neighboring community, since Chandler didn't have a home game—and had the new 6:00 p.m. to 6:00 a.m. shift. Up by noon that Friday, Sam asked Chuck if he'd meet her for a game at the tennis complex.

When Chuck had first been divorced they'd played every week. Until rumors had started that there was something going on between them.

Half-afraid Chuck was behind the rumors, Sam had called off their regular dates.

If he'd been interested, he took the hint. And they'd been good friends ever since. She wasn't sexually attracted to Chuck, but she liked him. Respected him. He was truly dedicated to the town. Her people. The job.

He was also a damned good tennis player and had her at six-zero after their first set.

"You want to quit?" He met her at the net.

"Hell, no, do you?" She'd beat Chuck to the complex earlier and had talked to Delia, the full-time equipment manager who'd been there since the complex first opened.

Delia told Sam about the tennis club for underprivileged kids who couldn't afford to play sports at their high schools.

She'd shown Delia Maggie's picture, and the woman confirmed that Maggie was a member of the club.

Chuck served. Sam returned long. He served again and she managed to fire a shot straight down the line, just out of his reach. And then to break his serve.

They were tied three-three when two young men, dressed in basketball shorts and T-shirts, took the court one over from them. The boys looked to be about sixteen, had rented rackets and balls and, in the next half hour, didn't manage a single volley. Not one returned serve.

Nor did they seem to know how to serve. Or to care to learn.

They took turns slamming shots across the net and chasing balls.

But what Sam noticed most, as she won the next two games, was that both of the boys had tattoos, long hair and used despicable language.

After she lost the second set by a respectable six-five, she joined Chuck for a burger and soda at the place across the street and told him what she thought about some of today's youth.

She was going to tell him about the tennis club, too, leaving Maggie out of things for now because of her promise to Kelly. Like Kelly, Sam understood how easily a kid with Maggie's background could be branded and she wasn't going to do that to her.

"Life is sure different than when we were kids," Chuck agreed, biting into his double-size burger. He'd foregone the fries for more meat.

Sam, who'd insisted on paying for her own lunch, though Chuck had intended differently, had given in to the fries and passed on the burger, ordering a salad instead. She'd also traded the soda for coffee, which was so rancid it needed four creams.

"Crime's different," Chuck continued. "Life for a lot of people doesn't seem to be about following the law so much as finding ways to do what you want without getting caught. Or just ways to get around the law."

He was right. Things had changed from her father's day when right was right and wrong was wrong and everyone knew that. "It sure makes our jobs a lot harder," she said, thinking of those tennis players who couldn't play tennis.

She was also thinking of Maggie Winston. Talking to Kelly about an older man and being curious about sex.

And the tattoos on those kids on the court that morning. The piercings and long hair. She was judging by appearance. Stereotyping. But something about those kids bothered her.

She asked Chuck if he'd heard of the club.

"Sure. They call themselves the Ramblers," he said, surprising the heck out of her. "Because they're from all parts of the Dayton area."

"How'd you know about them?"

"Remember Shane? That boy we busted last Friday who sold the Hatch girl the meth?"

Sam nodded. She wasn't likely to forget.

"Shane's mom was telling me about the Ramblers," Chuck said. "The group is part of the reason I decided not to press charges against the kid. He's one of their charter members. The idea actually came from a conversation Shane had had with his mom when the school levy failed and he knew they wouldn't be able to afford for him to play football this year."

Sam listened, finishing her fries and looking at the salad, trying to talk herself into wanting it.

And trying to keep from showing any sign of the adrenaline rush she felt to learn that Shane Hamacher, who'd just been busted for selling drugs, played in the same tennis club that Maggie was in.

"Football to tennis is a pretty big stretch," she said, trying to put the pieces together.

"A group of the kids went around with a letter Shane's mother helped him draft, looking for anyone who would let them participate in a sport for free. They went to the Y, to a soccer park, bowling alleys. Delia's the only one who did more than shake her head and wish them luck. So they're learning to play tennis."

"You're sure that's all they're doing?"

"Absolutely. I talked with Delia and a couple of the other parents—all single moms, by the way."

Parents, sponsors, didn't always see what was going on right under their noses.

"Shane's dealing. Maybe the others are involved with drugs, too."

Please God, no. She couldn't just sit and watch them fall, one by one.

Not sweet girls like Maggie Winston.

"Shane made a mistake. A one-time thing. He's not a dealer."

"How can you be so sure?"

"He told me all about it and his story checks out. He got the crystals from a guy in Indiana. Some guy he met while he was at his dad's for the weekend." Sam already knew Shane's dad was an ex-convict.

"The guy was offering five hundred dollars to anyone who could sell one thousand dollars worth of meth. Might as well have offered Shane a million dollars right then.

His mother had just told him that they were facing eviction because she couldn't pay the rent. He figured this was their answer. He didn't have to make any contacts. There were notes left in his locker at school. He just had to deliver and collect."

"So how does a guy in Indiana get notes into a locker in Chandler, Ohio?"

"Obviously he has someone in the school system working for him. I'm checking on that. And looking at other schools, too, to see if there are similar setups throughout the area."

"Have you found anything?"

"Not yet. But I'm not giving up."

"Shane could be lying."

"I don't think so."

Chuck was sharp. The best.

But Sam wasn't as apt to believe the kids.

The drugs were here. No one could argue with that. And if they were being produced here, as Sam suspected, their problem was not just identifying a delivery service. They had to find and shut down an entire company. If there was a superlab in Ohio, they were only seeing the beginnings of a spike in drug use. And it was already nearly impossible to keep up with what they had.

She opened the packet of dressing. Put it on her salad.

"And Shane has no idea who left the notes?"

"None."

"I don't suppose he kept any of them, either."

"No. He'd been told to flush them."

With the plastic fork she'd just taken from its wrapper, Sam mixed the dressing into the salad.

"Whoever's behind this is thorough."

"Nobody wants to get caught. Stops the money flow."

"Yeah, but you have admit, this is a pretty elaborate setup. Money splitting in several ways. Seems like big business to me."

"I grant you that," Chuck said. "But maybe now they'll know we're on to them. If we make it hard for this guy to do business here, he'll move on. The last thing he wants is cops on his trail."

Sam wanted to believe him. To be relieved of her suspicion about the superlab.

"I don't know, Chuck. I look at the child welfare statistics and the Holmes case and…this isn't just in the schools. Or one guy selling drugs. With the quantities we're seeing, the lower cost, the use across all sectors of society, I'm really afraid we have mass production going on right here in Fort County."

She wasn't telling him anything he hadn't heard before. From her.

With a quarter of his burger lying uneaten on the paper in front of him, Chuck looked at her.

"What?" she asked.

"Just…I wasn't going to say anything, but…"

"What?" she asked a second time.

"You need to let that idea go, Sam. The whole superlab thing." He wiped his hands on his napkin and leaned forward. "People watch you, don't you know that?"

"People? You mean my brother. And Kyle."

Shaking his head, he glanced away, and then, as though he'd made a decision, pinned her with his most serious look. .

"I figured you knew, but…everyone watches you. From the sheriff on down."

Shocked, she just stared at him. "Why? I've never done anything wrong. My record's exemplary."

"It's not about anything you've done. Or not done, for that matter."

"Then what?"

"You've been under scrutiny from the day you put on a uniform. Surely you knew that. You have to try harder, be more perfect than anyone else."

Chuck was right. She did seem to have to answer a lot of questions about routine things. Always had.

She'd just thought the sheriff was looking out for her.

"Because I'm a woman." Chandler was a small town. A little old-fashioned.

But she wasn't the first—or the only—female cop in the area.

"No, not because you're a woman. Because of your dad."

The quietly spoken words hit her hard.

"You idolized your old man," Chuck said. "Everyone knows that. Some of the older guys say you're just like him in your loyalty to the job. Your refusal to relax and let anything go. Your passion for police work. And they're afraid that—"

"I'll be just like him and make a mistake."

"From what I hear the job was everything to your father."

"Just as it is to you."

"With one difference," Chuck said. "I do the job I'm given. I don't go looking for more."

Sam's father had. Which had made him a better cop in Sam's opinion. The best. He gave over and above. And the people of Chandler had been safer for it. She had the medals and awards he'd won that showed their gratitude.

Just because he'd had a problem, as well, a sort of personal vendetta, didn't take away from all the lives her father had saved.

"Like it or not, you are your father's daughter."

She'd give anything to be as good a cop as her father was. "I was ten when he died, Chuck. Hardly enough time to model myself on him."

"But aren't you doing just that? You've talked about your meth lab suspicions to everyone. And I know your brother is worried. You aren't on meth-lab detail, Sam."

"I'm asking questions. Which is what any good cop would do if he or she had suspicions."

"And in anyone else, it would just be put down to being a good cop, but not for you, Sam, don't you see? They're looking at you. Looking for a sign that you're going over the top, as he did. And you're giving it to them."

Sam forked a bite of her salad. What could she say?

"They don't want to lose another cop. Or have to visit your mother a second time with the news that a member of her family is dead in the line of duty."

"So I'm guilty by association."

"Just be careful, Sam," Chuck said, picking up his burger. "Don't feed them. Drop this meth thing. I'll talk to the sheriff again, tell him that we need to dig a little deeper about a possible superlab nearby. In the meantime, I promise you, I'm aware. If I see anything, feel anything, hear anything that raises suspicion I'll be on it."

Sam nodded because she had to.

Not because she'd made up her mind to let go.

11

I was tired when I got home Friday night, but picked up the call that came in just as I was sitting down with a glass of wine because Sam's name popped up.

She sounded all cop and official-like. "As far as I can see Maggie spends a lot of time with that girlfriend I told you about, and she plays tennis. I haven't seen her so much as smile at a man across a street, let alone be in contact with one."

"I've seen her a total of three times," I said. "Talked to her mother twice. Neither of them mentioned that she plays tennis." Didn't necessarily mean anything, though.

I took a sip of wine, glad I had a full bottle. I might need a rare second glass tonight. "It's an expensive sport."

"Yeah. But not for the kids Maggie plays with. There's a group of them." Sam told me about the tennis club the kids had formed. Said she'd gotten a list of their names from some Delia woman who worked at the complex.

"Do they have an adult sponsor? A coach of some kind?" I was pretty certain there was a man in Maggie's life, and that she was savvy enough to know she had to be discreet. I also knew that if I was going to help my young client, we had to find this guy before Maggie had sex with him.

Camy lifted her head from my lap—her usual place when I was sitting at our dinner table.

After a questioning stare and a cursory sniff that revealed no food was being consumed with my wine, she settled back down.

"No," Sam reported. "They're on their own. But there's more."

Of course there was. Sam wouldn't be telling me about it otherwise.

"What?" I asked, twiddling a pen between two fingers.

"I busted a kid last week for selling drugs at a high school football game. He's a member of this tennis club."

Okay. I didn't like it. But… "When we played basketball that Miranda girl was a user. Remember? Heck, these days, it's pretty much impossible for a kid to go to school without being exposed to users. And probably dealers, too."

"I saw a couple of the other kids in the club this afternoon. At least, I think they were from the club. If I met either of them on the street, I'd keep an eye on them."

"Not someone you'd want your fourteen-year-old hanging out with?"

"Nope."

"But not adults, either."

"No."

Fine. We were looking for an adult. Period.

"Who else works at the courts besides this Delia woman?"

"Some kids work part-time. Mostly doing cleanup stuff. But that's not what I'm worried about."

"What are you worried about?" I asked.

"I think that tennis club could be a front for drug dealing. And if it is, this guy Maggie's going for could be their supplier. Or a client."

Overreaction. I made my first note since the conversation had begun.

Sam was seeing drugs everywhere.

I wondered if maybe I should consider giving her that prescription she'd been after me for.

She didn't seem to be shaking the Holmes case.

She'd told me about practically accusing Kyle of being involved with meth production.

"I'm not sure how it would work," Sam said. "I haven't figured it all out yet. But I know that one of the kids was busted for dealing within the past couple of weeks. I mean, it's kind of a stretch, a bunch of these kids suddenly wanting to play tennis. And they don't seem interested in learning the game. Watching them on the court, it's like they couldn't care less."

I said nothing, just let Sam talk.

"How they get their drugs and what they do with them, I have no idea. And how does tennis fit in? Why not just deal drugs? Unless they deliver at the club. Maybe buyers come to the courts to make the deals."

"It seems kind of far-fetched to me."

"Yeah?"

"Yeah."

"It probably is. Kel? Do you think I'm irrational?"

"Absolutely not."

"Obsessing?"

"There's a difference between being dedicated and being obsessive," I said.

"Which do you think I am?"

"Dedicated. And overtired. And I think you're worried about the upswing in drug use. You're overwhelmed with your seeming lack of ability to do anything about the problem, and like any good cop, you're brainstorming every possible scenario you can think of."

"Thank you."

"You're welcome."

"You'll tell me if you think I'm losing it, right?"

"Not that you'll listen."

"I know. But you'll tell me?"

"Yes. You know I will."

"Gotta go," Sam said abruptly, as she'd done many times before. I could hear the crackle of her radio in the background. "Chuck needs backup on a domestic-abuse call."

The line was dead. I hadn't had a chance to ask the deputy if she'd found out anything about Maggie's mom.

One of the things Kyle had managed to keep after his divorce—thanks to David Abrams—was the state-of-the-art combine that his father had purchased the year before his death. With careful planting this year, so that the rows and combine head were equally matched, he'd been able to bring in a little more than his estimated harvest, and the feed corn had already been delivered to Bob Branson.

And now Kyle could concentrate on his future—the experimental crop that he'd been working on since high school. To minimize loss and kernel damage, he would handpick the acre filled with the prototype seeds' growth. This year, he had a winner. Bob thought so, too.

The older man was coming for Monday night football that evening and bringing a steak dinner courtesy of the saloon in town, plus a hamburger for Grandpa. Now that the major crop was in, Kyle could easily grill them a couple of slabs of beef, but Bob insisted, and Kyle wasn't about to argue.

The divorce was taking its toll on Bob and, to Kyle, he looked frail, though Bob insisted he was fine. The eighteen-hour days he was putting in seemed to support that.

It was the first time in the almost two years since the stroke that had initiated Grandpa's downward spiral that Bob had agreed to have dinner with them at the farm.

Kyle had just finished his breakfast and was listening to Clara sing to Grandpa as she bathed him when he first smelled the burning.

His initial thought was that he'd left a towel or plastic utensil too close to a stove burner. But the stench was unusual, acrid, and it wasn't coming from the kitchen.

"Zodiac!" His urgent call was met by silence. Kyle couldn't remember whether the dog had been underfoot while he was cooking breakfast. But then, the eight-year-old German shepherd came and went as she damn well pleased since Sam had given her a doggie door for her birthday.

Kyle rushed past the table and outside. The smell was worse. Pungent. Like chemicals. At the barn door, he skidded to a halt long enough to haul the big door aside. The warm interior seemed to be just as he'd left it. Rad and Lillie popped their heads over the stalls, telling him good-morning—as they did every day. But Lillie's nostrils flared and her eyes darted with an uneasy glint.

Zodiac was nowhere to be seen.

"Easy girl," Kyle said softly, stroking the mare's nose as he checked her stall, Rad's and the six empty ones. All fine. Not wasting a second, he let the horses out to the pasture and went to check the supply barn. Maybe there was a clue...

Kyle coughed, inhaling the distinct smell of smoke. And that's when he saw the cloud on the horizon—above the land the government paid him to leave unplanted as part of an ecological program to regenerate the earth.

There was nothing out there to burn but dirt and clover. Nothing that would send up such a stench.

The dirty gray plumes of smoke were shooting higher into the crisp morning air while he stood there, reasoning to himself why there couldn't be a fire.

Making a run for the house, Kyle called to Clara to keep Grandpa in his room, grabbed his cell phone off the kitchen counter and dialed 9-1-1.

Sam was at Kyle's place before the fire was out. She wasn't on duty until noon. But he'd called.

"Did you find her?" she shouted as he met her car in the drive. Zodiac was still missing.

"Not yet." His face was grim. "I can't get anywhere near the fire," he added.

"I know." The authorities had ordered Kyle to stay away from the site because of the chemical odor he'd reported. But at the moment, the fire wasn't his only concern. "I've checked all of her haunts," he continued, his long hair more mussed than usual. "She's not down by the stream or in either of the barns."

"What about with Grandpa? You know she likes to sleep beside his bed in the mornings."

"Checked. Clara's here, anyway."

"Did you look at your mole traps? Could she have gotten caught in one of them?"

"I checked. Nothing."

"I've never known her to leave the property."

"She doesn't. Unless she's with me."

One look at the pinched skin around his mouth and she said, "You think she's at the fire."

"It's a damned good possibility, wouldn't you think? Zodiac is missing at the same time there's a fire on our property. If someone was out there, and she heard them…"

"If she's there, the authorities will look out for her, Kyle. They're trained to deal with animals. I drove a mile on both sides of your property and didn't see a sign of her," she told him. At least she hadn't found the dog dead on the side of the road, Sam thought.

Hands in his pockets, Kyle looked toward the smoky horizon and she knew how hard it was for him to just stand there when his family's land was in danger.

"The fire's contained," she told him. "They should have it out soon."

"Have they said how far it spread?"

"No more than an acre." Which was good news.

"Any word on what caused it?"

"Not yet." But from the call that had come in over her radio, she knew chemicals had been involved. They'd called in hazmat. Sam didn't want to think about that. Not now.

Not until Zodiac was found.

Chuck's cruiser pulled up behind Sam's Mustang and the deputy climbed out, a limp dog in his arms.

God. No.

Kyle's movements were stilted as he approached the deputy.

"She's alive," Chuck called out. "But she needs the vet."

"I'll drive." Sam had the engine going and the car

turned by the time Kyle, his unconscious German shepherd cradled in his arms, climbed into the passenger seat beside her.

Zodiac had no broken bones. No cuts or other external injuries. But she was suffering from acute smoke and chemical fume inhalation. The vet had given her oxygen therapy and had her on respiratory support. An IV attached to her left front leg, just above her paw, was filling her with a combination of drugs to clear fluid from her lungs. Sometime in the past few hours she'd been given electrolytes and bicarbonate.

If she made it, they'd probably be looking at daily nebulization therapy for a while.

If she made it....

Sitting beside the dog in the special room they'd set up as a favor to Kyle, he watched his unconscious friend struggle for her life and wondered how in the hell he was going to pay the exorbitant vet bill.

Wondered, and worried, yet knew he would spend whatever it cost to keep the dog alive. Zodiac was going to make it. As soon as she woke up, he could take her home.

"Hey, they told me I would find you here." Sam stuck her head in the door before coming the rest of the way in. In her uniform, her hair back in its bun, she must have just gotten off work. "Dan says she has a fifty-fifty chance."

He didn't want to hear about chances. The dog was going to make it. Kyle asked for very little. Expected very little. Didn't need much. But Zodiac was family.

"Is it past eight already?"

"It's almost ten. You need to go home. Get some rest."

"I told Dan I'd stay with her." The veterinarian had

known Kyle since he was a toddler. He'd been the only vet Kyle's dad had allowed near his prized horses, and had agreed to let Kyle stay at the twenty-four-hour clinic for as long as he needed to. One of the benefits of small-town living, he supposed. "Clara's staying with Grandpa for now. James and Millie will relieve her at bedtime and stay the night, if it comes to that."

James and Millie Turner were Kyle's next-door neighbors.

"I see that the bench has a pad." She motioned to the orange plastic cover upon which he sat. "But it hardly looks comfy."

Her voice was light. Her eyes told another story.

"What's wrong?"

Shaking her head, Sam closed the door behind her and sat down beside him. And he was glad.

They'd brought him a night-light, taken from the boarding kennel section of the clinic, but Kyle hadn't yet turned off the bright overhead examining light. He was watching Zodiac's intravenous drip.

"Bob Branson called me."

Oh, hell. "I completely forgot. He was bringing dinner."

"Yeah, but he heard about the fire and phoned first. When he didn't get you, he tried me and I told him about Zodiac. He says to tell you that if you need anything, let him know."

Much earlier that day Kyle had left briefly with Sam to retrieve his truck and feed the horses and check on Grandpa while Dan was with Zodiac. Everything else could wait.

"Have you eaten?"

"No." He'd been nauseous on and off for most of the afternoon. Probably a result of the smoke he'd inhaled when he'd run out, cell phone in hand, to the site of the fire, before he'd been ordered back to the house.

He had a hell of a headache, too.

Both symptoms would pass. Kyle had taken enough chemical safety classes during college to write the manual. If things got worse, he'd see a doctor.

"So what's wrong?" He knew the woman beside him as well as he knew the smell of rain.

"It was a chemical fire."

That was hardly news.

"Arson?"

"It doesn't look like it. More likely someone threw a lit cigarette out of a car window."

It didn't make sense for a piece of land to go up like that from a lit cigarette.

Zodiac's ribs rose and fell. Rose and fell.

He just needed her to open those damned eyes so he could take her home. To the old white house that needed a coat of paint and had nail dings in the walls from all of his school pictures and his dad's before him. To a frail old man who didn't know who he was half the time.

Home.

Where they belonged.

"So what are you telling me?" he asked.

"That field was a toxic landfill."

"Toxic landfill. As in contaminated ground? Up until two years ago I was growing corn on that land."

"I know."

"I tested it regularly. It was fine. Healthy."

"I know."

"Was it something with the groundwater?"

Gases rose. It could happen. But what a nightmare if that was the case. God, his entire property, his recent harvest...the experimental crop...

Where did the pipes run on the land? He tried to envision site plans he hadn't looked at in years.

"It was being used as a dump site for used chemicals, Kyle."

Someone was dumping on his land?

What the hell.

And because of it, Zodiac was lying here fighting for her life. Tired way beyond his years, Kyle yearned for his backyard, stars in the sky and a beer.

"What kind of chemicals?" he asked. He remembered Sam's accusations. And the chemical missing from his barn.

"It's a meth lab waste dump."

Shit. The string of words that mentally followed would have shamed Kyle in his younger days.

"I have a warrant to search your property, Kyle. I just want you to know I'll take the inside and make sure that Grandpa isn't upset."

Kyle heard Sam's voice. He saw the beige polyester pants on the seat beside him.

And almost threw up.

God, he hated that uniform.

12

"Hey, you busy?"

Startled, I looked up at Deb from the file I'd been reading. I could count the number of times my receptionist actually walked down the hall to my office. Her preferred mode of imparting information was to let her fingers do the walking to the intercom button on our ancient phone system.

"No," I said, pushing aside the transcripts from a deposition I'd taken part in a few days before in a child endangerment trial. I had to be completely sure of my findings before I'd write anything that could take a child away from her mother. "What's up?"

"Maggie Winston's here."

Deb hadn't been around any of the three times Maggie had been there. "You know her?"

"Cole went to school with her mother." Cole, Deb's husband. "Until she dropped out their freshman year to have Maggie. He says she was a straight-A student. The mother, that is." The woman Deb had previously referred to as *WT*.

I blew the bangs off my forehead. I should probably just cut them. But I liked them long. They'd always been that way. "Did Maggie say what she wants?"

"Just to see you. I know you have to get that report in and didn't know if you have time. I couldn't find where she had an appointment."

I was kind of surprised she'd looked. Deb wasn't really particular about that type of thing.

"I'll see her," I said, curious and relieved at the same time.

Deb nodded and left and I wondered again what was up with her.

Then I'd turned my thoughts to Maggie.

I'd talked again to Jim Lockhart at Maggie's school. He'd said the girl had all female teachers that year and he hadn't seen her interacting with any of the male personnel. Sam had found the same. So a crush on a schoolteacher seemed unlikely.

"I can come back another time if you're busy...."

Maggie hovered in the doorway. A startlingly changed Maggie.

"No." I stood and walked over to the couch as if I had all the time in the world. For now, I did. "Come on in. Have a seat." I motioned to the cushions beside me.

Maggie, wearing jeans, a low-cut sweater and flip-flops despite the cool temperature outside, settled on the opposite end of the couch.

"You've changed your hair." The highlights were still there, though probably touched up.

"My friend cut it for me. Just to give it some body. So it doesn't always just hang flat around my face."

Still long, Maggie's hair curled around her cheeks, little wisps giving her a waifish air.

"And the makeup?"

"She helped me with that, too."

I was going to ask about the tight sweater, but didn't. Maggie's body was slightly turned away from me and she clutched her purse on her lap. *Defensive,* I jotted in my mind.

"I'm glad you came by. I've been thinking about you."

"Why?"

"Because I care about you."

"You hardly know me."

"Sometimes you don't have to know a person long to recognize there's something about them that speaks to you."

"You pro'bly care the same about all your patients."

"Are you one of my patients?"

"No." The answer was instantaneous. And accompanied by a tightening of the pink Coach knockoff against her body. "Yeah. Maybe. I don't know. I don't need to be."

"Tell me why you're here."

"It was either that or be grounded."

"Your mother sent you here?" That surprised me.

"Yeah." Maggie's head turned as she glanced straight at me. "She said you probably wouldn't see me if she asked. What'd she do, call you up and blame you for something?"

That sort of covered it. She'd been upset about Sam's surveillance and I was to blame for that.

"She wasn't happy with me the last time we spoke," I said. "She's worried about you."

Maggie stomped her foot on the floor where she sat.

"She doesn't have to be. I'm perfectly fine. I'm not going to screw up or anything. She's, like, obsessed that I'm going to ruin my life like she did."

Understandable, given the circumstances of Maggie's life. The run-down trailer park where she lived. Her lack of supervision while her mother worked. No siblings or a male father figure that experts said kids needed.

Of course, I'd done just fine without that male influence in my life. But then, I knew better than most that the experts were only making educated guesses. No one could be one hundred percent certain about anything.

And not all people needed the same things.

"Anyway, she says that I have to find a way to get you to talk to me because if I don't I'm grounded." The girl was looking right and left.

"Okay, you did. We talked. Does that cover it for you?"

That got her attention. "Don't you want to know why Mom wants me to talk to you?"

She was such a sweet child. A combination of intelligence and insight and naïveté all rolled into one. Self-sufficient and needy at the same time.

Strong and craving support.

She reminded me of someone and I didn't want to admit it might be me.

"Of course I do," I said to her now. "But only if you want to tell me about it. I'm not your enemy. I want to help, but I can't do that if you don't want the help."

She let go of her purse. "It's not that I don't want help, it's just that I don't need it. My mom's wasting your time and I feel bad about that. She's always using people. I don't want to be like her."

I don't want to be like her.

More Maggie notes.

"So tell me why your mom thinks you need to talk to me."

"Because of my hair, of course. And my makeup. She won't let me grow up. Any change at all and she freaks out. I was the only girl in my class who'd never worn makeup. I felt like a freak."

"And this friend who helped you—is she in your class?" Sam had mentioned a friend who drove.

"No. Glenna's a senior."

Glenna. The girl Sam had talked about. The one who babysat for David Abrams.

"How'd you meet her?"

"I've known her almost forever. When I was little my mom took me to dance class for a year. Glenna was the student aid. She was really nice to me."

"So you're still close."

"Very. She's like the first friend I've ever had that I can actually talk to. She doesn't care where I live, or that the trailer has a hole in the bathroom floor that looks down to the dirt underneath."

Her mother had mentioned that hole, too. I wondered why they didn't just get it fixed. Or put a board over it.

"I told Glenna about my chat loop with the sick kids and she talks to them sometimes, too. Glenna's an only kid like me and lives alone with her mom, but her mom's sick."

"What's wrong with her?"

"I don't know, but she can't work and Glenna babysits, like, every day because they always need money."

"So the hair, the makeup—Glenna helped you with all that?"

"Yeah." Maggie's eyes darted to the left again.

There were two reasons that I knew of for young girls to change the way they looked. Peers. Or a boy. Or both.

"Does Glenna have a boyfriend?"

"No. She did. But they broke up. He was a jerk."

"What made him a jerk?"

"He plays football and thinks that makes him great when it really just makes him do stupid things."

"Like what?"

"Drinking. Partying. Driving fast."

"And Glenna didn't like that?"

Maggie looked at me again. "No. She's not that type. She wants to go to college, to be a teacher. She loves kids."

So maybe we just had a case of hero worship here. A young girl being mentored by a slightly older teen.

"I heard you're playing tennis."

She clenched the purse up against her torso again and started to bounce the foot. "Yeah. Why? Is there something wrong with that?"

"Of course not. I have a friend who plays and she mentioned seeing you at the complex."

"Oh," Maggie said, nodding. "Yeah, I play out there."

"Does Glenna play, too?"

"No. She…doesn't…have time with babysitting and all."

"How are the courts?"

"Good. Do you play tennis?" The foot tapping increased.

"Nope. Never picked up a racket."

"Oh." Her foot relaxed.

More comfortable knowing I won't be hanging out at the complex?

"Anything else going on in your life?" I asked.

Maggie had an energy about her, a sense that she was holding back, and that made me nervous.

"Not really."

"Now that school's started, have you met any boys that interest you?"

"At school? Hardly." The derision was obvious.

"Any teachers that stand out?"

"My English teacher's pretty cool. She's making us journal every day."

"Anyone else?"

She shook her head. "My teachers are all nice. Just kind of boring."

So Maggie was safe at school. At least, from what she told me. But I believed her.

"How about out of school."

Silence.

"Maggie?"

"It's not like it's anything..."

Except that she seemed to want to talk about it.

"What's not anything?"

She turned on the couch so she was facing me, like two girlfriends having a chat. "There's just this guy. He's... I don't know. I just like him. He's exactly the kind of man I hope to marry some day."

Uh-oh.

"Is this the same one you didn't want to talk about before?"

"I guess."

"So tell me about him."

"There's not much to tell. I just— We talked."

Trouble's arrived.

"On the Internet?"

"No."

"You've met him in person, then?"

"Yeah."

"Where?"

"At the park. I was there for a party with these kids I

babysit. The little boy has Down syndrome and wandered off and he brought him back."

"So he wasn't with you."

"Of course not. I told you, he's just a guy I talked to."

Funny how an older guy Maggie had a crush on just happened to turn up at the park while the girl was there.

"So tell me about the kids."

"They're just these kids I watch sometimes."

"Does Glenna babysit for them, too?"

"No. She doesn't have time. She's a nanny to one family and there's her mom and stuff."

"So what was this guy doing at the park?"

"He was just there. I don't know. It's not like Chandler is a big place."

"Did he say anything to you? Touch you in any way?"

"No! He's not like that. You're making me wish I didn't tell you."

"Does your mom know you take kids to the park?"

"Yeah."

"Does she know about this guy, too?"

"No. Of course not."

"Why not?"

"Come on, Dr. Chapman. The whole reason I'm here is 'cause my mom's whacked about me and boys. She thinks I'm two steps away from being a slut or something. If she knew some guy helped me in the park and that I actually liked him, she'd lock me in my bedroom until she dies. Besides, it's not like it's anything. I'm way too young."

"So this guy…is he a dad?"

"No. I don't know. I didn't see him with any kids."

"Are you going to meet again?"

"How would I know? I just ran into him."

"Does he know how you feel about him?"

"No."

"Has he ever given you any indication that he likes you?"

No answer. I sat forward.

"Has he ever touched you, Maggie?" I asked again.

"No."

"Would you like him to?"

The girl shrugged, her shoulders closing in on herself. "I don't know. Maybe. Someday."

"But not now."

"No."

"Do you know how old he is?"

"No."

"And he's never said or done anything to you that would lead you to believe that if you'd agree, he'd have sex with you?"

"He wouldn't do that. He's a good person. Not a creep."

Okay. So maybe all we had was a normal schoolgirl crush. Girls had them. Often on safe, innocuous authority figures who posed no threat.

"Can you tell me his name?"

"Do I have to?"

"I'd like it if you would. At least his first name. Just so I don't have to worry that you're hiding something. Or that he is."

"It's Mac. I asked him and that's what he said. I don't know his last name."

Mac.

I was sending Sam on a manhunt. Immediately.

13

Sam wasn't the only one to search Kyle's place. But she'd managed to be assigned to the barns and house, while Todd Williams and Chuck had covered every inch of the fields.

If Kyle was making meth, she wouldn't cover for him. But she wanted to be the first deputy who knew—to protect him.

And she'd had to make Grandpa think she was just there visiting him while Kyle tended to Zodiac. James and Millie, who'd only known the police were investigating the fire, had taken advantage of the chance to go home and shower.

The search was conducted first thing Tuesday morning. She'd felt like an intruder going through Kyle's personal things without him there. At any other time, she'd have touched them as easily as if they were her own.

But at any other time, she'd have felt as though she was a part of him.

She wasn't sure what she was now.

Except a cop.

When it came right down to it, that's all Sam was. Anyplace. Anytime. A cop.

She reminded herself of that fact at five minutes after eight Tuesday evening when she changed out of her uniform into the jeans and black sweater she'd brought with her to work. Her plan was to head straight out to Kyle's. She'd spoken to him briefly that morning. Zodiac was awake and Kyle had been ready to take her home, but not until Sam and her fellow officers had vacated the place.

She and her fellow conspirators. There was no reason for her to feel guilty. She was doing her job. Nothing more.

She wasn't the one who'd bought questionable amounts of dangerous chemical—not that she'd told anyone about that yet. The toxic waste in the field was reason enough to search the premises. Not that Kyle was a suspect, but his land was.

And she wasn't the one who'd kept a little thing like another lover a secret for fifteen years. A lover who'd turned up possessing enough meth to be selling the stuff.

Still, she'd offered to collect Kyle and Zodiac. To take them home. Truth be known, she'd needed to see them. To be near Kyle. And to look Zodiac in the eye.

He'd said Dan was taking him back to the farm. The vet was going to help him set up a bed and IV for the dog in the kitchen.

Sam didn't ask if she could drive out after her shift. She wasn't giving Kyle the chance to tell her no a second time. Technically, if he insisted he didn't want her on his property, she'd be breaking the law by visiting him.

The Mustang faltered a bit at the slow speed up the long dirt drive, but Sam wasn't in a "roaring up" mood. Hell, for all she knew, if she showed her power, her proud and sensitive sometimes-lover might meet her outside with a gun.

Order her off his land.

He'd be within his rights to do so.

He didn't meet her car. Not even when she parked by the house. Turned off the engine. Lights were on in the kitchen. Sam climbed the steps to the back door. And stood, staring at it. Should she knock?

She hadn't knocked in years.

So she didn't.

Pulling open the old-fashioned wooden screen door, she pushed the heavier one inward.

"Kyle?" she called softly, stepping into the mudroom, but no farther.

Grandpa should be down for the night.

Still…

Kyle's boots were there. Just like they always were when he was in the house. Ready and waiting for him to slip into them to get to the barn.

They never crossed the threshold into the house. Kyle believed that a man's boots didn't belong in his house.

Because his father and grandfather had believed the same.

There was no answer to her call.

She tried again, moving a little closer to the archway that led to the kitchen. "Kyle?"

"Yeah."

She saw him then, sitting in the handmade wooden rocking chair that had been in his living room ever since she could remember. He'd pulled it over to the far corner of the kitchen where a makeshift bassinet sat with an IV drip beside it.

Grandpa's door was shut—a monitor on the table beside Kyle. When Grandpa had first come home from the hospital after his stroke, Kyle had slept in the front room so he could hear if the old man stirred during the night.

Sam had bought him the monitor so he could go back to sleeping in his own bed.

He didn't smile when she entered the room. Hardly looked at her at all.

But he didn't tell her to leave.

"How is she?"

"Sedated. Her throat and lungs are burned pretty bad. Dan wants to give them a day or two to heal before seeing how she does up and around."

Peering over the side of the long wooden crate on top of a saw table padded with sheets and bedding, Sam looked for signs that Zodiac was better.

The dog looked just as lifeless as she had the day before.

"Has she been awake at all?"

"An hour the first time. 'Bout the same, the second."

A cereal bowl with cooked chicken and rice sat on the edge of the table.

"Has she eaten anything?"

"A little bit. Can't give her too much. Throwing up would hurt her throat."

"Did she seem to know you?"

"*She* knew me." The implication was clear that someone else in the room didn't.

And that's what happened when a person kept fifteen-year-old secrets.…

She had to let it go. It was past. Over a long time ago.

She just couldn't believe that Kyle hadn't told her. That he'd impregnated a woman and…

But she didn't know that for sure.

She looked back at Zodiac. "She's going to be okay, right?"

His gaze, when it met hers, lacked his usual confidence. "I don't know."

Swallowing, Sam wasn't sure what to do with herself. Take a seat at the table? Rub Kyle's back and neck? That's what she'd have done a month ago. He had to be exhausted, aching, after spending the night in a tiny exam room at the animal hospital.

Leaving should probably be an option. It wasn't.

"Can I touch her?"

"Suit yourself."

Okay, she would. She'd done nothing wrong. And she'd loved Zodiac since she'd watched the dog come into the world, the pup of Kyle's dad's dog, Missy, who'd since passed on.

She'd been caring for Kyle a whole lot longer than that.

Instead of its usual silkiness, the German shepherd's fur felt kind of sticky. Zodiac didn't flinch, didn't move at all, as Sam stroked her, rubbing gently along the dog's chest between her front legs. Zodiac's favorite spot.

The dog was so strong. Had seemed invincible. Smart enough to keep herself safe in any situation. And to keep Kyle safe, too.

Look what had happened to them both.

"I don't know the rules here." His voice was even. Unemotional. "Do you tell me the results of your search or do I find out when you show up at my door in uniform?"

"I'm here as a friend, Kyle."

"So you can't tell me what's going on."

"I didn't say that. It's just…this doesn't seem like the right time. It's not like we can do anything tonight."

"You found something."

"I didn't say that."

He shot up, the chair knocking into the wall behind

him. "Dammit, Sam. What's the big secret? And how can there be a right time for a friend of twenty years or more to show you they don't know you at all? That you could think, even for a second, that I would—"

"Wait just a minute, buster."

She should have told him before now. Shouldn't have let it fester.

"What? You come at me like I'm some kind of criminal and I'm supposed to just take it in stride?" His quiet tone didn't take any of the anger out of his voice. "I can't believe you didn't trust me."

"Don't talk to me about secrets, Kyle," Sam said, her own throat burning. "Or about not trusting someone."

"What? I've got nothing to hide?"

"Oh, yeah? What about Sherry Mahon?"

His face paled.

"Name ring a bell, Kyle? Now let's talk about good friends and secrets."

He didn't say a word. And any hope that Chuck had somehow been wrong, confused his stories, was dashed.

Sam fell to a chair that had been pulled away from the kitchen table to make room for the makeshift dog bed. "You want to talk to me about how I could possibly doubt you, Kyle? About how it feels to have a friend for so long and then discover you don't know them at all?"

"Sam…"

"No, I don't think I'm ready to hear about it yet. Which is why I didn't tell you when I first found out."

"When was that?"

"The morning I discovered your chemical purchases."

He nodded, his face grim and filled with disgust. But

Sam had a feeling the negative emotions were no longer directed at her.

"Did you use protection?"

"No."

That hurt. More than it should have. He'd… With his… That had been hers… And the very next night he'd put that used thing inside Sam.

What was the matter with her?

She was acting like a fifteen-year-old virgin, not a thirty-three-year-old woman.

It had been different when Kyle got married. She'd been over him by then. Or thought she was.

She'd been starting her career—so certain that when he'd forced her to choose between her life's calling and being his wife, she'd made the right decision.

"I just need to know one more thing," she said.

"What?"

"Did Sherry Mahon have a baby, Kyle? Your baby?"

"No." He was staring at the tips of his socks. One had a hole in it.

"You're sure about that."

"Of course."

Kyle was ashamed.

Good. He should be.

So it was true. One night after they'd broken up, Kyle had bedded another woman. And then slept with Sam again the next night.

He could have given her a sexually transmitted disease.

Her mind reeled as he silently cleared away the dog's food. He turned off the overhead light in the kitchen, leaving only the small fixture above the kitchen sink. A light he left on all night.

Was he just going to go to bed and leave her standing there?

They were both upset. He'd probably had very little sleep. His beloved friend was lying there fighting for her life and he could do little to help her. He had financial pressures.

And a possible arrest on the horizon?

"I'm sorry." He stood in the center of the room, arms folded across his chest.

Because he'd slept with the woman? Or because he hadn't told her.

He'd changed from the jeans and flannel shirt she'd seen him in the day before into fresh jeans and a corduroy shirt. His stocking feet might make him look more defenseless, but Sam couldn't let her heart rule her.

Couldn't get overly emotional.

That's how cops made mistakes.

Put others in danger.

Like her dad had.

That's why she wasn't married. Why she lived alone.

That's why she was always a cop. Only a cop.

She had to remember the choice she'd made years ago. The choice to be a cop—rather than a wife.

"There's no evidence of a lab or former lab anywhere on the premises."

His arms dropped. And he actually looked at her. Fully.

She wondered if he heard the *but* that was coming.

"There is, however, a significant amount of chemical missing."

She'd gone over his records. The subpoena had given her the right. He'd told her where to find them.

"Forty-five gallons of methanol," she said when he

remained silent. He didn't give an explanation. Or show undue surprise, either.

Sam's heart sank.

"And a large percentage of anhydrous ammonia, too."

His gaze sharpened as if he hadn't known about that.

"Traces of both were found in the fire."

"Do I need a lawyer?"

Sam was shaking. Her hands. Her knees. Her lips. "I don't know, Kyle. Do you think you need one?"

"Am I being charged with something?"

"As far as I know, it's not against the law to purchase legal chemicals and have quantities unaccounted for."

"So what's the big deal?"

They were in a standoff. All that was lacking were holsters with guns that they could pull simultaneously and see whose trigger finger was fastest.

"There's circumstantial evidence, Kyle. You purchased five times as much ammonia as usual. And you've never bought methanol before. Large quantities of both are missing, though all storage tanks appeared secure. And you have a toxic fire on your property with evidence that could point to the making of methamphetamine."

"Do I need a lawyer?" If his words were bullets, he'd just hit her hard.

She was tired, too. Tired and scared. And she didn't know him. Which scared her most of all. "You tell me! Talk to me, Kyle. Give me something. Anything."

She didn't want to believe her best friend was making illegal drugs. Didn't want to believe anything bad about him. Didn't want to know that he'd slept with Sherry Mahon.

"Why should I give you anything? You already believe

I've done something wrong. I'm not going to change your mind."

"I love you, dammit!" Shit. The words weren't supposed to have escaped.

With narrowed eyes, he turned away from her. "And we've known for a long time, Sam, that, for us, love isn't enough."

14

"I wish you'd just go." Kyle's bones ached. His entire body ached. He wanted to sink down into his chair, tilt his head back and go to sleep.

If he could. ·

"Do you mean that?"

Did he? Sure. He wanted her to get the hell out of his house. Out of his life.

And he wanted her to stay, too.

He was scared to death. Couldn't fathom a single day in jail—let alone a string of them.

He had an ailing grandfather to take care of. Kyle's arrest would kill the old man.

He'd lose his home. The farm. Zodiac. Lillie and Rad.

His whole life would be gone.

He'd never survive being locked inside.

Intending to stand strong until Samantha Jones was out of his sight, out of his home, Kyle dropped down to the rocker his grandfather had made for his grandmother when Kyle's dad was born. His father had been rocked in that chair. Kyle had been rocked in that chair. The upholstered pads had been changed a couple of times over the years, but the chair, the rockers, the steady rhythm of its movement, the sound of wood against wood floor, remained exactly the same.

He heard Sam move, expected to hear the door close behind her. He'd earned her desertion.

He should have told her about that night.

But when she'd come back to him, begging him to take her back, to love her for the rest of his life, he'd been so afraid of losing her again.

Because losing her had almost killed him.

And there was more. Thank God she didn't have access to his bank records. Those would require a subpoena. And even if she got one, she'd have to go back a ways to find anything. She couldn't know about the payoff. She'd have him in jail for sure....

He opened his mouth, not sure how to start, and felt her arms on his thighs as she lowered herself to the floor beside him. "Talk to me, Kyle. Help me."

"I don't know where the chemical is or what happened to it."

"But you knew it was missing."

As soon as he admitted that, she'd have more reason not to trust him. And that was his own fault.

But Sam was obsessed with this meth-lab business. And she couldn't see it. How could he hope she'd understand why he'd kept silent?

And yet, if he didn't gain her understanding, she had the power to take his life away from him.

"The hose cap on the holding tank had been chewed. I thought the gas had evaporated."

"Forty-five gallons' worth?"

That was a stretch. But he'd hoped...

"Don't lie to me, Kyle."

"I didn't tell you because I knew you'd think exactly

what you're thinking now," he finally said, too tired to fight her.

He'd go to battle for his grandfather. For his land. For his life. They weren't going to take any of it away from him.

He just needed some sleep so he could figure out a strategy.

"I didn't discover the missing methanol until a week ago Tuesday—after you'd been out here accusing me of buying the stuff to make meth."

"I didn't say that."

"You didn't have to. It's what you were thinking. Suspicion was written all over you."

"Because I'd just found out about Sherry. She was arrested last week, Kyle, for possessing large quantities of methamphetamine."

He swore.

"What about the ammonia?"

"I didn't know about that until tonight."

"You don't keep tabs?"

"Yes, I do regular checks for leaks, things like that. But I don't worry about it being used without my knowledge. It's in pressurized tanks. It's not like it would be real easy to steal."

"So you're saying it was stolen?"

"Who's asking?"

She frowned and Kyle's uneasiness increased. Sam was never just a woman, just a friend. She didn't know how to be.

But in the end, his answer didn't change.

"I'm saying that I didn't use it."

"Do you know who did?"

"Of course not! God, Sam, what do you think I am?" He wanted to snatch the words back the second they left his mouth. He knew damned well what she thought he was.

And yet, he still craved the feeling of her body leaning on his. Still needed her touch. Her scent.

Masochistic. That's what he was.

And stupid.

"I hope to God you aren't going to be the one to come pick me up," he said aloud. "As a matter of fact, I'm telling you right now. Send someone else."

"No one's going to be picking you up." They were the first words she'd said all night that he wanted to hear. "At least, not yet."

She could have left out the last part.

"Why not? With such pointed circumstantial evidence?"

"Because no one knows about the chemicals."

His entire body stilled. "That they're missing?"

"That you even purchased them."

He stared at her.

"I… The investigation into purchased chemicals was done on my own time. I'm under no obligation to report my findings. Unless I know that something illegal is going on, of course."

Pierce's concern that Sam was working on her own without departmental direction or support to find a methamphetamine superlab came back to bother Kyle.

Yet he was relieved, too. Hugely relieved.

"I made sure I was the one who searched your house and barns this morning, just like I told you I would, for Grandpa's sake," she continued, her hands folded together.

Kyle had to ask. "Why did you do that?"

"Because if you're in trouble I want to help you."

He was just curious. "Help me how?"

"I'm not sure. I can't cover for you. Once I know for certain there's illegal activity involving this farm, I'll have to act upon that knowledge. But for now, it's only a possibility, and if I can help you, if there's anything I can do to make certain that you're protected, I'm going to do it."

The sincerity shining from her eyes was the only thing that kept her in his house.

"You really think I'd make methamphetamine."

"You've got a degree in chemistry. A history of purchasing the chemicals. You're desperate for cash. There was an alleged toxic waste dump on your property."

She had no idea how desperate he was for cash. Or why. Like everyone else, she thought he was strapped because of the divorce. And Grandpa's care.

"You think I'd do that to my land?" He was calmer now. Gathering information rather than panicking. He looked at Zodiac. "You think I'd risk her health by dumping dangerous chemicals where she runs?"

Sam didn't back down. Didn't look away or even blink. "What I know is that you'll do anything to save this farm, Kyle."

Including break up with her.

Thirteen years ago, Kyle had chosen his farm over her. He'd wrestled with the decision for months, grieved for a love he couldn't find a way to have, cursed at fate. He didn't want to be married to a cop. Didn't want to have to worry about what she'd be facing every single time she left the farm to go to work. Didn't want a wife who had to carry a gun on the job. He hadn't wanted the mother of his children to be a woman who knowingly put her life in the line of fire.

He'd grown up without a mother. Sometimes it couldn't be helped. But in Sam's case, the risk of him raising motherless children would have been significantly higher.

He wanted, needed, a wife who stayed on the farm. Who worked side by side with him.

Sam had wanted a husband who'd spend half the week on the farm and half the week in the city.

And in the end, he'd done what he thought he had to do. Honored who he was over a relationship that asked him to be something he was not.

And he'd asked the ultimate of her. Him or her job.

He'd suspected that some day he was going to have to answer to that decision. He'd just never thought it would be with his life.

"You've been crying."

Mac had been thinking about this meeting all day—the couple of minutes when he passed the package from his hand to Maggie's.

"No." She looked down. As though she could hide anything from him. Didn't she know he could see straight into her deep and lonesome soul? Was he the only one in her life who saw how incredibly special she was?

"Tell me what's wrong."

She liked him. He knew it. He saw it in her eyes.

That day at the park—he'd wanted to stay with her. Play with the kids.

And her.

"Nothing's wrong."

Wait. How could she lie to him? She never had before.

Maybe she'd met someone.

The thought depressed him.

She'd made so many changes lately. The hair. The clothes. The makeup. He'd thought the curls, the tight shirts, were for him. He'd been flattered. And a tad amused.

But if there was someone else…

"It hurts that you'd lie to me. I thought we were more to each other than that."

They'd never talked a lot. Never seen each other for more than the brief time stops she made during her paper route.

But every time he looked in her eyes, it was as if they'd talked.

Her glance darted up and, connecting with it, he breathed a little easier.

"I…just… You don't need to hear about my stuff."

"I want to hear it. I care about you." He'd spoken the words aloud. "I care about all of you."

"I'm fine, really." She reached for the bag he held.

He pulled back.

"I can't send you to work upset. You might miss something. Deliver to the wrong house. Accidents happen that way and I won't have you, or anyone else, hurt."

"You'll think it's dumb."

"Hey." He lifted her chin with his finger and let his hand linger. Just for a moment. For a touch of the skin that haunted him. Skin he now had to think of every time he had sex so he could get it up. "When are you going to understand that there is nothing you could do or think that I would find dumb? If something's upsetting you, it's important to me."

Those big brown eyes stared up at him and he could hardly breathe. His mouth was dry and he forgot, for an instant, that he was the leader. The one they all relied on.

He had a job to do.

A strict set of rules.

He was a grown man with the responsibility that came with age.

"My friend, Glenna, just told me about a little boy with ADHD who was locked in a closet for five months because his parents couldn't keep him from hurting himself and couldn't afford medication to help him." She teared up again.

"Jimmy Williams."

"You know him, too?"

"We're going to help him, sweetie."

"We are?"

"Yes. We'll be delivering meds to his house, soon, just like we do with the other folks that need them but can't afford them. It's your help, yours and the others, that let us do this so cheaply. We don't have to pay doctors and pharmacists and distributors. We just pay you guys. That's why it's so important that you not open the packages," he added for good measure, not that he worried about her following the rules. "We can't take a chance on having any of the medications contaminated or we'd have to throw it away and then it would cost more money to replace."

It was the story he gave Maggie. That she was delivering meds to sick kids. Because she was different. The rest of them were just happy to make the money. They knew if they touched the packages, they'd lose their jobs. Ones that paid more than any minimum-wage job they could get.

Some of them might suspect, but they didn't care. As long as they were paid.

"Jimmy's already on our list, sweetie," he said, gazing down at the young woman in front of him.

As happy tears trickled down her face, he longed to kiss them away and satisfied himself with slowly wiping them instead.

"I have to talk to you about something." He'd had a scare. This time her tears had been for a young boy who was sick. Next time it could be an older boy, or man, who caught her interest. Her heart.

He couldn't take that chance.

Not with this one.

"What?" Her concerned and completely trusting look gave him strength.

"Your clothes. Your hair. The makeup."

Her expression fell. "You don't like them?"

So they had been for him.

"I do like them," he told her, careful of her fourteen-year-old budding ego. "Too much. And that's why they have to go."

"You don't want to like me." Her voice was as glum as her expression.

"Hey." He lifted her chin again, this time because she was hurting at his expense and that was something he could never allow. His fingers trailed softly along her neck. "It's not me I'm worried about.

"I love seeing this." He pointed to the young, firm breasts beneath the tight black sweater and fought the temptation to accidently brush against one of the rigid nipples. He was a good man. A decent man. "I don't want anyone else to have that same privilege. They'll use you. Take advantage. You'll get hurt."

And when she continued to stand there, looking at him, he pointed lower to the curve of crotch that was outlined in the low-cut jeans. "This is too much temptation. You're perfect. Gorgeous. And I can't send you out like this in front of other people. I don't trust them not to touch."

And, just in time, he remembered himself.

"If you get hurt, you won't be able to help anymore," he said, stepping back.

"I'll tone it down," she said. And then smiled at him.

A burst of unexpected sunshine.

And because she was a good girl who'd understood him, because she was having an emotional day, because the project needed her…he broke one small rule. He pulled her into his arms and hugged her.

He did it for good reasons. Logical ones. Compassionate ones. He did not do it for himself.

15

After a phone conversation with MaryLee Hatch, facilitated by Sam's old schoolmate Roberta Gainey, who was MaryLee's younger sister, Sam picked up Nicole Hatch in the cruiser on her way home from school Thursday afternoon and took her to the county sheriff's office, which also housed the administration offices and county jail. The complex was in Chandler and not far from the high school.

Samantha had decided not to charge the child the night she'd been brought in almost two weeks before and had released her to her mother's care, but Nicole had not yet been told that she wasn't going to be charged. As far as the girl knew, she was waiting to hear what was going to happen to her next.

Sam and the sheriff and Nicole's mother had all decided to give the girl a couple of weeks to be afraid for herself and her future. Two weeks to think about what she'd done.

MaryLee wanted her daughter scared. Really scared. Since the motorcycle crash that had killed her husband, the woman was trying to hold on to a full-time job and raise four kids single-handedly. She couldn't afford to go lightly on her second youngest. Not for a moment.

"Why am I here?" Nicole's face was white. Sam had her in a private consultation room. There was a table. Some chairs. And little else. Fort County couldn't afford extravagances.

The beat-up desk Sam shared with a couple of other deputies was located down a separate hallway.

"You're here because I want to talk to you," she said, dead serious. "Your mom tells me you're thirteen." MaryLee had given Nicole's vital information on the night she'd come to collect her daughter after she'd been brought in for the drug exchange. MaryLee also asked for police help in disciplining her daughter.

Nicole nodded.

"In eighth grade?"

"Yes."

The drug epidemic wasn't just in high school anymore. It had spread to blue-eyed, blond-haired innocents in junior high.

And maybe even younger kids.

"Do you have any idea what can happen to you now that you've broken the law?"

The girl's lower lip started to tremble. Sam wasn't going to be moved by tears.

"Nooo." Nicole drew the word out on a soft wail. "Wendy says I could go to jail until I'm eighteen and not get to finish school or anything. But Daniel says that's not true. He thinks I can't go to jail since I've never been in trouble before."

"Who are Wendy and Daniel?"

"Wendy's my best friend. Daniel's my brother. He's in high school."

"Does Daniel do drugs, too?"

Eyes wide, the girl shook her head. "He runs track. He says drugs'll kill you. He wanted Mom to ground me for the rest of the school year."

"Did she?"

"I don't know. She hasn't said yet. I just can't go anywhere or do anything until she says so."

"Well, just so you know, Wendy's partly right. You could go into detention for drug possession. But she's wrong that you couldn't finish school. They have school in juvenile detention and every inmate is required to attend. Juvenile offenders here in Fort County generally range in age from eight to seventeen. All the girls are housed together. You'd have to sleep in a cell...."

Nicole started to cry.

"On a cot. You can't wear shoes, only slippers made out of paper that the guards give you. They give you clothes to wear, too. You have to eat when you're told. And only what they give you. You have to go to bed and get up exactly when you're told. You have to shower out in the open. No privacy. You can't go outside unless it's a sanctioned function with a guard present at all times, and you can only have visitors a couple of times a week for a short period. No unauthorized phone calls are allowed and no e-mail." The girl was sobbing, staring at Sam through her tears.

Sam had considered taking Nicole through juvenile detention, to show the girl what her fate could be as a result of drug use, but after seeing the girl's raw fear, she changed her mind. She wanted to scare Nicole, not give her psychological issues for the rest of her life.

"And then, depending on your sentence, if you get out before you're eighteen, you'll have a criminal record. Do you know what that means?" Sam handed the skinny kid a tissue from a pile she'd stashed in her back pocket.

Nicole shook her head.

"For one thing, it means that if you get in any more trouble, any little thing at all, they'll throw the book at you."

Thank you, television.

"Have you ever heard of an aggravator, Nicole?"

Another shake of the head.

"Hey." Sam touched the teenager's forearm. "Look at me."

Nicole did as she was told. Her face was blotchy and tears continued to pour down her cheeks.

"Aggravators are things that happen that make a crime a more serious offense. Do you know what an aggravator for drug possession is?"

Nicole's head shake was barely discernable through her sobs. Sam concentrated on the girl's trembling chin, not the eyes that stared at her with naked fear.

"Buying or selling drugs near a school is an aggravator," she said, hoping her voice was as firm as it had been when they'd begun this conversation and did not, in any way, reflect her compassion for the child's obvious suffering.

A day's misery for the girl was one hundred percent better than a life ruined by methamphetamine.

"That means you're in extra trouble and the sentence the judge gives is more harsh."

Sheriff Hale, Sam's elected boss, passed by and glanced in the window, brow raised. Sam shook her head and he moved on.

He'd offered to up the pressure if Nicole gave her any attitude.

This little girl didn't seem to have a microfiber of attitude. She was a sweet, frightened child who'd somehow been convinced to buy a dangerous drug.

MaryLee Hatch was going to be relieved to find out that she did know her daughter, after all.

And Sam was going to find out whatever she could from Nicole.

It was up to all of them, working together, to keep Nicole, and children like her, safe in a dangerous world.

Chandler, Ohio
Thursday, September 16, 2010

Lori Winston, I was finding, was a hard woman to get ahold of. Without a home phone, she could be reached only by cell, and didn't pick that up much. At least, not when I dialed the number—which I'd done multiple times since my Tuesday afternoon meeting with Maggie. I needed Lori to confirm that she knew about Maggie's visits to the park.

Thankfully Sam hadn't been so hard to reach. Since dinnertime Tuesday, the deputy had been on a "Mac" hunt and city-park detail. I'd told her that I believed Maggie had met the man in the park originally and that she'd only seen him once.

My high school buddy hadn't sounded good. She still wasn't sleeping. I wished she'd let me help her and was now determined that if she didn't come to me soon, I was going to have to get pushy.

With a pen between my teeth, I dropped my office phone in its cradle and pushed the intercom button. "Deb, you busy?"

I had half an hour before my last appointment of the day.

"Of course."

Which could mean anything from bookkeeping or licking envelopes to filing her nails. I didn't much care.

Deb got the work done.

I asked her to come to my office.

"What's going on?"

She was dressed up today. Wearing a red sweater and red boots with her jeans. Her short black hair, longer in front than back, curled around her face, giving her an elfin look.

"Just wanted a minute. Everything okay with you?"

"How do you mean? Did I screw up something?"

"No. Of course not. Do you ever?"

"Not that I'm aware of."

"Not that I'm aware of, either." I'd had a couple of secretary/receptionist/bookkeepers. Professional ones. And probably more respectful ones. But none of their work equaled Deb's for accuracy and precision. And none of them were as loyal. "But you seem edgy. Is something wrong?"

"I'm not sure."

She came in and sat on my old couch. I joined her, pad in hand. I didn't have to worry about doodling in front of Deb. She knew me. Heck, she'd be more uncomfortable if I didn't write something now and then.

"I'm worried about Cole."

Deb's husband of four years worked for the state as a road engineer.

"Why?"

"He just doesn't seem as interested in me all of a sudden. He used to insist on holding my hand everywhere we go. Now half the time he doesn't—and doesn't seem to notice that he's not. We used to make love at least four times a week. Now I'm lucky if it's once…"

It was nice to talk to a friend who didn't have to be coaxed to open up to me.

But I didn't want to hear this. Not from Deb. She and

Cole had been so clearly devoted to each other. They seemed a perfect example of the true love that I still believed in, in spite of all the evidence to the contrary that I saw in my practice.

"Is he spending more time away from home?" I asked, expecting an affirmative answer. I knew which signs to look for. It just remained to be seen whether a who or a what had replaced Deb in Cole's affections.

"No."

"More time on the computer?"

"Nope."

"How about a new hobby? Or sport?"

"Uh-uh. Unless you count the cooking lessons we're taking at the Y."

"You're taking them together? In the same class at the same time?"

"Yeah."

"You guys still spend all your free time together?"

"Yep."

Oh. Well, then. Life could still surprise me.

Too sure of yourself. I jotted. And followed the words up with two more. *Jaded. Ineffective.*

Which was what I would be if I handled all my patients like I'd just handled this situation.

"How are your finances?" I said aloud. Not a usual boss-to-employee question, but this was a counseling office. We did things differently.

"Okay. But I don't think they are at Cole's work. There've been a lot of cutbacks. He says that with all the layoffs he's been given a lot more to do. He's valuable because he knows how to do most of the different jobs so they can just move him around."

"Have you asked him what's wrong?"

Should have been my second question. After "how are you?"

Deb nodded. "He just tells me not to worry about it. And I wouldn't. I mean, I'm not needy or anything, it's just that…with the physical stuff…"

Deb was worried about once a week. I hadn't been held in…well, this wasn't about me.

"In most cases, after the first year or two of a relationship, the sex settles down to a level that can be sustained through a lifetime together."

"But it doesn't seem like settling in. It seems like he's lost interest in me. Which is what I told him."

"What does he say about that?"

"That he still wants me. That there are just times when other things take precedence. He said that when guys are focused on changes at work, the economy, finances, sex sometimes doesn't happen as often."

"That's true."

"It is?"

"Of course."

"But…studies say that men have sexual thoughts once every seven seconds and—"

I shook my head. "Studies don't say that. Urban legend does. The Internet does. Any studies I've read only point to the fact that men *report* a higher percentage of sexual thoughts than women. Just as women report a higher percentage of emotional thoughts than men."

As I might have mentioned, I was not fond of the Internet. For all the good it might do, what I saw was the huge amount of damage created by too much easily accessible, dangerous information.

The damage created when kids like Maggie felt safe speaking with pedophiles.

I saw the cesspool hiding behind the websites. From

sexual deviants to psychological statistics, incorrect self-diagnoses and self-cures, even companies manipulating people's fears for financial gain through fancily skewed statistics and surveys...

But I couldn't get sidetracked right now.

"A lot of things affect the male sex drive." I told my friend what I'd learned in books, because they were really all I had on this one. "Financial worries are one of the biggest desire suppressors. Job and life changes also affect sexual desire. A lack of sleep, lack of exercise, hormonal imbalances and diet are a few others."

"So you don't think it's me?"

"It doesn't sound like it. I'd guess it's the economy and work."

"Really?" I hated the doubt and hurt I saw in her eyes because it reminded me once again of the fragile state of the human psyche. Deb was questioning her attractiveness.

"Really."

"Cool!" Deb smiled and I did, too.

"I'm happy to speak with him if you want me to."

"No." Deb relaxed back into the couch, as though relief had left her exhausted. "I don't want to put any more pressure on him. I'm good with once a week. I was just scared I was losing my husband."

"There are no guarantees, you know," I felt compelled to tell her. "Without speaking with Cole, I can't be sure...."

"No, it's okay. I feel a lot better. Cole said the same things you did. I just thought he was, you know, making excuses because he didn't want to hurt my feelings by admitting that I didn't do it for him anymore."

"Once a week is hardly not doing it." I said drily, because she was my friend. "Anyway, I could have told you this weeks ago. Why didn't you just ask?"

Deb's expression sobered. "Because…people…they take advantage of you. A lot. I'm not going to do that."

People didn't take advantage of me. "I help because I want to, Deb." This was new—the idea of someone looking out for me. Even with Sam, I was always the caregiver. "Please, come to me anytime. It'll hurt my feelings if you don't."

"Well, hopefully I won't need to, but—"

She was interrupted by the pealing of the office phone and she waited while I jumped up to answer it.

"Lori, thanks for calling me back," I said, recognizing Maggie's mother's voice on the other end of the line.

Turning back to let Deb know I'd be a minute, I saw that she'd already left the room.

"I would've called sooner, but Mags has been around," Lori said, and I could tell from the long breath she took that she was smoking a cigarette.

I started to ask her about Maggie's volunteer activities, but she cut me off.

"Listen, I was going to call you, anyway, to thank you," she said, sounding more up than I'd ever heard her. "I don't know what you said to Maggie, but it worked. It's like I have my daughter back. I went to work yesterday morning and said goodbye to this girl all done up like a tart and came home last night to a fourteen-year-old in jeans and a baggy T-shirt with no makeup and her hair back in a clip like she used to wear it."

"Maybe she'd just gotten comfortable for the night."

"No. She went to school that way this morning, too. And she told me that I was right about not wanting her to get all dolled up and that she was going to be more careful."

Inexplicable behavior change. Maggie's file was on my desk. I jotted the note on the inside cover. In red ink. I hadn't encouraged Maggie to change her appearance.

So who had?

"Are you aware that Maggie spends time in the park with the kids she babysits?" I asked instead.

"Yes." Was that sharpness I heard in the woman's tone? Or a quick intake of nicotine?

"And you're okay with that?"

"What? Yeah, I played in that park as a kid."

"Times have changed."

"Not that much. Not in Chandler. Besides, Maggie's a great kid. I just… I might overreact to the guy thing, but I'd rather overreact than have my kid end up like I did. I called you because I needed a professional opinion—you know, in case I missed a sign or something, since I didn't do so great in that area myself."

The woman was rambling.

"Being a single parent is mostly okay, but I know how easy it is to fall into the whole being-loved thing and not realizing that it's not love at all until it's too late. But other than that, there's nothing to worry about with Maggie. She doesn't do anything wrong and wouldn't get into trouble. She's the best."

"I agree—you've got a great daughter, Ms. Winston. You're very lucky."

I just wished I felt that Maggie was equally blessed. Or even half as certain that Maggie was okay.

I wished Samantha Jones would call with news on Mac.

16

After exacting a promise from Nicole Hatch that she would never again knowingly be in the vicinity of illegal drugs, and getting it in writing, Sam finally told the distraught girl that she was not going to press charges.

"But I can't let you get away without paying for your crime," she said.

Nicole's tears had stopped, but she glanced up nervously from the table where she'd written her statement in elaborate cursive that looked as much like art as it did handwriting.

"You can't?"

"No. You have a choice. You can volunteer at either of the two assisted-living places in town one day a week, for two hours, until the end of the school year. You'll be reading to older folks who have trouble seeing."

The arrangement had already been okayed by Nicole's mother.

Frowning, Nicole said, "You told me I have a choice. What is it?"

"You can decide which place you're going to volunteer."

"So I don't really have a choice."

"That's right."

"Okay, but I don't know if my mom will let me…"

"She'll let you, Nicole. This is the law talking. You do understand that, right?"

"Yes."

"And if I ever, ever see your name anywhere near a police report in the future, I'm coming after you personally, you got that?"

"Yes, ma'am."

"Okay, now tell me how you got connected with Shane Hamacher."

"I just know him. You know, from school."

Shane was in high school. "You mean from last year?"

"And before that. He's just one grade ahead of me."

"So how did you know you could get drugs from him?"

She had Shane's version through Chuck and wasn't satisfied.

"I didn't. There was this number to call if you were having troubles with a class and needed help."

"Where'd you find it?"

"Kids were passing it around. It wasn't like a secret or anything."

Sam was confused. "Where did they pass it around?"

"At school. In classes, or the lunchroom—whatever."

"In front of teachers?"

"Yeah. I thought it was like tutoring or something. I'm really good at English, but not so good at math, and I have algebra this year and I got my first B ever. Daniel doesn't have as much time to help me since he's working now and still staying in shape for track, and my older sister, Tanya, she's babysitting all the time to make extra money and she's not so good with math, anyway. And Mom's working and always has chores to do when she gets home even though we all help out, so I called the number."

I liked the kid. She communicated.

"And Shane gave you the number?" So much for notes in his locker. "Or did he answer when you called?"

"No." Nicole shook her head, her eyes clear as she looked at Sam. "It was a recording. You could leave a number and what you needed and someone would contact you."

"So did someone call you back?"

"Uh-uh. There was a note in my locker that told me if I wanted help, to wait after school on Friday by my locker. So I did. And this girl showed up from the high school."

"Do you know who she is?"

"Nope. I've never seen her before."

"Did she tell you her name?"

"No."

"Did you ask?"

"No."

"Why not?"

"I don't know. She was from high school. You know, a lot older than me. Like a teacher, sort of. And…I didn't ask your name. I just see Jones." Nicole glanced at the name bar pinned above Sam's left breast.

Point taken.

"So then what happened?"

"We talked about my problem and stuff, and after a while she told me that there was this drug I could take that would help different functions in my brain to work better so that I could get straight A's no matter what the subject. She told me it was perfectly safe or else we wouldn't be able to get hold of it so easy. She asked me if I wanted to try it."

"And you said you did."

Nicole nodded. "Then she told me how much it was."

"And that's when you took the money from the emergency fund in your mother's bedroom." Sam had already heard all about the family theft.

And had cautioned MaryLee against keeping any substantial amount of money where her kids had access to it.

"Right. She told me to wait behind the bleachers at the football game and someone would come. That's what I did, and then Shane came up and told me he'd been sent to help and to kiss him, and I did, and then you were there."

Sam had to find the older girl. And to trace the phone number.

And to acknowledge that Chuck had been right about Shane.

Thank goodness. She should have known.

"Why'd you kiss him?"

"I don't know. Because he's cute. And…I don't know."

Sam wanted to relent, to give the girl a hug, but as tough as it was being an adult in today's world, it was tougher being a kid. Nicole Hatch had to be able to hold her own. To discern right from wrong a whole lot better than she'd been doing.

"I'm going to bring you some yearbooks and you see if you can find that girl for me, okay?"

"'Kay."

"And I want the phone number you called, too."

"I don't have it anymore."

Sam frowned and Nicole's eyes filled again. "I promise,

sir…ma'am, I'd give it to you if I did. I'd give you anything you asked for. I threw it away as soon as I knew I was in trouble because I didn't ever want to call it again."

No worry. Sam would find it another way. If it was that easy to come by at school, she shouldn't have too much trouble.

Sam opened the door, heading for the records room where five years' worth of Chandler yearbooks were on file.

By Friday morning, Zodiac was almost back to normal. She was up before Kyle, nudging his arm at the side of the bed before the alarm went off. And she ate a full breakfast. She watched as he fed Grandpa, who hadn't recognized Kyle and was not able to get out of bed that morning. Then, after greeting Clara, the dog trotted next to Kyle when he went out to the barn to take care of the horses. She stood just inside the fence as he worked with Rad. And watched as he oiled and adjusted the tractor, readying it for Monday's harvesting of the experimental corn.

He'd been on the phone the day before with an ethanol manufacturer who'd agreed to run Kyle's corn through a line he wasn't currently using, with the agreement that if the corn produced as well as Kyle suggested it should, then he would get first refusal on all of Kyle's future production.

It was a shot in the dark.

But then pretty much everything great that had happened in history had been the same. You didn't get to new places by walking along the same old roads.

Out of all the ethanol manufacturers he'd contacted, one had returned his call.

Sam called Friday morning, just as she had each

morning that week. She was checking up on Zodiac and, Kyle figured, on him, too.

He hadn't contacted her. He'd screwed up. Betrayed her trust. And she still didn't know the whole of it.

The fact that she didn't trust him now, when he needed her protection, was partly his own fault and partly a product of who Sam was—a cop, no matter what. Even if it meant investigating her lifetime best friend at the first hint of criminal activity rather than automatically believing in him.

Sherry Mahon and fires and chemicals and meth labs aside, they'd broken up all those years before for good reason. He'd been stupid to let himself fall back into friendship with her.

"I interrupted a drug deal under the bleachers at the football game two weeks ago today," she said, seemingly out of the blue. Normally, Sam's conversational twists amused him. Today he figured her statement was leading him up a row he didn't want to hoe, so he said nothing.

"A thirteen-year-old girl called for help with algebra and ended up stealing a hundred dollars from her mother for a bag of meth."

Thirteen. Holy Christ. When he'd been in junior high, they'd been hard-pressed to find an opportunity to down a swig of beer without getting caught. Later, in high school, there'd been a little pot circulating. How in the hell had that progressed to football drug deals?

"It was a fifteen-year-old kid who sold it to her."

She sounded so depressed.

"You're doing the best job you can, Sam. You can't keep criminals off the streets and run the school system, too."

"They're not pressing charges against either kid. But the boy will be spending his Saturdays at the dump until next summer, and there's a record of the arrest. If he gets in trouble one more time, he's done."

"I'd say his life was off course before he made that drug deal," Kyle told her, falling into the role of talking her down without even realizing he was doing so. It was what he'd always done. The relationship they'd developed.

When the job got to be too much for her, she called him.

And he was there for her.

"Chuck says the kid insists that he got the stuff from a friend of his in Indiana, but I don't believe that."

"You don't?"

"No. He's getting it right here in town, Kyle. I'm sure of it."

Doing an emotional backup, Kyle said, "You are." She was coming in a different door, but still engaging him in drug talk. What'd she expect? That he'd suddenly confess if he knew kids were involved?

"Yes. The kid plays tennis, Kyle."

Was she nuts?

"What does playing tennis have to do with meth-amphetamine?"

"I'm not sure, maybe nothing. But there's this group of underprivileged kids who have a club at the Tri-County Tennis Complex. Supposedly they met on the Internet and came up with this idea on their own. But I don't believe it."

And this was one reason why life out on a farm appealed to him. He wanted no part of her life. The constant crime. Mistrust. A life where everyone was a possible bad guy.

"They were on a site for kids with single parents and a bunch of them who couldn't afford the fee for sports, known as 'pay to play,' that went into effect with the school systems this year decided to start their own club," she continued.

And this upset her, why?

"How'd you find out about it?"

"I was watching one of the kids. I'd actually followed her there."

"Because you suspected she was doing meth?"

"No. I'm keeping an eye on her for something completely unrelated. It has nothing to do with this case. I just happened upon the tennis thing."

"I'm still not following how tennis and meth are connected."

"Maybe they aren't. But the activity at the complex is suspicious. And now we've got a dealer who's in the club."

"A coincidence." He cursed himself as soon as he let the word slip. And mouthed her reply as she said it aloud…

"I don't like coincidences."

"Have you talked to Chuck about this?"

"Yeah."

"And?"

"He's as concerned as I am about the increase in drug offenses, but he doesn't think the tennis club is involved. He thinks the club is a good and healthy outlet for kids who were cut out of sports."

"Sounds reasonable."

"Yeah, well, I'd agree, but…"

"Your instincts are telling you differently," Kyle said, knowing her well enough to anticipate what was coming next.

"Yes, they are, but it's more than that."

"What else is there?"

"Chuck was telling me about what this fifteen-year-old

and his mother told him about the start-up of the club. He says the mom helped the kids write up letters that were delivered to all the sports facilities around here, including both bowling alleys, asking for free or discounted services."

"And the tennis complex agreed to give free court time?"

"Right. But on a hunch, I went to both bowling alleys yesterday, talked to several people, and neither of them received letters from these kids. Neither did the Y, the golf course or the soccer club."

"Maybe Chuck misunderstood the mother. Or maybe the kids didn't really mail the letters. It doesn't necessarily mean anything, Sam."

"I know. I'm just worried. We've got to find the source of these drugs, Kyle. I feel like we're running out of time and we're getting nowhere."

So maybe she was just talking to him. Like the old days. Not stringing him out to get him to confess something.

"You're doing everything you can," he assured her. "Following every single lead."

"It's all I know how to do," Sam said. "Chuck's following up, as well. But there are only the two of us on it."

"Does Chuck now think there's a mass production operation close by?" Kyle hoped to God her fellow officer had put an end to the obsession. Or that Chuck agreed with Sam and she wasn't obsessing, after all.

Not that that helped his current situation and the suspicious activity on his farm.

"No, he doesn't. He still thinks we're looking for a distributor who's moved into the area. But it's more than that, Kyle. There's just too much of this stuff showing up at too affordable a price for it to just be some new distributor."

"What about the sheriff? Did you talk to him?"

There was a pause before she replied. "Chuck did."

"And?"

"He wasn't convinced there's enough evidence to warrant an investigation into a superlab. But they're wrong, Kyle. I know there's an operation. I can't ignore what the evidence is telling me. The bust at school wasn't the first, and you know as well as I do that drugs weren't a problem there, even ten years ago. And Holmes isn't the only meth-related death we've had in the area—he's just the closest to Chandler. And lived the cleanest life. And there's the fire at your place, the chemicals missing."

She took a breath. "I already told you about social services and three-quarters of the child welfare cases being associated with methamphetamine in some way. That's up a quarter from last year. And why are all these disadvantaged kids suddenly playing tennis? It's a perfect front for getting the drugs to the kids. The tennis complex could be the pickup point. Can you think of a better way to traffic illegal goods right under our noses than by using our kids? Sherry Mahon had way more meth in her possession than only personal use would suggest. Drug arrests like hers are so commonplace these days they don't even make the news. When you take these things by themselves, they're nothing, but added together…"

Sherry Mahon again. Kyle felt the sting, intended or not.

"They're signs of a hurting economy, Sam. Maybe, like Chuck says, there's a new distributor. This is Chandler, Ohio, not Mexico City. And the tennis club actually gives me hope for a generation that has been touted as having no work ethic."

"I watched them play. They're not interested in tennis. And your kind of thinking is what they're banking on."

"Who?"

"The cooks. They're counting on our ignorance as they work their trade right here in front of us. Taking our money, our kids, even our lives."

The cooks. Did her indictment include him? He was afraid to ask.

"If you know something, Kyle, you have to help me."

So she *had* been trying to close in on him? This had been a professional call all along?

He almost hung up on her.

"If I knew something, I would already have told you," he said instead, driven by some slim hope that he could still reach her.

She used to listen to him.

"This meth disease is not just a moneymaker, Kyle. It's not just feeding druggies who would find the stuff, anyway, or adults who make their own choices. It's infiltrated the kids. Sweet innocent little girls who just want help with homework. I can't let that continue. I can't pretend I don't see. Not even if your farm is implicated."

"Then I guess you'll have to keep looking, Sam. But I can't help you."

This time Kyle did disconnect the call.

17

Staring at her reflection in the mirror Saturday morning, Sam sipped from her second cup of extrastrong ground Colombian and faced the truth.

She'd reached a point in life where she had to decide who she was, a decision that was going to define the rest of her life.

She could back down from her convictions, play the game the way everyone seemed to want her to do. Spend her free time looking for a drug distributor while the evil substance continued to be produced in large quantities right here in the county.

Or she could risk her job, her friendship with Kyle, the respect of her peers and her family by continuing to look for a superlab. She wasn't Joe Blow cop. She was the daughter of Peter Jones, a man who'd lost it in the line of duty and paid the price.

So did she do the reasonable thing and just let the hunch go? Bury her head in the sand as Chuck and the sheriff wanted her to do, accepting that there wasn't time or resources to act on a mere possibility? Did she please her loved ones, her mother and Pierce and Kyle, and play it safe?

Or did she carry on the legacy of her grandfather? A legacy her father had bequeathed to her as surely as he'd left her having to live down the fallout from his last act.

Both her father and grandfather had served the public their entire lives by trusting hunches. Acting on them. Countless times.

Just as Sam had done during a routine traffic stop that had turned into a shoot-out. This wasn't about ego. Or needing the big plays. She'd turned that one over to an officer wearing a bulletproof vest because she'd had a hunch to do so.

There'd been other times, as well. Many of them.

Peter Jones had been a great cop—just like his father. The best. He'd been a natural.

He'd just let a personal crisis interfere with his good judgment and acted on a misguided "hunch" rather than relying on solid police work.

Did that mean Sam was somehow genetically predisposed to make a similar mistake?

"Who are you?" she asked the blue eyes staring back at her.

And she knew she was going to have to make a call.

Chandler, Ohio
Saturday, September 18, 2010

Camy and I were lying in bed reading on Saturday morning. Or rather, I was reading. The princess, pressed up against my side, slept. She wasn't interested in the newest selection from my book club. Neither was I, to tell the truth, but I slogged on diligently, trusting that I'd benefit from the ensuing conversations regarding its readability or the motivations behind it.

thing is, I've always sort of known that was the case. It just never really bothered me before because I knew the truth."

"What truth?"

"That my dad had issues because of…a personal grudge. But I don't have any hot buttons like that. And other than that one emotional trigger, he was the best damned cop this county has ever had."

I'd heard about the many exemplary-service awards Peter Jones had earned during his career. Awards that largely blinded many of his peers, including his superior, to his growing obsession with single-handedly preventing every rape in Fort County.

"So what's changed?"

"I don't know that anything has changed," Sam said now with more raw honesty than she'd ever allowed with me before. "I don't feel changed. I know there's a super-lab somewhere close by us, Kel. But before I risk possibly hurting my professional reputation, or upsetting my brother further, or losing Kyle completely, I just wanted a second opinion. I'm not saying it's going to make any difference to what I ultimately decide to do, but do you think I'm obsessing as some sort of post-traumatic stress from the Holmes murder-suicide?"

"No." I had to be honest. "Obsession infers irrationality, and just by the fact that you're listening to those around you, questioning yourself, speaking to me, you've shown yourself to be rational." And then I added, "I do think, however, that the experience is probably affecting your judgment in that it's made your need to stop the local drug trade that much more acute. And I think it's causing a bit of sleep deprivation, which will affect your judgment."

"So what are you saying?"

"That I think you're rational and doing your job well,

but that you need to be careful that it stays that way. If I were you, I'd weigh very carefully every decision I made right now."

"So you don't think I've crossed the line yet, or anything."

I didn't think so, but I wasn't positive.

"I'm just one person, Sam."

"You're a shrink. You're supposed to be able to see these things."

"I'm a professional, but I'm not perfect. And you're my friend."

"I'm going to pursue this thing."

"I know that."

"I have to."

"I know."

"Do you think I'm making a mistake?"

"I hope not."

"Yeah, me, too."

I was worried about her. "Sam?"

"Yeah?"

"Keep in touch with me, 'kay? Let me know what's going on with the investigation?"

"Keeping an eye on me, Doc?"

"And if I am?"

"Thank you."

Sam had Saturday off that week. It was an every-three-week pleasure she shared with the other Fort County deputies, two at a time. Dressed in jeans, her black work boots and a black sweater, with her hair up in a bun—and a renewed confidence after her talk with Kelly—she went first to the tennis complex. There she sat in her car with a full travel mug of coffee and watched to see if any of the kids in the Ramblers club had any suspicious interactions.

When nothing transpired, she got her racket and balls out of the trunk and hit the court. She worked on her serve on an empty court, and eventually managed to talk to a couple of the kids there.

Both were part of the tennis club. They'd heard about it on the Internet. Neither of them knew Maggie. Or Shane. Both had part-time minimum-wage jobs—one at a fast-food place, the other doing yard work. Some of their club mates had paper routes. Neither had heard of a guy named Mac and both would rather be playing football.

One asked Sam out. A kid and a thirty-three-year-old woman. What in the hell was the world coming to?

Extricating herself with a smile and a comment about her boyfriend probably not liking that idea, Sam gave up and moved on to Chandler city park.

After an hour with nothing new to go on, she drove to the deserted house on Mechanic Street. The address she'd found scribbled on a paper on Holmes's coffee table. She searched the grounds again, nosed around the house again, but noticed nothing out of the ordinary.

And she drove out by Kyle's place, just as she'd been doing every day since the fire. Watching for any sign of suspicious activity.

Back at home with her espresso machine, she gave herself a break from the drug investigation and pored over registered sex offender logs and census records for Ohio, looking for anyone named Malcolm or Mackenzie—even MacDonald.

Eliminating any male younger than twenty and older than forty, and setting a reasonable range for distance, she ended up with an entire page full of possible Macs in Fort County. One was currently incarcerated, so she checked him off the list.

Only one, a Malcolm Hardy, was a third-tier registered sex offender living right there in Chandler.

Samantha knew the street. It was less than a mile from Maggie's home. It took Sam ten minutes from the time she read the address on the sex-offender list to reach her destination. But only because a train was passing through town and she had to take side streets to detour around it.

She parked in front of the house and checked that her weapon was lodged against her side under her black sweater. The crumbling cement steps led up to a peeling wooden porch that had once been white and had probably hosted many relaxing social gatherings on summer evenings fifty or so years ago. Now it should probably be torn down.

The house, one of several just like it in town, had been built shortly after World War I. It featured a big window on one side of the front door and two smaller windows on the other.

With her identification badge in hand, Samantha rang the bell.

The muscled, trim man who pulled open the door looked more like fifty than the thirty-nine on the registration Sam had pulled up. His hair, graying at the temples, was short and styled and his face clean shaven.

"Samantha Jones from Fort County sheriff's office." Samantha introduced herself straight off, showing her identification badge. "Are you Malcolm Hardy?"

"Yes." Irritation turned to resignation. "What am I suspected of now?"

"Nothing that I know of," Sam said.

"Why can't you people just leave me alone?" Hardy asked, still just showing his face behind the door. "I register every three months, like I'm supposed to. I meet with my parole officer."

"Do you stay away from kids, Mr. Hardy?"

"One thousand feet. Always. I can't even do my own shopping anymore. Seems like every time I was in the store somebody accused me of looking at their kid. Now I gotta pay someone to get my groceries for me."

Hardy's teeth were straight. White.

Sam had read the man's record. Someone should have broken those teeth. And shoved them down his throat.

"I'd like to feel sorry for you, sir, but I don't," Samantha told him. There wasn't a lot she could do. She had no case. No evidence. Not even a hunch.

The visit was based on pure logic. A girl had a crush on a probable pedophile named Mac. A registered sex offender in the area was named Mac.

"Tell me about Maggie."

"I don't know no one named Maggie."

"You have a computer?"

"No. I'm not allowed to own or access one."

She knew that.

"Mind if I check?" She could only search the place without a warrant if he allowed her to do so.

He pulled open the door, stepped back. "Be my guest."

Walking on a recently vacuumed carpet, Sam made a quick study of the house. A couch, table, chair and television, without cable, in one room. A single bed and chest of drawers in another. The third was completely vacant, closet and all. The kitchen had a dinette with two chairs.

There were no pictures. No mementos on the walls.

No electronics.

Except a cell phone on the table in the living room.

"This your phone?"

"Yes."

Samantha picked it up. Flicked it open. It was as simple a phone as you could get—a freebie giveaway for signing up for cell phone service. There were no pictures. And no Internet capabilities.

He stood there, arms crossed over his chest, not saying a word as she invaded his privacy.

"You ever go to the coffeehouse in town?" she asked him, setting the phone down.

"Nope. Can't. Free wi-fi."

"And if I go in, show your picture around, anyone going to recognize you?"

"Not from being in there. Coulda seen 'em at the gas station, though. Or at the pub."

She gave him that. Chandler was a small town.

"What do you do in your spare time, Malcolm?" The man was too physically fit to just sit in that chair in front of the television all day.

"When I'm not looking for work, you mean?"

"Your file says you work at the paper plant."

"I did. Until someone complained that I'd brushed against them in the cafeteria."

Sucks being a tier-three offender. Sam had to bite back the words. Sucks being your victim even more.

"So, yeah, when you're not looking for work, what do you do?"

"I climb. Mountains. No one up there to accuse me of doing something I ain't doin'."

"You been climbing lately?"

"Yeah, as a matter of fact." He opened a drawer, pulled out a permit for an all-adult campsite in southern Ohio. Sam had heard of the place. A retirement resort for RV'ers mostly. "Been there the past month." He named the hills he'd hiked.

She looked at the date of the receipt. He'd checked in to a tent campsite in the middle of August.

And checked out yesterday.

Didn't mean he couldn't have been talking to Maggie somehow while down there. Sam could call and check the log-in access records for any public computers on the premises. And he could have befriended some trusting older couple who'd allowed him access to their computer.

But even then, he wouldn't have been available to see Maggie Winston in the past month as Kelly had claimed.

Unless he'd driven home and back to the campsite.

Leaving his alibi intact.

She'd call. She'd check up on him.

And she'd add Malcolm Hardy and his home to her watch list.

At four that afternoon, after a stop home for a latte and a peach, Sam was once again knocking on a door. This one belonged to MaryLee Hatch. She'd called ahead and Nicole's mother was waiting for her.

"Did you find the number she dialed?" MaryLee asked worriedly as soon as Sam was in the door. The woman was a much older version of her blonde, blue-eyed thirteen-year-old.

Sam nodded. "It's a pay-as-you-go cell phone and has been disconnected."

"So there's no way to trace it."

"No." She hated having to admit the bad news to this single mother who was relying on Sam to keep her daughter safe.

She was not going to fail.

"And what about that other kid? Shane Hamacher. Did he tell you who he worked for?"

"Says he was on his own. That he didn't know of any girl meeting Nicole at her locker. He says that Nicole asked him for the drugs."

"Do you believe him?"

"No, but the deputy that questioned him did. He put him on civic duty and let him go."

Seeing the other woman's distress, Sam continued. "He's not going to rat on his contact. He'd be in danger if he did. But don't worry. I'm watching him, and working on several other leads. We'll get these guys. I promise you."

MaryLee's grateful—and still frightened—look would go in the portfolio that kept Samantha awake at night.

She hefted the large stack of yearbooks from schools in the county that she had under her arm.

"She's in here," MaryLee said, leading Sam to a homey, lived-in family room. Nicole was curled up in a chair in a corner, reading.

The girl took an hour going through the photographs, having spent as much time with the Chandler yearbooks at the station.

And the result was the same.

She didn't recognize anyone who resembled the mystery female who'd shown up at her locker at the junior high eight days before.

When Kyle heard car tires on his gravel drive early Saturday evening, he expected to see either a county cruiser coming to pick him up or Sam's Mustang. As far as he knew, she was off duty.

And off duty wouldn't stop her from investigating him, or even calling for his arrest.

It wasn't Sam that pulled up to the barn. It was her brother, Pierce. Kyle was only slightly more happy to see him.

Pierce was an okay guy. More than that, he was the closest thing to a brother Kyle had ever had. But Pierce loved his sister. And right now Kyle was trying to stay as far away from that woman as he could get while still living in the same county.

Sam didn't trust him—his own fault.

She was on a witch hunt. There had been inexplicable happenings on his farm. And he hadn't been completely honest about Sherry Mahon.

He hadn't wanted to give her any more reason to doubt him, and telling her the truth would have done that. It would have made her feel as though she didn't know Kyle at all.

When it came to that part of his life, he didn't even recognize himself.

Zodiac, who'd been no farther than a few yards from Kyle in the two days she'd been back on her feet, ran up to welcome their visitor. Her raspy bark and perhaps some weight loss were the only visible signs of her life-threatening ordeal.

Pierce greeted her while still in his car, checking her over, petting her, telling her what a good girl she was.

Zodiac soaked up every drop of affection and then returned immediately to Kyle's side.

"How about a game of darts?" Pierce asked, climbing out of his sedan, a bag in each hand. "I brought pork and caramelized-onion crostini, some Parmesan and prosciutto bread-stick bites, cucumber cups and some tarts." He held up one bag.

Grandpa loved Pierce's tarts. The old man was already in bed for the night, but Kyle would love to have tarts waiting for him for breakfast in the morning. They'd have a better chance of having a good day if it started off on an up note.

"Got any of those homemade potato-chip things?" he asked.

Pierce lifted the other bag.

"I'll get the beer."

He'd thrown one dart when Pierce mentioned the fire.

"Sam tell you about it?" Kyle asked. With a careful aim, he set a second dart sailing. Bull's-eye. Except the excessive force he'd used caused the dart to bounce right back off the board rather than sink gently into its brushed bristle depths.

Pierce stood beside the card table laden with the food he'd brought. "No. I ran into Chuck Sewell at the gas station. He said the fire department declared the field a toxic waste dump. He asked me if I knew anything about it. If you'd said anything about it."

So Sam wasn't the only cop checking up on him.

Kyle did not want to talk about or hear what anyone thought—firefighters or cops.

Which was why he hadn't set a foot near town since bringing Zodiac home.

He was going to have to go within the next day or two, though. His grandfather was out of cookies and they'd need milk.

"What did you tell him?" he asked Pierce.

What in the hell would happen to Grandpa if Kyle got arrested? He hadn't done anything, but with the circumstantial evidence they had they could still press charges.

"I told him that was the first I'd heard of it," Pierce said. "You got any idea what's going on?"

"None." And then, because he was speaking with Sam's older brother, a person who would understand the painful dynamics of Sam's role in the investigation, he said, "Sam thinks it's meth-lab waste. Apparently everything used in illegal meth labs could pretty much pass for household waste, so I'm not sure with only charred remains if they'll be able to tell for sure."

He'd done a lot of reading in the past couple of days and now knew more about methamphetamine than he'd ever thought he'd know. Recipes, warnings, ingredients, types of equipment, dangers, laws, costs, availability, even the contents of a report from the Environmental Protection Agency to the president of the United States and the Speaker of the House.

"But they know you're not involved, right?"

"I'm not so sure about that."

"I didn't get the idea from Chuck that you were in any kind of trouble."

"But he was asking about me just the same."

"Yeah, but it was more about the fire than about you. He just wanted to know if I knew anything. What did Sam say?"

"She didn't come right out and say it, but I was left with the impression that she thinks I could be a cook." That word rankled.

"As in making meth? She doesn't think you have anything to do with this superlab she's talked about, does she?"

Kyle's silence, accompanied by a perfectly thrown dart, was his answer.

"That's fucking crazy!"

18

Fucking crazy. Kyle wouldn't have put it quite like that. But the sentiment fit. He stopped throwing long enough to shrug nonchalantly in his friend's direction. And then had to defend Sam. "There was some bust at the high school a couple of weeks ago. She's pretty freaked out about it."

"Oh, God." Hands to his head, Pierce took a seat in one of the lawn chairs set up along the wall opposite the dartboard. Zodiac settled down beside him, watching Kyle. "She's doing it," Pierce wailed. "Just like Pappy feared she would."

Frowning, Kyle threw a dart. And then another. And then, helping himself to the stash in the cabinet behind him, six more. Samantha Jones was an old friend. Nothing more.

"She's just so one-dimensional. Pappy said that's the way Dad got, too. Everything you are is about police work. The job is your top priority. Without the force, you cease to exist."

Kyle couldn't speak for Pierce and Sam's father, but the description sure fit Sam.

"Your dad sure seemed to love you kids."

"He did. I was only fourteen when he was killed, but I

remember him laughing at the dinner table, playing Santa Claus, tucking us in at night. When he was at home."

Didn't sound one-dimensional to Kyle. He retrieved his darts and started in the twenty spot this time. Might as well have a goal. Aimless projectiles were wasteful and he couldn't afford waste.

Of any kind.

"Problem was that we came second to the job. Always. If the phone rang, or he heard something on the scanner, he'd be out of there. It was like we ceased to exist. Birthday parties, in the middle of the night when we were sick, Christmas Day—it didn't matter." Elbows on his knees, Pierce stared at the hay on the barn floor. Kyle aimed. And launched.

"Even without the phone ringing, he'd have a sudden epiphany at random times and have to go check something out," Pierce continued, as though talking to himself. Kyle let him ramble, glad to be talking of something other than Samantha. Out of nine darts, six hit the twenty mark, two in doubles, one in triples.

He retrieved. And aimed for three. Zodiac was sound asleep.

"Dad was married to the job. Even Mom's tears didn't matter. He always said he was doing it for us...."

Pierce finished his beer. Helped himself to another.

"Sam never said much about any of that," Kyle half muttered, grudgingly participating in an evening he hadn't planned. He'd heard about the good times. Countless trips to the police station, rides in the cruiser, pushing the button to turn on the siren, wearing his badge...

"She didn't know some of it," Pierce said. "The rest she ignored. Dad was her hero. He could do no wrong. She was only ten when he died."

He'd known that, too, of course. But somehow ten sounded so much younger when Pierce said it.

Coming from Sam, the memories left an impression of maturity, when, in fact, she was merely relaying childhood memories through an adult's perception. Funny how he'd never realized that before.

And how, almost imperceptibly, it made a tiny chink in the armor that surrounded her.

Gave a hint of vulnerability where she'd have you believe there was none.

But then, Kyle already knew better than that. Until recently, he'd been the one she ran to when life got too much for her. Like the night of the Holmes murder-suicide.

"Pappy was frantic when you and Sam broke things off."

Kyle's dart misfired. Hit the wall beside the board. Zodiac lifted her head.

What the hell.

"It was his worst nightmare coming true. Sam choosing police work over life and love. He'd been so certain she'd be different. That she'd be like him—a good cop and still committed first and foremost to family. Able to balance the two. To know what was most important."

She knew all right. For Sam, being a cop came first. And second and third, too. But their breakup wasn't all her fault. He was the one who'd given the first ultimatum.

"From the minute he heard the wedding was called off until the day he died, he blamed himself for Sam's choices. For ruining her life. He blamed himself for my dad's death, too. Said he should have seen the signs sooner. Should have done something about it. But Dad had always been so strong, solving the most difficult cases, and Pappy, like everyone else except maybe my mom, had let the fact that Dad was a great cop blind him to the fact that he was crossing a line when it came to protecting the county from rapists."

While Kyle hadn't really warmed up to Sam's grandfather, he'd respected him. And hated to think of anyone dying with a heart full of guilt.

Maybe because he knew what it felt like to live with a guilt-filled heart.

"Pappy always said there'd be one incident, one crime, one problem, that would get Sam. He told me to watch out for her. To catch her before she ended up like Dad. He made me promise. And I've watched her like a hawk. But I still didn't see it coming until it was too late."

Kyle tossed a couple of bull's-eyes and grabbed that beer.

"The fact that she'd really believe you had anything to do with this lab…" Pierce's voice trailed off and Kyle tried to think about the chips the other man had brought, to work up an appetite for them.

Anything to stop thinking about Sam. About the fact that he'd lost her trust.

He hadn't told her about Sherry all those years ago because he'd been afraid he'd lose her forever. The fact he'd slept with another woman during their one day apart would look as though their breakup had meant nothing to him.

Who'd have thought that, more than a decade later, the thing he'd feared back then was happening because he hadn't risked exactly that? Because he hadn't told her what had happened?

Pierce opened another beer. Kyle was going to have to let the man stay overnight or take him home.

"I always thought it would be the rape thing that would get her," Pierce admitted.

"What rape thing?" Kyle asked.

Sam hadn't been raped, had she? She'd have told him. Like he'd told her about Sherry?

God in heaven…

"Dad's obsession. Didn't Sam tell you about it?"

"I know nothing about any rape." Sam was only ten when her father died. Just a little girl. Kyle felt the bile rise in his throat.

"Our mother was raped.…"

Pierce's words brought a swell of heady relief. And then, as Kyle thought of Grace Jones, he felt compassion, pity…and finally…understanding. The woman had always been so fragile. So…frightened. Of everything.

And Peter Jones had been killed when he'd attacked a man who he'd thought was raping a child.…

"That's how my mom and dad met," Pierce said, looking over at Kyle with a half-embarrassed expression as emotion momentarily choked him. "She was seventeen and he was one of the officers who answered the call. He'd promised her he'd catch the guy, but he never did."

Pierce stood and grabbed the handful of darts Kyle had abandoned. He threw hard and missed the board completely. His air shots didn't stop him from slamming the darts again and again. Sometimes landing within the vicinity of the board.

On another night, Kyle might have reminded his friend that those dart tips were expensive.

"The night Dad died," Pierce said after a good ten minutes of silence, "he'd been out on a domestic-abuse call and was heading back to his car when he heard a scream. Or at least that's the best anyone can figure. He must have taken off in the direction of the sound. He rounds a corner, sees a tall guy with someone in what appeared to be a headlock. He didn't identify himself as police. Didn't tell the man to stop. He just attacked. And the man did what any guy would do when jumped from behind. He fought back. Grabbed a mallet from the ground and swung. My father was dead before he even knew what hit him."

Pierce had thrown all nine darts. He didn't hit the board once.

"And the person the man was attacking?" Kyle sat in the chair his friend had vacated.

"A girl. She was the guy's daughter, which was why he was so fierce in his defense of my dad's attack. He'd been protecting his daughter against my father. Father and daughter had just been playing around. They were fixing some landscape lighting, which is why the mallet was on the ground, and she kept poking him, trying to tickle him. He retaliated with a headlock. The mother saw the whole thing from the front window. She'd been guiding her husband on how to position the floodlights so that they didn't shine into the living room."

"What happened to the guy?" He'd killed a cop.

"Nothing. He was on his own property, acting in self-defense. No charges were filed."

Kyle had heard bits and pieces of the story, like pretty much everyone else in Chandler. He could still remember his own family's shock when they'd heard the news that Peter Jones was dead.

But he'd never known the details. Obviously the sheriff's department had done what it could to protect one of its own. And his family.

"He died for nothing," Pierce said. "But beyond that, if he'd followed police procedure, he would still be alive. All he'd had to do was say that he was a cop when he approached. The most basic training."

"Maybe he thought the element of surprise would help."

"He didn't think." Pierce threw again and hit the bull's-eye. "He was obsessed with stopping every single rapist in the county with his bare hands. There wasn't a rape call that came in that he didn't answer, even if he wasn't first on the scene. He refused to let a case go cold. Some of them were older than I was and he still put them in the system for DNA checks on a regular basis. He was going to get every single rapist if it killed him."

And in the end, it had.

Kyle now understood Pierce's fear where his sister was concerned. Pierce had just been lying in wait for the day when his sister let her job consume her to the point that it obscured her judgment.

"Help me." Pierce pulled another chair over, opened two fresh beers and handed one to Kyle.

"Help you?"

"With Sam. We have to stop her. If anyone can get her to listen, it's you. The first day she met you we all knew without her even telling us. She'd changed. She'd talk about things you said as though you'd created the earth. For the first time in her life, there was someone whose opinion mattered to her as much as her own."

"That was a long time ago."

"But that much hasn't changed," Pierce said. "Samantha puts stock in what you say, Kyle. In what you think. She gives you way more credit than she ever gives me. Or Mom, for that matter. She loves us. She humors us. She'd die for us. But a lot of the time she doesn't think we have a thought worth percolating."

"Samantha doesn't trust me anymore."

"Deep down she does. She's just losing it over this drug problem. The fact that she thinks she can't trust you is proof that she's lost her ability to think rationally on this one."

"No, it isn't."

"What are you saying? You *are* involved with meth?"

"Hell, no! You know me better than that."

"What, then?"

Kyle had kept quiet about Sherry Mahon for so many years he'd almost convinced himself his stupid mistake hadn't really happened.

Except that there'd been consequences he was never going to forget. Maybe because he couldn't figure out a way to forgive himself.

"You remember back when Sam first announced she was going to the academy?"

"Yeah. You two broke up. She spent the weekend alternating between biting our heads off and crying. I'd never seen her cry like that before. Even when she was little."

"And then on Sunday she came to me, begging me to take her back, telling me we'd make it work somehow."

Pierce's look was assessing. "I remember."

"When Samantha walked out on me that Friday I felt like the sun had left my world forever," Kyle said. "I honestly couldn't imagine life without her."

"I figured as much."

"Well, Chuck and some of the other guys from school stopped by that Saturday, offering to take me out to forget about Sam. I went. And I drank. Way too much."

"A lot of guys would have done the same."

"I slept with someone else that night, Pierce."

"I know that." The man spoke as though Kyle had just told him he'd fed Grandpa that morning.

"You know."

"Of course. I'm Sam's older brother, Kyle. All those guys you were with—you didn't think that at least one of them would tell me what you did?"

"But you never said anything to me."

"I didn't figure I needed to."

"And you didn't tell Sam."

"I thought you had."

Kyle shook his head.

"Oh, shit." Dropping the darts back on the table, Pierce sat down. "I'm guessing she found out."

"That's right. And it gets worse."

Pierce's eyes looked weary as he glanced over at Kyle. "Can it?"

"The woman I slept with was just arrested for possession of a large quantity of methamphetamine."

"We're fucked."

Chandler, Ohio
Monday, September 20, 2010

Sam called again. Told me about the checking around she'd done over the weekend with no further developments.

She'd been keeping Kyle's place under periodic surveillance and was going to be speaking with some of his neighbors that day.

And she'd subpoenaed his bank records, which she'd be going through as soon as she had them. Sam's dad and the local judge had gone to school together. He generally gave her what she asked for. And she could trust him not to mention her every move to the sheriff. He believed in her.

When I asked, she said that she hadn't found anything further to implicate him. I could tell she was missing her friend.

But I couldn't do anything to help her trust him again. That would be up to him. If it could happen at all.

Trust, once betrayed…

And then Sam told me about Mac, the tier-three

pedophile. And that she'd found nothing to link him to Maggie, or even to any current deviant sexual behavior. But she'd be keeping an eye on him. There were others on her list. She was still checking. She'd still be watching Maggie.

Just the thought of a tier-three sex offender setting his sights on Maggie—a man who lived less than a mile from her—sent cold chills through my body.

I wasn't waiting around to hear more. Telling Sam to keep in touch, I rang off and called Maggie's cell phone and told the girl I had to see her. That afternoon. I told her that it had to do with Mac. I knew that would get her to respond. Maybe I was skirting propriety by not calling Maggie's mother first. But the woman had asked me to help her with her child's burgeoning sexuality.

And one thing I knew for certain. Maggie hadn't suddenly changed the way she dressed out of a desire to please her mother.

Something else was going on.

If there was even a slight chance that a registered offender was involved, I had to talk to Maggie.

Laws, procedure, meant nothing to me if a child was in danger.

Let Lori Winston sue me.

Just as her mother had reported, Maggie hardly resembled the sophisticated teenager who'd been in my office the week before. In nondescript jeans, striped sweater and tennis shoes, with her hair back in a clip, she could have passed for twelve.

"What's up?" the high school freshman asked, plopping down on what had become her end of the couch.

"I have some questions and I need complete and total honesty from you." There was no smile on my face. Or in my voice. I had a pen in one hand, and a photograph in the other, as I joined her.

I'd put on the jacket to my maroon suit, freshened up the little bit of makeup I wore and tamed down my blond mane. I couldn't be Maggie's friend that day. Her confidante.

I had to be the enforcer.

I did all I could to make sure my voice and expression followed suit.

"Okaayy." The girl drew out the word, her gaze darting from my hands back to my face. "Is something wrong?"

"I'm not sure, yet."

"You're scaring me."

Forthright was the only way to play this one.

"I'm scared."

"Of what?"

I turned around the picture of Malcolm Hardy that I'd printed off the Internet list of Ohio sex offenders. "Do you know this man?"

She leaned in. Looked closely, and then, with an expression that showed puzzlement, not recognition, said, "No. I don't think I've ever seen him before. Who is he?"

I didn't answer right away. I gave her a couple of minutes.

"Is he someone my mother knows?" Maggie was frowning. Looking a bit frightened, but still not engaged with the picture.

"I'm dead serious here, Maggie. You're sure you haven't seen him recently?"

"Completely. Why? What did he do?" She wrapped her arms around her middle, rubbing her hands against her elbows. "What does this have to do with me?"

"This isn't your Mac?"

Eyes huge, Maggie sat back. "Oh, my gosh! No! Mac's nothing like that. He's…he's…you know… He wears suits and…" And then, as though realizing how much information she was giving me, she was silent.

But I had my answer. At least on this one.

Folding the sheet of paper in half, I sent up a prayer of thanks.

"Who is that guy?" Maggie asked again.

I debated. The child wasn't involved with Malcolm Hardy. But she was seeing someone, not just talking to him on the Internet. She knew he wore suits.

"He's a registered sex offender who lives a mile from you."

"Eew." Mouth open, face skewed with a combination of fright and aversion, Maggie glanced toward the folded page. "Why would you think I'd have anything to do with him?" And then, as though ramifications were raining down on her, said, "Or did someone see him around my house? Around me?" Her voice rose.

"No." I was quick to reassure her, yet glad that she was beginning to see the possible dangers. "He isn't allowed anywhere near kids and appears to be adhering strictly to the requirements of his release. But you told me your guy's name is Mac and I couldn't take any chances."

Nodding, Maggie seemed to be okay with that.

"So now we need to talk about this man, Maggie."

"What about him?"

"Just the fact that he exists. I need to know how old he is."

She shrugged. "I don't know."

"Maggie, I'm not fooling around here."

"I really don't know."

"Guess."

"Twenty-five. Thirty, maybe."

I waited.

"Okay, probably more than thirty. He seems older than my mom and she's thirty."

"Older how?"

"Like he knows stuff that she doesn't know."

Which could merely mean that he was more educated.

"Do you know what he does for a living?"

"Not really. Just that it's business. He's always dressed nice."

"So you see him a lot?"

"No, hardly at all." And then. "This stuff that I tell you. It's confidential, right? Because I'm not saying anything else if it isn't."

"Why? Is something wrong with this man? Is there something you're hiding?"

"No! I just don't want trouble, that's all. There's nothing wrong. Nothing happening. And I don't want to get anyone in trouble just because I told you I kinda, you know, thought someone was hot."

"If a thirty-year-old man is romantically involved with a fourteen-year-old girl, there is something wrong, Maggie. It's against the law. Period."

"He's not romantically involved."

"That's not what you said last time we spoke."

"I said he likes me. That's all. He's not... There's nothing, you know, physical or anything..."

"He's never touched you? Kissed you?"

"No! Mac wouldn't do that. I've run into him a couple of times in the park, is all. We say hello. That's it."

Pen in hand, I was shaking too much to write. I believed the girl.

Maggie sounded far too offended to be lying to me.

But I was listening to a fourteen-year-old's perspective. What about the man? Did he know Maggie had a crush on him?

Was he doing anything to avert the situation?

Or was he a pedophile creep who was wooing a vulnerable and naive young girl?

"He's never asked you to do anything physical for him?"

"He asked me to dress more conservatively," Maggie said, her tone as defensive as the look on her face. "He says girls that wear so much makeup and tight clothes are sending out the wrong signals. He says that I need to protect myself so that I'm not taken advantage of."

Things I should have told her when I saw her last. This mystery man, this Mac, was keeping Maggie safer than we were.

"And you're sure he didn't make any advances."

"Mac isn't like that. I'm telling you. If he did like me that way, he'd wait until I was older. He doesn't break laws."

"You sound sure about that."

"I am sure."

We'd overreacted.

"So, these feelings you were telling me about having, the kind of attraction you felt, the being curious about sex…they were all just you."

"Yeah. That's what we were talking about, right? Me?"

Out of the mouths of babes. And teenagers.

"Do you have a crush on Mac?"

"Yeah." Maggie sounded relieved, as though now that she figured we understood each other, she could speak freely.

"So how about if you call him and ask him to meet you in the park. Let me meet him."

"I don't have his number. Heck, I don't even know his last name."

"Or what kind of car he drives?"

"Nope."

Then she hadn't been in it.

So maybe it was just as Maggie said. A crush.

A schoolgirl crush. We'd all been expending valuable hours investigating a schoolgirl crush.

Wait until Sam got a load of this one. She'd really be after me to pay up with the sleeping-pill prescription.

Maybe I was the one who should be worried about obsessing.

Especially considering the fact that I wasn't going to tell Sam. Not yet. I wasn't ready to call off the watch.

19

Sam had spent the day driving county roads, pointing a speed gun, watching for unusual traffic or activity on farming property and thinking about the Mac names she had yet to investigate. She'd also been thinking about the local pharmacy records she'd obtained a warrant for, and was now perusing one by one on her own time, looking for suspicious purchases of pseudoephedrine drugs. Or the kind of plastic tubing used for IV drips. She was also thinking about the girl who'd approached Nicole at school. And how to find her.

About tennis clubs and drugs and pedophiles.

And Kyle. Whoever had been dumping chemicals on his property had stopped.

Chuck and Todd Williams had checked every inch of his land.

But there were neighboring farms. She had to speak to James and Millie and some of the others. If Kyle wasn't dumping on his own land, surely a neighbor had noticed something on the property.

The same went for the missing chemicals. Hard to believe someone had managed to steal that much hazardous material without being seen.

She just couldn't figure how someone could get into Kyle's locked barn without alerting Kyle or Zodiac.

She'd stopped for lunch with Pierce and her mother and had used up what extra energy she had chatting about the weather and local football scores, not leaving a breath for them to jump in and ask a single question about her career.

She was tired of her family thinking she was still a child, needing their protection. Tired of them making her feel as though she couldn't think clearly, do her job thoroughly. Tired of having babysitters.

Thirty-three was a little old to still be requiring child care.

By Monday evening all she could think about was Arabica beans and milk and cinnamon, with a touch of nutmeg. And a bagel laden with fresh vegetables.

If she had the vegetables.

Coffee was the most important part of the menu.

She was using decaffeinated beans after five these days.

Anything to get some sleep.

Exchanging her uniform for the long white terry robe her mother had bought her for Christmas, she stretched out on the couch in front of an *I Love Lucy* rerun as soon as dinner was done. At least she was resting. And Lucy could sometimes hold her attention all the way through to commercial break.

Unless her scanner, which was always on, bleeped with something important. Or her phone rang.

Or headlights shone through her front window as they did just now. Living in a trailer park meant that cars went by frequently. The lights only shone in her bay window when someone was pulling onto her lot.

Not dressed for company, Sam peeked through the

partially closed blinds and didn't bother running for clothes when she recognized Kyle's truck.

Undressed with Kyle. Exactly what she'd have ordered up as a stress reliever.

"Hey," she said, standing there with the door already open by the time Kyle climbed the steps onto her porch.

She saw his gaze take in the gap at the front of her robe, showing more cleavage than anyone but Kyle was allowed to see. And then he looked away.

Hmmm.

"Come on in."

He did. And stood, hands in his pockets, just inside the door. Like he didn't know what to do with himself.

It hadn't been that long since he'd been there. Six weeks, maybe.

"Take off your jacket." The temperature had dropped down to the fifties, but was expected to go back up to near seventy before winter finally set in.

Throwing his denim jacket on the back of her rocker, Kyle settled on an end of the couch, sitting upright, his hands on his knees.

"Can I get you some coffee?"

"No, thanks."

"A beer?"

"No, I'm good."

"You been in town?" Maybe he'd already had his two-beer driving limit.

"No. I came in the back way."

"James and Millie with Grandpa?"

He shook his head. "Clara's there tonight. Monitoring his blood pressure every hour."

"His usual quarterly check?"

Kyle shrugged, and Sam took the answer as a yes.

She eased back on the couch, not quite at the other

end, but not too close to Kyle, either, and tucked her feet up underneath her robe.

On the TV, Lucy was trying to sell Vitameatavegamin. Of all the episodes, this one was Sam's favorite.

"It's so tasty, too!"

Sam laughed out loud at Lucy's loud and perky sales pitch.

"Why didn't you ever tell me about your mother?"

She blinked. Looked over at Kyle. If he wanted to have an attitude because she'd had to search his place, that was fine.

But he'd better not talk to her in that accusatory tone, trying to make her feel guilty for withholding information.

She wasn't the one who'd done that.

"What about my mother?" she asked, watching Lucy continue shooting a commercial, taking sips of the magic potion she was trying to sell, unaware that she was getting drunker by the minute.

Pretty soon she'd be asking the audience if they "popped out at parties."

"Her rape."

Not a Lucy topic. Not even close.

And not something that anyone needed to know about.

Old news. History. Long before Sam was born.

"Who told you?"

"Pierce."

That made no sense.

She and Pierce knew about the attack. Their parents had been so obsessed with their children's safety that they felt the need to instill fear in them in order to keep them safe.

But she and Pierce didn't speak about the rape. Ever.

Their mother was afraid of her own shadow—she didn't need anyone reminding her why.

Yep. Lucy was really drunk now. She asked if someone was "unpoopular." The line was Sam's personal favorite.

"He told me how your father died."

"I told you how my father died," she said, her attention still on the television set. Or at least she pretended it was. "He was killed in the line of duty."

"Attacking a man who was horsing around with his daughter in his front yard."

"It was after dark. The girl screamed."

"And your father jumped the man without telling them he was a cop."

"He had on his uniform."

"Like you said, it was dark. And he jumped the guy from behind."

"Pierce gave you the long version."

Her brother was really starting to piss her off.

"Did he tell you how the mother saw it all? How she called the police, and that the county tried to use the recording of the 9-1-1 call to avoid paying my mother the money allotted to widows of officers killed in the line of duty since he hadn't followed procedure?"

"No."

"But then he didn't need to, did he? You guys weren't talking about money. My brother was enlisting your help in getting me to drop this 'meth thing.'" She mocked Pierce's voice.

Flipping the television off, Sam threw down the remote and turned to the man who alternately invigorated and infuriated her. "Let's get one thing straight, Kyle. I'm a good cop, following up on a hunch. I'm not off on some misguided mission.

"And for the record, I don't think my father was, either. He heard a scream and saw a potential attack. Adrenaline pumping, he made the decision to act first and ask questions later. The same decision I would have made. If that man really had been attacking that girl, her neck could have snapped in the time it took for my father to announce himself.

"Any cop involved in any case gets caught up in it to some extent," she continued, because Kyle seemed to be giving her words serious consideration and she so badly wanted him to understand. "The art of good police work is to be all in, and remain outside at the same time. To get inside the minds of those who break the law in order to predict their moves so that you can get a step ahead of them and stop them, without becoming one of them. Take that night my father died. Had he pulled his gun and shot the man on the spot, without announcing himself or giving the guy a chance to put his hands up, he'd have become a criminal. He'd have saved the girl, though. Instead, he risked his life to save her in the way he thought best after assessing the situation."

"Your father made a mistake that cost him his life, Sam. And it cost you and Pierce your father. Your mother her husband. You think like him, by your own admission. So how do you know you aren't making the same mistake now?"

And she'd actually thought he might understand? But she was mostly angry at herself for needing something from Kyle he wasn't able to give her. "I'm guessing Pierce called you this afternoon, after I was there for lunch and wouldn't give him a chance to harass me."

"No. I haven't spoken with your brother since he was out to play darts Saturday night."

Saturday night. She'd seen Pierce twice since then.

Today and Sunday, when she'd joined her brother and mother for dinner.

As she did every single Sunday she wasn't working.

Pierce hadn't mentioned visiting Kyle either time. But then Pierce had had a friend over for dinner the day before. A male friend. Their mother had been comfortable with the guy, joking with him, as if she'd been around him a lot.

Sam had never seen the man before in her life, but she'd liked him.

She'd wanted to ask her brother if he and Paul were more than friends. But hadn't.

If she'd opened that door, he'd have felt entitled to interrogate her in return.

"I get that you and Pierce hate what I do for a living," she said now, using every ounce of self-control she had to keep her voice level. Calm. "Personally, I think the better cop I am, the more you guys hate it. I even get why. My job is sometimes dangerous. And I'm a woman. I know that you both think you're looking out for my own good. But have either one of you ever looked at me? Really seen *me,* the person I am, not the person you want me to be? Being a cop makes me happy, Kyle. It fulfills me. Why can't you guys just accept that and love me for who I am?"

"You're a cop and I think it's fairly obvious that I love you."

His words silenced her. Instantly.

Kyle hadn't spoken of his feelings since the day he'd come to tell her he was marrying a girl who'd been four years behind them in school. A girl he'd only dated for a few months. A girl too eager to get out from under her father's control and who thought farm life seemed like a hoot.

Amy Wilson hadn't been in love with Kyle, but then, Sam had never believed that Kyle loved her, either, though he'd tried to convince himself he did. Kyle had been in love with the fantasy life he'd imagined for himself. A wife working side by side with him on the farm, day in and day out. Delivering animals and birthing babies, cooking and cleaning and helping bring in the crops.

With his mother dying so young, Kyle had never had a woman around. He'd built a fantasy of the ideal farm wife and thought Amy could fulfill it.

But once Amy had gotten a taste of real farm life, she'd decided it wasn't what she wanted at all. She'd only lasted a few months.

Soon after the divorce, when Sam had ended up back in Kyle's bed, they'd made love—but he'd never spoken of love.

And not in the thirteen years they'd been sleeping together since then, either.

"I love you, too, Kyle. You know that." She should be holding him. Feeling his arms around her.

"James and Millie stopped by this afternoon," he said. "They said you'd been to see them."

"We have to find out who dumped those chemicals on your land."

"They seem to think I'm in some kind of trouble."

"I never said anything like that."

"Maybe not, but the questions you asked led them to conclude I'm a suspect, not a victim."

She'd asked the questions she'd had to ask.

"What did you find out?"

"Nothing. But I'm not done looking. Until we find out who's dumping the waste, and perhaps stole chemicals from you, it's an open case, Kyle. I've been granted a subpoena to look at your bank records."

Kyle stood, an imposing figure in her relatively small living room. "Just in case you decide I'm a bad guy, I'm lawyering up. If you have any further questions, call David Abrams."

He wasn't smiling. He didn't trust her any more than she trusted him. The truth was looking straight at her from the eyes of the only man she'd ever loved.

But she heard his voice again, telling her that he loved her.

"I know your lawyer, Kyle. As a matter of fact, I spoke with him a couple of weeks ago."

She couldn't let it end like this. He'd just admitted, after thirteen years of silence on the subject, that he loved her. And they'd get through this case. One way or the other, no matter what, she'd do what she could to protect him.

She wanted to tell him that, but knew he'd just throw the words back at her. He wouldn't believe her.

"Susan's pregnant again," she said instead, grasping for a more neutral topic

"I know."

Kyle had always wanted a house full of kids. Sam hadn't wanted any—not while she was working the streets. She'd never have been able to make the tough decisions if she knew she had babies at home who needed her.

"Are you envious?" she asked.

"You want the truth, Sam?" His gaze bored holes into her heart, and she could see the tension he barely held in check. "I ran into David early Wednesday morning at the grocery store a few weeks ago. He was there getting diapers after having been up all night with a sick toddler. He'd spent the past thirty-six hours at home tending to the boy. And had to be in court at eight. He looked like hell. And I'd have given my right arm to be him."

Alarm bells rang in Sam's brain. A Wednesday morning a few weeks ago...

"Was that the first? You always stock up on the first of the month...."

"Yeah," Kyle said. "Clara was there early, running a test on Grandpa."

She'd followed Maggie Winston to David's house on Tuesday, August 31. The day David was at home with his son. But when she'd asked him about the girl on Thursday, the second, he'd said he'd never heard of her.

Of course, she could have her dates wrong.

But she didn't think so.

20

"Come here."

She was beautiful today. More so than ever before. Makeup improved some women. On her it had only messed with perfection.

Mac watched as Maggie came toward him.

Sweet, angelic perfection.

"What?" Her smile lacked coyness, artifice. It lacked sexual invitation. But her eyes gazed at him with such adoration that, God help him, he felt an answering surge of affection deep within him.

"I just wanted to have you near for a moment," he told her. "To feel your energy close to mine. Do you believe in personal energy?"

Eyes wide, she nodded.

"Yours is filled with love," he told her. "With all of the love and care you give to the kids you deliver those packages to."

She nodded again.

"You know they couldn't get the medication any other way."

"Just like Jeanine couldn't."

"And as long as you don't ever open the bag, don't ever

see what's inside, you can always honestly say that you don't know what's there."

"I thought I wasn't supposed to open the bag so the medication isn't contaminated."

"That, too. But…we're taking risks, doing this."

"I know."

"I just want to make certain that you—and the others—are protected."

"I know. But I'd take the risk, Mac." Her eyes teared and he longed to pull her onto his lap. And keep her there, secure. "The last month Jeanine was alive…you should have seen her. The sounds she made when the pain got so bad…I still hear them sometimes. Mostly in the middle of the night."

He needed to be there for her. In the middle of the night.

But he couldn't be. It wasn't their journey.

"You hurt for all the sick kids whose parents can't afford to help them."

"Yeah. It could be me, too, you know. My mom doesn't have insurance for us, either."

"I can feel your hurt, Maggie. And your worry. It makes me want to help you not hurt so much."

She just stared. And he knew he had to be careful. So very careful. Many great men had fallen because of lust. And maybe even because of love. In the wrong time and the wrong place.

And sometimes, men were made great by the love of an angel.

"Would you like that? If I helped you not hurt so much?"

"Yes." Her voice was raspy now. As if her throat was as dry as she made his.

Another inch and his arm would brush her breast.

That's all he needed. Just a hint of intimacy between them. To comfort him in the dark of night. And in another woman's arms.

Because he wasn't going to take from his angel. He wasn't going to hurt her. Or anyone else. He was a good man. Born to help others.

He moved the inch. Heard her intake of breath. She'd felt him.

And hadn't retreated.

The harvest of the prototype took two days to bring in because Kyle picked it by hand.

He worked alone, by choice, and at one point it occurred to him that in his own way he was as driven as Sam. Not wanting to go there, he turned his thoughts to the shipping arrangements he'd made to see his product safely to his ethanol-producing partner.

When the crop was processed, he would know, finally, if he really was capable of growing a corn that could produce twice the starch per kernel. He'd been told to expect a report within a month of shipping.

After all the years of planning and attempts at implementation, one more month should seem like no time at all. Instead, it loomed longer than the years that had preceded it.

He was losing Sam again. Who'd have thought it could possibly hurt more the second time around?

And he lay awake at night planning what he'd do if he was arrested. James and Millie would stay with Grandpa. And surely he could be out on bail almost immediately. Assuming he could use the farm for collateral.

If not, as much as he hated to, he'd ask Bob Branson for help.

He'd have to come up with money to pay David Abrams, too.

And thoughts of money inevitably led to the knowledge that Sam had requested access to his bank records. For all he knew, she already had them.

And depending on how far back she went...

He wrestled with the idea of coming clean. He'd learned his lesson. Keeping secrets from Sam didn't pay in the long run. But she'd also shown him, unequivocally, that he couldn't trust her to trust him. If there was a chance that she didn't have to know the rest—at least while she was investigating him for methamphetamine involvement—he had to take that chance. The warrant allowing her access to the bank records had been open-ended. But Sam was really only interested in the past six months. If that was as far as she looked, he'd be okay...

This was generally where Kyle got out of bed and put an end to all thought with a bottle of whiskey at the kitchen table.

In spite of the lack of restful sleep, he stayed busy the next week. Tuesday he finished cleaning and organizing the storage barn. He worked with Rad every morning. And every afternoon he rode Lillie along the entire perimeter of his property. It took a while. Didn't matter. The land was his. He wasn't going to have its health, or his life, put in jeopardy by any drug-dealing jackass.

On Wednesday, he rode toward the site of the fire with Sam on his mind. Maybe he should've told her the rest about Sherry Mahon. But what good would it have done? It would only hurt her more. Make her doubt him more.

Kyle could hardly stand to look at himself in the mirror when he thought about the aftermath of his one hour of drunken indiscretion. How could he possibly face the condemnation, the disappointment, he would see in Sam's expressive blue eyes?

Drawing close to the site, Lillie jerked her head on the reins, and Kyle noticed the doe rummaging through the dirt-covered charred remains. With a light touch of his hand on the bridle, he stopped Lillie and watched. The fire department had cleared the land of any damaging chemicals and covered the ground with new earth. The deer was safe. But would she find anything of benefit to her in the new land?

He heard the car before the doe did. Recognizing Sam's Mustang, he watched as the deer hopped off across the field, heading for a cove of trees.

Dismounting, Kyle held Lillie and waited while Sam pulled off the road and climbed out.

"Checking up on me?" he asked as she skirted the edge of the field and came up to them.

"How's my girl?" Sam rubbed Lillie's nose. And Kyle's horse nuzzled her back.

"I've been driving by as often as I can," she said, still fondling the mare as she looked up at Kyle. "Someone dumped that waste, Kyle."

"I know. I've been making rounds, as well."

She was in uniform. And still looked beautiful to him. His horse, his senses, were working against him.

And then she buried her face in the mare's neck, breathing deeply as though shoring up her strength, and Kyle started to sweat.

Her eyes, when she turned back to him, were blazing.

"Mind telling me why you paid Sherry Mahon ten thousand dollars last year, Kyle?"

She'd gone back far enough. There'd always been that chance.

"Who's asking? The cop or the friend?"

"How about the woman you've been sleeping with for the past thirteen years?"

"I'm not sure who that is."

"Ditto. You're scum, Kyle. Lying scum. I…can't find words to tell you what I think of you right now."

Samantha's wrath wasn't new to him. Her passion in bed was a hundred percent more acute than its shadow side.

"Tell me, Kyle. Tell me why you risked everything— your farm, Grandpa, your last chance with the experimental crop…us. Why would you throw all of that away by giving that woman every dime you had left in savings?"

"Why don't you tell me?" She wasn't going to hear anything he had to say. Not right now. Not when she was glaring at him and shaking and trying not to cry.

"I'll tell you why," she said. "I think she's blackmailing you. That's what I think."

She'd surprised him. He'd expected her to think he'd been supporting the woman on the side. Like a mistress.

"Blackmailing me? For what?"

"I'm not sure about that." She looked down and her voice lowered a couple of decibels. "I just found out about this an hour ago. I haven't had time to work through all the facts. It's probably got to do with the drugs somehow. Like she found out you were involved with the meth she's dealing and is extorting your silence."

Kyle had lain awake in bed so many nights lately, imagining his life unraveling. He'd never envisioned anything like this…this calm, almost slow-motion spiral. He stood, as though outside himself, watching the whole thing. He was no longer just imagining.

"Is that what you really believe?" His voice sounded a lot calmer than he felt.

The seconds that Sam stared up at him were interminable. "I don't know what to believe. I can't believe my Kyle would ever have anything to do with drug production, distribution or use. But then, my Kyle wouldn't have screwed another woman the day after we broke up, either. Or gotten back together with me the next day without owning up to the mistake."

"Dammit, give me a break, Sam." The words were wrung out of Kyle. "I was as devastated as you were when you gave me your ring back that Friday night. It was like permanent darkness descended. All good feeling was gone out of my life. I made a horrible mistake. I was too drunk. Had a disgusting lack of judgment. I get that. But if I'd told you about it that Sunday when you came over asking for your ring back, would you have taken it? Would you have gotten back together with me?"

She didn't blink. Didn't lower her gaze as she considered his question. "No."

If he'd told her the truth, he'd have lost her. By not telling her the truth, he'd lost a part of himself.

And that was the choice he'd made.

"Why did you give her what was left of your life's savings, Kyle?"

It wasn't any of her business. Not now. His shame was his own. He didn't have to share it with her.

And if he didn't, the cop standing there with tears in her eyes as she gazed up at him would run with her theory that he was being blackmailed by one of his distributors.

"She called me. About six weeks after that night. Told me she was pregnant."

Sam's shoulders dropped and her expression went dead.

"She wanted money, support for her and the kid. She suggested that we get married."

He gave Sam a chance to say something. She didn't.

"I asked her how sure she was that the baby was mine. After I told her I was going to ask around at the bar where I'd met her, she admitted that she'd been with someone else, but swore they'd used protection."

Another pause met with eerie silence.

"I told her that I wanted a paternity test. And that if the test showed I was the baby's father, I'd help pay for the birth and would support the child, help raise it, but that I couldn't marry her."

"So the ten thousand was only last year's installment on child support? You've been paying her all these years?"

"No. There is no child, Sam."

Hands in his pockets, he swallowed bile. "I called her back a week later to see how she was doing. She'd had the child aborted."

"Was it yours?"

"Probably. But there was no way of knowing for sure. Last year, after all these years, I got a call from her. Said she was having female complications due to the abortion and needed surgery. She didn't have insurance so I gave her everything I had left to pay for it."

"Did you go see her afterward?"

"Hell, no. She's nothing to me, Sam, other than the biggest mistake of my life."

"And you haven't seen her since?"

"No."

"Sherry Mahon was in jail for most of last year, Kyle. I'll check on the surgery story, but I'm guessing your ten thousand dollars paid for one hell of a lot of methamphetamine."

Kissing Lillie goodbye, Sam turned her back and left him standing there.

21

David Abrams finally returned Samantha's call Thursday morning. She'd had three days to investigate a man she'd known, in passing, for most of her life and, as far as she could tell, he'd never defended a methamphetamine case.

There were no obvious signs of an influx of cash in his life. The new house was nice, but not flashy, and was in the moderate range of what he should be able to afford given his case list and hourly rate. He'd been driving the same car for a couple of years. Hadn't taken any recent vacations, except to see his parents in Florida.

He worked and volunteered and donated ten percent of his income to various charities. He spent time with his family and was active in a local political party. A trustee at his church, he was also a member of the parent organization at school.

Sam found no scandals, rumors, no professional complaints against him, according to the Ohio bar association website. Not even a speeding or parking ticket marred his record.

The judge, his colleagues and even the police spoke highly of him.

But he'd lied to Sam—a deputy sheriff.

And everyone had secrets.

At this point, after her experience with Kyle, if someone told her David Abrams was a mass murderer, she might believe them.

She'd left her cell number with him a number of times that week and he called while she was in the Mustang, having followed Maggie Winston from her home to the school. Her shift didn't start until noon so she'd watched Shane arrive, as well, cruised by Malcolm Hardy's rented home and checked out the park just to make certain Maggie hadn't backtracked to meet her Mac. Sam had also already been out to the sports complex to see if there were any kids making rendezvous when they should be in school.

"I'm following up on a previous conversation we had," she told the lawyer as she switched lanes, made a U-turn and headed out toward Mechanic Street and the vacant house a couple of blocks from Abrams's new place. She'd look for any changes at the empty residence, any sign of temporary occupancy, and then head out to Kyle's part of the county.

"Is this for a case?"

"Not really." She sipped from her favorite of the many thermal coffee mugs she owned. "This isn't an official call, David. I'm just checking up on something for a friend and thought maybe you could help."

"Sure, if I can."

"Do you remember when we talked a couple of weeks ago?"

"Of course. You were asking about a girl. A teenager. I can't remember her name, but I remember that she wasn't old enough to drive."

Right. Because he and Susan had agreed to hire only babysitters with a license.

"That's the one," Sam said, making a turn and then another. Chandler was quiet that morning. Peaceful. "You told me you weren't at home the morning she stopped by your house."

"I didn't tell you that."

She pulled over to the side of the road. "You didn't?" Of course he had. He'd said he'd never seen or heard of Maggie Winston. And that Susan had told him about meeting the potential babysitter.

"No, what I said was I didn't see the girl. Susan answered the door because I was upstairs with Devon, who was throwing up. As I recall, you didn't even ask if I was home. You only asked if I knew the girl."

He was right about that.

"Are you at home now?"

It was early enough, but she knew the attorney had a habit of being in his office at the crack of dawn.

"No, I'm on my way to the office."

"Oh, sorry, do you mind holding on for a second?"

"Sure, no problem."

Clicking her cell phone to put the call on hold, Sam dialed David's home phone from her contact list. If his story checked out, she could just have given everyone around her reason to believe their concern about her being obsessed was credible.

David and Chuck were brothers-in-law and played darts with Kyle and Pierce. There was no chance that the morning call would go unreported.

Susan Abrams answered on the third ring.

After asking how the other woman was doing—and making an inane joke about Chuck, Susan's brother—Sam asked if Susan knew Maggie Winston.

"Yes, she's Glenna's friend."

"Your babysitter?"

"Yes. Why? Is something wrong? Glenna's not hurt, is she?"

"Nothing's wrong," Sam said. "A friend of mine was asking about Maggie and I'd heard she'd been at your house. Were you home alone when the girls came by?"

"No, the kids were here. And David was, too, as I recall. He was upstairs. I remember because Devon was sick and David had had to reschedule a couple of court hearings to stay home and help me with him. I couldn't take the time to talk to the girl after she'd come all the way over to meet me."

Confirming David's rescheduled court cases would be easy.

Thanking Susan, and apologizing for interrupting her morning, she returned to David.

"I have to be honest with you, David. I just called Susan to check up on what you told me about Maggie Winston. I've been watching out for the girl, not as a cop, but as a favor for a friend, and I got a little crazy there when Kyle told me you'd been home the day that Maggie visited. I thought you'd lied to me and—"

"Why on earth would I do that?"

She couldn't be that honest. "I had no idea. I was hoping you were going to tell me."

"Is she in some kind of trouble?"

"Not trouble. She's a great kid. But she might be in danger."

"What kind of danger?"

"I'm not sure. But there've been some strange things happening and her mother is worried about the possibility that she's falling under the spell of a pedophile."

"A pedophile? Here in Chandler?"

"Maybe. Maybe not. Truthfully, I have no proof of anything. It's just some things the girl has said."

"What kind of things?"

He cared. And she owed him after practically accusing him of being involved with Maggie himself.

"Just that she has feelings for this older guy. Stuff like that."

"Has she said who he is?"

"Just a first name. Mac. We've checked every Mac, MacDonald and Michael, in the vicinity and—"

"You think she's seeing him?"

"I know they've met at least twice. But she doesn't have any way of getting in touch with him. She insists there's nothing going on. That she just made an offhand comment that's been taken way out of proportion."

"Is that possible?"

"Of course."

"For what it's worth, I think you're doing the right thing, Sam. There are a lot of despicable crimes, but sexual impropriety with a minor is at the very top of the list."

"Yeah, well, I'm really sorry I involved you."

"I'm not. You're a good cop, Sam. Don't let anyone make you feel any differently."

He had no idea how much his words meant.

"Thanks, I appreciate that."

"I mean it."

"I know. Give your kids a hug for me."

"You got it. And tell my brother-in-law that he'd better get himself out to the house for dinner or I'm going to come looking for him. Susan worries about him, and she doesn't need any extra stress right now."

"I'll tell him."

*** *** ***

Kyle was cooking bacon Friday morning when he got the call.

"Kyle?" He didn't recognize the number on his caller ID. Or the voice, either. At first.

"Yeah."

"This is Viola…"

Bob Branson's wife. He'd been meaning to call her—Bob, too—to find out if there was anything he could do to help hold their marriage together. With everything going on at the farm, he'd lost touch with the Bransons over the past year.

"Yeah, Viola, what's up?" he asked. She sounded as if she'd been crying, and it was before dawn. This wasn't a social call.

"It's Bob…" He could hear her blowing her nose. "He's dead, Kyle."

The fork in his hand dropped to the pan of sizzling bacon. Kyle moved the pan to another burner. Turned off the stove. "What?" He couldn't believe he'd heard right.

"I found him half an hour ago. The paramedics have just taken him away and I…I don't know what to do, Kyle. I couldn't call the girls. Not yet. He was their daddy and things have been so… They haven't been speaking with him and now they won't ever have that chance and—"

"Sit tight. I'm on my way.…"

Kyle speed-dialed Millie. The minute she arrived to finish preparing Grandpa's breakfast, he grabbed a denim jacket off the hook, slid into his boots and was out the door.

The back door to the Branson farmhouse was unlocked and Kyle let himself in, making his way to the beam of light coming from the kitchen. The room was huge—enough counter space to cook for an army, double oven, top-of-the-line appliances and a massive, mahogany kitchen table with matching chairs that had been the focal point of life in the Branson home.

Viola sat in her chair at one end of the table, eyes open but unblinking.

"Hey." Kyle bent over to take her into his arms. She started to cry, to sob, and he slid onto the chair next to her, pulling her onto his lap. "Shhh," he said. "It's okay."

And then he just held on, lending her his strength.

"Today was our anniversary." Viola, her eyes still pool-ing with tears, sat back in her chair at the table an hour later, a cup of freshly brewed coffee in her hand. Kyle sat with her. "I came over here to make breakfast for him. To surprise him."

"You two were talking, then? Trying to work things out?"

She shook her head, her face still wrinkle free and beautiful. "Not really. Because of me, not him. Bob didn't want the divorce. He didn't want me to leave at all. But I just couldn't stay here and take it anymore. Maybe if I had…"

"Couldn't take what?" He sipped coffee he couldn't taste in a kitchen that was at once completely familiar and totally foreign to him.

"The mood swings. The broken promises. The mania."

A strange description for the reliable, responsible, calm man Kyle had known. "He told me he had a problem that got the better of him. I thought maybe he meant cards, or horses or something."

"I know," Viola said, her expression so filled with sad-ness he could hardly stand to look at her. "That's all he told anyone. And all I ever said, too. Including to our girls.

Maybe that was wrong. I just… I wanted to spare him. To protect him. Instead, I guess I killed him."

"Viola, what are you talking about? Bob had lost a lot of weight. Was he sick?"

But that didn't make sense. Viola Branson was the ultimate nurturer. She would never have left her husband if he were ill.

"He was addicted to methamphetamine, Kyle."

"What!" His first thought was that Samantha was behind this cruel and very sick joke. She and Viola were staging this whole thing to get him to confess.

The thought flew by the wayside without landing.

"I didn't know about it at first. I knew he was taking something, but he told me the doctor had prescribed it for fatigue."

"Fatigue? Why would Bob be so tired he needed medication?"

"After Jaime moved out a year ago July he went into a funk. And then when Shauna miscarried last fall and they told us she wouldn't be able to have any more children, he started to withdraw. Like it was all somehow his fault. For the first time in his life he couldn't make something right for his baby girls, even though Shauna's fate was completely out of his control. With the kids gone, our sons-in-law pretty much running things here, he felt worthless."

Kyle understood. Sort of. He couldn't imagine not having a day's worth of work facing him every morning.

"And then last winter Chuck Sewell had a parolee who needed a place to stay," Viola continued, "and he asked Bob and me if he could work on the farm for his room and board. It wasn't the first time. We've taken in several young men over the years."

"Why don't I know that?" Kyle asked.

"Because we never told anyone. The idea was to let first-time offenders with a good chance of rehabilitation work without a criminal reputation hanging over them. So much of the time, it's the reputation that's a barrier to a productive life. To anyone outside our family, Yale was just another worker on the farm."

Viola sighed. "Bob probably needed him more than he needed us. Yale was like the son we'd never had. Bob insisted that he have dinner with us every night. And pretty soon he was at the breakfast table, too."

"Did that bother you?"

"No. The house was empty with the girls gone. And Yale was so sweet, so grateful. He'd grown up in foster care. Never had a real home or a dinner table he felt welcome to come to every night. He was eager to learn and worked tirelessly."

"What had he been in jail for?"

"Stealing tires off cars and selling them. Nothing violent or anything. Chuck wouldn't have asked us to take him if he'd thought Yale would be a danger to us."

She was right about that.

"Then last spring Bob found out that Yale had been cutting corners, sending out eggs without meeting the strict health standards. Thankfully Bob discovered the lapse before the department of agriculture did, which saved the farm's reputation, but he had to visit each supplier personally, take back all of the possibly contaminated stock. And then he purchased another, smaller farm in Indiana in order to make good on all the orders. Between here and Indiana and all the traveling, he was going about nineteen hours a day."

"I could have helped. Any of us could have."

"He felt like such a fool for allowing it to happen. And

he insisted on protecting Yale. He said the boy had only been trying to save them money and he couldn't bear the thought of Yale ending up back in prison. Everyone had down times, he figured, and he wasn't going to crucify the young man for one mistake."

"How old is this guy?"

"Twenty-two."

"What did your kids think of him?"

"They all liked him."

"Where's Yale now?"

"I'm not sure. I caught him in my purse and told Bob that he had to go. Yale claims that he was only looking for a pen. Bob believed him. But the next day Yale was gone and his room was empty. Bob never mentioned him to me again."

"Was anything missing out of your purse?"

"No, I caught him before he had a chance to take anything."

"Do you think he took things from the house?"

"Not that I know of. But look at this place. Someone could take a car load out of here and it'd probably be years before anyone noticed. The attic's full, too."

Kyle had to agree with that assessment. Viola kept a clean house. And she kept everything else, too. After thirty years, every room in the farmhouse was cluttered.

"Anyway," she said, "this past June, Bob fell asleep at the wheel, driving home from Indiana. He went off the road, but got lucky and ended up in a field with minimal damage to his truck. He wasn't hurt and thankfully neither was anyone else. But he got checked out by the doctor once he was back home, and next thing I know, he's got this stuff to take to help him stay alert."

Kyle could see the train wreck coming.

"I didn't like him taking anything, but he insisted it

was perfectly safe. And since I thought it came from the doctor, I didn't say much. By the time Bob told me the truth, it was too late."

"Where'd he get the meth? Did he tell you?"

"No. I accused Yale of getting it for him. Bob insisted that it was no one in Chandler. But he never did tell me where it came from. He said I was better off not knowing anything."

Viola looked at Kyle, tears falling down her face. "That stuff is a synthetic version of chemicals in your brain, and once it gets in, it's not long before it takes hold. Sometimes one or two highs is enough. By July, Bob was fully hooked. I was watching him kill himself, and I thought that if I didn't do something drastic, he'd be dead by Christmas."

And so she'd threatened divorce and moved out. The meth had won.

She started to sob.

After the research he'd done, Kyle could give her statistics to show her that the fault wasn't hers, but he figured she already knew them. Numbers that spoke of death and destruction.

He just couldn't believe Bob Branson was one of them.

22

Things were changing. He had thought what he did was safe, but no longer. He'd been weak and fate was stepping in.

Mac headed for his rendezvous.

So many questions with no answers.

And there she was. Fresh. Innocent. Ordinary, yet otherworldly at the same time. She knew none of the questions and had all of the answers.

They'd been at this for months, with no problems. But he couldn't shake his uneasiness.

What if something went wrong?

What if she got hurt?

What if they got caught?

People were watching her.

"We have to stop."

The fear in her eyes pierced his heart. He had to protect her.

"Why?"

"Because it's time."

She wasn't his.

"But…the kids. They need us." And I need you, her eyes told him, when they shouldn't.

She wouldn't look like that if she were older. More experienced.

Someone was going to break that heart.

Unless he took care of it.

For all time.

"New health-care plans will help them." It wasn't a complete lie.

"What new plans?"

"Government policy. The new president has been working on it for the past eighteen months." He took a risk, betting on her lack of knowledge.

But then, he'd been taking a risk all along that she'd figure out there were no sick kids.

Just addicts who were going to use regardless of where their drugs came from.

At least his way, the money stayed home and paid for services that supported prisons and law enforcement. Programs that helped the sick kids Maggie cared so much about. The money paid for new computers at Maggie's school and financed so many other public services that people took for granted until they lost them.

People were so stupid. Everyone waited for someone else to do something. It had taken him, a relative nobody, to make a plan.

Their work these past six months had saved the Chandler library from closing. Paid the public defender and the sheriff. Kept lights on in the court building.

"And you're sure these new health-care plans will help poor kids?"

"Positive."

"What about me? Will I qualify?"

"It depends on your mom's job. But if you get really sick, you'll get the help you need."

He hoped he was right. He'd do what he could to see

that there was extra money in the Fort County public health coffers.

Funny how anonymous donations were accepted without question.

"Oh." Maggie wasn't arguing. Wasn't fighting him. She was going to walk away. Out of his life. He'd never see her again. He'd make sure of that.

And she would be hurt. By life. By her mother.

That woman should burn in hell for her sins.

Selling this child.

This precious spirit.

"So should I go?" She was staring at him, her big brown eyes consuming him.

She was too vulnerable to be alone out in the jungle the world had become.

Someone would steal her innocence. Take her gift. She would have scars that would never heal.

He wanted to tell her that. To warn her.

He couldn't change the world, but he could help take care of her. He could make certain that no animal deflowered her in a way that would leave her wounded.

"Do you want to go?"

"No."

"Why not, Maggie? Why don't you want to go?" But he knew.

She was young. And so wise.

"Because I'll never see you again."

Their thoughts were mirror images. Two souls in one.

"And that matters to you?"

"Yes." She didn't move closer. But she didn't move away.

"Why?"

"I don't know."

Her honesty called out for an answer.

"Do you want to know?"

She nodded, her neck so fragile looking with her long dark hair trailing down over her shoulders. Touching her breasts.

Oh, those breasts. He dreamed of them. Nightly. Touched them. And woke up with his hands empty.

In other countries it was perfectly acceptable for men his age to love women her age. In this country, years ago, women Maggie's age were marrying.

Age was just a number.

"Come here." He wouldn't go to her. That would be wrong.

He wasn't surprised when she didn't hesitate.

His penis started to fill. And he knew that something else was changing. His life was altering course.

He didn't turn away. Didn't even look away.

She drew closer, watching him. Letting his eyes draw her to him.

This was no child. She was a woman with needs that she might not fully understand, but that she was powerfully aware of.

"If I were to kiss you, what would you do?"

"I don't know."

He couldn't make love to her here. Not now.

"Do you want to find out?"

"Yes."

He'd have to be very careful with her. Pick the perfect time and place. Soon.

"Are you sure?"

"Yes."

It was her lack of hesitation that sealed their fate.

A blood test showed large amounts of chemicals commonly found in methamphetamine in Bob Branson's system. They were enough to explain the hypothermia and convulsions that ultimately sent him into cardiac arrest. The death was ruled an accidental drug overdose, not a suicide.

An autopsy was done and by Monday the body was released to the local funeral home.

The obituary, which was all that was reported in the paper, spoke of Bob's life, not his death.

Rumors flew around town, but those who'd known and loved Bob all their lives quickly squelched any talk of drug use.

And on Tuesday, Sam stood beside Kyle at the cemetery just outside of town where Bob was being laid to rest.

The minister from the local Presbyterian church, where Bob had been a member all of his life, spoke at the grave site. Kyle, hands clasped in front of him, didn't move. He was a pallbearer and had been tight-lipped through the funeral. Through the past several days.

But when they were lowering Bob into the ground, Sam looked over and saw tears in his eyes. She saw something else, too. Anger. Determination.

But no guilt.

Surely, if he'd had anything to do with making methamphetamine, he'd be remorseful standing there.

Watching him, she saw the teenager he'd been. The fiancé. The lover. The man. The Kyle she knew was not someone who would get involved with illegal drug making.

Ever.

He just wouldn't.

But then, she reminded herself, she'd never have believed Bob Branson would be addicted to meth.

* * *

"We need to talk." Sam wanted to wait a few days, at least give Kyle time to grieve in peace, but she was afraid, with Bob Branson's death, that the cooks would get nervous. Move out of Fort County.

That wouldn't be all bad. She wanted the fiends out of her territory. But there were two problems with that.

First, they'd only set up shop somewhere else and hurt other people.

And second, now that they'd established a customer base in Fort County and had distributors in place, they weren't going to let them go.

The cooks were only going to become harder for her to find.

"What's up?" Kyle asked. They were at his place sometime after eight on Tuesday night. Sitting in their chairs in his backyard, a fire crackling in the pit. The first time they'd done so since the night of the shooting.

He had asked her to come home with him after the funeral to help with Grandpa.

So she had.

"Methamphetamine." She braced herself for his verbal lashing, prepared to listen, then press on.

"What about it?"

That was it? All the flack she was going to get? She watched Kyle, trying to decipher his expression in the glow of the fire.

"I wonder if someone is setting you up."

"For what?"

"Using you as a front for their operation."

"Based on what?"

"Your chemicals are missing. You say you haven't used them. But I have to assume someone has."

"I don't see what that has to do with a setup. I bought

methane so I'd be the one using it. A thief wouldn't figure he'd get caught. He had no idea you'd be researching my purchases or getting a warrant to search my place."

"He might. Whoever stole that chemical could have set the fire to the waste dump, Kyle, because he knew you'd be the focus of the investigation."

Although, truth be known, because of understaffing in the county, Kyle's fire was not at the top of the list. Insurance wasn't involved. Other than cleanup, there'd been no damage. The official report read that the fire was started by a match or cigarette thrown from a passing vehicle.

"A more likely possibility is that a thief didn't set the fire," Kyle said. He stared at the flames dancing a foot in front of them. "Maybe the methane evaporated because of a faulty valve. I used more ammonia for fertilizer than I realized. Made a mistake in the math. And the toxic waste was no more than someone looking for a free dump to avoid the forty-dollar-a-month pickup fee we have to pay out here in the county. Up until this year that field has been planted, so it wouldn't make a good dump spot. But now it's a bunch of clover on the side of a little-traveled country road."

"Who's had access to your barn in the past three months?" Sam asked.

"You just aren't going to give up, are you?" Kyle's tone held no accusation. Just resignation.

She liked the accusation better.

Maybe he was right. Maybe they were all right and she was losing perspective.

She had with David Abrams. And probably with Kyle, too—at least in thinking that he was involved with illegal meth production.

She was still no closer to finding Maggie's phantom pedophile. Maybe he didn't exist, either.

"Instead of spending so much of your time and energy looking for a lab that might not exist, why not try to find the dealer who killed Bob Branson? We know he's out there somewhere."

She could do as he asked. Give up.

Maybe she should.

And then she thought of Nicole. Of the disconnected phone number. The mysterious girl who'd met Nicole at her locker. And Maggie Winston talking to a man in the park and belonging to a tennis club with a drug-dealing player.

Mr. Holmes, who'd been an engineer with a six-figure income before he shot his brains out.

The sound of the gunfire reverberated once again in Sam's mind. As it often did in the darkness.

The problem was bigger than just a drug dealer.

"Getting the dealer would be like putting a bandage on a wound that's going to bleed out if it doesn't get stitches. One that will get infected if it isn't surgically closed up."

He took a swig of beer.

"Humor me, Kyle. Tell me again who's had access to your supply barn."

"We've already been through all of this. Your brother. David Abrams. Dan." The vet. Sam hadn't looked at him, but she would. "The two guys who transported the feed corn from here to Bob's."

Pain and disbelief passed briefly across Kyle's expression before he became expressionless once again.

"The older guy I hired to transport the hybrid."

Bob Branson had been Kyle's biggest champion on the project since he was in high school and first started talking about possibilities. Kyle's father had thought his son was filled with pie-in-the-sky ideas, but not Bob. Sam could remember Kyle telling her how Bob had listened to him, asked questions and told him to keep working on his theory.

"James and Millie Turner. You. I carried Grandpa out to the barn when Lillie foaled. He sat there for an hour or so. And that's about it."

She'd already talked to James and Millie and had harassed David Abrams to the point of embarrassment. She wasn't going down that road again. Pierce was obviously out. She'd check on the transport companies, but that didn't seem likely.

Now that she knew the true state of Kyle's finances, he had more motive than ever. Desperate people do desperate things. Facing the loss of his farm, of Grandpa's home, Kyle could most definitely have become desperate. But she was around the farm too often. There was no stench. No signs whatsoever of a meth lab on any scale.

Sam sipped her beer, staring at the flames as though an answer awaited her there. If she wasn't already crazed with obsession, the circles her mind was traveling in were going to send her over the edge.

"I'm sorry, Sam."

"For what?"

"Not telling you about Sherry Mahon."

"I know. I checked on her medical history," she added. "There's no record of any surgeries last year. And with the amount of time she spent incarcerated, there'd be a record of any medical procedures in her prison medical history."

Kyle barely moved. "I'm not surprised," he said. "After what you told me, I kind of suspected I'd been had."

How could someone be so angry, so hurt and so filled with protectiveness at the same time? "I want to help you," she said.

"I need you to trust me. And not just because of this whole meth craziness." He glanced over at her, no life in his eyes. "I miss you."

"I miss you, too," she told him.

But she couldn't tell him that she trusted him. She was too consumed by the hurt of betrayal to know how she felt.

She didn't leave, though.

And when Kyle reached for her hand, she gave it. When he leaned over and kissed her, she kissed him back.

She walked side by side with him into his bedroom and undressed of her own free will. Climbing into bed with him, Samantha loved him fiercely, taking him into her body again and again, as though somehow, in the ancient ritual, they could obliterate the wrongheaded choices that had brought them to this point.

She had an orgasm. More than one. And held on to Kyle while she took his release inside her.

And then she got up. Got dressed. And left.

23

I decided to walk to work that morning. The unusually blue skies and bright sunshine, together with a balmy seventy-degree temperature, helped convince me. October was looming, and with it would come falling leaves and chilly air that limited my time outdoors.

Besides, I needed a little time to relax. I'd been up and down all night. Camy, who normally never stirred, had barked three times—each time just as I was drifting off. I blamed her restlessness on my tossing and turning.

I had more than thirty active cases to deal with and I couldn't get Maggie Winston out of my mind. I had such a strong feeling that the girl was in trouble but I couldn't prove anything.

By all appearances she was a normal fourteen-year-old girl experiencing her first crush. Many youngsters subconsciously chose an older man to test their wings on. Mostly because he was safe. A sure bet that nothing would materialize beyond the fantasies in their minds.

But Lori Winston had been concerned enough about

Maggie to risk opening their lives, and her daughter's confidences, to me. Granted, the woman was panicked that Maggie would make the same mistake she had—limiting her choices, her life. Everyone had their hot spots. Maggie having sex was Lori's.

So maybe I was just overreacting to the mother's anxiety.

But why was Lori so outraged by Sam watching her daughter? If Lori had nothing to hide, why would it matter?

Unless it was just the widespread perception of people with histories like hers that cops were the bad guys, out to get them.

Maybe Lori was afraid the police would discover she'd been tapping illegally into the local cable line.

But that didn't give me the answers I needed about Maggie. Just who was this guy she'd met in the park on at least two different occasions?

If it was only two. And if they'd really met in the park…

Was Maggie lying to me?

I'd just turned on to Main Street when I heard the voices. One male. One female. They were coming from a doorway about a block away. I couldn't make out the words, but the anger was clear. On both sides.

My office was around the next corner, so I slowed down, wanting to observe, make certain that no one needed assistance.

The man's voice sounded, crisp. Curt. And then he stepped onto the sidewalk and walked away. That's when I saw his uniform. The same as Sam's. And recognized the walk, too.

Chuck Sewell.

The woman waited a bit, then left the open doorway and headed down the street.

Lori Winston.

Maggie's mom having a run-in with a cop?

I pulled my cell phone out of my bag.

"Hello?" Sam's voice was groggy.

"Did I wake you?"

"Yeah. What time is it?"

"Almost eight."

By now I was at my office, unlocking the door. Deb should have already been there. We had another full day.

"I didn't get to bed until six," Sam said. "What's up?"

"I just saw Lori Winston having an altercation with Chuck Sewell. They were outside the pub. We need to know what he caught her doing. And why she was downtown, looking like last night's clothes at eight in the morning on a school day."

"Let me get the coffee on," Sam said. I could hear her rummaging around in her kitchen. And waited for the electric grinder to sound while I turned on the lights in the suite. Got my soda from the fridge in the large closet that doubled as a kitchen.

I sat at my desk, grabbed a pencil and listened to a toilet flush.

"Okay," she said a minute later. "I've had my first couple of gulps. I was going to call you, anyway," she continued, sounding more alert. "I was up most of the night, going over things, and I think I'm on to something. Listen to this."

I heard a bar stool scrape the floor, pictured her sitting at her counter. And figured it was loaded with the night's work.

"I started out listing everything I know. I compared the list I have for Maggie with the things I know about the kids in the tennis club and the info on Shane and the high school meth bust, and the list with Nicole, and the Holmes case. I just kept making links and I know I'm on to something, Kel. I can feel it."

"What are you thinking?"

"They've all got to be connected. Even the kids having paper routes. That could be a cover for running drugs. Ingenious really, to have kids delivering papers and drugs at the same time. In the tennis club there's one kid per burg who has a paper route. They've got the entire tri-county area covered."

Maggie into drugs?

Sam had mentioned the idea before. I just hadn't given it an ounce of credibility.

If we were talking about Maggie's mother...

But, like Sam, I was pretty sure something bad was going on with Maggie. And I'd rather it be drugs than sex. Drugs we could get rid of. Treat an addiction. Sex abuse would scar the girl forever.

My pencil bore new teeth marks but I didn't taste lead.

"I'm figuring that the guy in the park—Maggie's Mac—is their supplier."

Dickens's *Fagin*. I'd hated the story the first time I'd read it. But the author had exposed the very real abuses in the society in which he lived.

The city's street kids were being taken advantage of, even killed.

"You think all those kids playing tennis go to the park to get their drugs?" That didn't make sense.

"Maybe Maggie lied to you about where she meets up with Mac. Maybe it's at the tennis complex. Maybe that's why they're all playing tennis. It's a meth distribution point."

Maybe Sam needed to get a lot more sleep. I had to admit, there were coincidences I didn't like, but her theory had a lot of holes. Like the fact that there were a lot of kids in the tennis club who *didn't* have paper routes.

"I don't know, Sam. You know a lot more about the drug world than I do, but I can't imagine any dealer always delivering to the same place. Especially somewhere public like tennis courts that are frequented by the local police. Doesn't make sense."

"Maybe not. And neither Maggie, or Shane, look anything like druggies. If they're living in that world, they'd have had to deal with stuff that would have toughened them up. From what I've seen of Maggie there's no sign of drug use. Her hair's healthy and shiny. She's got no meth mite marks on her arms or legs."

"I agree. I'd bet my practice that she's clean. There aren't any physical signs of addiction. She's thin, but not too thin. She looks me straight in the eye. Her gaze is clear. Except when she's feeling defensive, she holds her hands in her lap. She gets good grades. Her attention span is good…."

When I heard myself going on so much, as though I had a personal stake in Maggie's life, I stopped. Maggie was just a client.

But then, all my clients were very important to me. Maggie was just the one we were talking about.

"I need you to speak with her, Kel. Find out what's going on."

"In the first place, I'd have to see her to do that, and even then, I can't guarantee she'll tell me anything more. I've pushed as much as I can. In Maggie's case, my job is to look out for her, period. Not solve a crime." It felt good, too.

"If Maggie Winston is running drugs, having you in her corner couldn't hurt."

Sam knew how to play me. "I just don't believe Maggie's a part of that world." I was worried about Maggie's sex life and Sam was talking drugs.

"It all adds up, though, doesn't it?"

"You've concocted a scenario that incorporates most of your evidence."

"What have I left out?"

"Maggie's mom, for one. Why was she just having a run-in with Chuck? You think she's in on it, too? And that he interrupted something?"

"Could be," Sam said slowly. "If he'd found something, he'd have arrested her, but she might have been waiting to make a deal and he just happened to be there. She could have mouthed off. He'd retaliated, told her to move on. She'd be pissed for missing her deal. Think about it. That would explain why she flipped out when she heard I was poking around."

"Doesn't make sense. I mean, I can believe she'd deal drugs, but there's no way she'd involve Maggie in any of this. Whatever else I might say about that woman, she loves her kid. And why, if there was some drug scheme going on, would she have contacted me?"

Lori Winston would risk everything to prevent her daughter from having sex at fourteen and ruining the child's life.

"And it still doesn't tell us where the superlab is," Sam said. "Or who's behind it. It's sure not located in that trailer Lori Winston owns. It's way too small. And I'd have noticed traffic coming and going."

"No, but I'm really wondering what Lori Winston's up to," I said, half thinking aloud.

"I'll give Chuck a call just as soon as I down another cup of coffee."

I hung up, frowning, and drew the shape of a tennis racket. Wrote Maggie's name in the middle of it. And wondered how I was going to get that kid to tell me the truth.

Sam wanted to be off work at four on the dot Thursday to get out to the farm to see Kyle. He'd spent the past two days going over the Branson operations at Viola's request. She wanted someone she trusted, someone besides her and her kids.

Sam might not completely trust Kyle. But she still loved him. And after the hours they'd spent together in his bed, she knew she needed to be a part of his life.

When her cell rang just after three on Thursday, she recognized MaryLee Hatch's number.

"Jones," she answered immediately.

"Nicole knows who the girl is," MaryLee said. "Her picture's in the paper today."

Flipping off the screen she'd been perusing on the computer, Sam stood. "I'm on my way."

"You're sure that's her?" Standing in full uniform in Nicole's living room, Sam stared at the thirteen-year-old, and then back at the newspaper in her hand. "That's the girl that met you at your locker and told you she had something you could take to help you do better in your studies. The one that told you when and where to meet Shane."

"I'm positive. That's her."

Shit.

"I looked through all the yearbooks, just like you told

me." Fear laced Nicole's voice. "I didn't see her there. I swear."

"You're sure," Sam said one more time.

"Yes."

"'Chandler High School senior wins scholarship to Ohio State,'" MaryLee read aloud. "And she's dealing drugs? Wow. I guess she's going to see how quickly she can lose a scholarship."

Yeah, that wasn't the half of it. Not only would Glenna Reynolds's promising future take a severe U-turn, but things weren't looking real good for Maggie Winston, either.

With a sincere thank-you to Nicole, Sam left the Hatch home, her cell phone already to her ear in a call to Chuck. The high school bust was his, too.

The next call would be to Kelly.

Sam was dreading that one.

Kyle had spent the past two days looking for Yale without anyone but Viola knowing. With her permission, and at her request, he spoke with everyone on the Branson farm. The three daughters. Their husbands. And the staff, from foremen to egg pickers. He wasn't a cop. He was a concerned friend. As far as he could tell, no one had seen the blond ex-con.

Bob had to have gotten the meth from Yale. Nothing else made sense. The older man had trusted the kid. He'd allowed him to live in his home even after Yale had stolen from him.

Kyle was convinced Yale was behind his friend's death, even if Chuck Sewell hadn't caught on yet. And Kyle was going to find the man and do what he had to do to get a confession out of him.

And then he'd turn him over to Sam.

She wanted her dealer. Kyle was convinced it had to be Yale.

Nothing else made sense.

He was going to do this for Bob. And for Viola. Bob's widow was falling apart. Her husband of thirty years had died before she could tell him she still loved him. Before she could tell him she didn't want the divorce. Before she could tell him that she'd stand by him, in sickness and in health, just as she'd promised to do.

Kyle couldn't give her back the lost opportunities. But hopefully he could give her a measure of peace.

And he was doing it for him and Sam, too. Not only to clear his name once and for all, but to win back at least a small measure of her trust.

He also hoped it would give Sam some peace. Maybe she'd accept a two-bit distributor and give up her search for a full-scale lab.

He hoped so.

The timing worked—Yale's release from prison coincided with the statistics Sam had spouted about the increase of drug arrests in Fort County.

He'd thought about contacting Sherry Mahon, too—even if he had to coerce information out of her. But considering Sam's probable reaction to him and Sherry in the same space, breathing the same air, he quickly dismissed the idea.

By Thursday afternoon he hadn't found Yale but he'd discovered the old storage building on Bob's land where he'd been living. Until the past couple of days, judging by the date on the milk in the mini refrigerator. Obviously this was where the kid had holed up after he'd been caught in Viola's purse.

The cot in the one-room building was unmade. Jeans and flannels were strewn around the floor. The seat on

the toilet in the corner was up, the bowl unflushed. The
door on the new-looking shower unit was hanging open,
a towel flung over the top.

A used condom was in the trash.

Had Bob known Yale was still around?

Had he allowed the man access to this makeshift
home?

Kyle chose not to tell Viola what he'd found just yet.
Why hurt her with the knowledge that when she'd given
Bob an ultimatum—Yale or her—he'd just moved Yale
out of sight?

If he had.

With Bob gone, there was really no way for them ever
to know for sure what he'd done.

His friend's death had left a lot of questions.

Chandler, Ohio
Thursday, September 30, 2010

Some days were just not good days. Deb had looked
like hell when she'd come in that morning and by four in
the afternoon she'd given up pretending to do any work
at all.

"Can I go, please?" The receptionist stood in my doorway, her eyes red rimmed as though she'd been crying.

"What's wrong?"

"Would you believe a cold?"

"No."

"Allergies, then."

"No."

She leaned against the doorjamb, head and all. "I'm
afraid Cole's having an affair," she said, her voice devoid
of emotion, her eyes full of pain.

Cole Brown, another bastard? I wrote on the sticky note in front of me.

"With who?"

"I don't know. But last night, for the first time since we got married, he went down to the pub. He didn't get home until five o'clock this morning. I know because I was still up. Sitting in the living room waiting for him."

"Had you tried calling him?"

"Yeah, his cell phone was dead."

"Off or out of charge?"

"I don't know. He says out of charge."

"The pub closes at two."

"I know."

"Did you ask him where he was after that?"

"Yeah. He says driving around."

"For three hours?"

"That's what I said. He swears that's all he was doing."

"But you don't believe him."

Raising her head, Deb looked at me. "Would you?"

"No." I answered her honestly. Deb was a friend, not a client. Giving the benefit of the doubt wasn't as easy.

"Did he give you any explanation for his unusual behavior?"

"Just that he's trying to figure himself out."

"Did he come up with any answers?"

"Apparently not. He just keeps saying he's confused."

"About you? Your relationship?"

"That's part of it. Mostly it's about him. About what he wants."

The man was way too young for a midlife crisis. Maybe he was having an identity crisis.

Or maybe… I froze as another thought occurred to

me. Lori Winston appeared to have been out all night when I'd seen her arguing with Chuck early Wednesday morning.

She and Cole had graduated high school together.

Could there be some connection between Deb's unhappy husband and Maggie's mother?

I didn't want to think so.

And didn't want to worry Deb until I knew more. I was starting to sound like Sam.

"So what does he want from you?"

"I know what he says he wants."

"And that is?"

"For me to be patient with him. He says he loves me. And that he wants our marriage to work."

"What are you going to do?"

"Try to be patient and believe in him."

Probably the best choice. Just not one I would have made.

But then, my perceptions were a tad skewed at the moment when it came to anyone within Lori Winston's sphere.

24

Sam put off the call to Kelly until she was through her shift, thinking maybe she'd just stop by Kelly's office on her way out to Kyle's. As anxious as she was to spend time with Kyle—and, let's face it, stay on top of everything going on at Bob's—the latest development in town was equally urgent.

She'd call Kyle. Tell him she'd be there, just later than she'd expected. First, she wanted to visit the holding cell where Glenna Reynolds waited to see the judge.

Chuck had arrested the girl—at Sam's request. She'd taken a run out by Maggie and Lori Winston's place, waiting until she'd seen Maggie inside the window of the trailer before she'd called Chuck. She wanted to make certain the girl was nowhere near her friend when the arrest was made.

Chuck picked the senior up at home, brought her in and booked her. She'd spend the night in a county cell by herself and then see the judge in the morning. She and Chuck had agreed that they wanted the girl charged as an adult.

Luring innocents like Nicole Hatch to an addictive, lethal drug was not something they could shrug off.

And then Chuck had gone to have dinner with his sister and her family.

Sam waited for him to leave, then headed to the jail. She wanted answers. Shane Hamacher might be able to get away with not knowing much. He'd been the last man on the totem pole and a year younger than Glenna. Glenna was the middle guy.

Sam wanted to know everything the girl knew before the system got hold of her, even if it meant breaking some rules. That's why she'd left Chuck out of her plan.

Walking by a couple of deputies, waving to the dispatcher on duty, Sam let herself into the cell block, swiping her badge as she went.

Glenna Reynolds. Maggie's friend. A babysitter with a sick mother. A straight-A student who'd cared about leaving pregnant Susan Abrams in the lurch.

Chuck had said the girl was in cell number three. He'd chosen it because it was off by itself, leaving Glenna relatively removed from anything else that might happen in the jail that night.

When Sam had asked, Chuck told her he'd caught Lori Winston sleeping in a doorway Wednesday morning. He'd ordered her to move on, and she'd taken exception to his disturbing her sleep.

Something else that made no sense. Why would the woman be sleeping in a doorway when she had a perfectly good bed to go home to?

A daughter to go home to.

Listening for any sound coming from cell three, sobbing maybe, Sam approached. "Ms. Reynolds?" She spoke in the direction of the one-foot-by-one-foot barred opening at the top of the solid cell door.

No response.

With the key she'd brought, she unlocked the door. Pulled it open. And felt the blood drain from her face.

The plastic cording from around the mattress had been ripped away and was hanging from a fire sprinkler on the ceiling. The slender body of the sixteen-year-old senior hung suspended, the plastic cord around her neck.

"Call an ambulance!" Sam called to the guard down the hall. "Now!" Rushing forward, she grabbed the teenager's legs, lifting the girl to relieve the pressure on her neck.

Please, God, let her live.

Sam repeated the words again. And again. Only those words. They were the single thought in her brain for minutes that seemed like hours until help arrived.

She's just a child. Let her live. All idea of charging the juvenile as an adult fled as she gave every bit of energy over to keeping the young woman alive.

The only guard, an off-duty deputy, raced in with a chair. While Sam held Glenna's feet, the man stood on the chair and freed the cord from the sprinkler.

But Sam already knew the girl was dead. The bodily waste that flowed upon death was all over Glenna's jail-issue pants.

Chandler, Ohio
Thursday, September 30, 2010

Deb had been gone awhile but I wasn't ready to face the long hours of quiet awaiting me at home. Deb was so confused, so scared, she didn't know what to do with herself.

I didn't know what to do with her, either. Except to help her draw on personal strength as she waited to see what the future would bring.

Considering how the day had gone, I wasn't surprised when Sam showed up just after five. I was at my desk, supposedly going over files for the next morning's appointments, but mostly just chewing on a pen and staring into space when I heard the bell chime out front.

I jumped up to see who was there.

The sleeves and front of Sam's uniform shirt were stained. Tendrils of her long hair had worked out of her bun and were hanging half in her face and half down her back. Her shoulders were rounded in, as though she could no longer bear the weight of them.

"What happened?" I went to her immediately, an arm around her back as I ushered her to a seat in the reception area, then sat down next to her. I tried to ignore the putrid smell, even while I was trying to place it.

"I just…" Sam's face turned white. "Do you have a restroom?"

"Yeah, first door on the right…"

My words followed Sam as she ran. She made it to the toilet, but didn't get the door closed. I stood just outside and listened while the toughest woman I knew lost her cookies.

And then I went into action. Cool towel first, and then a warm one. The first I handed to Sam, who cleaned her mouth. The other I held as I wiped her face, her eyes, her neck.

Like a child, she stood there and let me tend to her. And that scared me.

I helped her out of her clothes and into sweat shorts and a T-shirt—an extra skating outfit I kept around just in case I had an hour to get away.

We went to my office and sat on the couch, the stench still with us.

And when Sam glanced up at me, I knew that she had information I absolutely did not want.

"What?" I asked.

"Glenna Reynolds."

"Maggie's friend?"

She nodded.

"What about her?"

"She was the girl who met Nicole Hatch at her locker." Sam's words registered. I heard them. I just didn't know what they meant. "She's the one who set up the deal between Shane and Nicole."

"Who are Shane and Nicole? What deal?"

"The meth bust I made at the high school a few weeks ago. Shane was the seller. He's the one in Maggie's tennis club."

Right. I knew all about that. Fine. And the girl. Glenna. Maggie's friend, her mentor, was older. Into things that weren't good for Maggie. We could fix that.

"Shane's the one who said he got his drugs from a dealer in Indiana."

I knew what Sam was telling me. That she thought Maggie was like these other two. Into drugs.

"Maggie Winston would never be involved with illegal drug distribution," I said aloud. "Especially among kids. If you could hear her talk about sick kids her age whose parents can't afford treatment for them, about the pain and suffering. And she lectures her mother about her cigarette smoking…"

"We can't ignore what we know."

"Maggie is adamantly opposed to substance abuse. She just wouldn't do this. You're making her guilty by association."

I got the picture. I just didn't want to look at it. That was my prerogative.

Sam sat there trembling on my couch. Why was this one arrest tearing her apart?

"Sam? What's really going on?"

Her eyes filled with tears. "She's dead, Kel. Glenna's dead."

"What?" I tried to focus. To think. An overdose? "What happened?"

That would make two dead in Chandler in less than a week and—

"Suicide." Sam swallowed. "She hung herself. In her cell. I…"

And that's when I knew that Sam had been the one to find her. I knew where the terrible stink was coming from. I knew what the stains on her uniform meant.

And I knew that as soon as I got my friend settled, I had to get to Maggie.

It had been a long couple of days. A long week.

Kyle had been home less than half an hour when he heard a car in the drive. Zodiac, at his side, he went out to shoo away whoever had come.

He couldn't be sociable.

Not tonight.

He didn't recognize the car and thought for a second that they were coming to pick him up. That Sam had finally convinced someone to issue a warrant for his arrest.

Bob's death had cut her deeply—because she knew the man, but also because they'd lost one of Chandler's most respected citizens to the meth war she was waging single-handedly. She'd taken responsibility for his death. As though she'd injected the farmer herself.

Not that she'd admit that to Kyle. Or anyone. Probably not even herself.

But you couldn't know a woman, love a woman, for more than half her life and not figure out some things.

A blue Dodge Nitro pulled up to his side door. Kyle knew the driver. He'd graduated from high school with her.

But it wasn't Kelly Chapman that held his attention. It was Sam, in the passenger seat, wearing a T-shirt. She stared straight ahead. Her hair was down—out of its bun.

Something Sam only did when she went to bed.

Kyle almost stopped breathing. The woman's features said she was Sam. But this woman was broken, in shock.

Shit. What had happened? Who got to her? And what had they done?

Kelly Chapman climbed out of the driver side. Kyle knew the two women were friendly. But he couldn't tell if Kelly was there professionally or otherwise.

"She wanted me to take her home," Kelly said, as though Sam wasn't sitting right there. "I didn't think that was a good idea. I have to get back to town. To see… someone. I don't want Sam to be alone, and I figured you were the best shot at getting her to agree to that."

Arms crossed over her chest, Sam looked pissed. But it was the sense of loss in his longtime friend's expression that catapulted him into action.

Opening her door, he almost choked on the stench. But he didn't hesitate as he said, "Come on, Sam. Let Kelly get on her way and I'll take you home."

He wouldn't. Sam probably knew that.

Zodiac pushed in beside Kyle, nudging Sam's elbow, asking for her customary greeting of a rub.

Looking at the dog, and then up at Kyle, Sam got out of the car.

25

"Where are the drugs coming from, Kyle?" It was late and they were still at his place. She'd agreed to stay when he'd reminded her that if she didn't, he'd have to leave Grandpa alone. "They're taking over the county, just like I knew they would."

She lay back in a corner of the couch, dressed in his robe. He'd told her, straight off, that she had to shower. She hadn't argued but had refused his offer of help washing her hair.

She'd showered on her own with the door firmly shut but not locked.

He wouldn't allow that and she'd agreed. Which made him feel a bit easier. When he'd heard the shower running he'd slipped inside the door for her dirty clothes and walked them straight to the washing machine. They were in the dryer now.

Kelly had disposed of Sam's uniform.

"I told you, Kyle. I told you." He'd tried to interest her in a beer, hoping it would make her sleepy. She'd wanted nothing but water.

Food hadn't been an option. At least, not yet. Kyle wasn't giving up.

"Told me what?" He sat in his dad's chair and watched her.

"That they were going to kill people. I told you I had to find the superlab. I had to stop them or more people were going to die. And they're just going to keep dying, Kyle, do you get that? People we know and care about."

She sat up, holding the bottle of water as though she didn't know what to do with it.

He'd never seen Sam so lost. Not ever. Not even the night he'd told her he was going to marry Amy Wilson.

"Two deaths in one week. Both meth related."

He didn't discount that.

"One was a child, Kyle. Sixteen years old."

The bottle was on the table now. Sam fell back to the corner of the couch, resting her head but propped up so she could look straight at him.

"This is exactly what I've been trying so hard to prevent."

He understood. And didn't have any answers.

"I can't let it continue, Kyle. I don't care if everyone in the whole damn state thinks I'm nuts, I know I'm on to something and I can't just let it go."

Kyle didn't argue. He couldn't. Things had changed since Bob died. Everything had changed.

"I'm not asking you to."

"You aren't?"

"Nope."

She blinked as though waiting for the catch.

"Do you know who's behind all of this?"

She still didn't trust him. Didn't believe in him. And he couldn't blame her. He'd doubted her forever. Right from the start. Doubted that someone as glorious as Sam would ever really be happy to settle for a simple man like him.

That's why he'd accepted her ring back that long-ago

Friday. It was his doubt that had led him to find a drunken release in another woman's arms. And that same doubt had led to the secrets that had stood between them ever since.

"No, Sam, I have no idea. But I will do everything I can to help you find out."

"So you believe me?" The skepticism in her voice kicked him. "You don't think I'm nuts?"

"I'm the one who's nuts."

"What do you mean, you? Did you get into something you shouldn't have?"

"Not like you mean. I've done a lot of thinking these past couple of days." He wasn't sure how much to say. "The past week, really."

Years ago, she'd have tried to draw him out. Asked him what he'd been thinking about. He probably wouldn't have told her then. Most of what Sam knew about him she'd had to discover on her own.

Amazing that she'd stuck at it all these years.

Stuck by him.

"I've been angry with you," he said. That came out wrong. Wasn't what he'd meant.

"I know. Because I searched your place. Because I had doubts. But, Kyle, Sherry Mahon aside, I have to look at all of the evidence. I took an oath. I wouldn't have been doing my job if I'd let myself be swayed by the fact that I love you and—"

He held up a hand. "I was angry with you, like you say, for doubting me. For not trusting me. Even though I knew I'd deserved it. I still felt betrayed."

"I know, but—"

"Let me finish. Let me get this out."

Sam watched him, not moving.

Kyle wished he'd helped himself to a beer. He wished

a.lot of things. But wishing didn't get a man through life. Doing did.

"I didn't believe in you, Sam. I didn't trust you to love me enough to be a cop and a wife, too. And because of that, I betrayed you."

There were so many things to consider, to figure out. That's what happened when a man started to think.

"You never once doubted me back then," he said. "I didn't understand that, not until now, when you finally did doubt me and I realized that it was the first time. You always believed that I could be a farmer and your husband, too. You never once asked me to leave the farm and join you in the city."

"The farm is your life, Kyle. That's just a given."

"This farm is important to me, yes. But it's just land, Sam. It's not life itself. Bob's death showed me that quite clearly. I've been out there on his farm. It's a great property. A great business. And there sits Viola with all of it, just wanting her husband back."

She didn't say anything.

More likely she was probably sitting over there asking herself if she'd ever known him.

"Anyway, the point I was making is that we broke up because of me, and all this time I've been blaming you."

"I didn't blame either one of us."

She wouldn't have. That was so…Sam.

"If I'd had faith in your judgment, instead of being so scared at the idea of you being a cop and me losing you like your mother lost your father, I might have been a little more willing to find a compromise for us. Just as you tried to do."

She shook her head. "It wouldn't have worked. Look at Viola. She's a farmer's wife, Kyle. A great cook. A seamstress. A homemaker. Happy to spend her days out in the country in the same house, ready to take on whatever that life brings. Viola is the kind of woman a farm needs to be successful. Not someone who's out chasing down drug dealers and meth labs."

That's all he'd seen back then. Now he wondered if maybe he should have been looking at what he needed more than at what the farm needed. Because when his life was over, the farm would go on. Even if someone else took over.

"I realized something else this week."

"What's that?" She was tired, her eyes little more than slits.

"When I finally realized that you were really going to leave me to be a cop, I retreated to what I knew, the farm. When my father died, same thing. And through my divorce, the same. Then 9/11 came and the whole country was afraid and I was safe here on my farm. Or so I thought. In the past few years, as the economy suffered and the rest of the world seemed to rock off its moral axis, I retreated more, so smug that I had all the answers. I had what everyone else needed right here, and as long as I stayed put, I would be protected from the world's craziness."

She looked...confused.

"But you know what?" he continued. "The craziness found me, anyway. And there wasn't a damned thing I could do about it. Grandpa's stroke. Financial troubles. The missing methane. The fire. Bob's death. Everything. All out of my control. And hitting me right here at home.

"And I realized that I wasn't a hermit out here because it made me happy. I was just running from every damn thing in the world that I couldn't control." He hadn't meant to tell her all this, but it seemed right.

Sam leaned forward, and Kyle thought she was going to get up. Instead, hands clasped around her knees, she stared at the floor and said, "My mother has been running her entire life, too. Locked away in that big house, with my dad, and later Pierce, to care for her and keep her world safe. But she's not safe. The house could go up in flames tonight. Someone could break in with guns and kill Pierce and get to my mom. I always knew that."

She understood.

"And instead of protecting her, they've wasted her life," Sam continued. "My mother loves flowers, did you know that?"

He hadn't.

"She talks about flowers all the time. She watches television shows about them. She knows every variety, every scientific name and growing season and method. She knows which plants come back year after year and which ones need direct sunshine. But she's never grown any of her own. She's had indoor plants that my father brought her. And ones Pierce and I have brought her. Her entire apartment upstairs is filled with pictures of flowers. But she's never had her own garden. And do you know why?"

He shook his head.

"Because she was afraid to spend time outside alone. My father didn't want her to. He wanted her protected. And with the hours he worked, he didn't have time to help her with a garden."

This was a far different picture of her family. And yet he couldn't think of a time he'd ever seen her mother out and about without her father. Or Pierce. Or Pappy.

"You know why Pierce is a chef?"

"No."

"Because the only things of original beauty my mother could create in the house were meals. Her outlet was cooking. It was safe. And she could lose herself in her recipes. She couldn't grow flowers, but she could create wonderful dishes in the kitchen, with gorgeous presentation. The entire time I was growing up, the only place I really remember spending time with my mother was in the kitchen. She was there when we left for school and when we came home."

How could he have known Sam for most of their lives and not seen any of this?

"Pierce was fine with it all. He inherited her love of cooking, while I was more interested in the fire extinguisher on the kitchen wall, or my grandfather's scanner."

"You're a great cook."

"Yeah, well, with the number of hours I had to spend in front of a stove I kind of learned by default."

"But you hate it."

"Not really. Not anymore. But I resent it. I guess that's why I'm so finicky about my coffee. It's my creative culinary expression. It's the part of me that's my mother—in spite of myself."

Why had she never talked with him like this before?

And even as he wondered, he knew the answer. Because he'd never provided the space for her to talk to him like this.

"You know the greatest tragedy of all?"

"What?"

"My dad and now my brother have always thought that they've been protecting my mother, but they've really enacted the greatest crime against her."

"How's that?"

"By enabling her fear, they've robbed her of her life."

Kyle would have liked to argue. But how could he? He was a victim of the same crime. Only in his case, he was the perpetrator, too.

26

It was the day that wouldn't end. I'd been by Maggie's place twice since dropping Sam off at Kyle's. Sam had said that Maggie had been in the trailer when Chuck arrested Glenna, but no one was there now. I suppose I could have gone on home. Had a bath and a read and done something that would in some way resemble having a life of my own.

But I couldn't just walk away from Maggie Winston. I had no idea if she knew about Glenna yet.

What I did know was that her mother had been out all night Tuesday and I couldn't take a chance that it would happen again. Maggie couldn't be alone tonight.

I didn't hang out in the trailer complex. That wouldn't have been smart. Not in my car. But I stayed close enough that when a car pulled in next to Maggie's place, I could see the headlights. And I was right behind it. A woman was driving. About my age. I didn't recognize her.

She handed Maggie some money and I watched as the woman saw her safely to her door.

Babysitting, I guessed.

A minute later, when lights came on inside the trailer, the woman pulled away.

And I pulled in.

"Your clothes are ready if you'd like me to take you home."

Sam sat in this man's house, completely naked beneath his robe, and she didn't really even know him.

At least, not the version he'd given her tonight.

But she wasn't sure she was complaining. She might like this new Kyle even better than the one she'd always known. If she were in a mind to like anything.

"I have to find that lab, Kyle."

"I know."

"Bob can't tell me anything. And neither can Glenna. Shane won't. Kelly insists that Maggie isn't involved in anything and I don't have any legitimate reason to access her, unless it's to question her about her dead friend, but if Kelly hasn't been able to get anything out of her, there's little chance I will. Assuming she even knows something."

"I've been looking around Bob's place. There's this kid he'd taken in, an ex-con. Viola said he'd been stealing from them. She made Bob kick him out this summer. I've been thinking he might be Bob's source. He was living in a shed at the back of Bob's property, but there's been no sign of him."

"Was he at the funeral?"

"Not according to any of the family and staff members I've talked to."

"What was he in for?"

"Tire theft."

"How old is he?"

"Twenty-two."

"How long's he been out?" He'd asked about her clothes. She was still lying on the couch in his robe. He didn't seem to mind.

"Almost a year. Bob took him in as part of his release."

"Is he still on parole?"

"I'm not sure about that."

"You got a name?"

"First only—it's Yale. But he won't be hard to trace. Your friend, Chuck Sewell, set him up with the Bransons."

She'd known Chuck had worked with the Bransons in the past. She hadn't heard about Yale.

"I'll see what I can find in the morning."

Speaking of which, she should get home. It was almost midnight.

"Stay with me tonight?"

In the past five years or so, that invitation meant sex. Sam didn't know what to say. She loved Kyle. But so much had happened.

Sex with him the other night had been different. Desperate. She didn't think she could handle a repeat.

"I just want to hold you. To feel you close. To hear you breathing beside me."

She wanted that, too. So badly.

What she didn't want was to lie sleepless in her bed at home, or more likely on the couch, and feel that girl's body growing cold against her. Didn't want to smell the smell. Or think the thoughts.

She needed to sleep.

"I can't have sex with you, Kyle."

"I'm not asking you to."

"Then I'd like to stay."

Chandler, Ohio
Thursday, September 30, 2010

Watching the lights go on in the trailer, I called Lori Winston's cell phone. Maggie's mom said she was at work. When I told her about Glenna she could hardly speak, but she asked me to be the one to tell Maggie.

She also asked me to stay with her daughter until she got off.

Maybe I should have taken offense at being an unpaid babysitter, but I didn't. I was glad to spend time with my young client, to care for Maggie as I sensed she needed to be cared for.

Maggie was quiet for the first few minutes after I told her about her friend. We were in my car. She hadn't wanted me to come inside their home. I didn't like her reticence. Afraid of what she was hiding.

And at the same time, I understood.

Maggie lived in poverty.

It was hard to share that.

"I'm so sorry, sweetie." The girl's head was bent, her hair just a shadow in the darkness of the car. She'd had on a sweater when she'd come home but had left it inside. The white of her T-shirt and tennis shoes were the only things distinguishable against the Nitro's interior.

"Where's my mom?"

"At work. I just talked to her."

"She was off at ten. She should have been home by now."

I wanted to ask Maggie if she knew her mother had been out all night the other night. If she knew where she had been. But this was not the time. At the moment, Lori Winston was my last concern.

"I just can't believe it. Glenna killing herself? She just wouldn't."

"Did you know she was dealing drugs?"

"Glenna? No way. You've got the wrong girl, Dr. Chapman." Maggie pulled out her phone. "Wait, I'll call her. You'll see."

I stopped her with a hand on her arm. Glenna's mom was terminally ill and facing the loss of her only child. She didn't need a phone call from a distraught teenager at midnight.

"It was Glenna, sweetie. She was alive when they arrested her. She had her driver's license on her. She admitted who she was and what she'd done. And according to a police friend of mine, her mother came in and identified her."

"Glenna wasn't doing drugs. Heck, she wouldn't even drink soda because of what it did to your body. She broke up with the cutest guy in school because he smoked a joint."

I couldn't speak for Glenna, but Sam had Maggie all wrong.

"I didn't say she was doing drugs, I said she was dealing them."

"There's just no way. Why would she do something like that?"

"I don't know. I wasn't told any of that. But maybe she did it for the money. Because her mom was so sick."

Maggie was quiet and I figured I'd hit a nerve.

"She did say her mom needed some new medicine. She was all worried about how to pay for it, and that if she didn't get it she might die. Then a couple of days later, she wasn't worried about it anymore. She said someone gave them the money."

"Do you think this someone could have been a drug dealer?"

Looking at me through teary eyes, Maggie said, "I would never have thought so. But if she was arrested, and confessed, maybe it was."

"Do you have any idea who that dealer might be?"

"No."

"Have you ever seen anything out at the tennis complex?" I asked, because Sam's suspicions couldn't be ignored with a girl dead.

And because I couldn't bear the thought that Maggie could be next.

"Drugs, you mean?"

"Yeah. Anyone passing anything. Anyone talking about it."

"Not about meth or drug dealing or anything." The girl frowned. "I mean, some of the kids are pretty rough looking, but if they do stuff like that, they don't bring it to the court. We just play tennis. Or try to."

"And you're sure you have no idea who the dealer might be?"

"Yeah. How would I know a drug dealer?"

"I'm not saying you know him. Or her. But you were with Glenna a lot. You might not realize how much you know. Whoever this person is that she was working for, he caused Glenna's death, sweetie. The police are going to want to catch the guy."

"I hope they do. I hope they catch him and he rots in hell...." Her voice broke and then the avalanche I'd been expecting hit. The teenager's shoulders started to shake and I pulled her against me as well as the console allowed.

"It's okay, sweetie, let it out," I encouraged, and sat there, holding her until her mother came home.

* * *

The first thing Sam did Friday morning was ask Chuck about Yale. He verified everything Kyle had already told her, plus added the name of his parole officer and a few facts about the charges against him, including a couple of drug-related priors. Chuck said the kid's last name was Conrad. And that he hadn't talked to him since he'd been released.

Chuck did check with Yale's parole officer, who'd said he had been a model parolee.

He'd been released the month before and no one had heard from him since.

Sam wanted to find the guy.

Chuck didn't think Yale had anything to do with Bob's drug use.

She drove by Maggie's trailer and saw Lori Winston's car there, then she turned up Malcolm Hardy's street, spun by the park and out to the tennis complex. She ended up at the local paper and asked to see their customer list. They could refuse her. She didn't have a warrant.

But they didn't.

Still off duty, Sam spent the next couple of hours at work, checking names on the list against a database of known drug users and dealers. Anyone who'd ever been picked up for drugs in the county was recorded. She executed cross-checks between the two lists and came up blank.

While she was there, the sheriff had a visit from the coroner. And because they ran an open ship in Fort County, she heard what the coroner had to say.

"That girl's death wasn't a suicide," she reported stoically. The doctor was an older woman, sixtyish, and had been at her job a long time. "The bruising on her throat, the way her neck broke, she might have been hung, but she didn't kill herself."

"You're sure?" the sheriff said. Sam sat frozen, her hand on the computer mouse, and waited.

"Positive. There's more. Her arms were bruised up pretty badly, too."

"Had she been raped?"

That would have been Sam's question.

"No. She was a virgin, actually."

A child. Who'd barely started to live.

Calling up the county jail prisoner database from the night before, Sam read every profile, looking for someone who had a reason to kill a sixteen-year-old girl.

It took Chuck five minutes to come up with the answer. He'd arrived at the tail end of the coroner's visit and was as upset as Sam about the turn of events.

They'd been responsible for bringing the girl there. Locking her up.

"Hank Long," Chuck said, wheeling his chair over to Sam's and taking the mouse from her hand to scroll down her screen to the man in question. "He made a couple of comments when I walked through with Ms. Reynolds. Apparently she'd stiffed him on a deal a few months back...."

Hank Long. She looked at the profile on the screen. *Wanted for robbery, attempted robbery, assault...and drug trafficking.*

The man was thirty-five years old and had already done ten years for rape.

"Look at this," Chuck said, pointing to the screen. "His career, locksmith. Explains how he could get in and out of Glenna's cell."

Or he could have stolen keys from the deputy on duty. Fort County jail hadn't been updated since the days of

The Andy Griffith Show. They didn't usually keep hardened criminals there.

The city jail, across town, was brand-new and housed both county and city inmates whose crimes were of a more serious nature.

"Why was he here?"

"He'd just been brought in on OVI," Chuck said. "Williams brought him in and was still processing him, but locked him up because he was being so belligerent. That's how I knew the guy's name."

"So where was Williams, or whoever was in charge here, when the guy had enough time to kill a helpless girl? And why would he do that? Risk a murder rap over a few bucks worth of drugs?"

"He'd have done it if he's way more involved than we know and the girl was going to snitch."

So this Long guy could be the cook? Or at least know who the cook was.

"And it wouldn't have taken a guy like that long to knock someone off," Chuck added, and the sheriff nodded. "A couple of minutes, tops. He could have been in, done and out while Williams took a piss."

There'd be an investigation of course. Fingerprints taken. DNA would be sent to the major forensics center in Cincinnati that processed most of their evidence.

Sam sat there, listening to the two men analyze the death of a sixteen-year-old girl as though they were solving a crossword puzzle, and feared that a year ago she'd been just like them. And for the first time in her life, she wondered why she'd wanted to be a cop.

27

Chandler, Ohio
Monday, October 4, 2010

After two weeks of hell, that weekend in Chandler was
the calm after the storm. I was home most of the time, not
wanting to be far away, in case Maggie or Lori Winston
called. I'd told the girl's mother when I'd left them just
before midnight on Thursday night that I'd be available
any time if Maggie needed me.

I hated leaving the girl.

But she was my client. Not my child. I was only there
to facilitate.

And so I went home and worried about her. And prayed
that her mother would keep her close all weekend.

Lori Winston had been sober when she'd pulled up not
all that long after I'd called her—not even a hint of alcohol on her breath. She'd been immediately attentive to
Maggie, taking the child under her care as only a mother
could do. I'd been impressed, in spite of my doubts about
the woman.

And I wondered about the girl Glenna. About Shane,
and tennis courts and drugs. I agreed with Sam. Something

was going on. I just wasn't sure what. And I wasn't sure how my client played into the scenario. Maggie wasn't dealing drugs. Of that I was sure. But the fact that two of the people with whom she associated had been involved with a meth deal made me nervous.

Really nervous.

Which is probably why I was so startled when I escorted a client out to the front office Monday after school and saw Maggie waiting there. Deb had left early—she and Cole were going to see a counselor—and the door was unlocked. Again.

Maggie waited silently while I finished with the middle-aged woman who'd just found out her son was gay.

"Are you busy?" Maggie asked as soon as we were alone. The girl looked all right. A little tired, maybe, but her hair was clean. She had on a blouse under her hoodie instead of a T-shirt, and she was wearing her usual tennis shoes.

"Not for another half hour. Come on back." I led her to my office and tucked my long cotton skirt under me as I settled with her on the couch. My arms ached to hug her, but that time had passed when I'd left her with her mother.

She didn't seem very huggable today, anyway. The three days since I'd seen her seemed to have changed Maggie—distanced her. Or matured her. Death had a way of doing that, but I hated to see it in this special young woman who'd already had to grow up so fast.

"I'm glad you came by," I told her. "I've been worried about you."

"I'm fine."

"How was your weekend?"

"Okay."

"How about school today?"

"They had grief counselors in Friday and today. It was pretty stupid. They told us all it's not our fault. That we shouldn't feel like, as Glenna's friends, we could have done something for her. But how do they know?" Maggie's tone had a new, bitter note.

"I mean, really," she continued, "that's what they're always telling us. Things aren't our fault. If our parents get divorced it's not our fault. If someone commits suicide it's not our fault. Jeanine's suffering wasn't our fault. Being alive and healthy when she had to die wasn't our fault. Like our actions have no effect at all, you know?"

Maggie had never been so talkative. I hoped that she was finally comfortable enough with me to open up, but knew that she was also rambling her way through a difficult situation. Death wasn't easy for anyone and most particularly children, who so often had perceptions of invincibility.

"We do matter, Dr. Chapman. And we can make a difference, too. One of us probably could have helped Glenna. And kids are sometimes partly responsible for parents' divorces, too."

"What about you?" I asked her as she sat, feet flat on the floor, toying with the zipper on her dark blue hoodie. "Is there some way you could have prevented what happened to Glenna?"

"I could have paid more attention when she talked about her mom. I could have told her that she could stay with me if anything happened to her mom. Maybe I could have taken more babysitting jobs to help with the money so she didn't feel so alone."

"And how about your mom?" I asked, listening between the lines. "Is there something you could do to help your mom?"

"Grow up," Maggie said without hesitation. "I ruined her life, you know."

Eyes narrowed, I ached for a pen. A pad.

"Did she tell you that?"

"No. She didn't have to. It's just obvious, you know?"

"Obvious how?"

"She was like Glenna, Dr. Chapman. A straight-A student. She didn't have much at home. No money or anything. But she could have gotten a scholarship just like Glenna did. Except that I came along and she had to quit school."

"Tell me this." I chose my words carefully. "Did you have anything to do with the fact that you came along? Did you put yourself here?"

"No. Of course not."

"That's right. You didn't. Your mother made a choice. And you were conceived as a result of that choice."

Maggie was quiet for a moment and I hoped I'd pierced the shell she'd wrapped around herself.

"Still, she chose to keep me, to raise me even though it was hard for her."

"Yes. Which tells you she must love you very much."

"And that I have to love her back that much and hurry up and grow up so she can still have time to have her own life."

My chest tightened.

"Did she tell you that?"

"No, Dr. Chapman, she didn't tell me any of this. Mom doesn't even know I think about things like this, but I do and they're true, and now, with Glenna...I don't know, I just have to try harder. To make sure that what I do is the best thing for the people I care about. Look at Glenna.

I was so wrapped up in my own stuff that I just let her suffer all by herself."

"No, Maggie, you didn't. You were her friend. The rest—taking care of her—wasn't your job."

"Whose job was it? Her mom's? She couldn't help that she was sick."

"Her mom could have asked for help for Glenna. The school could have done more. The minister at her church. All people who are qualified and responsible to her in different ways. It wasn't you."

"I had no idea she was dealing drugs."

And that hurt. I understood that completely. "You couldn't know, because she didn't want you to. I'm guessing she realized how you feel about illegal substances since you knew how she felt about them. She probably also figured that you'd think less of her if you knew what she was doing. She didn't want that, so she didn't tell you."

"I should have noticed something."

"How? If she chose to deliberately hide it from you?"

"But everybody hides things."

Ah. Hah. "I suppose so."

"So how do you ever trust someone?"

"Trust is something you give, Maggie. It's not based on something someone gives you first. And sometimes the person receiving it doesn't recognize it, doesn't know you gave it or doesn't want it. Those are the times you get hurt.

"And there are other times you give your trust and the person knows the value of it and takes care of it like you'd take care of a newborn baby, or maybe a pot of gold. And that's when people are really happy. When they can give trust, and have it cherished."

"So how do you know when to give your trust?"

"You don't always. Sometimes you just give it because you feel, deep inside, that it's the right thing to do. That's how it is with things like faith and trust—there are no guarantees. Except for one."

"What's that?"

"I can guarantee you that if you never trust, if you never have faith in anything, you'll never be happy."

Her brow creased, she sat still for a long moment. And then nodded.

I had to say more because she was a child and I knew she was on the verge of trouble.

"There's another side to trust, too," I said. I might confuse the issue but it was a chance I had to take. "If someone knows that you're lonely or hurting, he might pretend that you can trust him, and then take advantage of you and use your trust to gain something for himself."

She was listening, her mouth slightly open, her hands still on the couch.

"Because trust is one of the keys to happiness, you have to be very careful with it," I continued. "You can't just give it to every person you meet."

"I don't trust our landlord. I think he wants to sleep with my mom."

I figured he already had.

"Right. Sometimes it's obvious who not to trust. Like strangers on the street. They might be perfectly nice, but in today's world you just can't take that chance. You don't hitchhike because you never know who's going to pick you up."

"Or take candy from strangers, I know," the girl said drily.

"But that's not really what we're talking about here, is it?"

Maggie's silence warned me, but I think, in some way,

I already knew. I'd known since I saw her face that afternoon. I just… I thought if we kept talking…maybe we wouldn't get there.

Ever.

As if the girl could sit safe and sound in my office for the rest of her life. Safe and virginal.

"So why don't you tell me what we *are* talking about," I said softly, rearranging the colorful yards of cotton skirt around me.

"I…"

No.

"I… This weekend…Saturday, my mom had to work and I…well, it had kind of been building and he was so sweet, Dr. Chapman. He understood all of it. About Glenna. And my mom. And he knows me. He understands me. He…"

Loves me.

"…loves me."

Shit. Total shit.

"Did you have sex on Saturday, Maggie?"

"Yes."

"Full intercourse?"

"Yes."

Okay.

"With this man, Mac, that you told me about?"

"Yes."

I was a doctor now. Under oath.

"Did he tell you his last name?"

"No. I didn't ask."

"Does he know yours?"

"Yes."

This was getting worse and worse.

"Where did you meet up with him? How?"

"I went to the park, hoping he'd be there, and he was.

That's how I knew it was meant to be. Like some force had told him how badly I needed to see him."

"Where did you have sex?"

"In a tent. Out on some road I'd never been on. He was so sweet, Dr. Chapman. He had everything done up and it was so romantic. He had sleeping bags on the floor, and candles and music that I like, and chocolate and cream sandwich cookies because he knows I love them. He just wanted to take care of me."

Take care of her, my ass. The slimeball was going down. Way, way, way down.

I didn't get angry often. But I was now. Well and truly, one hundred percent angry.

He'd premeditated the entire thing. A tent. Romance. Sleeping bags. Candles and music.

I wanted to vomit all over the jerk.

And to cry.

I was devastated. But that emotion had no place in my practice as a psychologist.

"Did you see what kind of car he drove?"

"No. He was on a bike and so was I, and we rode out to this place in the woods outside of town."

Because he knew damned well that what he was doing was illegal. Immoral. The sin of all sins.

Just plain wrong in any terminology.

"What color was his bike?"

"I don't know. Blue, I think. It had speeds. Mine doesn't."

"Did he say why he was in the park?"

"He said he was just out riding and started thinking about me. Like I was out riding and thinking about him."

Or the pedophile knew that Glenna had been killed. He'd known that Maggie was going to need a friend.

And he'd gone looking for her in a place he was sure to find her.

He'd known about Glenna because he'd been her dealer. Just as Sam had thought.

"He was so gentle," Maggie said, and it took everything I had to keep a neutral look on my face so that I could get every drop of information out of her. "I thought it was going to hurt, and it did just a tiny bit at first, but he knew how to take care of that and…then it wasn't bad at all."

Wasn't bad at all. Just what every mother wanted for her daughter's first experience at love.

A fourteen-year-old should be thinking about highlights and makeup and playing tennis. All of the things we'd worried about with this sweet child.

"It's like you said, Dr. Chapman, it's a matter of trust, and I know, deep inside, that I can trust Mac."

No, you can't. But you can trust me. Though, very shortly, you aren't going to think so.

Everything she told me had potential information in it for Sam to use in her investigation. Because Samantha Jones, Chuck Sewell, the entire Fort County sheriff's department, the Chandler police and the FBI were going to hunt this fiend down. And when they found him, he'd better hope that he never came face-to-face with Kelly Chapman.

"Did he use protection?" I couldn't retrieve Maggie's virginity, give it back to her. We had to move on. The future was what mattered now.

"Yes. Of course. I'm not going to end up like my mom."

Sad thing was, the child was making choices exactly like her mother had made. And probably for the same reasons.

But there was one major difference. Maggie had me.

28

Recognizing the number on her cell phone display Monday afternoon, Sam picked up on the first ring. She was out in a cruiser, on speed-gun duty, where she'd found herself every shift since Friday's disclosure from the coroner.

She understood. The sheriff. Chuck Sewell and Todd Williams. They were all worried about her. Thanks to her dad and Pierce. And the Holmes suicide. They had no idea what she'd do now that a child had been murdered due to the meth lab that didn't exist in their county.

"Deputy Jones?"

"Yes."

"This is MaryLee Hatch."

A car passed. Doing fifty-six in a forty-five.

"Is everything okay?"

"Daniel just called. A girl approached him at school today. She asked him if he needed help with homework and gave him a flyer like the one Nicole had."

"He didn't call the number, did he?"

"Not yet, but he said he was going to. I'm afraid he'll do it, ma'am. He's just so mad at what those guys tried to do to Nicole, and now that that Glenna girl's dead—he heard about it at school—and with my husband dead, Daniel thinks that as the man of the house he has to protect us...."

Sam's mind raced. The flyer had been given to Daniel. Specifically him? Had he been sought out?

"Tell him not to call," Sam said, her voice as firm as it had ever been. "Better yet, let me talk to him." Was Daniel being targeted? Because of Nicole?

"He's home, if you want to just stop by."

She put the car in gear. And then stopped. Someone, maybe Hank Long, had killed Glenna Reynolds because the police had her. Hank was in jail, but he obviously had others helping him. This organization—killing Fort County citizens one person at a time—was not small.

Did they know Nicole was working with Sam? A cop?

"No, no, I can't really do that right now," she said, her mind working furiously. Suddenly the emphasis was not on the meth. It was on keeping Nicole and Daniel safe.

And Maggie.

Thank God Sam hadn't had any personal contact with Maggie. No one but Kelly—and Kyle—knew that Sam had been watching the girl. Not even Maggie's mom knew which deputy had been watching her daughter.

"Listen, Mrs. Hatch. I don't mean to frighten you, but I'm not taking any chances with your children."

"What?"

"I need you to phone Daniel back. Tell him that if he calls that number I will have him arrested and shipped out of town immediately. We're dealing with very dangerous people here. People with money. And they mean business. If they'll kill a girl in jail, they won't hesitate to go after someone on the street if they think that person is talking to the police."

She was getting worked up, but she knew she wasn't exaggerating. It had come down to life and death.

As she'd known it would.

"Do you have any relatives in another state?" she asked. "Someone who wouldn't mind some company?"

"Wait. I can't leave. I have to work and—"

But now that the idea had taken root, she couldn't let it go.

"Mrs. Hatch, listen to me. I'm afraid your kids could be in danger. Nicole talked to me. I've been to your home. Please…I think we're going to find these guys. Soon. But until then, get those kids out of town. Just to be safe." If Daniel had been singled out to get that flyer… If they knew he was Nicole's brother and that Nicole had identified Glenna…

"I have a sister in Kentucky. She's been asking us to come there to live. She says there's a job in her office. Maybe we could go down for a couple of weeks. Check it out. Fall break's coming up, anyway."

"I think that's an excellent idea. Just let me know where you are so I can keep you posted. And, Mrs. Hatch?"

"Yeah?"

"Get me that phone number, okay?"

"I'll call you right back."

Within five minutes she had the number. And an assurance that MaryLee Hatch's children were already packing.

Viola gave Kyle access to all of Bob Branson's financial and personal records but asked that, for now, he keep the information to himself. She wasn't sure what her husband had gotten into and didn't want the police all over the farm without first being able to make plans. She had to think of her kids, who depended on the farm for their livelihood.

"He wrote a lot of checks to the city," he told Viola Monday evening as he ate the meat loaf and mashed potatoes she'd brought over. Grandpa had already eaten and was in the living room, watching football.

Or at least staring at the television screen.

"Bob's been donating to the city for as long as I can remember. He didn't believe in supporting a political party. He said the money spent on campaigns was a waste and would be better used for worthwhile services rather than popularity contests."

"Here's one from last month to David Abrams."

"I'm guessing he hired him to represent him in the divorce." The woman teared up and Kyle put down the notes he'd taken throughout the long afternoon.

"You know what I couldn't find…?"

"What's that?"

"Any missing money." She took a deep breath. "My husband wasn't a thief. Nor would he have had to steal from himself. We always had what we needed."

"I understand. But with no missing money, how did he pay for the drugs? It's not like you can write a check for that particular purchase. And it doesn't look like Bob carried enough cash to support a drug habit."

"No, ever since the advent of credit cards, Bob's been a firm believer in carrying one card to pay for everything and paying it off at the end of the month. He's always insisted that I do the same. He said that if a wallet or purse gets stolen, we can just call and cancel the card. We wouldn't lose any cash."

"He's right about that. But it still doesn't explain how he paid for the drugs. I wonder if he was selling things.…"

"Not that I'm aware of. One of the girls or I would've

noticed if he'd been selling anything of value from the house. And if any of the farm machinery was sold, there would be a record in one of the farm books."

"And you keep those books."

"That's right. If money was missing from there, I'd know about it."

It felt like a dead end to Kyle.

But he had a feeling that what he'd found would mean something to Sam. He called her as soon as Viola was in her truck, heading down his drive. He hoped he could talk her into driving out to the farm for the evening. He hadn't seen her since Thursday night.

And knew that was intentional on her part.

For thirteen years he'd been pretending to be Sam's ship in the night, when, in fact, he'd been little more than a rotting piece of driftwood.

Chandler, Ohio
Monday, October 4, 2010

When Maggie Winston had sex with Mac, she took away my ability to protect her from investigation.

By law, because she was a minor, I had to report the incident to the authorities. Her mother would have to be told, as well, but I had to call Sam first. When and how to inform Maggie's mother would be Sam's call.

So, yeah, I was buying Maggie some time, maybe, by not telling Lori Winston right away. Buying Sam and me more time was more like it.

I tried her cell while I was still sitting at my desk. She didn't pick up. And I didn't leave a message.

I tried again on my way home. And then, instead of pulling into the garage, I pushed the automatic button to lower the door again and headed back out—much to

Camy's chagrin. I could hear her high-pitched welcome since she thought Mama had come home to feed her.

Thank God for Camy. She kept life in perspective.

Sam wasn't at her place, either, so I went by the county building and from a block away saw her Mustang parked in the side lot.

My phone rang and Sam's number popped up.

"Don't pull in," the deputy said, just as I was about to signal my turn.

"Okay, but I need to speak with you. Urgently."

"Fine, but I don't want anyone to know. I don't want them to associate you or Maggie Winston with me."

With my Bluetooth on for talking, I grabbed a pen from my console and tapped it against the steering wheel, worried that my friend had pushed herself too far. The woman had been teetering on the edge of a breakdown for weeks.

Sleep deprivation could do that to you.

"What do you suggest?" I asked, considering a phone call to Chuck Sewell. I knew him in passing. Trusted him.

I'd just hoped that Sam, being a woman, could speak with Maggie.

"Just keep driving. We can talk this way. I'm on my way out to Kyle's. You head somewhere in the opposite direction."

"How about if I just go home?" Why hadn't Sam thought of the obvious?

"Fine. Yeah, that's good. You didn't tell anyone that it was me watching Maggie, did you?"

"I didn't tell anyone except her mother that she was being watched, and I didn't give her a name."

"Okay, good. I was going to call you, just in case."

"You sure we can't meet? Talk in person?" I wished

Sam would give me the chance to assess her face-to-face. She was scaring me. I'd been to her house. She'd been to my office. It was a little late to pretend we weren't in touch.

"No, I have to get out to Kyle's. I— Listen, Kelly, stuff is happening, worse than you know. Maggie's friend Glenna didn't commit suicide. She was murdered."

"What!" I swerved, barely missing the car in front of me. I hadn't even seen it.

"The coroner came in on Friday with the news. We're looking at one of the inmates but until tests come back we can't be sure it's him. And even if it is, it's certain that he has others working with him. More fliers turned up at the school today. There's a different number for kids to call if they need help. It's confirmation that someone besides the inmate is involved. In spite of the deaths, in spite of the fact that the sheriff's office is pursuing things, these folks aren't the least bit intimidated. They're continuing to peddle their wares right under our noses. They're that bold. Which means that, at this point, no one involved is safe. These guys have an elaborate scheme going here. And they're willing to kill to protect their business. They aren't going to let some small-town kids, or cops, get in their way."

She sounded completely rational.

"I've got some other leads and I'm following up on kids in the tennis club. None of them have priors that I could see. I just have to figure out how to keep them all safe until I figure out if they're involved in any way. But the quickest and most sure way I'm going to protect anyone is to find this damn superlab. My time's running out."

"We've got another problem."

"I didn't figure you were calling me to check on the weather."

"Maggie had sex with Mac."

I'd never heard the expletives that followed come out of a woman's mouth before.

"Tell me everything she told you," Sam demanded through what sounded like gritted teeth.

"While you're driving? Don't you need to write something down?"

I'd seen Sam's lists.

"I never take notes when I'm getting information. Only when I'm compiling it."

Seemed completely backward to me.

"If I'm focusing on what I'm writing, I'm taking my attention away from what's being said," she added.

I tapped my pen and related everything Maggie had told me.

"Wait just a goddamned minute."

"What?" Feeling rattled by Sam's nervous energy, I turned onto my street. I wanted to be home with Camy.

"The guy knew that Maggie needed him? Then he knew about Glenna."

"That's what I figured, too."

"Oh, God, Kel, this is bad. This is so bad. We had grief counselors at school on Friday, just in case someone heard something, but we didn't make any announcements until today. We kept things out of the media, too. There's no way for Mac to have known by Saturday…unless he's involved."

I was in my garage, waiting for the door to close behind me, before I opened the car door.

"Maggie's Mac is the dealer," I guessed, barely above a whisper.

Camy's bark had turned into a high-pitched yelp, signaling her growing distress. She was hungry. And tired of hearing garage doors.

"He might be the cook." Sam sounded as worried as I was. "Makes sense, too," she continued. "I'm pretty sure the tennis kids are his distributors. And I think at least some of the drugs are delivered as part of regular newspaper routes. I just haven't figured out how the kids pick up their packages. Or where the lab is."

"So this cook, or dealer, somehow targets potential users from people who take the paper?"

"No, he has his customers sign up for the paper. I've got the *Journal*'s distribution list, just no subscription dates." Sam named the Chandler weekly that had been in business since before I was born. "I can't ask for a warrant yet. People already think I'm crazy, but I'm going back into the *Journal* tomorrow, hoping they'll give me a breakdown of longtime customers versus new customers. I'm guessing that if we keep a watch on the new ones, we'll find drug deals."

Which meant that Maggie was dealing, after all? With her newspapers?

I just couldn't accept that. Maggie could never be that duplicitous.

"Which still doesn't help us find Mac," I said. Locating the pedophile before he did something even worse to Maggie—like sell her to his friends or to strangers, kidnap her, kill her—was my first concern.

"No, and if he's having sex with Maggie, he's probably already done so with some of the other kids. Or will be."

"How many girls are there in the tennis club?"

"Three."

"What can I do to help?"

"Find a way to keep Maggie away from tennis, from the paper route, from Mac, until I can get this figured out."

If life were that easy. "Someone has to inform her mother."

"You're right. Someone does. But do you want to tip the woman off, when she's a suspect in all of this? Or at least exhibiting suspicious behavior for which neither of us have found an explanation?"

"No, of course not. Neither do I want to lose my license to practice."

"You're under obligation to report sexual behavior with a minor to authorities. Not to parents."

Technically.

"What if Maggie lived with her dad and you suspected that he was Mac?"

What Sam was describing was despicable. But it happened more often than I'd ever have imagined. Even in Chandler.

"Would you tell him what Maggie told you?"

"Of course not."

"This isn't really any different, then, is it? We suspect that Lori Winston could somehow be involved in drug trafficking. And that her daughter might be, as well. Lori might know Mac, Kelly. She might have been afraid the man was the type to take advantage of her daughter and hired you, hoping you'd be able to keep Maggie safe while she delivers drugs for her."

"Which means even more that we should go to her. If she can tell us who this Mac guy is…"

"That's too big an *if* for me right now. Because if she's working for Mac, and Mac is somehow behind Glenna Reynolds's death, he'll kill Lori Winston for sure before he'll let her snitch on him. You want to take a chance that the woman is willing to die to protect her child from having sex?"

I wanted to argue. To find a way out. I wanted to feed

my four-pound squealing housemate, curl up with her on the couch and watch *Mary Poppins*.

"Do you?" Sam asked again. Was I willing to risk Maggie's life on the belief that her mother loved her enough to die for her?

"Of course not."

"Then do something to get Maggie out of there for a few days. Tell her mother that you suspect some kind of mental disease and need to hospitalize Maggie for a few days of observation or something."

"I can't do that."

But the idea was tempting. Really tempting.

"Do something," Sam said, and rang off without saying goodbye.

29

Sam was going out to Kyle's place for one reason. She needed him. Life was flying out of control and Kyle was her grounding point. Always had been. Didn't seem to matter whether she could trust him or not.

Or maybe, what she was discovering was that, deep down, she did trust him.

Truth be known, at the moment, it didn't matter if Kyle lied to her or not. She needed his calmness. Needed him to quiet her own frenetic pace so that she could think. Find the missing link.

She also needed to use his unlisted landline without him around to hear her. The number MaryLee Hatch had rattled off was replaying itself like a billboard announcement running across Sam's brain.

But first, she put in a call to Jim Lockhart, the Chandler high school counselor who'd helped her a time or two over the years. He was at his home just outside of town.

"I need a favor," she said.

"Anything. I assume you're working on the Glenna Reynolds case."

"I'd rather not say what I'm working on. I just need a favor."

"You got it." Jim had been a counselor at the high school when Sam was there. He had to be close to retirement, but she'd hate to see him go.

"I need a locker at the high school."

"I'll see what I can do."

"Thanks."

Before she'd reached Kyle's place, Jim had called her back with a locker number and combination.

And she had her chance to use Kyle's phone when he went out to the barn to feed the horses.

She had a good five minutes. Probably ten, because he'd take time to ask Lillie and Rad about their day and to apologize for neglecting them. Not that she knew Kyle well or anything.

She didn't need five minutes. The call took less than one.

"I'm Sally Ingalls," she said, raising her voice several octaves. "I'm staying with my aunt and uncle for a while and didn't do the same math at my school that they do here. I need some help catching up, please. My locker number is two-twelve at the high school." She delivered the information following instructions from a voice recording.

Now all she had to do was get into the high school tomorrow and check that locker without anyone being the wiser. She'd find out what time and where she was supposed to meet her perpetrator.

Sam's breath caught as she thought of Glenna. And wondered who Mac had recruited to take the young girl's place in his system.

And that was where it was going to stop. She'd play along until she had what she needed. She was going to have to be very, very careful not to jeopardize another teenager's safety. Obviously Glenna's position had been important. Shane had been in jail, too, and was still alive. Glenna was not. Which told Sam that Glenna had information that the dealer didn't want known. Like his identity.

Smart guy, this "Mac." He'd kept an extra layer between him and his seller to safeguard his identity.

Stupid guy to continue doing business as usual after a child working for him was just killed.

Or was he simply that confident the law wouldn't find him?

"I know exactly what it means," Sam said over sloppy joes at the big, scarred table in Kyle's kitchen later that evening. He'd just told her about the absence of missing funds in Bob's account.

"It means either he had money stashed away that Viola didn't know about—" she popped a chip in her mouth, looking more like the Sam he knew than the nearly broken woman who'd been delivered to him the week before "—or that Bob got the stuff for free."

"For free? I didn't figure anyone gave that stuff away."

"They don't. Unless the guy was a personal friend of Bob's. Maybe Bob found out what the guy was doing. The guy sold him a bill of goods about how it wasn't dangerous. It was just like moonshine. Would get him through a bad spot. He got Bob addicted to keep him quiet."

Kyle hadn't thought of that.

"Or he could have just been a good friend who was buying a bit of insurance. Bob had a lot of clout in the community and, if trouble arose, the cook would have someone with enough power and or money to return him the favor."

Kyle ate—hungry all of a sudden—and listened. Really

listened. Not just to Sam's words, but to the way her mind worked.

"He could have been given the stuff with the hope that he'd get addicted so he could be blackmailed into doing something illegal if the need arose."

Her thoughts didn't stop or settle. They never did.

"It's also possible that he didn't pay for it because he had ample supply."

"How would he manage that?"

"If he, or someone on his farm, was making it."

Okay, that was…

"Yale Conrad."

"I've wondered."

He put down the sandwich. "Viola is being understandably protective of Bob's possessions and records right now, of the business, but I know she'd let me back into the shack Yale was using. I told her about it and we changed the locks, but I left everything inside just as it was."

"You'll search the place for me? You'd raise less suspicion than I would."

"I don't think Viola would let you on the farm without a warrant, anyway. Tell me what to look for."

She did. He nodded. And they finished their dinner.

Chandler, Ohio
Monday, October 4, 2010

A message from Deb was waiting for me when I got home. Cole's problem, which he'd finally admitted in counseling, was that he wanted a baby. He and Deb had been adamantly opposed to having kids and had agreed before they were married that they'd never ask the other to do so.

Turned out, after having been married to Cole for a

while, Deb wanted his baby, too. My receptionist wasn't going to be in the next day.

I was glad for the validation that there was good in the world.

But Sam's words weren't far away.

"Do something." She basically wanted me to kidnap Maggie. And to lie to her mother. I couldn't do either.

I compromised. As soon as I'd fed Camy and sat my butt in front of a frozen dinner that I eventually pushed away uneaten, I called Lori Winston.

"Is Maggie there?" I asked.

"No. She's at home. I'm still at work."

I took that as a sign that I was doing the right thing. Even though I didn't believe in signs. They were excuses, justifications for a decision a person was not sure about.

I didn't have time to get sure.

"Do you have a minute?"

"Yeah. I can take a break."

I waited while the woman told someone she was clocking out and then did so. "I'm back."

"I don't want to alarm you, Ms. Winston, but I know how much you love your daughter and are concerned for her well-being...."

"Is Maggie in some kind of trouble?"

"Nooo." I was not good at subterfuge. But one thought of Maggie losing her virginity on a sleeping bag in a tent in the woods and I was refortified.

"But I think she's going to be. Very soon. If we don't intervene."

"What kind of trouble?"

The only kind the woman seemed to care about where her daughter was concerned.

"Sexual trouble."

"I knew it. Goddammit, I knew it."

"Wait, Ms. Winston," I said quickly. I couldn't go too far or I'd blow everything. And if Sam was right, if lives were at stake, I'd be responsible.

I wished to God the deputy had given me a little more help in the "do something" department. I wasn't a police officer. I didn't think like she did.

"I'm not saying anything has happened. Only that Maggie came to see me after school today and I sense that she's on the verge of making a major decision."

"Great. On the verge. What am I supposed to do? Just sit around and wait for something to happen? And then have it be too late…"

I understood the sentiments so forgave the overly aggressive tone.

"Can't you stop her? You're supposed to be some kind of expert.…"

An expert witness. I gave opinions for a living.

"I've talked to her, but Maggie needs more than that. She needs constant supervision. To be taken to school. Picked up from school. And not left alone."

"I can't do that. I have to work. I'm barely making my rent as it is. And I sure as hell can't afford to hire someone."

"Is there a friend who could help you?"

"Uh-uh. Not anyone I'd trust with Maggie. What about sending her somewhere? I've heard of places that take troubled kids. My brother had to go to one once. I hate to think of Maggie in a place like that, but they watch them closely there. And I'll do anything to get her away from this guy. Whoever he is."

Maggie did not belong in a group home. Not one like her mother was describing. She wasn't an offender. She'd never last there.

Or her innocence wouldn't.

But if it would get her away from Mac…

"I can make some calls tomorrow, see what I can do, but the homes in Dayton are suffering from overcrowding as it is, and without a court order…"

"What about your place?" Lori Winston blurted into the silence that had fallen.

"My place?"

"We could tell Maggie that I have to work third shift for the next few weeks. And that I asked you to keep her for me. I wouldn't ask if I weren't desperate, Dr. Chapman. Or if I had money to send Maggie somewhere, or take her somewhere. If she was with you, you could take her to work. She could help out or do homework in your lobby. You could take her to school and pick her up and work with her one-on-one. You know what to say to her. All I do is piss her off.…"

The woman had stepped way beyond her boundaries and right into a plan that would fit Sam's edict.

"I can't do that, Ms. Winston. Maggie's my client. I—"

"Please, Dr. Chapman! I thought you cared about her! I thought—"

"I do care about her."

"She talks about you a lot. She feels safe with you. And with Glenna dying and… If she's with you I can still see her and…"

Sam had told me to do something. And the idea of being able to help Maggie myself, to have the right to keep her safe…

"Okay," I finally said, hoping I wasn't making a grave error. "She'll need to cancel any babysitting she has set up."

"That's not a problem."

"She wouldn't be able to play tennis.…"

"It doesn't matter what she's got planned, she'll cancel it," Lori Winston said. "How soon can you take her?"

Everything was happening so fast. But I couldn't risk giving Mac a chance to get to Maggie.

"I'll go get her now, if you want to call and let her know I'm coming."

It was finalized. I'd done something. Just like Sam had ordered.

Whether or not it was the right thing remained to be seen.

Maggie came without much fuss. She seemed kind of excited to be spending some time at my place while her mother worked nights. I wondered just how bad things had been at the Winston household.

The girl was already packed and waiting for me when I got to her place.

I picked up the duffel on the outside step by the one strap that wasn't broken and loaded it in the back of the car. "Is that it?" I asked, nervous someone was watching us, but glad to be getting the girl away from there, as well.

"Yep." She reached for something just inside the trailer—a lined denim jacket—and, wearing her backpack, locked the door behind her.

"Your mother told you you'd be staying with me for a while, right?"

"Yeah."

So the girl packed light.

We got in the Nitro. Fastened our belts. "Did she tell you that you'd be missing your paper route?"

"Yeah. I'm probably going to quit, anyway. I can make more money babysitting."

So Sam's idea that Maggie was delivering drugs with

her papers must be wrong. Unless Glenna was Maggie's contact and Sam had been exactly right.

I drove toward my house. It wasn't huge, but it was custom-built and had a hot tub on the back deck. Probably my reaction to my own poverty-stricken childhood.

But, like Maggie, I didn't often invite people inside. No one had ever spent the night with us in the three years since Camy and I had moved in.

"Did your mom tell you why you were staying with me?"

"She thinks I need counseling and can't afford for me to be in a real program. But she didn't seem to know about Mac." The girl looked at me. "Thank you for not telling."

"I'll have to tell her at some point. But I thought we could try changing your environment first and see how we do. How do you feel about that?"

"I'm okay with it. I mean, if it was anyone else but you, I'd be pissed, but this is okay, I guess. If it'll make my mom feel better and get her off my back."

"You won't be going anywhere else while you're with me, except for school. Just as if you were in an official program."

"I know."

"And you're okay with that?"

"It's only for a few days."

"And no computer, either."

"I know."

For someone who'd just been completely cut off, Maggie seemed unusually content.

I didn't know if that was good or bad.

"Did you tell Mac where you'd be?"

"I don't have his number."

I found that hard to believe. "You know, at the place

in the city that your mom was talking about, the group home, they take the girls' cell phones. I'll need you to give me yours."

Without a word, Maggie reached into her pocket, withdrew the phone and handed it to me.

If Mac had called the girl, or if Maggie had called him, I'd soon have his number.

Samantha was on duty the next morning and asked Jim to keep an eye on the locker. He called her at just past nine to tell her that there'd been a note left for her. If she still wanted help, she was to be at her locker at four-thirty that afternoon.

At least it was after school. And gave her time to get home and get changed. Showing up in uniform with a pistol in plain view would be a sure tip-off to a potential drug dealer to hightail it out of there.

At home she put on her tightest jeans. They were so low-cut the zipper measured about an inch. It was a pair she'd bought on sale without trying them on. She wasn't fond of shopping, and even less fond of fitting rooms, but since the jeans episode, she'd been more careful. Adding a long-sleeved white T-shirt and blue hooded sweatshirt that zipped up the front, Sam put on a pair of real tennis shoes.

She took her hair down and combed it until it was shiny and full of static electricity. And she pulled out the bin of makeup she kept under her bathroom sink just in case she felt like looking girlie. It rarely happened. As a last touch, she added a pair of sunglasses her mother had given her for Christmas and that she'd never worn. They had jewels on the sides. Tucking her badge in the pocket of the hoodie and hooking her gun to her waist beneath the sweatshirt, she was on her way to pass as the new kid in town long enough to meet her contact.

She wasn't following procedure. At all. No one knew what she was doing. She wasn't under assignment. Didn't have approval for an undercover job at the high school.

But they wouldn't have given her the approval. They'd have sent her out to Siberia to work a crosswalk. If she was lucky.

Kyle went through every inch of Yale's place. He found a couple of plastic bags in the trash that looked as though they'd contained crystals. There was a white powdery film on the inside of the bags. Kyle didn't open them.

Nothing else stood out. A picture of some woman. A girlfriend? Sister? He didn't know.

Didn't care.

Yale had left a few other things lying around. Some clothes. A small wooden box with mementos. A cross on a chain. An old driver's license.

Kyle looked out the back window of Yale's makeshift home. He saw nothing but weeds.

And something else. A piece of plywood? With a handle? He leaned in for a better view. Was that a door? It was some kind of storage on the side of the shack. Maybe it gave access to the bathroom plumbing—the new shower.

Heading outside, Kyle pulled open the unlocked door— and verified his plumbing theory. About to close the rickety wooden panel before a rat appeared, he noticed a glint of metal in the corner where the setting sun shone. All thoughts of rats fled as Kyle stepped into the small space to see what was there besides pipes.

He reached into the corner and his hand met the cool metal of a small tank.

Grabbing the handle, he pulled it out.

And was looking at one of his own portable storage tanks for anhydrous ammonia. He recognized it instantly because of the line of rust along the bottom edge. Rust meant the possibility of leakage. He'd set it out at the back of his barn, planning to dispose of it, then forgotten to do so.

Probably because it hadn't been there to remind him.

Reaching for his phone, Kyle dialed Sam's number.

And cursed when she didn't pick up.

30

Sam didn't recognize the young woman waiting by locker two-twelve until she was almost face-to-face with her.

"Ariel?" It had been a couple of years since she'd seen Chuck Sewell's daughter. Hadn't even known the girl was back in town.

"I thought you were living with your mom in Michigan."

"I was. I just moved here over the weekend. My mom and I aren't getting along so well."

Odd that Chuck hadn't mentioned his daughter had arrived. But then, they'd been preoccupied with a sixteen-year-old's death.

Odder still that Chuck's daughter was here…making a drug deal?

Sam's head felt a little cottony. As though there was something she was missing here.

Did Chuck know his daughter was in trouble? Was that why she'd come to Chandler to live? Because she'd been using drugs in Michigan and her mother couldn't control her?

But… If she'd only arrived that weekend, how had she gotten hooked up so quickly?

"My dad asked me to meet you here. To give you a message."

"Your dad?"

"Yeah. He said to tell you that he just saved your, uh, backside and that if this had been a real call you could have lost your job."

That hurt. It was much worse coming from a teenager. As Chuck would have known.

She'd considered the idea of a setup, of course. Had been pretty certain the flyer was delivered to Daniel to get to her. But she'd figured since she knew what was going on, she'd be able to protect herself. She'd gone rogue. Acted alone. Just like her father had.

"My dad cares about you a lot."

Sam wasn't all that fond of herself at the moment, though. She'd been working practically around the clock and was no closer to finding a superlab. Or even a distributor.

And Maggie Winston had just had sex with a pedophile.

"You know Daniel Hatch?"

"No, my dad just asked me to look him up and give him some flyer about homework help or something. What's going on? Are you in trouble?"

"No, but I could have been, which is what your dad just showed me."

"Well, anyway…" Ariel moved back a couple more steps, obviously embarrassed. "My dad said that he's got something that will help you, and if you want to talk, to meet him out at Bob Branson's farm 'cause that's where he is tonight. He said you'd know where it is."

"He's right. I do," Sam said. "Did he happen to mention where on the farm?"

"Oh, yeah. He said there's a building behind the barns

that used to be used for egg processing, but now it's used for storage. It's white like the rest but has a door big enough to drive a truck in. I hope I got that right."

"Thanks, Ariel. I'll find it."

"Well, I gotta go. Dad said I have to be home by five or I'm grounded. He's got some neighbor lady checking on me. He's worse than Mom."

Sam nodded. "Thanks for giving me the message. Welcome back to town," she said, and received an uneasy grin in return.

Kyle tried Sam a second time as he drove the truck with his rusty anhydrous ammonia container in the bed up to the farmhouse at the front of Bob's property. Viola wasn't there. She'd been staying at Shauna's the past couple of days, but planned to move back to the farm with Shauna and her family.

She'd given him free access to search everything and Kyle wanted to do it while he had the house to himself. For Viola's sake. Besides, poking into his friend's personal effects made him damned uncomfortable. He wasn't a cop. How would he even know what he was looking for? But he had to go through every room, every drawer, every closet and shelf, anyway. He needed to find something that might lead Sam to Bob's killer.

He entered the kitchen through the back door, letting himself in with the key Viola had given him.

And stopped as soon as his boot hit the tile. He smelled bacon. Viola hadn't cooked in the kitchen since Bob died.

And he knew for a fact she was at Shauna's. He'd talked to her half an hour before.

There'd been no vehicles outside when he'd pulled up.

"Hello!" he called out.

No answer.

With his hand still on the doorknob, he tried again. "Anyone here?" He couldn't see much of the room, but he noticed the shadow fall across the floor by the sink.

There was no sound. Or motion.

But mixed in with bacon was something more rancid. Body odor. Like someone hadn't showered in several days.

"Yale?"

Silence.

Kyle wasn't armed or trained. But he was a man who didn't accept someone hurting those he cared about.

"You're done, son," he said. "Come easy, or come hard, but make no mistake, you'll be in jail before you sleep again."

Figuring the fire extinguisher hanging on the wall was as good as any weapon, Kyle took a slow step into the room. A physical match between him and a twenty-two-year-old didn't faze him. Couldn't be any worse than wrestling a wild horse.

Kyle froze as he felt the prick of something sharp at his throat.

"At least I'll be waking up in the morning." The voice, a low growl, came from just behind him. The man's spittle sprayed Kyle's neck.

If he guessed right, he'd just met Yale.

"You should have minded your own business," the voice said angrily. "Now, walk!"

Sam let the Mustang have her way on the trip out to the Branson farm. She'd just been made a fool of by one of her fellow officers. A speeding ticket from another wouldn't be any worse.

And she was pissed. Really pissed. Who the hell did

Chuck think he was, using Daniel that way? And Ariel. Using *her* for that matter.

She was almost out at the farm before she calmed down enough to acknowledge that the message Chuck had just sent had been effective. And probably the only way to prove a point. They'd all tried talking to her. Reasoning with her. Pierce. Chuck. Kyle. They'd practically begged her to rein herself in. Slow down. Follow protocol.

And she'd ignored them.

What she'd done, working undercover on her own, was stupid. These guys had already killed. They wouldn't blink at killing a cop. And Sam could have been walking into a potentially deadly situation without backup.

Chuck could have just saved her life.

But did he have to use his teenage daughter to do it?

Coming in the back way on one of her favorite, rarely traveled country roads, she entered the Branson property from the west side—the one usually reserved for the semis that transported Branson product. She recognized Chuck's Taurus outside a building that fit Ariel's description. Eager to hear what he had found, to find the meth lab and arrest the pedophile who'd lured Maggie to a tent over the weekend, she jumped out of her car and headed toward the building at a trot.

And when all was done, she was going to tell Chuck Sewell what she thought of his little trick. She'd get back at him. Just give her time to think of something really good.

In the meantime, she was relieved as hell that he'd been able to do what she hadn't—make a break in this case. They couldn't afford to lose any more lives.

She pulled open the heavy wooden side door of the old processing building. "Okay, Sewe—"

"Sam! Get down!"

She heard Kyle's voice and ducked, barely registering
that he'd pulled himself away from the knife at his throat
and launched himself at the man pointing a gun in her
direction. A bullet flew past her shoulder and out into the
night. She felt it go by.

Heart pounding, Sam had her gun pointed and a shot
off before enough time had passed for thought. And then
she shot a second time.

Kyle was climbing slowly to his feet, blood on his neck.
Right beside him, in the dirt, was the man he'd tackled.
The one she'd hit with her first bullet. Blood oozed from
his chest, saturating his shirt.

Oh, my God. No!

It was Chuck Sewell.

Kyle grabbed Chuck's police-issue weapon from his
limp right hand.

"Call 9-1-1!" she screamed.

A second man, an unshaven punk, was also down—hit
by Sam's second bullet. He hadn't moved.

Shaking inside, but with iron-steady arms, she held her
gun out in front of her, letting it lead her over to the three
men on the ground, keeping them in sight as she prepared
to shoot anyone who might be lurking in the shadows.

Within seconds, she was kneeling at her fellow officer's side, shoving her finger into the spurting hole in his
chest, trying to stop the flow of blood.

Chuck looked straight at her.

"Good cop," he said, his voice raspy. He attempted to
raise his hand. Sam watched as the deputy's arm went
limp and fell across his abdomen. "Bad cop." He choked
and swallowed. Probably on his own blood.

"Just hang on. You're going to make it." Tears blurred
her vision. Chuck was her friend. Her fellow officer. She'd
just shot one of her own.

"You were going to kill me," she said, aware that she was probably in shock, but knowing that she didn't have time right then to give in to any kind of emotion.

"Had to." Chuck's words were barely discernible.

She could hear Kyle on the phone. Giving their location and describing the scene. The other guy still hadn't moved and Sam figured him for dead.

She hadn't put it together yet. But she would. Sam knew that more was coming. Much more. For now, there was only one thing on her mind.

"Just stay with me, Chuck. Dammit, stay with me!"

"For what?" She leaned closer, trying to understand the guttural whispers. "It's…all…over…now."

"What about Ariel? She needs you."

"Better…off…with…mother."

Tell me you love her, dammit, Sam thought. Give me something to tell her.

"Not…going…jail…"

And that was when Sam registered the apparatus surrounding them. The elaborate kitchen she'd burst into. Professional-size stoves. Freezers. Countertops filled with tubing and beakers and thermometers. A state-of-the-art science lab.

And she knew she could stop looking for her methamphetamine superlab. She was kneeling in it.

Chuck's sudden grin was off, lopsided. "Nice…shot," he said.

"Chuck. Damn you! You were behind this? It was you?"

And when he just kept grinning at her as blood spurted out of his mouth and dripped down his chin, she cried, "The kids. The deaths. How *could* you?"

"Would…'ve liked…to…fuck…you."

They were the last words the man said.

31

Sirens wailed. Lights flashed. Uniformed bodies burst into the room in some weird kind of organized havoc. Staccato questions and orders flew about the tall old cavernous building in as few words as possible. Everyone moved quickly with clearly understood tasks.

A couple of paramedics hurried toward Kyle. He'd never seen them before and wondered, briefly, if they were from Chandler, or if other squads had been summoned.

"We got two dead!" a female voice called urgently just as the big strapping man in front of Kyle said, "Sir, are you okay, sir?"

"I'm fine."

"You're bleeding. Let's take a look at that." It was his female partner. With gentle pressure against Kyle's shoulder she pushed him onto a stool that had somehow appeared behind him.

Kyle didn't much care what they did to him as long as he could keep his eye on Sam.

While the woman dabbed wetly at the wound on his neck, then placed a wad of gauze over it, he listened to the cacophony of voices echoing off the high ceiling of the barn, trying to sort out Sam's voice. Trying to hear what she was saying to the sheriff, Ben Chase and Todd Williams.

"Would you mind rolling up your sleeve?" the male paramedic asked. Kyle complied.

"Do you hurt anywhere other than your throat?" the woman asked.

"No. I'm fine. Really."

One officer was dead. Shot by another. There'd be an investigation. An inquiry. From the compassion on the faces of the officers circling Sam, carefully shielding her from the rest of the activity in the room, Kyle figured she'd have their complete support in the coming weeks.

"You're lucky the blade missed your artery," the woman said, applying a slightly painful pressure as she secured a bandage over the right side of his neck. "But you're going to need stitches."

Each grabbing one of his arms, the paramedics pulled him to a standing position. "Can you walk?"

"Of course."

"Then let's get you out of here and to the hospital."

They led him slowly, carefully maneuvering around what seemed like scores of people. Someone was drawing a chalk line around Chuck.

"Wait." Kyle stopped them as they neared Sam. Pulling free, he pushed his way to her side.

"You okay?"

"Yeah." Her eyes were haunted, though, when she gazed up at him.

"You going back to the station?" She'd have to give a report at the very least.

She nodded. "What about you? Are you okay?" She stared at his neck. "Oh, God, Kyle, you could have been killed."

"I know." And she could have been, too. That really scared the shit out of him.

He'd come so close to losing her. To…

"I…"

And then the paramedics broke through, ordering him to the hospital—and to the station afterward. He told Sam he would see her there.

Sam rode back to the station in her Mustang. She let Todd drive. Just this once. And she put up with everyone's pandering for the first half hour or so when they got there.

She told them what she knew. And said she had to get back to work. Had to tie up the pieces. With Chuck gone, she was the only one left on the case.

Going through Chuck's files could wait until morning. But his things had to be secured. His daughter removed from his house and arrangements made to return her to her mother. His house had to be taped off as a crime scene until the police could go through it.

She had some calls to make, at the very least.

Had to stay busy. To think.

Not feel.

The lab was already being dismantled. Crews would be at it all night and into the next day until everything was disposed of or destroyed.

"You should call your mom, and Pierce," Todd said, standing there with Ben and the sheriff, looking at her as if they half expected her to fall apart on them any moment.

"Not now," she said. "Not yet." And she glared at each one of them in turn. "I want every one of you to promise me that you will not call my brother."

They nodded.

"We're keeping this out of the news, right? At least until morning?"

The sheriff nodded. That was one benefit to small-town living. There wasn't a lot of media, and what there was usually cooperated with the law.

"Is Lori Winston here yet?" They'd sent a deputy for the woman at Sam's request.

"Yes. She's in the holding cell."

Sam looked up at her boss. "Do I have your permission, sir, to question her?"

He stepped back.

"Be my guest." But he didn't look pleased.

Sam understood. He'd have felt a lot better if she'd just gone on home and let him handle everything.

Especially now that he knew she'd engaged in a one-woman undercover act.

She'd be hearing about that one.

Sam wasn't around when Kyle was dropped off at the station by the police officer who'd accompanied him to the hospital. His neck stung a bit, but not badly, and he was impatient to be finished with protocol and get to Sam.

Alone.

James and Millie were with Grandpa for the night. And for as long as he needed them.

Ben and Todd, the two deputies he knew best, next to Chuck Sewell, took him to a conference room and offered him coffee. Hot chocolate. Anything out of the machine.

They asked if he was up to answering questions.

"I'm fine," he said, for what felt like the fiftieth time that hour. He figured he must look like hell.

Todd flipped on a recorder, and Ben, sitting beside him

at the table, said, "We need you to tell us whatever you can remember about the evening."

Sure he could tell them. In detail.

"Take your time, Kyle."

He'd been in Yale's makeshift lodgings. Had been thinking about helping Sam...

"Whenever you're ready."

Kyle nodded. He was ready.

He'd seen that trapdoor out back. The glint...

"We can do this later, man...."

No. He couldn't leave. He had to see it through. To find what Sam needed. *He stashed the can in the back of his truck and...*

"What's this about? Why am I here?" Lori Winston looked more irritated than scared. Which bothered the hell out of Sam.

"That's what you're going to tell me," she said, gritting her teeth in an attempt to stay calm as she circled behind the seated woman, ending up facing her across the table set in the middle of an open cell at the front of the jail.

"How can I tell you anything? I don't even know why I'm here. You can't do this, you know. I know my rights. You can't just barge into my trailer at nine o'clock at night and haul me down here and—"

"Shut. Up."

Lori's belligerent expression didn't fade, but her words did.

Sam went to work, relying completely on a combination of instinct and information she'd received from Kelly over the past weeks.

"Your daughter was screwed in a tent by a grown man this past weekend, Lori," Sam blurted derisively. And then she twisted a little deeper. "She says they used protection, but who knows if they really did?"

Tight-lipped, the woman didn't move.

"Maggie said the man was a little older than you. Think about it. A man that age, with his experience, pulling down your daughter's pants. Pulling down his own, and sticking that—"

"Stop!" Lori's chin trembled. Her lips trembled. "Stop!" she screamed again, her hands over her ears as she shook her head back and forth. She started to cry, to whimper. "Noooooo," she said, chin to her chest. "Oh, God, noooo. Please noooo. Not my baby. Not my…"

The woman's suffering was obvious. Sam almost had sympathy for her. On another day she might have.

Or not. She pulled the woman's hands away from her ears and held on to them.

"Tell me who he is, Lori."

"I don't know," the woman said, tears flooding her eyes, flowing down her face. "If I'd known who he was, I'd have stopped him long before now. Chuck wouldn't help me. He just kept telling me I was imagining things. That he was certain no one involved was on to Maggie or would hurt her in any way. Even after I told him about finding the condom. He just laughed at me. That's why I sent her to that shrink. That Kelly Chapman woman. I wanted her to use whatever hypnosis or brainwashing tricks she had to get Maggie to tell her who the guy was."

Chuck.

As in Sewell.

Lori did not yet know that the man was dead. But she was rolling on him.

"You know who he is, Lori."

"I don't. I swear to God, I don't. But when I find out I'm going to kill him. I will rip out his balls and cram them down his throat and leave him there to suffocate on his own sex...."

If Sam hadn't been a cop, she might have agreed with the woman.

"He's someone involved in the local drug cartel," Sam said. "He knew that Glenna Reynolds had been killed just hours after the murder."

"But...that doesn't make sense. Chuck was the only one involved. He swore. And Chuck would not sleep with Maggie. I know he wouldn't. And there's no way Maggie would have slept with him. She can't stand the guy."

"But you slept with him, didn't you?"

"Yes."

"What do you know about a vacant house on Mechanic Street?" She was playing a hunch.

"Chuck got access through the city. He used it sometimes, to meet people."

"He sold drugs from there."

"Yeah."

Didn't really matter now, but she'd had to know.

"You ever hear anyone call Chuck Mac?"

"Mac? No, I've never heard of any Mac."

"So, assuming you're telling the truth, there's someone else involved. Someone besides Chuck. Someone older."

"Yes, but I don't know who he is."

"Then help me find him," Sam said.

"How?"

"Tell me about the drugs."

"What do you want to know?"

"Everything."

Some time later Sam sat across from Lori Winston, watching while the woman wrote down everything she'd confessed and then signed her name.

Sam had to hand it to the woman. She'd just sacrificed her life to help find the man who'd so grossly hurt her daughter.

Of course, that was after selling her only child to a dirty cop to be set up on a paper route to deliver several packages a month filled with methamphetamine to two middlemen who distributed all over Ohio.

And once, to meet a man on a side street and drop a package in his car.

He was in the old processing plant, perched on a stool that had been shoved behind his knees, the blade of a very sharp knife against his throat. Any time Kyle moved, either because he was bumped, or because he breathed too heavily, the blade pierced a little more, went in a little farther.

And he was looking at what he assumed was Sam's superlab. She'd been right all along.

It didn't surprise him as much as he'd have liked it to.

"Come on, Chuck," Kyle said. "You aren't going to kill me. We both know that." He looked straight in the other man's eyes. In plain clothes Chuck looked small. Skinny. Nothing like the man Kyle had always taken him to be.

Not even the gun he held in Kyle's direction intimidated him.

"You're kidding, right?" blurted the young fool at Kyle's side, the one who'd gotten the better of him up at the house. "He killed a fuckin' sixteen-year-old girl in jail, man. He ain't gonna think twice about offin' you. You're just some country hick farmer pokin' around in business that ain't yours."

Yale, who'd confirmed his identity for Kyle on the painful walk over from the house, had already told him that he'd seen Kyle search his place. He'd seen him open the trapdoor and had headed up to the house to wait for him.

He'd also bragged about the chemicals he'd convinced Bob to take from Kyle's place one day when Kyle had been at a co-op meeting. They'd been low on supplies and had a large shipment due. Bob, who'd been privy to the information about Kyle's experimental crop, had known the chemicals were there. He'd also known he'd be the only one who could get by Zodiac without having to hurt the dog.

"You killed that girl?" Kyle asked Chuck, having trouble believing that one. Even with the deputy pointing a gun at him.

"That girl had a name," Chuck said. "It's Glenna. And yes, I killed her. I had to shut the bitch up. She was blubbering. Screaming at me to do something right there in the jail cell. Hollering about the fact that I'd said I'd protect her..."

"So this is the lab Sam was talking about, huh?" Kyle looked around, thinking of Sam. Of her theories and ideas. Her energy and dedication. Her love. He was waiting for a moment when one or the other of his captors was distracted and he could go after him. Or at least die trying.

Odd how in that, a life-and-death moment, everything seemed so clear. And he felt so...calm.

"It was all you, Chuck? Bob? Holmes? Seventy-five percent of Child Protective Services cases..."

"Hell, no, man. It ain't all him. It's bigger 'n that. It's—"

Chuck's gun fired. Ricocheting off the floor about two feet from Kyle's right. He had no idea where it landed.

"Shut the hell up, punk." Chuck's voice was deadly.

"I'd do it if I were you, kid," Kyle said. *"He'd kill a sixteen-year-old, he sure isn't going to hesitate to off you."* His palms started to sweat. Probably because his heart was pounding.

He had to get Chuck talking. To distract him somehow. To...

"Tell me about the tennis club," Kyle said, calling up anything he could remember that Sam had told him about her theories.

"What about it?"

"It's part of your operation, right?"

"Hell, no. It's a charity club. Started by a friend of mine. But when we came up with the perfect plan and needed kids, it was a fucking cesspool of possibilities."

"The perfect plan?" Kyle asked.

"Yeah, man." Yale, who was apparently more stupid than he looked, popped off again. *"A cop giving packages of drugs to kids to deliver. They're told to do their job and shut up or they'll be in jail. Or, worse, lose all the dough they're making and—"*

Chuck's gun fired again. Missing Yale's foot by about an inch. The knife slid along his neck. Kyle could feel the blood dripping down.

"And who'd ever think anything of a cop meeting with kids?" Kyle said quickly.

"That's right," Chuck said. *"And if one squealed, like Glenna was about to, well...you see what happened to her."*

"Glenna, did she play tennis, too?"

"Nope. She babysits for my little sis. And when I heard about the horrible time she was having with her mom so sick and all..."

"You just had to help out." Kyle didn't bother to keep the sarcasm from his voice. Wasn't much chance he was

going to live to see another day and he'd wasted too much of his life hiding.

"I needed another layer of protection," Chuck said. "That's how these things work. You never deal directly with anyone. There's always an extra layer, so if one gets peeled, there's another beneath."

"Even an onion runs out of layers eventually."

"Guess it's good I never acquired a taste for onions."

The man was smart. Too bad he didn't have a soul.

"So what's the plan, Chuck?" Kyle asked. *If he was going to die, he wanted it done. He was not going to sit here and sweat.*

"The plan, my friend, is for you to shut up."

"I'll shut up just as soon as you tell me the plan."

"The plan is…" Chuck moved closer, grinning in a way that made Kyle want to punch the guy in the jaw. "That you are going to sit right there like a good little soldier, country boy. And when Sam gets here—" he looked at his watch "—which should be in about half an hour from now, based on how fast she drives that machine of hers.… When she gets here—" Chuck took another step toward Kyle, the gun pointed at him "—you get to watch me teach her the lesson she just refused to learn. She isn't the savior of the world. She couldn't learn to listen. To follow directions. And look where it got us."

Kyle could see pretty clearly. He'd promised to stay silent as long as Chuck talked. Because as long as he was talking, he wasn't shooting.

"You'll never get away with this, Chuck. Sam has a lot of friends in this town. People with money and power who will ask more questions than were asked about the poor girl. Or Bob."

Chuck actually laughed. "You're such a fool, country

boy. You know why folks aren't asking questions about Bob? Because one or two of those 'important' people you're talking about don't want news of our little operation here to get around."

"They know?"

"Hell, yes, they know. It's why the whole thing started. Meth was everywhere. The people who were using it were going to keep using it. And they were making Mexicans rich while southern Ohio died a slow economic death. American money was going to Mexico and we couldn't afford to pay our cops. Public health was almost bankrupt. Hell, at the rate we were going, we couldn't pay the electricity at the courthouse. Where do you think the money's going, country boy? Do I look rich to you?"

Kyle wasn't sure whether to believe the man or not. "You didn't keep any of the money."

"Okay, well, sure, I kept some. It's put away safe. And when there's enough of it to last me the rest of my life, I'm moving to Florida."

"You're not going to get away with this," Kyle said again. He had to believe he was right. So they had some corrupt officials; Chandler was filled with good, honest people who'd take back their town. "When word gets out…"

"But we're the only ones who know, Kyle. You see? Just us and pretty soon Sam. So you see the problem."

"You're going to kill her."

"After I fuck her," Chuck said. "She'll learn her place before she dies. And you're going to watch, Kyle. You know why? Because all these years, she's been your woman and you just couldn't ever get it right. You couldn't ever teach her her place. You failed me, my man. So it's good, really—poetic justice—that you showed up poking around here today. And this evening, all will finally be

*well. I'll get Sam." The man cupped his dick. "And then
I'll kill her. And when you've seen what a failure you are,
I'll kill you, too. And stage the whole thing to make it look
like you killed her and then yourself. Because after I'm
done with her, I'm going to kill Samantha Jones with her
own gun."*

*Kyle knew one thing. Chuck Sewell was not going to
lay a hand on Sam.*

*He didn't have to pretend to sweat. Or to worry. He
went right ahead and let Chuck see his fear.*

And he listened for Sam's car...

Sweat poured down Kyle's back and he blinked against
the harsh light of the conference room, barely registering that he was sitting there with Ben and Todd. He took
the bottle of water that was offered him. And when Sam
walked in the door, he passed out.

Chandler, Ohio
Tuesday, October 5, 2010

It was after ten when my cell phone rang. Maggie had
been in bed for half an hour. But when Sam told me she
was on her way over and to get the girl up, I did.

"What's going on?" Maggie asked, wearing flannel
sleep pants and a yellow T-shirt with hearts stitched across
the front. She followed me, barefoot, out to the couch.

"I'm not sure," I lied, sick to my stomach with worry.
As I'd been pretty much all night.

Sam had told me they'd arrested Maggie's mom, but
we'd decided to wait to tell the girl.

Because we still couldn't finger Mac. Maggie was
going to have to tell us, even if it meant we took her to
jail for withholding information.

I didn't have any coffee to make for Sam. Wouldn't

know how to make it if I had it, since I can't stand the stuff. But I needed to keep busy so that Maggie wouldn't see how badly I was shaking.

I thought about putting Camy outside. But what if Mac was out there? What if he knew that Maggie was here with me? Like he'd known about Glenna's death. What if he was waiting for a chance to take the girl?

I put water on to boil to make hot chocolate instead. And forgot to turn on the stove.

The three of us—Maggie and Camy and I—were in the living room when I heard Sam's Mustang in my driveway. Not wanting her out there by herself, cop or not, I waited by the front door. She wasn't alone. Kyle Evans was with her.

I'm not even sure we said hello.

"What happened to you?" I asked Kyle, staring at the bandage on his neck.

"Later," he said. "I'm fine now, and there's something much more important we have to do right now."

I glanced at Sam. She nodded. "He lost a lot of blood, but we've filled him up with orange juice and the medic says he's good to go. We went out to his place and got him a change of clothes, then came straight here. We've had a car watching this place since early this evening."

Feeling as if I'd just fallen into Alice's rabbit hole, the nightmare version of it, I led the way into the living room.

We sat—me and Maggie on the love seat and Sam and Kyle on the couch.

Sam glanced at me. I nodded, but couldn't breathe.

"Maggie, your mother's been arrested," Sam said.

"What?" The girl's eyes got wide, and she leaned forward, her arms gripping her stomach. "For what?"

I tensed.

"For selling you."

"That's crazy. My mom didn't sell me. She'd never do that. And besides, I'm right here. If she'd sold me, I'd be gone or something." Her face was ghostly white. I took hold of her hand.

She pulled it away.

"Maggie, do you remember when that man joined your Internet group, the one you told me about?" I asked. "The one with the kids who are sick like Jeanine."

"What man?"

"We know, Maggie. We know all about the packages you deliver."

Maggie's gaze dropped to the floor. She rocked back and forth. "The man you met on that site, the one who told you about a way to help those kids who were in so much pain because their parents couldn't afford to pay for all of the medications that would help them—that man was Chuck Sewell."

Maggie's head shot up. "No, it wasn't," she said, staring me straight in the eye. And then she looked over at Sam. "It wasn't."

"Chuck's been selling drugs all over Ohio, Maggie," Sam said. "He used a lot of people in many different ways, finding dealers from all kinds of places, but mostly he used kids."

"I'm not surprised about that. I told my mom the guy was a creep. But I swear, I haven't had anything to do with him. I wouldn't. And there's no way I'd sell drugs." She turned to me, and I took her hand again.

This time, almost as though she sensed she was going to need the contact, she held on.

"Your mom gave Chuck the information to join that site, Maggie. And she gave him your screen name."

Maggie didn't say anything.

"And the tennis club your mom had you join? Chuck told her about that, too. Some of the other kids that were playing tennis were already delivering drugs, and Chuck thought that if you met them, and got to know them, then if you ever started to worry about what you were doing, you'd have a group of kids who were just like you, doing the same things."

"I didn't deliver drugs," Maggie said, head bent. "I delivered medication to families who had sick kids and no money to pay for it."

"That's what you were told."

"That's what I did."

I sat forward, like Maggie, letting Sam grill the girl. There was more coming, and it all rested on Maggie.

"Did you ever look in the bags?"

"No. I was told not to. If something got opened or dropped or contaminated, there'd be that much less to go around."

"You were told not to so you couldn't implicate yourself if you were caught," Sam said. "And so you wouldn't know that what you were delivering was crystal meth. Your mother told us all about the plan."

Maggie needed to understand that she couldn't trust anyone but us. It was the only way this was going to work. The only way to save her.

Sam had her man. But unless Maggie implicated him, he was going to walk. They had nothing on him but the hearsay statement of a dead man.

A statement only Kyle had heard. I assumed that was why he was here with us. Not that I cared. I was glad for his presence.

Kyle was one of those guys that instilled a sense of security just by being around.

"Chuck wasn't working alone, Maggie," Sam said, and

I tensed. "There was another man. We think it's the man you told Kelly about. Mac."

The girl's head darted up, her eyes filled with steel. "No way. Leave Mac out of this."

"These are bad men." I meant to let Sam do all the talking, but I butted in. "Sweetie, they killed Glenna."

The girl said nothing. Showed no reaction. Mac's hold on her was strong.

"They tried to kill Sam tonight, too," Kyle added, earning him a stare from Maggie.

"Chuck did," Sam said.

"He did?" My friend hadn't filled me in on that little detail.

"He took a shot at me," Sam said, watching Maggie. "Kyle tackled him, though, so he missed."

"He'd have killed her, anyway," Kyle said. "But Sam got him first."

"You killed Chuck Sewell?" Eyes wide, Maggie shifted her focus from Kyle to Sam, her voice filled with awe.

"Yeah."

Oh. God. I'd had no idea Chuck was dead. Or that Sam had... I'd be working with her for months on that one. Hopefully with her cooperation.

"He's really dead?" Maggie asked.

"Yes, he's really dead."

Maggie jutted he chin out. "Well, I'm not sorry."

"And that's okay, Maggie," I told her. "It's natural and understandable."

"The point is, Chuck wasn't working alone," Sam explained. "Your mother told us that another man gave you your packages to deliver. You were the only one that didn't take delivery from Chuck."

"Why?" I asked, giving Maggie time to digest what she was hearing. She needed to figure out for herself that

Mac was a liar—and that if he'd lied to her about the drugs, he'd probably lied to her about his feelings for her, too. She needed to process the fact that Mac was friends with Chuck Sewell. And I also asked because I wanted to know.

"Two reasons, according to the signed statement from Maggie's mom," Sam said. "First, because Lori knew that her daughter would never, ever work with Chuck."

I had to wonder about that, and made a mental note to myself to ask Maggie exactly why she hated the deputy so much.

"And second, because the number-one rule in the organization was to keep a distance. There was always someone between a contact and a point person. Chuck's partner brought in all the other distributors, so Chuck delivered. And Chuck brought Maggie to the party, so his partner delivered."

There, that should close the deal for Maggie. Should make the girl angry enough to deliver Mac to us.

Despair would follow. I knew that. And an inability to trust. We had a lot of work ahead of us, me and Maggie. I was worried sick about her. About the coming months.

About the next few days. With her mother in jail, Child Services would be looking to place Maggie in a foster home. I wanted her.

Period.

Sam sat forward, moving closer to Maggie. Instinctively, I moved closer, too. I was trembling. But then so was Maggie.

"Maggie, Chuck said his partner started the tennis club. My fellow deputies and I made some phone calls tonight and we found out the name of the man who made arrangements with the tennis complex for you kids to play for free. He agreed to take on responsibility for any damage that could be incurred, including stolen or broken rackets and stolen tennis balls."

"And you think it's Mac?"

"We know it is, Maggie," Sam said.

And what I also knew was that Sam had absolutely no concrete evidence to pin on the man. If Maggie didn't identify him, if she didn't admit that he'd given her packages, or had sex with her, the pedophile drug dealer was going to walk.

"I don't believe you."

"Because Mac loves you?" I asked, knowing that this was where I came in.

"Because Mac's not anything like you're describing. And because he didn't deliver drugs to me, and because he doesn't even know I play tennis and he's never been at the complex. Mac's a good man. He loves me. Really loves me. All he cares about is that I'm happy. And safe."

We were in trouble. The man had her. He'd sucked Maggie in while the rest of us were busy living our lives around her.

Sam pulled a photo out of a folder she'd carried in with her. "Who is this, Maggie?"

The girl looked at the photo. And then away. "I don't know."

As she turned, Sam turned the eight-and-a-half-by-eleven photo she held. I caught a glimpse.

And couldn't believe what I was seeing. Sam was watching me. She nodded.

"David Abrams?" I could barely speak.

"I don't know any David Abrams," Maggie said. But I could see that this second secret—this second lie—coming so soon after she'd found out that her mother had sold her into the drug trade, was too much for Maggie. She'd shut down as surely as if there'd been a switch to flip. She was fourteen. She'd just lost her best friend. And her mother. She couldn't possibly deal with another loss.

And I couldn't stop Sam from trying to break her, anyway. Not with a pedophile on the loose.

"Maggie, this is Mac," I said.

"No, it's not."

"Maggie, do you know what happens if you lie to an officer of the law?" Sam asked.

"No. But I'm not lying."

"You could go to prison. And because there have been at least two deaths that we know of resulting from the activities of these men, you would be charged as an accessory to murder. If you were charged as an adult, and considering your age you could be, you could spend the rest of your life in prison."

I was scared just listening to Sam. And she was my friend.

"I'm not lying," Maggie said. "That man is not Mac."

We worked the child for another half hour. And then I called it quits. Maggie wasn't budging. And nothing was going to make her budge. Her subconscious was protecting her from what she couldn't handle. I was convinced Maggie honestly believed she was telling us the truth. There was nothing anyone could take from her at this point that mattered to her except Mac.

I sent the girl back to bed. She had school in the morning.

"What do you think?" Sam asked as I walked her and Kyle to the door.

"My professional opinion?"

"Yes."

"Abrams is Mac, but right now she believes what she's saying to us."

"Do you think you can get her to talk?"

"Not anytime soon," I told her honestly. "We could put her in a room face-to-face with David Abrams at this point and she'd deny that he was Mac. Because in her mind, her Mac would never do any of the things we've told her David has done."

"You do realize that without Maggie's testimony we have nothing on David? He's a lawyer, Kel. He's covered his tracks completely."

"Except for Maggie."

"Right. She's the one time he veered from his plan."

"So what are we going to do?"

"I'm going to testify, that's what," Kyle said, even as Sam was shaking her head.

"It wouldn't stand up in court. All you know is what Chuck told you when he was holding a gun to your head. It's your word against his and he's not here to defend himself."

I couldn't believe this.

"So now what?"

"So now I call David Abrams, put the fear of God into him and keep looking."

"And what about Maggie?"

"We watch her like a hawk, Kel. If the man so much as comes near her, we've got him, which is why I don't think he will. And hopefully, as time passes, with no contact between them, his hold over her will lessen and she'll tell us the truth."

"So you think she's safe?"

"For now. Absolutely. The man's not stupid. He's not going to risk his whole life to have sex with Maggie."

"Are his children safe?" I hated to ask but had to know.

"I believe so. All the indications are that he's a good

father. It seems clear that his obsession is Maggie. Just Maggie."

"That doesn't make me feel much better," I said.

"Me, neither," Sam admitted. "Which is why I'm going to stick to him like glue."

"You know Sam, Kelly. She'll get him." Kyle's possessive grin in Sam's direction, his arm around her shoulders, was encouraging.

And I had something else on my mind.

"Sam?"

"Yeah?"

"You got any pull with Child Services?"

"'Bout as much as you do, why?"

"I want to keep Maggie here."

"I'm pretty sure that can be arranged."

"I thought so, too, but…you'll put in a word for me?"

"I have a feeling it'll be more like them asking me to put in a word to you. Lori Winston has already requested that you be given temporary custody."

Well, thank you, God.

And I'm sorry I thought you didn't hear me.

"I'm driving," Kyle said, heading to the driver's side of her car as they left Kelly's front door.

Sam handed him the keys.

"You coming to my place?"

They hadn't discussed it.

"Yes."

She had her phone out and dialed before she'd fastened her seat belt.

"Hello?" The voice on the other end of the line was groggy.

"David? Sam Jones."

"What? What time is it?" Sam could hear a rustle. And a "David, who is it?" from afar—Susan's voice.

"It's just after midnight," Sam said, keeping her temper in check. But just.

"I… Hold on a second."

She heard David say, "It's work, sweetie, the police. Someone needs a lawyer. Go to sleep. I'll be right back."

A door closed.

"Sam? What in the hell is going on?"

"Chuck Sewell is dead."

"What? You're kidding! What happened?"

For a man who'd just lost his brother-in-law, David didn't sound that shocked. Sam wondered who'd told him.

Most likely one of the city officials Chuck had mentioned to Kyle. And that the sheriff had already tracked down.

Only Chuck hadn't had it quite right. The city officials he thought would protect them hadn't known a thing about the meth lab. They'd been accepting anonymous donations. Period. They'd had no idea where the money was coming from.

And hadn't asked.

They'd been severely berated by a very frustrated and distraught county sheriff.

"Don't bother with the games, David," Sam said, her voice shaking with anger. "Just listen. I know who you are and I know what you did. I might not have concrete evidence at the moment, but I will. You mark my words. I am going to be watching your every move, every single day, until I find what I need to hang your ass. Until then, if you so much as look at Maggie Winston, if you go near her, contact her, read an e-mail from her, I will take it to the judge with the circumstantial evidence I do have. We have a statement from Maggie that she doesn't know you. If you get in touch with her, that'll convince us she's lying to protect you. I will call in expert witnesses to testify to the fragile emotional state of an at-risk young woman with no support at home being wooed by an older, successful man. I will—"

"I get your point, Sam."

"So we understand each other."

"Just for the record, I don't know what you're talking about."

"Do we understand each other?" She bit out each word.

"Yes, Sam, we do."

"Stay away from her, David. I swear I'll—"

"Already done."

She hated the prick. Like she'd never hated anyone in her life.

But she believed him.

Kyle drove Sam's car over the dark and peaceful roads between Chandler and home, listening to her threaten a man twice her size, with twice her money. He should be intimidated, but he wasn't.

He was proud of her. Comfortable.

And aware, in a way he'd never been before, that she needed him.

"Here's the thing," he said as soon as she hung up the phone and was still filled with fire.

"What?"

"I want you to conduct an investigation."

"Of what?"

"Me."

"Don't be crazy, Kyle. I believe every word you said

tonight. And even if I didn't, the information you gave us, together with the evidence that's been collected already, is enough to prove beyond doubt that Chuck..." She finally noticed that he was shaking his head. "What?"

"I want you to look into my history. You're the best damn detective I've ever heard of," he said. "You could ferret year-old bread crumbs out of a bird who'd been dead for six months."

She chuckled. "What do you want, Kyle?"

"I want you to know that in thirteen years' time, I have not, even once, slept with any other woman but you."

"Kyle..."

"It shouldn't be too hard a search, Sam. Not for someone like you. Other than the couple of trips we've taken together, I haven't been away from the farm in the past ten years. You wouldn't have to look far. Check every bar. Hell, get census records and randomly send my photo to every woman who currently or in the past ten years has lived in the area...."

He might be laying it on a little thick. But he was completely serious.

Sam turned, her face tilted up toward his. "Why?"

"Why what?"

"Why would I spend time and energy on such a search?"

"Because you love me."

"I'm not following your line of logic."

"Because I love you."

"Still not following."

But not denying his assertions, either. Not that he'd believe her if she did. The fact that he and Sam loved each other wasn't in question. They'd have to be dead not to know what the rest of the town had taken for granted for years.

"I need you to be able to trust me," he said. "And the only way I've come up with to earn back your trust is to prove to you that I love you so much that, for thirteen years, while I was free to bed another woman, I didn't. Because I learned a long time ago that you're the only woman for me."

"Why couldn't you have known that thirteen years ago?"

"Come on, Sam," he said, pulling into his drive. He stopped the car. Turned it off. But didn't get out. "Think about it. I'm just what Chuck called me—a simple country boy. And you—you've got enough energy and determination to wage a one-woman battle." The silence in the car was at once deafening. And comforting.

"Sam, you've always been out to save the world. To make it a better place for everyone. And all I've ever wanted is to grow corn, have babies and sleep with my wife in my arms every single night for the rest of my life."

"What about what you said earlier, about hiding out at the farm so you didn't have to face what you couldn't control?"

She'd listened. And remembered.

"I'm not going to lie to you, Sam. I still want to live on the farm. A farm. I like farming. But I don't have to live here. I know that now. I need your forgiveness, Sam."

"For Sherry?"

"And for being too much of a coward. I was afraid to face life away from the farm. And afraid to love you."

"Because you couldn't control everything and might get hurt."

"That's right."

"Well, you know what, Kyle?"

He was suddenly sweating worse than he had earlier that night when he'd faced Chuck Sewell's gun. Almost as much as he'd been sweating when he'd heard Sam's car outside that barn and known that he'd only have one chance to save her life.

"What?"

"The truth is, you're the one of us who has courage."

"Don't lie to me, Sam. You faced down two men tonight—one a coworker you trusted with your life— and you killed them both almost with a single bullet. You aren't afraid of anything."

"I'm afraid of the truth, Kyle. That's what came to me tonight, when I stood there in that barn with Chuck dead on the floor and knowing it could so easily have been you. When I saw that blood on your neck, I..."

Her voice was shaking and he knew she was crying. "Anyone would have been scared..."

"No, Kyle, it's not... Let me finish."

He nodded and picked up her hand. Her right hand. The one that had held a gun steady enough to kill men on either side of Kyle and miss him completely.

"What I realized tonight, Kyle, was that I didn't choose being a cop over marrying you because I wanted to be a cop more than I wanted to be your wife."

He didn't understand.

"I chose being a cop because it made me feel safe. See, if I gave my whole life to being your wife, spending my days here with you and our kids, and then lost you, like my mom lost my dad, like I lost my dad... I just couldn't take that chance. And what I knew, even back then, was that life can be gone in an instant. You could have had an accident with a tractor. Or been hit by lightning. Or…"

Kyle felt as if a bolt of lightning had just struck him.

"And the being a cop part—I suddenly got that tonight, too, when I realized that it was all a lie."

"What was a lie, babe?"

She laid her head back against the seat, staring out in front of her at the barn where Lillie and Rad slept.

"From the time I was a little girl, I knew that the only way I could be safe and happy and not like my mother, who was always missing the fun because she was afraid, who was always weak and vulnerable, was to be a cop. Cops saved people from the bad guys. But you know what, Kyle?"

She turned to look at him.

"What?"

"I am a cop and I still almost lost the only thing in my life that's ever really mattered to me."

"What's that?"

"You. And I almost lost you *because* I'm a cop."

"Sam, don't…"

With a finger against his lips, she shushed him. "Tonight wasn't the only time, Kyle. Don't you see? When I joined the academy and gave you your ring back, it was my decision to be a cop that made me lose you. And later, when we broke off the engagement for good—it's because I was a cop. I was letting being a cop do exactly what the rape did to my mother. It was making me a prisoner in a world of my own fear."

He didn't know what to say except, "Sam, tomorrow will you go with me to the courthouse and apply for a marriage license?"

"Yes."

His mind raced. His heart and body were still in shock.

"I'd like to stay out here for the time being, because of Grandpa, if that's okay with you.…"

"This is your home, Kyle. And mine, too, if I'd only seen that. We'll stay here for good."

"I want to be in town, Sam, on the nights you're working late.…"

Again, she silenced him, this time with her lips on his. "I'm leaving the sheriff's office, Kyle," she said. "I already put it in writing. I want to do what I'm good at, which is investigating. There's a detective position open with the county and the sheriff is going to recommend that I get it. I'll be able to keep an eye on Abrams, to spend what hours I need finding a way to connect him to Chuck, to the money, to the drugs, to Maggie, something. And I'll have time to take care of Grandpa. To help you train Rad. And to bring Mom out here and have her teach me how to plant beautiful gardens."

"And to have babies?" Might as well put his last regret behind him.

"As soon as we can get them made," she said, sounding more like the Sam he'd grown up with. Fallen in love with. And stuck beside through all the years.

"Want to start now?"

"You're injured, cowboy." Sam's fingers trailed along the good side of his neck. "You've lost a lot of blood."

"I'm fine."

"Okay, then I'll admit that I'm not. I'm beat, Kyle. And scared. And feeling dirty. What I want more than anything is to take a shower."

"Can I watch?"

"Of course. And then I want to bathe you—"

"Because I can't get these stitches wet..."

"Right. And then I want to crawl naked into bed, cuddle up to your naked body, feel your arms close around me and go to sleep."

He couldn't think of anything that sounded better.

"And make babies tomorrow?" he said, just because it was a Kyle thing to say.

"And every day after that."

He was quiet for a moment, letting it all sink in. Odd how one day could be the worst and the best of your life. Which showed that no matter how bad things got, if you just held on, paradise could come next.

"Should we wake James and Millie?" Sam whispered as they took off their shoes at the back door.

"No. They won't want to traipse home in the middle of the night."

"They're in the guest room, right?"

"Right."

"And are they going to make breakfast for Grandpa in the morning?"

"You sure you're going to make it to morning?" he teased, though he was completely exhausted.

"Let's get cleaned up and then see."

As it turned out, Sam bathed him first. And then he bathed her.

He started at her feet, with the intention of working his way up. She was asleep before he finished with her second foot.

But ten minutes later, she nestled up to him when he joined her on the bed.

His neck throbbed a bit. Not enough to make him get him up and find the painkillers he'd been given.

Wouldn't have mattered. He remembered he'd already thrown them out.

The only painkiller he would be needing from here on out was lying right there beside him.

* * * * *

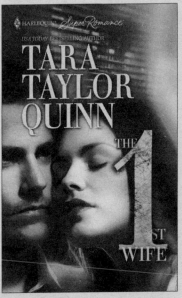

**To read more of Kelly Chapman's files,
watch for**

The Third Secret
This time a professional acquaintance of Kelly's
comes to her for advice. Attorney Erin Morgan
is about to defend Rick Thomas on a murder
charge. She believes Rick's been framed. She
also senses he's not exactly who he says he is....

Coming in November from MIRA Books.

The Fourth Victim
Kelly herself is at the center of this next case—
she's been kidnapped. And it's up to FBI agent
Clay Thatcher to find her. Which means he
has to figure out who did it...and why.

Coming in December from MIRA Books.

⸻

Award-winning author Maggie Shayne says,
"I consider Tara Taylor Quinn's books
essential to my bookshelf, and you will, too."

Tara Taylor Quinn writes books that readers
and reviewers describe as "riveting" and
"compelling" and "not to be missed."
Make sure you don't miss these next two titles
in The Chapman Files!

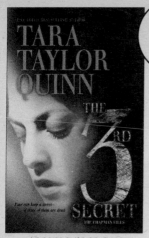

$1.00 OFF

MIRA®

Look for the next Kelly Chapman novel from *USA TODAY* bestselling author

TARA TAYLOR QUINN

THE THIRD SECRET

Available October 26, 2010, wherever books are sold!

$7.99 U.S./$9.99 CAN.

$1.00 OFF the purchase price of THE THIRD SECRET by Tara Taylor Quinn

Offer valid from October 26, 2010, to November 9, 2010.
Redeemable at participating retail outlets. Limit one coupon per purchase.
Valid in the U.S.A. and Canada only.

52609480

Canadian Retailers: Harlequin Enterprises Limited will pay the face value of this coupon plus 10.25¢ if submitted by customer for this product only. Any other use constitutes fraud. Coupon is nonassignable. Void if taxed, prohibited or restricted by law. Consumer must pay any government taxes. Void if copied. Nielsen Clearing House ("NCH") customers submit coupons and proof of sales to Harlequin Enterprises Limited, P.O. Box 3000, Saint John, NB E2L 4L3, Canada. Non-NCH retailer—for reimbursement submit coupons and proof of sales directly to Harlequin Enterprises Limited, Retail Marketing Department, 225 Duncan Mill Rd., Don Mills, Ontario M3B 3K9, Canada.

U.S. Retailers: Harlequin Enterprises Limited will pay the face value of this coupon plus 8¢ if submitted by customer for this product only. Any other use constitutes fraud. Coupon is nonassignable. Void if taxed, prohibited or restricted by law. Consumer must pay any government taxes. Void if copied. For reimbursement submit coupons and proof of sales directly to Harlequin Enterprises Limited, P.O. Box 880478, El Paso, TX 88588-0478, U.S.A. Cash value 1/100 cents.

5 65373 00076 2 (8100)0 11708

® and TM are trademarks owned and used by the trademark owner and/or its licensee.

© 2010 Harlequin Enterprises Limited

MTTQ1010CPN

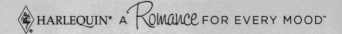

Debut author
Joshua Corin

IF THERE WERE A GOD,
HE WOULD HAVE STOPPED ME

That's the message discovered across the street from the murder site of fourteen innocent men and women in Atlanta. The sniper Galileo is on the loose.

Where others see puzzles, Esme Stuart sees patterns, a skill that made her one of the FBI's top field operatives. But she turned her back on the bureau eight years ago to start a family and live a normal life.

Now her old boss needs his former protégée's help. But is Esme willing to jeopardize her new family?

And what will happen when Galileo aims his scope at them?

WHILE
GALILEO
PREYS

Available wherever books are sold.

MIRA®

REQUEST YOUR
FREE BOOKS!

2 FREE NOVELS
FROM THE SUSPENSE COLLECTION
PLUS 2 FREE GIFTS!

YES! Please send me 2 FREE novels from the Suspense Collection and my 2 FREE gifts (gifts are worth about $10). After receiving them, if I don't wish to receive any more books, I can return the shipping statement marked "cancel." If I don't cancel, I will receive 3 brand-new novels every month and be billed just $5.74 per book in the U.S. or $6.24 per book in Canada. That's a saving of at least 28% off the cover price. It's quite a bargain! Shipping and handling is just 50¢ per book.* I understand that accepting the 2 free books and gifts places me under no obligation to buy anything. I can always return a shipment and cancel at any time. Even if I never buy another book, the two free books and gifts are mine to keep forever.

192/392 MDN E7PD

Name _____ (PLEASE PRINT)

Address _____ Apt. #

City _____ State/Prov. _____ Zip/Postal Code

Signature (if under 18, a parent or guardian must sign)

Mail to **The Reader Service:**
IN U.S.A.: P.O. Box 1867, Buffalo, NY 14240-1867
IN CANADA: P.O. Box 609, Fort Erie, Ontario L2A 5X3

Not valid for current subscribers to the Suspense Collection
or the Romance/Suspense Collection.

**Want to try two free books from another line?
Call 1-800-873-8635 or visit www.morefreebooks.com.**

* Terms and prices subject to change without notice. Prices do not include applicable taxes. N.Y. residents add applicable sales tax. Canadian residents will be charged applicable provincial taxes and GST. Offer not valid in Quebec. This offer is limited to one order per household. All orders subject to approval. Credit or debit balances in a customer's account(s) may be offset by any other outstanding balance owed by or to the customer. Please allow 4 to 6 weeks for delivery. Offer available while quantities last.

Your Privacy: Harlequin Books is committed to protecting your privacy. Our Privacy Policy is available online at www.eHarlequin.com or upon request from the Reader Service. From time to time we make our lists of customers available to reputable third parties who may have a product or service of interest to you. If you would prefer we not share your name and address, please check here. ☐

Help us get it right—We strive for accurate, respectful and relevant communications. To clarify or modify your communication preferences, visit us at www.ReaderService.com/consumerschoice.

J.T. ELLISON

VENGEANCE BORN IN THE DARK OF THE MOON

It is Samhain—the Blood Harvest. Nonbelievers call it Hallowe'en. The night when eight Nashville teenagers are found dead, with occult symbols carved into their naked bodies. It's a ritual the killers believe was blessed by Death himself.

When children are victimized, emotions always run high, and this case has the public both outraged and terrified—a dangerous combination. Recently reinstated homicide lieutenant Taylor Jackson knows she has to act quickly, but tread carefully.

Exploring the baffling culture of mysticism and witchcraft, Taylor learns how unchecked wrath can push a killer to his limits.

the immortals

Available wherever books are sold.